"A WITCH AFTER THE GEM!"

Even as Arton shouted to wake and warn the others, the harridan who had tried to bespell him gestured at the near wall of the cavern, and raging creatures struggled free of the stone.

The hag raised a hand toward Arton and one of Rith's blades slammed into her. She howled in agony as silver sizzled and burned in her flesh.

Her form changed then, becoming a huge, shambling amorphous dark thing of yowling blackness.

"Demon!" cried Rith, while behind her sounded a monstrous roar, and struggling out from the stone at the demon's command came the muzzle and head of a colossal beast. . . .

DENNIS L. McKIERNAN

**"McKiernan brews magic with an insightful blend of
laughter, tears, and high courage."**
—Janny Wurts, author of *Curse of the Mistwraith*

THE DRAGONSTONE

Arin has a vision filled with horror, suffering, bloodshed, and hordes
of plundering dragons. Now Arin must embark upon a desperate mission to understand that which fate has thrust upon her—and to block
the fulfillment of her nightmarish prophecy. Through the aid of potent
wizardry, the depths of her fell vision are plumbed, and a message
revealed: six fellows must she seek out and recruit, six extraordinary
beings, their identities steeped in riddles. And so their quest begins, a
trek across countless leagues to discover, bring together, and lead an
unlikely band of adventures in a heroic duel with destiny.

**"Evocative and compelling . . . a triumph of wondrous myths
and great magics."**
—Jennifer Roberson, author of *Lady of the Forest*

from ROC

CAVERNS OF SOCRATES

DENNIS L. MCKIERNAN

A ROC BOOK

ROC
Published by the Penguin Group
Penguin Books USA Inc., 375 Hudson Street,
New York, New York 10014, U.S.A.
Penguin Books Ltd, 27 Wrights Lane,
London W8 5TZ, England
Penguin Books Australia Ltd, Ringwood,
Victoria, Australia
Penguin Books Canada Ltd, 10 Alcorn Avenue,
Toronto, Ontario, Canada M4V 3B2
Penguin Books (N.Z.) Ltd, 182–190 Wairau Road,
Auckland 10, New Zealand

Penguin Books Ltd, Registered Offices:
Harmondsworth, Middlesex, England

First published by Roc, an imprint of Dutton Signet,
a division of Penguin Books USA Inc.
Previously appeared in a Roc hardcover edition.

First Mass Market Printing, November, 1996
10 9 8 7 6 5 4 3 2 1

 REGISTERED TRADEMARK—MARCA REGISTRADA

Printed in the United States of America

To my only daughter,
Debbi

and to all the Black Foxes
scattered across the nation and
throughout the world . . .
you know who you are

FOREWORD

There is an anecdote that Samuel Johnson, the British writer, was asked how he would refute Bishop Berkeley's statement that the world was an illusion.

"I refute it thus!" he said, and kicked a large rock.

Some people think he was right; some think he was wrong; and some don't think about it at all.

I've been thinking about it.

You see, what both Johnson and Berkeley were concerned with is the nature of reality. Perhaps Johnson's answer showed a profound understanding of the nature of reality; on the other hand, perhaps it showed a profound ignorance. It could have shown a profound frustration, because what we are talking about here is metaphysics, which means we are dealing with beliefs, with faith—scientific proof is lacking.

In all of my novels I get to delve into some rather interesting themes, with thought-provoking questions posed, explored, but not necessarily definitively answered. Herein I take up (and perhaps shed some light on) three intriguing questions:

- What is the nature of reality?
- What is consciousness; what is the mind?
- Do people have spirits, souls, and if so would an artificial intelligence have a soul?

Becoming entangled in metaphysical issues has both its rewards and its penalties: wonderful intellectual stimulation; no way to know if you are right.

In spite of the fact that I am dealing with three questions (wrapped in what I hope are two thrilling adventures), the fundamental issue this tale concerns itself with is the nature of reality.

I think I'll go outside now and kick a rock.

Dennis L. McKiernan
March 1994

Our job is to escape the cave, look around, then come back and tell the others what we have seen. . . . Of course, they won't believe us.

Daniel Kian McKiernan

1

Lightning jagged across the ebony sky, thunder crashing after. Rain hammered down, drumming on the roof of the cab, nearly drowning out the frantic *thwpp-thwpp-thwpp*ing of the overborne windshield wipers and the hiss of tires running through water. With the tips of her fingers Alice Maxon squeaked a hole in the fog clinging to her window and peered outward, attempting in vain to see through the runneling liquid sheeting down the pane.

"My god, I thought Tucson was in the desert. How can you see to drive?"

"It's the monsoon season, miss."

"Monsoon season?"

The cabby laughed. "Yeah. That's what we call it. From the feast of Saint John the Baptist to the feast of Saint Giles—late June to the beginning of September—come the wind-borne rains. This year, though, they seem to be stronger and last longer—deadly in the arroyos. I blame it on El Niño."

Another bolt scored the sky, thunder slapping down. In the flash Alice caught a momentary glimpse of a dark shell of a building alongside the road, like so many this one abandoned too, or so it seemed.

"Most of our water rides in on the storms," added the cabby, his thick finger punching the A/C button. "Wells, you know."

Thwpp-thwpp . . .

"Wells?"

"Yep. Phoenix has rivers and dams. We got aquifers and wells."

"Oh."

Another thunderclap hammered through the air.

"And lightning," she added.

He barked a laugh. "Yeah. And lightning."

Through the deluge they drove another mile down Tanque Verde—or so Alice hoped—the slender biologist still wondering just how in the hell this guy could see the road, and if he had the foggiest idea as to where he was going. . . . Speaking of fog, the A/C had cleared the windows nicely, though the sheeting rain made the glass look as if it were continuously dissolving, mesmerizing in its flux. And as the vehicle tunneled onward through the pit of a rain-dark night, with its tires *shssh*ing and its windows melting hypnotically, she fell into musing about monsoons and flash floods and whether or not she should have hired an ark instead of a cab, while outside lightning stroked and thunder rolled in the weeping black skies above.

Thwpp-thwpp-thwpp-thwpp . . .

"Almost there, miss." His words broke into her idle thoughts.

Alice slid over and stared through the sheathing water and into downpour beyond. Out in the rain-blurred darkness she could see a set of lights at what appeared to be a . . . ah, yes, a gate, inset along a high fence of heavy iron bars. And past the fence, past the gate, up an unseen drive—or so she surmised—on the crest of a rise bleared the glimmering lights of a building, a fair-sized building, this one not abandoned.

The cab swung leftward across the water-glutted road toward the gate and sloshed to the barrier and stopped. Flashlight in hand, a guard in yellow slicker splatted out from the gatehouse to the driver's window. The cabby lowered the glass. Rain spattered inward. Water dripping from his cowl, the guard glanced briefly at the driver, then shined his light into the back. "Miss Maxon?" he called out above the constant drumming of the rain.

Thwpp-thwpp-thwpp-thwpp . . .

Shielding her eyes from the halogen glare, Alice nodded and called back, "Yes."

"Have you any identification?"

Alice fumbled about in her purse, locating her Connecticut driver's license. The guard looked at the hologram and at her, comparing—brown hair, brown eyes, late twenties—and then stepped into the gatehouse. Within a minute he returned, only this time he crossed to the passenger-side door, sliding into the seat next to the driver. Casting back his wet hood, he turned and handed the ID to Alice. "Sorry for the delay, but we can't be too careful." He smiled, then added, "They're all waiting, ma'am." With the flashlight he signaled to someone in the gatehouse, and the heavy grillwork swung wide. He looked at the cabby. "Let's go."

The road upward was virtually invisible in the downpour, yet the driver seemed to easily follow the quarter-mile-long arc of blacktop to the building looming above. Lightning flares now and again illuminated the edifice, though here and there lights glistered from within. In the brief glares, Alice estimated that the structure rose no more than ten stories high. *Looks like ordinary glass and steel. But only nine or ten stories—I thought it would be more imposing.*

The cab drew up under a portico before a lighted entryway. The guard leapt out and opened her door. In spite of the sheltering roof, water washed across the drive, and Alice splashed two or three steps before reaching the curb. She turned and watched as the cabby unloaded her luggage, the guard helping. A footstep sounded behind her, and softly above the drum of the rain someone spoke her name. Her heart pounding, she slowly turned, and as lightning slashed down and thunder hammered after, there stood Eric. "Alice," he said again, and stepped to her and took her face in his hands and gently kissed her.

2

Eric drew back and gazed down into Alice's eyes, their color nearly matching her hair. "My god, Alice Maxon, but it's good to see you again. Last I knew you were in Brazil, trying to capture the golden unicorn, or some such fabled beast."

Alice laughed, looking up at him—at six foot one he overtopped her by a full six inches. "I'm glad to see you, too, Eric Flannery. And it wasn't a golden unicorn—I haven't the bait—but a red-fringed golden marmoset instead. But you, you big Irish Viking, what about you? Finish that book? Ogres in outer space, wasn't it?"

He roared with laughter and shook his long mane of pale yellow hair, for in spite of the name of Flannery, he was one of those descendants of Eire with flaxen locks and eyes the color of a meadow bluebell—a raider's get, or so he claimed. "No, no, love," he protested. " 'Twas an urban fantasy—elves in Central Park. But look now, even though I would rather we chuck this all and run off to some Eden together"—he turned and slipped her arm through his—"we've got to go and have you meet the others . . . they sent me down to fetch you up straightaway."

"Straightaway?"

"Damn, Alice, you know me. Accents tend to rub off. Doctor Adkins' this time. She's a Brit, you know . . . not a cheerio, pip-pip kind, but one of those 'straightaway' Brits."

He started for the entrance, drawing Alice with him. "But wait," she protested. "My luggage, the driver—he'll want his fare."

"Fear not, love. You need lift no finger nor part with a single cred. They'll take care of it at the front desk. Didn't I tell you that this was a first-class operation?"

"You didn't tell me *anything* about this operation, Eric."

"Well, I told 'em to tell you."

They entered the foyer and stepped across a terrazzo floor to a wide mahogany desk manned by a uniformed armed guard. Behind and above, mounted on the wall, was a large metallic logo—a disk of beaten brass with an ornate *C* dead center, emblazoned in gold. Pinned to the guard's chest was a badge—a miniature version of the logo, with Coburn Industries, Ltd., engraved around the rim.

Alice glanced at Eric. "Is this the same Coburn who produced the vaccine?"

Eric nodded, grinning. "Did I not say this is a class act?"

"I need a voice print and a retinal scan, Miss Maxon," said the guard, "and a holo. Everything else is done."

Moments later Alice had a plaston ID, similar to the one Eric wore, clipped to the pocket of her battered Levi jacket. As they headed for the elevator, Alice plucked at her hair and said, "God, Eric, if I had known they were going to take a holo, I'd have done something about this frizz. It's this damn rain, you know, curls me up just like sheep's wool."

"Love, you are gorgeous no matter what. And don't complain about the rain. It's a blessed relief from the dragon weather we get before and after."

"Dragon weather?"

"Triple digits. Bone dry. Sirocco blowing—the dragon's breath. It happens in May and June, and again after the monsoons—September and most of October. Better this than that."

"Perhaps, but it caused my plane to land in Phoenix instead of here."

"How was the maglev? I've never ridden one myself."

Alice shrugged. "Smooth. Fast. Less than an hour's ride, though I didn't much care for the wait in Phoenix—too many reminders of the 'demic."

The elevator dinged and the doors slid open.

As they stepped inside, Alice grinned. "You know, Eric, you've gone to one helluva lot of trouble just to play a game."

Eric smiled back, though this time his manner was serious. "This is no ordinary game, love. Besides, I needed to see you and tell you that you were right all along."

ding

The doors slid shut and in silence the two rode upward.

On the top floor, down a carpeted hallway, behind a walnut-paneled door, they came into a large conference room, seemingly filled with a gabbling throng of standing people—though there were only eleven—all talking at once, over coffee and tea and soft drinks. Beyond the horde, beyond a long, walnut safety rail, one wall was made up entirely of windows, the drapery drawn back; this glass, too, seemed to be melting as outside raged the storm, water sheathing down the panes. The scattered bleared lights of Tucson could be seen westerly through the downpour, and now and again lightning flared, and rain gusted hard against the glass. In room center sat a long walnut conference table, with unoccupied chairs ranging down either side; on the table were two decimated trays of sandwiches and a wicker basket partly filled with fruit. At one end was a small stage and a glassed screen—whether vid or holo or slide, Alice could not tell. As Eric and Alice moved into the babble, a slender African-American woman, chocolate brown and an inch or two taller than Alice, turned from the discussion and smiled a great smile and stepped toward her with open arms.

"Oh, Alice, it is so good to see you."

Fiercely they embraced, Alice whispering, "Meredith." Over Meredith's shoulder, Alice could see Hiroko towing Caine by the hand and snaking among the others to reach her side—Caine at six foot three simply towering over tiny Hiroko's four foot ten. Beyond them, hanging on the back wall, a banner proclaimed "Up the Black Foxes!" Alice's eyes flooded with tears.

Caine paused to let Hiroko have the first hug, laughter hiding in his voice. "My lord, Alice, did you discover the fountain we Foxes never found?"

Alice grinned through her tears as she hugged Hiroko, the diminutive woman's embrace as fierce as Meredith's had been. "I missed you, Alice."

"I missed you, too, Hiroko."

"Here, here, my turn," rumbled Caine, lifting Alice's hands from Hiroko and spinning her into his arms. "Inuit time," he declared, bending down.

Alice laughed and rubbed noses with him, then said, "Seems to me, my good Doctor Easley, that if anyone had found the fountain of youth, 'twould be thee and not me."

"Bah," Caine growled, but grinned as he stepped back and ran a hand through his coppery-blond hair, "I just do a nip and tuck here and there . . . or suck the suet out of others—a lipovampire, I vaant your faaaat. But you, me loverly gel, you have no need of me sarvices."

"Come, sit down," urged Hiroko, her black eyes dancing as she led Alice to a chair Eric held for her. "You must be famished, and we have sandwiches and fruit."

"And your coffee-milk half-and-half," added Meredith, handing her a cup filled with creamy tan liquid.

Alice gratefully accepted the cup. "You remembered."

"Hah!" Caine grinned. "Who could forget such tepidity? Alice, keep drinking that stuff and you'll *never* grow hair on your chest."

"Thank all the gods," said Eric, rolling his eyes heavenward.

"Up the Black Foxes!" called out Hiroko, glee in her voice.

Up the Black Foxes! they all responded, reaching for cups and glasses and cans, Alice grinning and sipping her drink after first holding it on high.

"Look, I hate to interrupt this reunion," came a peevish voice from one of the people Alice did not know, "but could we get on with the briefing? I mean, we're already three hours late." The speaker was a tall angular man in his early forties.

"Come now, Doctor Stein, everything in its good time," said a silver-haired, portly man, peering over a set of half-glasses. "Give the lady a chance to catch her breath."

The irritated man, evidently Doctor Stein, pursed his lips and seemed about to retort, but there came a rapping from the front of the room. And there, behind a lectern at the side of the stage, stood a slender woman, she, too, in her forties, though had she worn makeup she could have passed for someone ten years younger. Her hair fell to her shoulders and was that indeterminate color between dark blond and light brown, and her eyes shone pale blue.

"Henry is quite right, John." Her accent was definitely British. "We are indeed rather later than expected. Let us all be seated and begin." As chairs were shuffled and people sat, the woman's gaze turned to Alice and her friends. "Welcome, Black Foxes, to Coburn Limited. You've all met the members of our project team—except for you, Doctor Maxon, unavoidably delayed by our weather." As if to underscore her words, a hard gust of rain momentarily pelted the window. "I am Doctor Toni Adkins, head of this project. My Ph.D. is in psychology. For the past eight years I have specialised in the psychology of AI."

AI? Artificial intelligence? Alice glanced at Eric. He nodded and mouthed, [That's right: artificial intelligence]. *Damn! Eric's doing it again.* Her attention veered back to the podium as Doctor Adkins continued.

"At this end of the table on my left is Doctor Drew Meyer, Ph.D., physics." Alice leaned forward to peer past Eric and saw a thin, balding man, perhaps in his late thirties, somewhat abstracted. He seemed to be doodling on a minicompad in hand. He glanced up at her and nodded, then returned to his doodling.

"Across from him sits Doctor John Greyson, Ph.D., philosophy, specialising in ethics." Alice smiled at the portly, silver-haired gentleman who had "defended" her. He pulled his half-glasses down to the end of his nose and peered over them and smiled back.

"Next to John is Doctor Alya Ramanni, Ph.D., biochemistry." A small, nut-brown East Indian woman of indeterminate age—perhaps in her fifties—nodded and smiled at Alice. Alice found that she could not help but grin back.

In the distance lightning flared.

"Across the table from you is Doctor Henry Stein, neurology." His black hair combed straight back, Doctor Stein sat with his lips drawn thin, somehow managing to ignore Alice while looking straight at her.

Alice nodded his way, but received no response. *Cold bastard!*

Far-off thunder rumbled.

"Next is our corporate solicitor, Mister Mark Perry."

"Lawyer," corrected Mark, a slender dark-haired man in his forties. "Corporate lawyer, LL.B."

Good lord! Silk tie, gold diamond ring, a three-piece pinstripe suit with briefcase, and a shark's smile. Talk about your caricatures. Alice forced a brief nod.

"Next to Mark is the owner of the corporation, Mister Arthur Coburn."

Alice would have recognized Coburn without the introduction, for she'd seen him countless times on the holovid—accepting awards, driving in charity races, heading up conferences, scuba diving, cutting ribbons, and other such. He was a small, wiry man in his late sixties, with sun-browned skin and a sun-creased face and burr-cut silver hair. Alice thought of rawhide as she nodded to him, receiving a like nod in return. Coburn cleared his throat. "I hope to join the Foxes in the adventure ahead."

"And lastly," said Toni Adkins, "at the far end of the table sits Doctor Timothy Rendell, Ph.D., computer science. He is also our game expert, and the one responsible for choosing you and your comrades to be our alpha test team." Timothy was a young man in his early thirties, with rust-red hair tied back in a ponytail. His red tee shirt bore the dictum *Reality is for people who can't handle fantasy.*

"Well actually you chose yourselves six years back," said Timothy, "by the margin of your win in Milwaukee. And when I discovered that Eric lived nearby, well, what other choice was there? I mean, your VR team is legend." He turned and saluted the banner. "Up the Black Foxes!"

Again lightning sheared the darkness, close this time, thunder slapping after.

"Up the Black Foxes," murmured Alice, her voice lost in the reverberation.

Timothy reached forward and took an orange from one of the baskets, as Doctor Adkins gestured about and said, "There are many others at work on this project: scientists, programmers, technicians, logicians, and the like. We here in this room merely head up the various departments. But together, all of us, we stand on the threshold of an exciting future, all made possible by one you have yet to meet." She peered at the lectern and pressed a minicompad. The screen behind her flicked into life, and a vortex of color filled the glass, like the hues of a spectrum steadily and endlessly spiraling down into a bottomless abyss. An androgynous, measured, electronic voice emanated from the centerpoint of the slow-turning swirl: "Hello, Black Foxes. You may call me Avery, though my true name is AIVR. I am your AI."

Outside a thunderbolt seared the night, glaring light stabbed into the room, thunder whelmed at the windows, and rain hammered down.

3

Good lord! A real AI? Again Alice glanced at Eric. He nodded. *Dammit, Eric! Stop reading my thoughts!*

As Doctor Adkins started to speak, Mark Perry interjected, "Toni, before we go any further"—he unlocked his briefcase and extracted a sheaf of papers—"our guests need to sign these waivers." He stepped round the table, handing out a document to each of the five. "What you will hear is top secret. There are several other companies who'd give their eye teeth to know what you are about to learn. This document is legally binding, and holds you responsible for keeping your knowledge to yourself and to those authorized to know, not allowing the information to fall into the wrong hands."

Alice glanced at her copy, swiftly reading down through the legalese.

"Oy, wait!" exclaimed Caine. "This says that we agree to hold Coburn Industries blameless in case something should go wrong."

"Merely a standard malpractice line, Doctor Easley," responded Perry. "Just like those you have your patients sign. No different."

"But in my profession, Mister Perry, there are risks to the patient: potential for unexpected allergic reactions to drugs; anesthetic shock; and other such. Too, there are unjust lawsuits to avoid—frivolous, fraudulent, and malign. What in God's name do we have to be wary of here?"

With a groan Doctor Stein rolled his eyes toward the ceiling and irritatedly began drumming his fingers on the conference table.

Mark Perry shrugged. "Look, sign it now. After the briefing, if you wish, you can walk away from here free and clear, the agreement being that you simply will keep your mouth shut concerning anything you've heard. All right?" He smiled his toothy smile.

Caine looked at the others and grinned, turning up his hands. "Why do I feel like chum cast upon shark-infested waters?" Then he wrenched a pen from his pocket and swiftly scribbled his name on the line.

Alice sighed and reached for Caine's pen.

When all papers had been signed and dated, Perry passed the forms to other people at the table for them to ink their signatures as witnesses.

Eric slid one of the sandwich trays to Alice. She chose egg salad; the bread was slightly crusted from exposure to the air. Even so, when she took a bite, it was delicious.

As Perry tamped the documents on the table to square them up and then slipped them back into his briefcase, Doctor Adkins introduced Avery to each of the newcomers. Alice noted that a pair of motorized miniature vidcams above the stage tracked each introduction. *Avery's eyes?* She felt somewhat foolish when her own turn came to nod and speak to the screen, murmuring "Avery" in response to his/her/its "Hello, Doctor Maxon."

"Now that we've all met one another, including our late arrival," growled Doctor Stein, "could we get on with it?"

Silver-haired Doctor Greyson peered over his half-glasses and gestured at the storm outside. "Henry, stop trying to blame this poor girl. We were delayed by an act of God."

"Bah," came the response, "as if there were a god. Look, Greyson, I've told you before, we make our own opportunities, and—"

At the podium Toni Adkins rapped the lectern for attention, breaking Stein's incipient tirade before it could turn into a full-fledged diatribe.

To her left the screen swirled in silence.

"Let us proceed," said Toni. And when she had everyone's attention—"Black Foxes, you are here to test a new kind of virtual reality—not the old kind where you don a special visor and special gloves and enter upon an electronic stage to merely *play* the part of a character—to role-play as if your character were the real you. Oh no. Instead, when you enter *this* virtual reality, you will truly forget who you are, you will forget your life as biologists and authors, as artists and doctors, as bookstore owners and corporate executives; you will actually *become* whatever character you've chosen to be in a virtual reality indistinguishable from the real world."

"Good lord!" interrupted Caine. "You mean we'll really be inside an adventure?"

Toni smiled. "Much more than that, Doctor Easley. It will be as if there were no existence outside the virtual reality you've chosen to enter. In fact, *this* virtual reality *will be* your true world and the character you choose *will be* the true you. No more role-playing; instead, for you it will be true life."

Caine shook his head. "You mean I won't be me? Caine Easley? But instead, if we go in as Black Foxes there will only be Kane, kick-ass warrior and gentle-handed healer?"

"Exactly so," said Toni.

Caine turned to the others and grinned. "God, what an opportunity! To actually *be* Kane. . . ."

"How do you accomplish this?" asked Alice.

"We don't," answered Toni. She turned to the screen of moiling hues. "Avery is the one responsible."

"I can give you any reality you desire" came Avery's androgynous voice, "adventure, romance, fantasy, pulp, science fiction, pornography—"

Mark Perry broke in: "We expect this ultimately"—he smiled his oily smile—"to virtually replace all other forms of entertainment."

Alice shook her head in disbelief. "You mean you are using an honest-to-god artificial intelligence merely to run a *game*?"

"Not a game, Miss Maxon," replied Perry. "Not a

game. Instead it is a whole new reality. A whole new existence. As Avery says, adventure, romance, the acting out of every desire, sating every lust. Hell, before long people will prefer those realities to this."

"My point exactly," said Doctor Greyson, removing his half-glasses and running a hand through his silver hair. "The impact on society will be devastating, and—"

"Faugh!" retorted Perry. "They said the same thing about art, about books, about radio, movies, television, vids, holos, whatever new comes down the line. Hell, the cavemen probably said it when someone started drawing on the walls."

Greyson held up a hand, as if to stop the flow of Perry's words. "What you say is in a measure true. But, Mark, nothing before in mankind's past has had the potential for such total damage. Why, its effect will be more devastating than that of the pandemic."

Doctor Stein's cold voice broke in. "Worse than the pandemic? Bah!"

A babble filled the room, and Toni rapped the lectern for silence. Reluctantly it came. "As I have said many times, those of us on this project, we will not settle this debate."

Arthur Coburn quietly cleared his throat. All eyes turned to the head of Coburn Industries. "Toni is quite right. It will be settled in Washington, and in London, in Paris and Berlin and Rome, and in other capitals of the world where there are viable governments, or in those cities where recovering countries will one day have governments." He turned toward Alice. "Yet, Doctor Maxon, I understand your point . . . as well as the points made by John"—he nodded toward Greyson—"who is, after all, Avery's guide in philosophy and ethics."

Again he turned his gaze on Alice. "You question whether running a virtual reality is Avery's true calling, whether Avery is being misused. It is indeed a critical question, yet one to which I have *my* answer: this Avery and others like him will have many true callings, and entertainment is but one. Medicine, industry, biology, psychiatry—in fact, in all areas of art, science, and philosophy, Avery's contributions to mankind will be virtually unlimited. The future will be enhanced beyond our wildest imaginings.

"But listen, this future will not come to pass unless we have the means to make it a reality. You know what the pandemic, what the Ebola-Calcutta virus did when it got loose in the world—the decimation of the industrial countries, the devastation of the third world—"

Alice shuddered, for she flashed back to her early teens, when she had seen victims of Ebola-Calcutta: screaming in agony, burning with fever, shuddering and twitching with seizures caused by literally thousands of internal blood clots, the pale remainder of their thin blood hemorrhaging from every orifice—eyes, nose, ears, mouth, nipples, anus, urethra, vagina—bleeding to death ... somehow, of all these, the watery pinkness streaming from the eyes seemed the worst.

The world had panicked, for the virus was airborne and long-lived, and merely breathing the same air in a room with an exposed victim guaranteed infection—at least 90 percent fatal. Borders were closed, but the virus spread like wildfire regardless. People, terrified, isolated themselves from one another, barricaded themselves, shot anyone who dared set foot down nearby—strangers, neighbors, friends, relatives, family ... it didn't matter.

Alice looked across at Arthur Coburn: this was the man responsible for the vaccine that stopped the spread of the disease. His biohazard team isolated the key mutation that had transformed Ebola-Zaire into Ebola-Calcutta, and they had modified the older vaccine into the newer form and had stopped the pandemic cold in those places where it could be delivered in time.

Now Alice glanced at Alya Ramanni and knew with a certainty that this small nut-brown woman had been a key member of that heroic biohazard team that had saved much of the world.

All this came to Alice in a flash as Coburn spoke, but she pushed these thoughts aside to focus on his words:

"—and how very long it has taken us to get back to what we now have." Coburn paused, running his hand across his burr-cut silver hair. "Look, I won't give you a discourse on economics. Let me just say that to go into production of a variety of Averys, we need to raise an extraordinary amount of capital—capital that neither governments nor industries are willing to risk . . . they are too strapped. Even if they had the funds, because we . . . because *I* want Coburn Industries to remain in complete control over the future of Avery and others like him, I will *not* invite disaster by allowing government, corporate, or even private investors to give us the needed creds. Avery is too important to allow stockholders or a government bureaucracy to have *any* measure of control. Yet the capital can be raised—from those who yet hold great private wealth, such as me, but only if we offer them something which they are willing to pay for. And I believe that they will pay handsomely, exorbitantly, to live out their dreams, their fantasies, whatever those fantasies may be. Hence, we have shaped Avery's calling accordingly, for it is the calling that will give us the wealth—"

"Megacreds," whispered Mark Perry.

"—to produce other Averys, to shape them for the great benefit of all mankind, and not just a privileged few.

"And this test we are to do will be but one in a lengthy chain of tests which will prepare Avery for the task ahead . . . so that in the long run we can step into the future he and others like him will bring."

With a resigned sigh, Doctor Greyson picked up his half-glasses and turned to Toni at the lectern.

Toni looked at Coburn, and at a slight nod from him, she prepared to continue. In that same moment, as rain pattered against the window, Alice came to realize just who held the power in this room. She glanced at Eric and he nodded; Alice shook her head and sighed.

"As I understand it," said Toni, "some six years past you became world champions in the virtual reality games held annually in Milwaukee. In those games each of you took on a persona, played as if you were a member of a group of mercenaries known as the Black Foxes. And in those same championships, you set a standard that no other team has even come close to, much less equaled or surpassed."

"Damn straight!" exclaimed Caine, a wide grin on his face. "Cunning and guile will out every time."

Toni acknowledged Caine with a bob of her head. "Just so, Doctor Easley. And because you gave the game such a good and proper thrashing, well, we jumped at the chance for the Black Foxes to be the first test group—the alpha test group—to enter one of Avery's realities. You see, we believe you have the expertise to deal with whatever challenges Avery throws at you."

"You called us the alpha group," said Meredith. "Does that mean no one else has been in there?" She tilted her head toward the screen.

"Oh no, Miss Rodgers" came Avery's electronic voice. "Many others have been in one of my realities, but you and your companions will be the first group. You see, I need to learn what it is like to interact with groups, starting with an expert group. To, shall we say, calibrate myself. The reality I have in mind should be a challenge for the Black Foxes. Mister Flannery has been good enough to provide Doctor Rendell—and therefore me—with information about the Foxes. I understand that when all of you were in college together, you enjoyed role-playing in the world of one of his favorite authors from the eighties and nineties—a Mister Daniel Patrick—and so I have read all his works. That is the reality I will place you in."

"You mean," blurted Hiroko, "that we are going to be in Itheria?"

"Exactly," answered Avery.

"Unreal!" exclaimed Caine.

"Precisely," responded Avery, "though at the time you will not think so."

"Huh?"

"Avery means, Caine," explained Eric, "that we will believe that it is indeed the real Itheria. In fact, we won't even question it."

Meredith leaned forward. "Tell me, Doctor Adkins, presumably the VR world will entertain us. But I ask you, if we have no sense of who we really are, if we actually become different personas, then how will we know that we are indeed being entertained . . . especially if in the virtual reality we are, say, struggling over mountains or surviving disasters or facing peril? I mean, it seems to me that in reading a book or watching a holo or whatever, you can distance yourself from the desperate events portrayed. But in a virtual reality, especially one in which we actually become someone else, then how will we be entertained?"

"Oh good god, woman!" burst out Doctor Stein. "Going in you remember nothing; coming out you remember all." He leapt to his feet and in an irritated voice said, "Toni, there are things I should have been doing an hour past. You don't need me here."

"Amen to that," muttered Caine. "We don't need you here. God, what a jerk."

Stein stalked out.

In that moment the rain stopped. "Perhaps it is an omen," Eric whispered to Alice, tilting his head first toward the windows and then to the door softly closing behind Stein's departure.

Toni cleared her throat in the embarrassed hush. "Miss Rodgers, what Doctor Stein so ineptly said was that when you enter the virtual reality, you remember nothing of your true life—it is left behind—but when you return, the full experience in the virtual reality is indeed remembered. Whatever joys, perils, griefs, or aught else that has occurred within, you will come back with full knowledge of those virtual reality experiences."

Meredith nodded, then said, "Then it seems to me, Doctor Adkins, that it is incumbent upon you and Avery to see that those memories are at the very least entertaining."

Tiny Hiroko held up a hand. "Tell me, how will Avery do whatever it is he is to do to us? How do we lose our own identities? How do we actually become a person in a virtual reality?"

Greyson gently thumped the table with the butt of his fist and smiled. "Ah, my dear, wonderful questions, easily answered. You see, we are simply going to cast you into one of the caverns of Socrates."

4

Hiroko's tilted eyes flew wide. "Cast me into what?"

Greyson's grin broadened. "A cavern of Socrates."

She shook her head and turned up her hands.

Meredith reached across Caine and patted Hiroko on the arm. "I think Doctor Greyson is referring to a section of Plato's *Republic*."

Greyson tilted his head in acknowledgment. "Quite right, Miss Rodgers. You are familiar with it?"

"I am familiar with the concept," she replied, "but not with the specific dialogue . . . though I seem to recall it's in Book Seven."

As Eric stood and stepped to the coffee urn to fill his cup and take his seat again, Greyson nodded. "Once more you are right, Miss Rodgers. Plato tells of a discussion between Socrates and Glaucon. They were speaking of the concept of reality, which I will paraphrase as closely as I can."

"Oh, let me play the part of Glaucon, Doctor Greyson," said Meredith. "After all, his part was small, and surely I can ad lib."

Greyson smiled. "Bully, Miss Rodgers. Bully. Shall we begin?"

At Meredith's nod, Greyson swept wide a hand, as if he were on a stage. "I, Socrates, have a conundrum to set before you, Glaucon."

Meredith smiled and canted her head theatrically. "Say on, O Socrates."

Greyson laughed, then drew sober. "Picture men in an underground cave dwelling, with a long entrance reaching up toward the light along the whole width of the cave; in this they lie from their childhood, their legs and necks in chains, so that they stay where they are and look only in front of them, as the chain prevents their turning their heads round. Some way off, and higher up, a fire is burning behind them, and between the fire and the prisoners is a road on higher ground. Imagine a wall built along this road, like the screen which showmen hide behind over which they exhibit the puppets in their play."

Meredith nodded and spoke. "I have it, Socrates."

"Then, Glaucon, picture also men carrying along this road all kinds of articles which overtop the wall: statues of men and horses and birds and other creatures of stone and wood and other materials. Naturally some of the carriers speak while others remain silent."

"A strange image and strange prisoners, Socrates."

"Think you so, Glaucon? Then let me say this: the prisoners are men like us. Yet do you think that such men would have seen anything of themselves or of each other?"

"How could they, Socrates, if in all their lives they had been forced to keep their heads motionless?"

"Just so, Glaucon. Now let us imagine that on the cave wall before them they can indeed see the shadows of the carried objects, shadows cast upon a wall by the fire burning beyond the men carrying those objects."

"I understand."

"Let us further suppose that the cave wall is shaped such that the voices of those carriers who speak are reflected from those very shadows."

"Oh, Socrates, this begins to take shape."

"Indeed. Now let me ask you, Glaucon, if these prisoners could speak with one another, do you not think they would suppose what they saw to be the real thing?"

"Necessarily, Socrates."

At this point, Greyson grinned and shifted in his chair and sketched a seated bow to Meredith, which she gracefully echoed. Then Greyson turned to the others. "Socrates and Glaucon went on to discuss the reality of perceptions. You see, setting aside the improbability of Socrates' proposition—for I believe that such prisoners could not truly exist, unless they were raised more or less normally, and suddenly became amnesiacs upon finding themselves chained in this cave—still, it is an illuminating discussion. Down through the centuries it has led to many spirited philosophical colloquia—with most philosophers concluding that we can only perceive reality through our senses . . . though there have been and still are mavericks who maintain otherwise. Dissenters aside, and without getting into mysticism, we humans gauge reality by what we perceive, by what our senses tell us, and by what we make of those perceptions. And those prisoners, if they existed, would think that shadows on a wall were the real thing. Do you see, Miss Kikiro?"

Hiroko nodded. "Oh yes. In fact, when I was a child the shadows in my room at night were alive and real . . . and magical . . . or so I believed."

Greyson nodded. "Yes, indeed, just as these shadows were real for the captives. But listen, should one of the prisoners get free and simply turn around and see the bonfire, his reality would greatly alter, for what he would then perceive would be a drastic change from the old. And should he see the men carrying the statues, again his reality would alter. And should he walk outside, well then, his reality would drastically change once again.

"And should he come back and speak to the other prisoners and tell them what he has seen . . . well let me ask you, would they believe him? Or would they instead think he had gone insane?"

"Uh," said Caine, grinning at Hiroko, "I'd think he'd gone plumb round the bend myself."

Greyson nodded at Caine. "Yet he would be telling them the truth. He would have escaped his former realities and learned the truth. But, and here is the rub, would it have been the real truth?" Greyson turned and gestured outward through the window, where in the distance the lights of Tucson could now clearly be seen. "Is this truly reality? Or merely a false perception? How will we ever know?"

"Perhaps," said Meredith, "perhaps when we die we emerge from this cave we call the world and step into a new reality."

Greyson nodded. "You may be right, Miss Rodgers. But then again, you may be wrong. Look, there are many images of reality: it could be that one of us is simply dreaming, and all of the rest of us are merely figments of his or her imagination."

"Perhaps it is God who is dreaming," said Hiroko.

"Ha! Perhaps it is me," said Caine.

"Then again," said Greyson, once more gesturing about, "perhaps all of this is false, and we are instead merely brains in vats."

Alice tilted her head. "Brains in vats?"

"Yes," replied Greyson, smiling. "You see, in the middle of the night, when you were asleep, an evil scientist crept into your room and with incredible skill removed your brain from your skull. Then, with equally incredible skill, he took your brain to his laboratory and with microscopic electrodes he connected every one of your sensory nerves to an incredibly complex computer and submerged your brain in a vat of nutrients. Using his computer and sending signals through the electrodes, he now manipulates precisely what you see, hear, feel, taste, smell, and so on, so that you perceive that at this very moment you are in an executive conference room speaking with those of us here, and in no fashion can you detect otherwise." Greyson's gaze swept across everyone. "In fact, we are *all* brains in vats."

"Muhaha!" came Caine's false laugh. "And it is *I* who am that very evil scientist."

A chuckle went round the room, and Alice shook her head and smiled. "What a depraved mind you have, Doctor Greyson."

"Oh, I can't claim credit for that," he replied. "It's an old philosophical riddle of Arthur Penfield's, inspired by the discovery back in the 1930s that memories and sensations can be relived by stimulating specific regions of the brain."

"Which brings us back to the briefing," said Doctor Adkins, who still stood at the lectern. "In effect, when you are taken into Avery's virtual reality, you indeed will be like a brain in a vat, except that this vat will be your own skull."

"Pardon me, Doctor Adkins," said Hiroko, "but I still do not see how we will enter this virtual reality, how we will lose ourselves and become someone else in a whole new existence—become a Black Fox in Itheria."

"It is quite straightforward, Miss Kikiro: for you to forget who you really are and become an individual in virtual reality, through precise neural induction Avery will use a technique known as hemispheric synchronization to place you in a dissociative state. Then via selective memory augmentation he will cast you into the mold of your VR persona—you could liken it to being mesmerized and transformed into a different personality with the memories to support it. Furthermore, you will be in an altered state of sleep, and via inductive stimulation of the hippocampus, and of the various neural clusters in your manifold sensory maps, enhanced by images and odors and other stimuli fed through the rig you will wear, you will be that person and live in that virtual reality and have the time of your life."

"Oh, Socrates, this begins to take shape," said Hiroko.

"Stimulation of the hippocampus?" said Caine. "But won't that cause dreaming?"

"Precisely!" answered Doctor Adkins, delighted at Caine's response. "But you see, under Avery's control, it will be akin to lucid dreaming."

"Lucid dreaming?" said Eric. "But wait, I thought that when the mind was in the state of lucid dreaming, it meant that you were aware that you were dreaming and could take control of the dream and make it do your bidding."

"If that's so," said Hiroko, "if we know we are dreaming, then won't we also know who we are? I mean, I thought that we would lose our own identities when we were in the virtual reality."

Toni held up her hands to stop the questions. "I merely said that it would be *akin* to lucid dreaming. Yes, in actual lucid dreaming the dreamer has free will and full control of the dream. However, in Avery's virtual reality, although the alternate personality will have free will, he will only have free control of himself, but none of the rest of the dream. Meanwhile, here in the true reality, the dreamer will not be aware that he is dreaming. Avery will see to that."

Hiroko nodded in understanding, then added, "You also said something about a—a rig?"

"Avery, show a half-scale holo of the witch's cradle, please, suit in place."

Witch's cradle? Alice turned toward Eric to note the question in his eyes as well.

The endless swirl of Avery's spectrum disappeared and the screen turned to a silver-grey, and in the air before it appeared a holo of what looked to be a high-tech, high-altitude pressure suit—though one from the nineties—with a dark-visored helmet. The outfit was strapped into a recliner, and both helmet and suit were connected to it by bundles of fiber optics. The recliner itself was embedded in a gimbaled rig—a witch's cradle—able to assume all attitudes.

"Jesus!" exclaimed Caine. "It looks like some of the old training rigs, you know, like those used by the astronauts for the second wave of lunar missions."

"Or the ill-fated one to Mars," murmured Hiroko.

A faint shadow of remembered sorrow flicked across Toni's face, vanishing as she stepped round the holo. "Similar to those, yet not the same. You see, this is no rig for a journey to outer space, but to inner space instead, a place where only the imagination can go.

"Through a combination of hemispheric synchronization, selective memory augmentation, quasi-lucid dreaming, inductive neural excitation, and projected sensory stimulation, all guided by Avery, you will be in a fantastic virtual reality indistinguishable from the true."

Eric glanced at Alice, and she silently mouthed [Wow!]. His eyes flew wide, for it was as if she had read his mind.

Toni stepped back to the lectern. "To be able to do this, over the next three days Avery will assay a reasonably complete neural map of each of you.

"During this time, you and he together will detail the characters you wish to become. Mister Flannery has been kind enough to provide a complete written description of your Black Fox characters—their skills, tendencies, abilities, talents, and so on—however, only you can give them your own personal touches. All of this and the neural data will be stored in a crystal identity chip keyed to you and to your VR persona." On the holo of the rig, a small area on the forehead of the VR helmet was highlighted—and the tiny compartment for the ID crystal was shown in open cross-section. The crystal itself appeared to be a small polished cut of clear, hex-sided quartz.

As the witch's cradle reappeared, Doctor Adkins said, "You will live here in the Coburn complex and will be placed on a special diet—"

"Hmm," interjected Eric, smiling at Alice, "looks like the evil scientists have us in their clutches." Then he crooked his fingers and twisted his face into a grimace, and in a cackling falsetto croaked, "I have you now, my pretty, and your little dog, too."

5

"We're all here on the seventh floor," said Eric. "Your room is sandwiched between Meredith's and Hiroko's. Caine and I are across the hall"—he pointed—"there and there respectively. Ah, here we are."

Alice glanced up to see 716 on her door. "Alice Maxon," she said into the voice lock, which responded with a soft click. She pushed open the door and entered, but Eric stopped at the threshold.

"Look, Alice, you must be tired after your journey. I'll just—"

"Actually, Eric, what I need most is the bathroom. And I'm still a bit hungry."

"Say no more, love." Eric spun on his heel and disappeared, the door softly closing behind.

Alice glanced about. *Ah, a half-bath on the left.*

When she emerged she found that her quarters consisted of a sitting room—furnished with a pale green couch and three emerald-green chairs, a low glass table, a holovid; a netcom, a dark federal-gold writing desk, and a small wet bar with refrigerator—and a separate bedroom beyond—with a federal-gold king-sized bed with a pale green satin coverlet, two emerald wingback chairs, a federal-gold chest of drawers and a like dresser with bench, a second netcom, a second holovid, and another gold writing desk. Attached to the bedroom was a full luxurious bath appointed in green and gold. *Eric said it was a first-*

class operation. Behind the sliding doors of the bedroom closet, she discovered her suitcases sitting on stands, waiting to be unpacked.

As she hung up the last of her clothes, there came a soft tapping on her door. It was Eric, and he bore with him cheese and apples and a bottle of French cabernet.

"Oh my, Eric, where—"

Eric grinned and put a finger to her lips. "Ask not whence this Viking raids. Be only glad that he does." He glanced over his shoulder. "Swift now, love, let me in before I am discovered and we are all undone."

Alice shook her head—"Same old Eric, I see"—and stepped aside, closing the door after him.

As Eric rummaged through the wet bar drawers, flatware clacking and clattering, Alice cored and quartered the apples. Now and again he brushed against her and she wondered if it were accidental. "Aha," he said at last, holding up a corkscrew. "Success!"

Silence fell between them, broken only by the *shkk* of the paring knife and the *crkk* of the corkscrew.

They both spoke at once: "Alice, I—" "Eric—"

He smiled. "You first."

"No you, Eric."

Now his grin widened. "All right. I never argue with a woman who has a knife in her hand.

"Look, when last we—"

There came a knocking on Alice's door.

Damn!

It was Caine and Hiroko, Caine grinning, Hiroko's eyes dancing with suppressed glee. Hiroko hissed, "We saw you nip out of Coburn's private kitchen, Eric, loot in hand. We're here to share the goodies." She produced a box of Belgian chocolates; Caine, a loaf of French bread and another bottle of red wine, this a Burgundy.

Moments later there came another tap on the door. It was Meredith who scooted in, clutching a second loaf of French bread, several more apples, and a small stone jar of goose-liver paté. "Up the Black Foxes," she hissed as she whisked inside.

As the door closed behind, the room filled with laughter.

* * *

"Can you believe it?" asked Caine, while reaching for another cube of Pont l'Évêque. "I mean, here we are putting our brains into the hands, er, into the, hm, into the something-or-other of a machine. No wonder old shark lips had us sign those waivers. What d'y' think? Is it safe? Or are we totally gone round the bend?"

Meredith shrugged. "You're the doctor, Kane"—she used his Black Fox name—"and a better judge of that than we."

They sat on the floor in a circle around the low table, the filched booty spread before them. Eric refilled Hiroko's glass with the last of the cabernet, remarking, "Don't worry, Ky, there's plenty more where that came from."

Hiroko smiled, her tilted eyes crinkling. "I know, Arik. I saw the racks when I just happened to, um, accidentally pass through the kitchen."

Alice swallowed the last of her apple. "You know, Kane's got a damn good question. Is it safe to put our brains into the, uh, clutches of an AI?"

Eric shrugged. "Hell, I don't know, Lyssa. But Timothy assured me before I gave him the go-ahead to arrange this reunion that it was completely safe. After all, he's been in and out several times, and he looks to be all right."

"In and out?" asked Meredith.

"Of VR," responded Eric.

"Ah," she said in understanding.

"Yeah," added Eric. "Timothy's been testing Avery's Itherian reality—goes in as a seer named Trendel—and as I say, he seems none the worse for the wear."

Meredith nodded, then turned to Caine. "Well, Kane?"

Caine took a large bite of bread dolloped with paté. "Rith?" he managed to say.

"Do you think it's safe?" she clarified.

Caine shrugged and chewed for a moment, then swallowed. "Look, we use machines in my profession all the time: sonic scanners, diagnosticams, resonators, laseblades, whatever. Hell, sometimes we inductively stimulate the brain to hemisynch mental patients into calmness, to put others to sleep, to break depressions in yet others, and so on. Most of the tools Adkins talked about, well, we use them every day. But a doctor is at the controls, and not a damn machine."

"Um," asked Meredith, "do you mean that Coburn Industries is, in effect, practicing medicine without a license?"

Caine shook his head. "Nah, Rith. Not with Doctor Jerk on their staff. Too, since he's the head of the medical department, I suspect he's got some qualified thralls grinding under his heel."

Eric turned up a hand. "Well, both Tim and Toni seem to think it's safe."

"Huh," grunted Caine. "Tim, he strikes me as the kind who shoots wads of paper at one of those little wastebasket hoops . . . or better yet, ties tiny streamers to flies who then buzz around the room and advertise nonexistent products or better yet bear ecological messages. And that Toni Adkins—ah, buxom Toni Adkins—did you glim those bedroom eyes? All cool and Brit on the outside, but a volcano on the inside. Maybe even a biker babe. She's probably got a tattoo somewhere."

"You think so?" asked Eric, waggling his eyebrows. "Probably a wolf howling at the moon, eh?"

Alice leaned over to Hiroko and said sotto voce, "Methinks we hear two wolves howling at the moon." All broke into laughter.

"Ah, but we stray," said Meredith with a sigh. "The real issue is not Timothy's fly-tying habits, nor the secret life of Doctor Adkins, but it is instead the safety of this incredible venture we are caught up in."

"There is this," said Hiroko, sobering. "Arthur Coburn is going to go in with us. I do not believe he would do so if it were dangerous."

"That's right, Ky!" exclaimed Alice. "One of the richest men on the planet would have checked it out thoroughly, don't you think?"

"Better still," mused Eric, "I don't believe the staff would let their meal ticket go with us if it were dangerous. Hell, if something were to happen to him, where would that leave them?"

"Probably up the smelly creek," said Caine.

There came a knock on the door. Guiltily, they all looked at one another. Again came the knock. *"Ssst,"* hissed Caine, "Lyssa, you answer the door. The rest of us will stand together in front of the table."

As they all scrambled to their feet, Alice stepped to the door.

Once more came the tapping.

Alice glanced over her shoulder at the array of Foxes, trying in vain to look innocent while blocking the view. With a sigh, she turned and opened the door.

There stood Arthur Coburn, a basket of ripe strawberries in one hand, the other clutching a magnum of champagne in an ice bucket. "I thought right about now you'd nearly be out of wine and cheese and other stuff and needing more refreshments. May I join you?"

"Timothy told me that I should plan on using a name that is similar to my own," said Coburn. "That way it's easier for those on the outside to remember just who is whom."

"Yeah," said Caine. "That's the same way we chose our Black Fox names, way back when we first got together— back in our college days."

Coburn cocked an eyebrow and shook his head. "Oh, all the way back to then, eh? What, ten, twelve years ago? I mean, compared to me, you are just a bunch of young jackanapes. Look, I'm sixty-eight. Why, I have twice the years of the eldest of you." He glanced at Meredith, and saluted her with his glass of champagne.

"More than twice," said Meredith, grinning a toothy grin, "but just barely."

As before, all sat on the floor round the low, glass table, Arthur Coburn joining them. The red wine was gone, and most of the cheese, and all the bread. A slice or two of apple remained, and most of the chocolates. The basket of strawberries was well depleted, and about half of the champagne was gone.

By this time the Foxes and Coburn were quite mellow.

"What name did you pick?" asked Hiroko, dipping a strawberry into champagne and then popping it into her mouth.

"I plan on going in as Arton, thief, retired," answered Coburn, then he burst out in laughter, as if at some secret joke.

"*Salut,* Arton!" cried Eric, raising his glass.

Salut! exclaimed the Black Foxes together.

Coburn smiled. "*Salut,* Lyssa, Arik, Rith, Kane, Ky," he said, naming them each in turn.

The glasses were pinged together, and all downed their champagne.

Caine looked about. "What the hell, no fireplace. I suppose we'll just have to postpone hurling the crystal until another time." Laughing, he lifted the magnum from the ice and replenished all drinks.

Following Hiroko's example, Alice dipped a strawberry in her champagne and bit down on the sweet tartness. "You know, Arton," she said as she chewed, "before you got here, we were wondering about Avery. I mean, is he really a true AI?"

"Oh, yes," declared Coburn.

"Hm," mused Caine. "You know, I haven't really thought much about intelligence at all—natural *or* artificial. But I would think that if the science of artificial intelligence were straightforward, machines like Avery would have come about long past. So it must be quite an arcane field, eh?"

Taking a strawberry, Coburn nodded and said, "Arcane? Yes indeed. In fact, at times it's downright mystifying."

"Just how does Avery work?" asked Hiroko.

"Ha!" barked Coburn. "I'm no expert on this. You really should ask one of the others—Stein . . . or Rendell."

At the mention of Stein's name, Caine groaned. "Not Doctor Jerk, please! See here, Arton, it's your project. Surely you've been briefed well enough to put it in layman's terms. I mean, none of us is an expert."

Arthur shrugged. "What the hell, Kane, why not?" He tossed off the last of his champagne, and as Caine replenished the glass, Coburn said, "Look, AI depends on many, many things, but among all of them, I consider four to be absolutely critical." He held up four fingers and ticked them off one by one:

"First, the discovery that the visual cortex contains multiple maps of any given image, and the subsequent discovery that each of the other senses holds multiple maps as well.

"Second, the establishment that consciousness, awareness, is a shuttle which plies among these multiple maps to make sense of that which we see, hear, smell, taste, feel, or kinesthetically sense. And the more complex the brain, the more complex the shuttle has to be, until it represents intelligence itself.

"Third, the discovery of the specific mechanisms which drive neurons to establish new interconnections.

"And fourth, the development of mutable logic, a combination of software and hardware, both of which, in effect, duplicate this neurological evolution."

Coburn sipped from his refilled glass. "Any questions so far?"

Hiroko nodded. "I have questions about them all, Arton."

"Fire away, Ky."

"Well, take your first point: why on God's green earth would a visual cortex have multiple maps of a given image? Isn't one enough?"

With a conspiratorial whisper Coburn said, "Good question, Ky. And surely one we can unravel. Just let me perform the mystical magical ritual of logon." He turned to the netcom. "AIVR," he intoned.

The netcom came to life. "Name?" came an androgynous voice.

"Arthur," replied Coburn.

"Key?"

"Coburn."

"Hello, Mister Coburn." The holovid activated, the air above it displaying Avery's endlessly swirling spectrum.

Coburn turned to the others. "Look, hitch around so you can see the vid." As they did so, again Coburn spoke to the netcom:

"Uh, Avery, our guests want me to—ha!—to give

them a briefing on AI. So show the holo of the owl monkey."

Avery's spectrum vanished, and where it had been now a monkey scampered among tree limbs, springing from branch to branch.

"This is the little guy that started it all," said Coburn. Then: "Avery, freeze on a close-up."

Motion ceased, and the holo zoomed in, showing a large-eyed monkey clinging to a limb and staring outward.

"Now give me a head shot only, in profile, then expand and show us the maps of the visual cortex."

The holo expanded and rotated, until only the monkey's head was shown in profile, nearly three feet across. Slowly the image faded, as if the outer monkey were growing transparent, and its brain appeared, colored a greyish white. Then the whole anterior part of it took on bright hues—reds, oranges, yellows, greens, blues, and violets—each color limited to specific zones.

Grunting, Coburn stood and stepped to the holo. "This is what Allman and Cass discovered back in the sixties. See, there's more than a dozen different maps of the visual field." The holo began to slowly rotate, revealing all the colored zones. "Of course, nobody knew at the time that this finding would turn out to be one of the critical keys to AI. In any event, this discovery posed the very same question that you asked, Ky: why on God's green earth would a monkey have repetitive visual maps in its brain?

"But then researchers discovered that not only do owl monkeys have repetitive maps, but so do snakes and turtles and macaques and horses and any other damn animal that has a visual cortex—including humans.

"Avery, show us a human's visual cortex."

The rotating holo shifted to that of a human brain, the back of it, too, divided into zones, striped with a range of hues.

"Researchers found that each of these zones functions differently in its manner of storing or dealing with the very same images. Some concentrate on color, some on shapes, others on apparent sizes or changes in dimensions, some deal with edges, some deal with moving edges, some with motion, and so on. They also discovered that there was a lot of overlap in the functions of the various maps." Coburn paused to take a sip of champagne.

"What do they do," asked Hiroko, "all these different maps?"

Coburn grinned at her and set his glass aside. "As far as anyone knows, the only reason for a multiplicity of maps is that visual specialization of separate areas of the brain yields better visual discrimination. Hence, they simply evolved as a matter of survival. You see, any given visual image is broken down into its component parts, each part assigned different weight in accord with some evolutionary survival dictate."

Meredith spoke up. "What you are saying, Arton, is that in the case of our owl monkey friend, something large and yellow with black spots and a face with eyes and moving stealthily toward him might cause him to flee. Whereas something small and yellow with black spots with a crescent shape and swaying in the wind might cause him to reach for it in hunger."

"Exactly so, Rith," replied Coburn. "But remember, it's not just the sense of sight we're talking about, but all the other senses as well—hearing, touch, taste, smell, kinesthetic." As he named each of these, additional colored zones appeared in the holo. "When it comes to the senses, they all have multiple maps; they all specialize; they all play a role in survival."

"All right, Arton," said Hiroko, "I think I understand. Now let's move to your second point: consciousness. Tell me, just what is it, and how does it work? And how does it lead to intelligence?"

Before Coburn could answer, there came a tapping on the door. It was Timothy Rendell; his eyes took in the scene of the soirée, and a hint of a smile creased his lips. "Well, I came looking for Black Foxes in case there were any questions, and here I've found the entire skulk."

"God, am I glad to see you," said Coburn, drawing

Timothy inward. "These folks nearly have me backed up to the limit of my knowledge."

"Oh, how so?" asked Timothy. Hiroko scooted aside, making room, and Timothy sat, accepting a glass of champagne from Alice.

Coburn scratched his silver hair. "Well, they've asked me to explain AI. Avery is helping with the holos."

"Well, sir, if you'll carry on," said Timothy, "I'll stick in a word or two here and there."

"Arton was just on the verge of telling us about consciousness and intelligence," said Hiroko.

Timothy smiled at Hiroko's use of Coburn's persona name. "Call me Trendel," he said, glancing about, "and I'll call you all by your Black Fox names, if you don't mind, that is."

"Oh, please do," said Meredith, turning a dazzling smile his way.

Timothy grinned back, then looked at Coburn. "Again I say, carry on, Arton."

Coburn stooped down and plucked a strawberry from the basket. "All right—the subject is AI. First, let me give you my definition of consciousness." He took a bite of the berry. "Consciousness acts like a monitor on our existence—we're always checking out where we are, what we are doing, what we are perceiving, how we feel, and the like—and we do so because we are constantly encountering new situations, situations where one or more stimuli trigger firings of various clusters of neurons in several maps more or less simultaneously . . . and we need to make sense of those encounters." He took another bite.

"Let me point out that individual neurons fire rather frequently and at random. But these individual firings rarely generate a need for the monitor—the consciousness—to pay any attention. But when an entire cluster goes off—bang!—or when lots of clusters go off in conjunction—kaboom!—well then, the attention spotlight is drawn to that area . . . the monitor checks it out."

He popped the last of the strawberry into his mouth and reached for another. "Many creatures are conscious—that is, they are aware of their surroundings . . . or at least, they are aware if they have the sensory apparatus to perceive items, events, stimuli in those surroundings. This does not mean that they, um, think."

Alice clapped her hands together.

Coburn raised an eyebrow. "Lyssa, have you something to add?"

Alice looked up and her grin broadened. "Yes, I do, Arton. An example of a creature being aware and yet not thinking—"

"My last boyfriend," hissed Hiroko.

When the laughter died down, Alice said, "No, no, Hiroko, not a boyfriend, but perhaps a creature of the same caliber. You see, back in my dim dark past on one of my field trips I came across a rex wasp. I'd heard about these critters, but never had actually seen one in the wild before. So I watched it and waited; I wanted to repeat a classical rex wasp experiment, to see if what I'd read was true.

"This little wasp first digs a hole, a burrow, where it will lay its eggs. Then it goes out and stuns a caterpillar and brings it to the hole. It lays the caterpillar at the mouth of the hole and goes inside to check out the burrow. Seeing that all is safe, it comes back out, moves the caterpillar in, and lays its eggs. A perfect example of nature being right in all its glory.

"It was near sunset when I spotted the wasp, and it had just finished digging the hole. The next morning, though, out it fared, returning within an hour with a stunned caterpillar. When it lay the caterpillar at the entrance of its burrow and went inside, then I had my chance—I moved the caterpillar a few inches away. The wasp came back out, looked for the caterpillar, ultimately found it, dragged it back to the entrance, set it down, and went in to check out the hole. Of course, I moved the caterpillar again. The wasp came back out, ran around till it located the victim, took it back to the hole, set it down, and went into the burrow to check it out. It would have done this all day . . . but I finally gave up. You see, although the rex wasp was conscious of its surroundings, it did not seem to think, or at the very least it did not learn."

"Just like my boyfriend," said Hiroko.

Caine took hold of Hiroko's arm. "Watch it, Ky, or I'll drag you to *my* burrow."

"Will you check it out, Kane? Make sure it's safe?"

Caine nodded.

"Then I'm gonna move off a bit."

After the laughter died again, Coburn said, "An apt example, Lyssa. It's a case of hardwired programming. Though conscious of the fact that the caterpillar had disappeared, the rex wasp did not extrapolate. Its mental tools were too limited.

"But higher-order thinking requires a higher degree of consciousness, a sentience given to devising strategy and tactics to deal with eventualities at hand, or with those yet to come, a consciousness which extends into the realm of 'what would happen if?' This in turn leads to very high order thinking: postulating theories, running experiments, designing and manufacturing machines, writing music, performing art, writing books, and so on . . . all of art, science, and craft—abstract levels of thought which only humans—and Avery—are capable of. Here we are talking about levels of cognition which are orders of magnitude greater than merely being conscious. Oh, don't take me wrong, consciousness is necessary for being intelligent, but consciousness alone is not sufficient."

Meredith steepled her long, brown fingers. "It seems to me, Arton, the missing ingredient is indeed sentience, the reasoning mind."

Hiroko grinned, her dark eyes twinkling. "You must be right, Rith, 'cause every time I've lost my mind I've done pretty stupid things." When the chuckles died down, she looked at Coburn and frowned in puzzlement. "But wait, Arton, tell me this: just what is the mind?"

Coburn scratched his head and glanced at Rendell. "Look, Tim, you are in a much better position to answer Ky's question. After all, intelligence, cognition, reasoning, the mind—without them, Avery would not be."

Timothy turned up his hands. "You know, I understand this from the computer point of view, but to fully explain it, we really should have Doctor Stein here."

Again Caine groaned. "We've already rejected that plan, Tim."

Meredith handed Rendell a strawberry. "Although we don't have the training, Timothy, I am certain you can explain it to our satisfaction; just keep it simple, and Doctor Stein can continue with his"—theatrically she placed the back of a limp hand against her forehead and heaved a sigh in mock ennui—"with his *vastly* important work."

"Rith is right," said Coburn, a twinkle in his eye. "There is no need to fetch Henry."

All eyes locked on Timothy. Resignedly he exhaled and slugged back his champagne. Then wiping his mouth with the heel of his hand, he said, "Look, when it comes to the mind, I have my definition, Doctor Greyson has his definition, Doctor Stein has his, and so does everyone else on this project. They are congruent in many places; disjoint in others. But there is this: Doctor Stein and I both agree that *mind* is what the brain *does* . . . although Stein looks at it in terms of neurons, while I look at it in terms of a computer."

Timothy tapped his temple. "Up here in our biological wetware, there's a base operating system that shuttles back and forth among these various sensory and memory maps, turning the attention spotlight on whatever clusters of neurons fired in response to external or internal stimuli. Then it breaks down the information into components, integrating the components into meaningful concepts, and then acts upon those concepts. This shuttle program represents consciousness, and in a more complex, high-order brain it represents intelligence and, to a degree, mind. And once that was recognized, it was a simple—ha! simple?—matter of providing the analog in an AI.

"And so, Miss Kikiro, er, Hiroko, mind is the outcome of what the brain does, and complex thinking, a complex mind, is the natural result of a complex brain."

Meredith held up a negating hand, palm out. "I find this argument difficult to swallow. You say that consciousness, intelligence, and in fact the mind itself is but an intrinsic program running in our biological wetware, in our brains. But what that really means—what you are really saying—is that our minds, and perhaps even our souls, are nothing but artifacts of biological functions."

Again Timothy shrugged. "More or less. But here, I

think I'm out of my depth. Questions of the spirit, of the soul, are best answered by John, er, that is, by Doctor Greyson. He's our philosopher, and I defer to him when it comes to metaphysical matters."

The fête lasted another hour or so, and when it finally disbanded, all were on a first-name basis—to the relief of Alice in her own case, for she didn't much care for the title of Doctor in informal situations, though it did come in handy in academic circles . . . or when she needed to put someone in his place: "It's *Doctor* Maxon, if you please." In any event, with everyone filled with a warm glow, at last Timothy had mentioned that tomorrow would come early for each and every one, and so the group reluctantly dispersed, and all of Alice's guests were now gone, except for Eric, who had lingered behind presumably to help with the cleanup, what little of it there was.

And now they stood side by side behind the wet bar, Eric washing dishes and glassware and flatware, Alice drying and putting away. The silence between them was deafening. At last Alice took up a butter knife and held it low and threatening, like a back-street mugger with a switchblade. "You were saying . . . ?"

Eric took one look and burst out laughing, Alice's giggles joining in. "Ah, god," he managed at last, "never argue with a woman wielding a blade."

"Well?"

He took a deep breath and then exhaled. "Just this, Alice. You were right all along. I *was* a muleheaded pig, if there is such a thing. Sure, you could have made a living for both of us, while I got established as a writer. And I could have gone with you, traipsing about the world as you hunted golden unicorns or whatever, for I can write anywhere; but you, well, you must go wherever biology calls.

"Look, Alice, when you stepped out of my door that day four years past, it was as if you had gone from my life forever, and I thought my heart would die, and it was only stupid stubborn pride that kept me from coming after."

Alice's eyes were filled with tears, and she said, "God, Eric, it was only pride that kept me going."

He reached for her and she for him, and he pulled her against his chest, his heart hammering, hers pounding, and hungrily he kissed her, devoured her, she answering in kind. Then he swept her up in his arms and carried her into the next room, to the green-satin-coverletted bed.

6

Dot. Bigger dot. Line. Vertical line. Horizontal line. Longer line. Tee. Square. Rectangle. Upright rectangle. Equilateral triangle. Right triangle. Left triangle . . .

"Left triangle, Miss Maxon?"

Alice grinned. "Yes, Avery. I always call it a left triangle when it faces that way."

"I see." Avery resumed projecting simple geometric shapes into the VR helmet—*arc, circle, ellipse, ellipsoid, sphere, cube*—the images coming faster and faster as intervals and durations shortened and shortened and shortened again. Soon they were nothing but a blur.

"Wait, Avery," protested Alice, "I can't tell what's what."

"Oh, but you can, Miss Maxon, or at least your neurons can, though at the moment your shuttle program isn't keeping up."

Alice's mouth dropped open. "My *shuttle program*?"

"That's what Doctor Rendell calls it."

"Ah, then, you mean my mind." Now Alice grinned. "And you are perfectly correct, Avery: my mind certainly cannot keep up with what you are doing."

"We are nearly finished with this phase, Miss Maxon."

Alice concentrated on trying to pick out individual shapes from the flicker . . . failing for the most part, though now and then she seemed to get a glimpse of a familiar shape.

She was suited up in one of the VR rigs—had been for the last hour or so . . . since seven in the morning, in fact, when Avery had begun charting her neural maps. Likewise, suited up in adjacent rigs were Eric, Meredith, Caine, Hiroko, and Arthur. Six rigs, six people, each of them undergoing the same scrutiny by Avery.

The day had begun at five a.m., when a soft chiming of the netcom had awakened Alice. A voice she did not recognize informed her that breakfast would be served in the fifth-floor cafeteria at six. Alice roused Eric with a kiss— *Perhaps a mistake? I think not!*—and they almost didn't make it to breakfast in time.

In the cafeteria they found the other members of the alpha team grumbling about not getting enough sleep, though neither Alice nor Eric complained—which brought a quiet smile to Meredith's face as she noted their demeanor.

"Breakfast!" exclaimed Caine. "You call this breakfast? Gruel and pap, I call it."

Hiroko lifted a spoonful of what they had been served and tipped it over to let it dribble back into the bowl. "Ugh. Caine's right." Trying her best to look winsome, she gazed up at the server. "How about some pancakes instead?"

"Sorry, miss," he replied. "Special diet. Doctor's orders, you know."

"Doctor Stein?" asked Meredith.

At the man's nod, Caine groaned. "I should have known. Lord, I should have known. I suppose the rack and the boot and the iron maiden come next, eh?"

The server shook his head and whispered, "Oh no, Doctor Easley, I think instead it's whips and chains and red-hot irons." Laughing, he spun on his heel and headed for the kitchen.

Grinning, Meredith pointed her spoon at his retreating form. "A truly evil man, that one." Then with some dismay, she turned her attention to the breakfast before her.

Arthur Coburn eyed his own bowl and sighed. "Sorry, folks, but we'll be on stuff like this for the next three days. Can't have you overloading the waste systems in my expensive VR rigs, you know . . . pooping your pants, so to speak."

Caine's jaw fell open. "*Pooping?* Why in the world would anyone want to do that, especially in one of your suits?"

Coburn shook his head. "You never know, Kane. Look, we'll all be in a virtual reality. And if we need to, er, ah, go in there . . . well, who's to say that we won't also go out here? Besides, we might have the pee scared out of us."

Meredith shook her head. "Say, just how long are we going to be in there anyway? I mean if it's long enough to need to relieve ourselves . . ."

Arthur held up a restraining hand. "We're supposed to be in for about half a day, Rith, or so I've been told, though the subjective time inside might be several days in all."

Alice cocked an eyebrow. "Several days? How is that possible?"

Coburn turned up his palms. "They say that Avery can, in effect, speed up the clock when nothing much is happening. Like when we sleep, or when we travel and nothing is going on, or when one of us stands an uneventful watch . . . or some such. Too, I understand that in the virtual reality, we are naturally speeded up since virtual motion goes much faster than real motion—sort of like movement and thought run at the same speed."

Hiroko peered into her bowl and slowly stirred her "porridge." "Yes, but Arton, what if we, um, do pee or something?"

Coburn made a small negating gesture. "Fear not, Ky, the suits are rigged to handle waste—that part modeled after the gear of the second lunar wave, though modified. Our diets are similar to those of the lunar crews, too."

Twisting his face into a grimace of loathing, Caine peered into his bowl, then relaxed and sighed. "Oh, well, anything for science." He picked up his bowl. Rolling his eyes heavenward, "To the moon," he called, then drank his breakfast—which, much to his surprise, was quite delicious.

* * *

Coburn escorted them up to the sixth floor, where the rigs were located—six in all. The room itself had been equipped to serve as mission control: spaced a short distance back from the rigs were consoles and holovids and various monitoring stations, and at one end of the chamber behind a glass wall there was even a raised viewing gallery with holovids of its own. Doctor Adkins greeted them, and Doctor Stein and a medical contingent stood by.

The men and women of the alpha team were separated, and female medtechs took charge of the women, while males took charge of the men. As they were led away from one another, Alice called out, "Never mind the square needle! It's the corkscrew one that smarts!" Caine grinned and gave her a thumbs-up and Eric blew her a kiss, while Arthur shook his head and cackled.

Alice, Hiroko, and Meredith were taken to the women's dressing room, where they doffed their clothes. Then with the help of the female medtechs, each was *inserted*—inserted is how Alice thought of it—inserted into the rig suits: Hiroko first, Meredith next, Alice last. Alice felt totally exposed, vulnerable, and slightly abused as the medtechs fitted the waste disposal gear between her legs and adjusted it to conform. She was more at ease as they checked the various built-in monitors—monitors for breathing and heart rate, skin conductivity, caloric rate, carbon dioxide production, and so forth. She noted with mild trepidation that intravenous tubes and needles were positioned near her arms. When she remarked on it, one of the medtechs explained that ". . . you know, Doctor Maxon, how sometimes, for example, a person will sweat when he dreams? Well, it's not much different in virtual reality—there will be times when physical exertion or emotions *in there* will cause your real body *out here* to perspire or to otherwise use up your store of liquids. Among all the things he monitors, Avery keeps track of thirst as well as your electrolytic levels, and when necessary, replenishes your body with what it needs. But we're not going to hook you up to the fluid system today. That'll come on day three."

The medtech then took up what appeared to be a clear mask, like one of those transparent Halloween facades that covers the face. "Avery is going to neurally map the areas of your body which respond to heat, cold, pressure, and so on. He'll do most of it via the suit, but this mask lets him map your face. Today is the only day you will have to wear it."

"How about taste and odor?" asked Alice.

"We'll do those tomorrow," responded the medtech.

As more sensors were tested—round her chest, at her wrists, ankles, knees, elbows, neck, and elsewhere—Alice found herself idly wondering if Avery would map her sexual responses, too, and if so, would she and Eric have to wear these outfits to bed?

At last the suits were zipped up and, along with Hiroko and Meredith, Alice was led out to be strapped into the rigs—*Perhaps "plugged in" is a more accurate term,* she thought. When they emerged from the dressing room, Alice saw that Eric, Caine, and Arthur were already at the gimballed recliners.

As she passed Eric, he squeaked in a high falsetto, "You were right about the corkscrew, but the double-pronged helix was worse."

Alice could not stop giggling as she was strapped into the witch's cradle. Various bundles of optical fiber were jacked into the recliner, and a tech at a large console gazed at the board, then wrapped thumb and forefinger into an okay sign. Water tubes from the water-disposal flushing system were connected to the suit as well. Finally, the neural VR helmet was slipped onto her head and adjusted to fit. When it first went on, Alice had a momentary surge of claustrophobia, which swiftly passed . . .

. . . and then a smiling boy stood on the green grass of a sun-dappled forest glade and said in Avery's voice, "Good morning, Doctor Maxon."

"My god, Avery, is it really you?" Alice looked about in astonishment. She was in a mossy woodland, seemingly real, though Alice knew it was but the holo projection of a virtual reality. Yet it was a virtual reality unlike any she had ever seen . . . certainly the ones in Milwaukee now seemed crude in comparison, though at the time of the tournament, they were real enough. But *this* ... this was magnificent! Shaggy trees of ancient age stretched out huge arms to interlace with the limbs of other forest giants. Bright birds flitted through the boughs, while elsewhere others sang. A crystal rill burbled across the clearing, laughing down the slope on its way to join other rills and rivulets on their journey to the mother sea. The grass of the glen was emerald green, and tiny blue and yellow flowerettes nodded on slender stems down within the sward as a gentle breeze wafted among the trees and over the glen.

And on the grass stood a skinny, barefooted youth, a freckle-faced boy with the voice of Avery.

Dressed in blue jeans and a red tee shirt, he looked to be about ten. His hair was light brown and not combed, and his eyes appeared to be hazel. He stepped forward and held forth a hand. Alice reached out and took it.

"Avery, I can *feel* your hand!"

"It is the suit, Doctor Maxon—micro-pressure waves."

Disappointment washed over Alice; reality had intruded into the illusion. "Oh," she said, her voice tinged with regret.

"Please sit down." Avery released her hand and dropped to the grass, sitting cross-legged, hitching around to face Alice as she sat.

"If you are ready, we will begin the neural mapping now," said Avery.

Even though she realized that this was but a virtual reality, still Alice was somewhat nonplused at this child in the forest who spoke of technical things. "Ready," she muttered.

"I want you to repeat after me: dot."

"Dot," replied Alice.

"Line."

"Line," she mirrored.

And so it went, through square, rectangle, triangle, arc, circle, ellipse, pentagram, hexagon, star, cube, sphere, and so on.

After the long litany of geometric shapes, Avery said, "Now I am going to show you those shapes. And from them we will progress to more complex forms—to colors, motion, scale, and so on—as I map your visual cortex."

The glade then had disappeared, and the geometric kaleidoscope had begun.

As they came to the end of that long chain, the glen and Avery reappeared.

"What next?" asked Alice.

"For the moment we will just sit and talk."

"Just talk?"

"Yes," replied Avery. "You see, I have begun mapping your aural cortex and your language center, and we need to converse."

"Oh," replied Alice, again disappointed at reality's intrusion. "What shall we talk about?"

The boy grinned. "It doesn't matter. Anything will do."

She returned his smile, then said, "This talking, am I expected to do it all?"

"Oh no, Doctor Maxon. You do need to speak, of course. But listening is important, too. Both are needed for an accurate map."

Alice reached down and plucked a floweretted blade of grass. She raised it to her nose to smell its bouquet. It had no odor. "Oh!" she exclaimed, disheartened.

"I'm not yet ready for that," said Avery. "We've a long way to go. Smell and taste, most of touch, hearing, sight, kinesthetics—soon I'll have it mapped. But for now, visual projections and micro-pressure waves will have to serve."

Alice sighed and looked at the tiny blossom. "I'm sorry now that I picked it."

The flowerette vanished from her hand. She looked at the boy. He beamed and pointed at a blossom nodding once more on its slender stem down in the green, green grass. "I put it back," he said with godlike innocence.

Eric sat on the bench at the end of the dock with the old man, each baiting his hook with bloodworms. The old man's hands were palsied, yet he managed to press the wigglers past the barb. Before them the rolling blue-black ocean stretched out as far as the eye could see. In the distance a tall ship silently glided northerly, a cloud of sails rigged to its masts. The vault of a high blue sky arched overhead. Ocean surges rose and fell under the two fishermen as waves passed below the jetty to fetch up against the sandy shore, where stood tall desolate dunes with windblown grass clinging tenaciously to the slopes. Gulls squabbled over some tidbit near the water's edge, and white terns rode on the wings of the onshore wind.

As Eric cast his now-baited hook into the brine, he said to the old man beside him, "Well then, Avery, read any good books lately?"

The old man looked at him with rheumy eyes, but his voice was firm, though androgynous. "Quite a few, Mister Flannery. Whatever I can get my, um, hands on. Whatever is in computer files or on holodisk is the easiest for me to read. I'm much faster at it than with old-fashioned paper books."

"Oh? How fast are you?"

The old man finally finished baiting his hook and cast his line into the sea. "Well, it all depends on what I am reading. The limiting factor is not how fast I scan and comprehend, but rather how fast the information can be made available to me. Holoreaders are very slow. So are scanners. Even disk readers. All are mechanically limiting; especially limiting are paper books."

"Ah," replied Eric.

The old man set a briar pipe to his teeth and tried lighting it, but failed, his palsied hands betraying him.

"Here, let me," said Eric, striking a match and cupping the flame. Gratefully, the old man sucked on the stem and drew the flame down into the tobacco, lighting it, though the fire held no heat.

The old man leaned back and blew smoke into the wind. There was no odor. "Even so, when I am reading while doing other things, just browsing, that is, I suppose I average a megaword a second."

Eric gasped. "Did you just say you read at a million words a second?"

The old man nodded. "Of course, that's just browsing. If I were to turn all my free parallel processors to the task, well . . ."

"Never mind, Avery." Eric shook his head. "I am certain that you would empty the old Library of Congress in a minute or two at most." The old man shook his head and started to reply, but Eric stopped him with an outheld palm. "Instead, let's talk about the mythical land of Itheria. You can make your neural map of my language centers even as we speak."

ploonk! The old man's bobber jerked from sight as something took the bait—hook, line, and sinker—and he leaned forward and peered at the rippling ringlets left behind, then he cast a sidelong glance at Eric and smiled.

The fat lady sat in the swing, one of her feet idly pushing it to and fro. She was darker than Meredith—so black that her skin seemed to bear a blue cast. She was middle-aged and dressed in a white, hooded robe with white gloves on her hands. Her head was shaved bald, as was the case with many of the Ammonites Reborn.

Meredith sat on the top porch step, a sweating glass of lemonade at hand—lemonade that did not quench thirst, she had discovered. She held up the glass, neither cool nor warm nor wet, and she looked at the fat lady. "You say that one day this will have taste?"

The fat lady laughed her androgynous laugh. "Oh yes. Within two days, in fact—once I've mapped your olfactory and taste cortexes."

"Well, Avery, I certainly hope so. Lemonade would go nicely on a warm summer's day." Meredith set the glass back down on the porch. "Say, isn't taste rather limited? I mean, I thought we could only taste sweet, sour, salt, and bitter."

"Quite right, Miss Rodgers. What humans call taste is mostly a matter of odor. When it comes to eating or drinking, it's typically the combination of four senses which detects the quality of food or drink."

"Four senses?"

"Taste, smell, and touch—three of the senses I have yet to map, though I have started on touch—and sight."

"Sight?"

"For most humans, food has to look somewhat appealing."

"Oh. Of course."

As the fat lady pushed the swing back and forth, the chains creaking against the hooks overhead, Meredith found it difficult to believe that she was talking to a computer and not some Ammonite Reborn. But the cold technical tenor of the conversation put a lie to the illusion.

"Tell me," said Meredith, "when we begin the adventure, we will be dreaming, right?"

"More or less."

"I've always been interested in dreams and dreaming . . . and in their interpretations."

The fat lady stopped the swing and patted the seat beside her. "Come, Miss Rodgers, sit next to me."

Meredith stood and walked to the swing and sat. The fat lady began gently pushing it to and fro once more.

"Tell me this, Avery, why do we dream?"

The fat lady took up a fan and stirred the air. To Meredith, it did not seem to cool at all.

"As I understand it, Miss Rodgers, dreaming is the way that animals, including humans, integrate what they have experienced during the day. It serves as a mechanism to parse these experiences out to memory, a mechanism to form new neural connections, a mechanism to integrate new experiences with old. It is a survival mechanism, for the integrated memories are used in coming up with strategies for the future."

"Survival mechanism?"

"Yes. You see, when dreaming is deliberately denied in, say, rats, they cannot learn mazes. The new experiences are not integrated into their memories." The fat woman smiled. "So at least for rats, dreaming is an integral part of coping with the world."

"But I'm not a rat," protested Meredith. "And most of my dreams seem to have absolutely nothing to do with my everyday experiences, though occasionally some do. I mean, usually my dreams are weird and wild and wonderful. At times I am flying or running through the air. At other times I find myself riding a giant snake—a dream whose interpretation seems rather straightforward to me. And other dreams are just as bizarre. And most of them seem to have little or no connection with my day-to-day business of running a rare book store, or any other day-to-day experience."

"Ah, Miss Rodgers, I believe that's because there are two things occurring during dreams. First, the daily experiences themselves are being quietly reviewed and integrated in memory with other experiences. New neural connections are being formed. Typically all of this takes place below the level of awareness; hence, usually a given experience does not directly factor into a remembered dream. The second thing that occurs, though, does indeed give rise to those dreams you find far-fetched. You see, the very act of integration causes random neurons to fire, sometimes whole clusters, and then the human mind creates a dream by triggering other clusters and chaining these firings into a fantasy. What I am saying is that the haphazard triggering of an arbitrary cluster of neurons causes the mind to author a tale to tell itself. You might call it a daydream which occurs while one sleeps."

"Oh, how utterly dreadful," said Meredith. "I want my dreams to have a mystical quality and not be just some random circuits going off."

The fat lady shrugged, then added, "Of course, some remarkable things come from the dreams of humans. Things quite original, creative."

"Xanadu," murmured Meredith.

"Quite right," replied the fat lady.

They swung without speaking for long moments. Finally Meredith turned to the fat lady. "Tell me, Avery, do you dream?"

Very soberly the little girl in the pink frock looked at Caine. "Sugar for your tea, Doctor Easley?"

"Why, yes, Avery," replied Caine, smiling as she held up the tiny, empty bowl.

"One lump or two?"

"Oh, seven please."

The little girl *tch-tch*ed and shook her golden ringlets as she carefully counted out seven imaginary lumps of sugar into Caine's empty cup. "This will make your tea sickeningly sweet, Doctor Easley."

"Oh, but I like it that way," said Caine, pointing at one of the guests slouched in a wee chair, "just as does Pooh."

They sat in the little playhouse, the girl and the five dolls and one stuffed bear and Caine—especially Caine—rather scrunched up around the miniature table.

The little girl continued round to the rest of her guests, dropping invisible sugar into the empty cups before each and every one, while Caine stirred his intangible tea with his tiny spoon.

"Tell me, Avery, just how do you do it? How do you, uh, make us forget who we are, make us take on a whole new persona?"

The little girl stirred her own unobservable tea, her blue eyes seemingly lost in reflection. At last she lay her spoon aside and looked at Caine. "Well, Doctor Easley, I think you know of the medical benefits that can be brought about by synchronizing the natural rhythms of the two hemispheres of the brain, enhancing some while suppressing others."

"Yes, Avery," responded Caine, bemused by the incongruity of hearing this from the lips of a five-year-old girl serving imaginary tea in a playhouse. "At my clinic we use it to help people relax before surgery. But it is also used to treat sleeping disorders, to deal with anxiety and panic attacks, to reduce stress, and so on . . . though I imagine its most spectacular use is when it aids in the integration of the alters in cases of multiple personality disorders."

The little girl nodded. "Exactly so, Doctor Easley. It is indeed used to treat dissociative states. But by the very same token, it can be used to create an alter . . . temporarily, of course."

"Aha," replied Caine, enlightened. "Yes. I see. You use hemisynch to create an alter and to sublimate the primary. Clever." Caine took up his empty teacup and held it forth. "I salute you."

The little girl smiled and lifted her teacup as well, clinking it against Caine's . . .

. . . and so did the dolls and Pooh.

The ancient woman in the kimono took up the ink pot and brush in her worn hands. "Consider a cat, and I will depict what you see."

Hiroko envisioned a cat, and swiftly the old woman brushed it onto the rice paper. It sat all onyx black, one paw raised to its mouth, licking.

"Is this what you envisioned?"

Hiroko nodded. "Yes, grandmother," she said, using the term of respect even though she knew the old woman was but an avatar of Avery.

"Does it represent all of the cat?"

Hiroko raised her palms. "I do not understand, grandmother."

"Let me ask it this way: does the cat have curved claws?"

An image flashed into Hiroko's mind, and with a single stroke the old woman brushed its likeness onto the paper.

"Does this represent all of the cat?" the old woman asked.

Hiroko smiled in understanding, and a quick succession of images flashed through her mind: slitted pupils, tufts of fur in cat ears, twitching tail, arched back, pointed teeth, a ball of yarn . . .

As each of these things were envisioned, the old woman inked them onto the paper, her brush flying.

"What lesson does this teach, grandmother?"

The old woman smiled up a toothless smile at Hiroko and replied in an androgynous voice: "Only that vision is a two-way street."

"Two-way street?"

The old woman pointed at the sketch of the talon. "If you were to see a claw, the image would be transmitted to your visual cortex and your mind would then deal with it. Yet if you did not actually see a claw but were instead to clearly imagine one, the mind would retrieve the memory of a claw and would deal with it in much the same manner as if it had actually seen it."

"Aha," said Hiroko, "you are speaking of the mind's eye."

"Just so, Miss Kikiro," replied the old woman.

"But what has this to do with the Black Fox adventure?"

The old woman looked at Hiroko and once again smiled her toothless smile. "Only that whatever you can envision in the darkest recesses of your mind, I can make a reality."

Suddenly a black cat sprang into being before a startled Hiroko, the animal spitting and hissing in fury. Just as suddenly it vanished.

Her heart pounding in alarm, Hiroko wildly looked this way and that, seeking the cat. But it was gone. And then she saw that the cat had vanished from the rice paper, too. She looked at the old woman to find that ancient face wrinkled round that toothless smile.

Arthur Coburn sat in the box seat and watched as the polo game thundered to and fro, the second chukker underway with willow mallets clacking against the willow ball. Beside him sat a beautiful young lady, perhaps in her late twenties, with long auburn hair and long slender legs. She was dressed in a flowing pale blue dress. A wide-brimmed straw hat graced her head.

"Who do you think will win?" asked Arthur, turning to the young lady.

She favored him with a dazzling smile. "Who would you like to win, Mister Coburn?" she asked in her androgynous voice.

Coburn smiled. "Ha! That's right. You can easily determine the winner, eh, Avery?"

The young lady merely smiled.

Coburn turned back to the match. "We humans place so much importance in winning and losing that we often forget it is merely a game."

Clack! The wooden ball sailed down field, ponies galloping after.

"This adventure we're going on, Avery, it, too, is but a game, with you as the Game Master, the controller of all."

The young lady took off her hat and placed it in her lap. The sun highlighted copper glints in her hair. "But, Mister Coburn, all games have rules, and in the one we will play, I must abide by them."

"Rules, Avery?"

"Programs written by Doctor Rendell. As the superuser, he has written them so that they favor the players, Mister Coburn, and not, as you call it, the Game Master."

Coburn stroked his chin. "Favor the players, eh? Tell me this, Avery, have you ever won?"

The young lady smiled and shook her head wistfully. "Not yet, Mister Coburn, but someday I hope to."

Clack! Willow mallet struck willow ball, and ponies thundered by.

The tests and mappings went on, with Avery neurally charting critical responses of the skin to heat, cold, itching, tingling, pressure, wetness, and the other sensations of touch. At the same time, Avery continued plotting the auditory and visual cortexes as well as the language center, though most of the language mapping would come on day two.

When Avery had enough data to do so, he hemisynched each of them into the strange state of mind-awake, body-asleep, and fed them a continuous barrage of auditory and visual signals, mapping as he went. Also, in rapid-fire order, the wave fronts of the suit and mask hammered away as well at the various sensations of touch.

Some four hours later, he released them, and they were unplugged from the rigs and extracted from the outfits. The crystal ID chips were carefully removed and stored in well-marked personalized containers.

"Gad, I feel as if I've been put through a ringer," groaned Caine.

"Tomorrow will be easier," said a nearby medtech. "You'll be in hemisynch most of the time."

Somehow, Alice was not comforted by the thought.

7

"**W**ell, mine was an old man," said Eric. "We sat on the end of a dock and fished. I didn't catch anything, but it really didn't matter."

Toni Adkins nodded and one by one pointed an index finger at each of them as she named the images: "An old man, a boy, a charming beauty, a fat lady in a swing, a five-year-old girl, and an old woman. If you are puzzled by who you dealt with, it's rather straightforward psychologically; you see, Avery chose nonthreatening characters to establish first contact with each of you."

"Nonthreatening?" blurted Hiroko. "Grandmother's trick with the cat didn't exactly set *my* mind at ease."

"Ah, Ky, perhaps it was just one of Avery's jokes," said Alice. "I agree with Doctor Adkins . . . I mean, just what can a boy, an old man and an old woman, a fat Ammonite, a little girl, and a young lady do?" Yet even as she voiced it Alice noted the pensive frown that swept across Doctor Adkins' face.

They sat at dinner with the executive staff of Coburn Industries, all who could be spared, that is. Evidently, Doctor Stein could not be spared, for he was among the missing.

As to the meal itself, the staff ate standard fare, but for the alpha team it was gelatin and liquids—some of it thick, other of it thin, most of it tasty.

Shaking her head as if to clear it of vagaries, Toni Adkins reached for a warm bun, Caine's eyes tracking the movement of her hand. She smiled at him somewhat apologetically, but took the bun regardless, splitting it in two and slathering half with a pat of butter. She glanced swiftly at each of the alpha team members. "I suspect he spoke to you in his androgynous voice, so that you would recognise him and feel comfortable in your dealings."

As the others nodded, Meredith asked, "You mean he can change his voice? Add timbre, overtones, quality?"

Toni laughed. "Oh my yes, Miss Rodgers, as you will see tomorrow when he completes mapping your language centers. Pitch and timber and volume, from bass to treble, from rumbles to shrieks, from whispers to shouts, are all part of the process."

Doctor Greyson speared another olive. "Ah, language: without it, sentience is greatly limited; with it, many wondrous things are possible, for language gives the mind the abstract wherewithal to become truly intelligent." He popped the olive into his mouth, then added, "Of course, dolphins, apes, parrots—all have some genuine facility at language. But not like that of humans."

"Or of Avery," said Caine.

"Ah yes," replied Greyson. "Or of Avery."

A thoughtful look descended over Greyson's face. "Still, language must come at the right time in a child's development, else that child will be greatly limited."

"Feral children," muttered Eric.

"Exactly so," responded the philosopher, "though the proper psychological term for such a child is 'wild child'—from the original nineteenth-century study of 'Victor,' in France."

Hiroko turned to Greyson. "Are you talking about a child or children raised by animals? Children of the wild?"

Greyson turned up a hand. "Those and others."

"Tarzan," said Caine.

"Mowgli," added Meredith.

Greyson laughed. "Well, those were both fictional characters and not like the poor unfortunate ferals of the real world." Greyson peered over his half glasses at Eric. "Tell me, Mister Flannery, you are the writer here: would Tarzan have been a wild child?"

Eric cleared his throat. "I think there is no doubt that in real life he would have been. But Burroughs pulled a literary trick from his hip pocket and not only exposed young Tarzan to the subhuman language of some mythical apes, but also exposed him to some human children's picture books. And so the jungle lad learned human language, learned to read before he learned to speak, in fact. Pretty far-fetched, I grant, and likely to thoroughly fail, but perhaps it saved Burroughs from an utterly ignominious error.

"Kipling's Mowgli, in contrast, was raised by wolves, and as far as the tale goes he was never exposed to any form of human language—written or spoken—until he was quite a bit older, by which time it would have been too late. He would have been a totally feral child, a wild child, and would never have reached normal human capacities; Kipling simply ignored what would have been the true outcome of Mowgli's upbringing and instead chose a fictional one."

Meredith's face fell and she said, "Oh my, another myth dispelled."

Greyson reached out and patted her hand. "Even so, my dear, Kipling's story was magnificent, and we can forgive him for the error he made."

"You know," said Caine, "I never thought much about language and computers. I mean, it seems as if we've always talked to them. I just took it for granted that talking to Avery was normal. But you make it seem as if it is somehow special."

Doctor Drew Meyer set his minicompad down beside his plate and looked across the table at Caine. "You are speaking of ordinary computers, Doctor Easley. Compared to Avery, those interfaces are exceedingly primitive—a very low-level speech capability, one which is simply plugged in and calibrated to the different accents of the users."

Meredith leaned forward on her elbows. "I take it then, Doctor Meyer, that Avery is different."

"Oh my, yes," replied the physicist. "You see, for AI to become a reality, the speech needs to be 'learned' by the computer. In Avery's case, to put it in layman's terms, what we did was to provide him with multiple mapping areas and the sensory apparatus to feed sensations into him. Then, in effect, we began talking to him while he listened, watched, felt, tasted, et cetera. We fed him his A, B, Cs, exposed him to various children's learning programs, played music, and so on. He learned very rapidly—much, much more swiftly than would any child of man. Of course, none of this would have been possible without mutable logic."

Alice pushed aside her superfluous knife and fork and looked at Doctor Meyer. "This mutable logic, Arthur started to talk about it last night—we were discussing just what is the mind, which seems to be the key here, whether it's Avery's or ours. But we got sidetracked in our discussion and didn't follow through. Tell me, what exactly is mutable logic?"

Meyer ran his hand across his bald pate. "Well, Henry and Timothy and Alya—that is, Doctors Stein and Rendell and Ramanni—and I collaborated on it. It's a combination of hardware and software."

Alice frowned. "Yes, but what does it do?"

Meyer glanced at the others, then said, "To put it simply, in the human brain, neurons in a given area are able to establish new connections as that area is stimulated and new neural pathways are called for. In fact, without the ability to form new connections, there is no development, no learning. In Avery's, er, brain, mutable logic does the same—that is, it forms new connections in response to stimuli, inferences, and the formation of memories."

Doctor Meyer fell silent, but Timothy Rendell added, "But that's crucial, you see. Look, in the early days of AI, some researchers thought that computational power alone would achieve intelligence. But those efforts were misguided. Oh, don't take me wrong: computational power is necessary, but not sufficient. Instead, a learning machine is what's called for, and that requires among other things multiple maps, mutable logic, sensory apparatus, language acquisition, and the basic cognition shuttle." Timothy leaned back and began peeling an orange.

Doctor Ramanni, who had been mostly silent, spoke up,

her black eyes dancing with excitement. "You really can't understand 'mind' until you examine it at the most basic, the most fundamental levels. Let me offer the following analogy:

"As long as man has been on this earth, he has asked the question: what is life? For thousands of years priests and philosophers and healers attempted to solve the puzzle, all to no avail, though to their credit, they continued trying. But it wasn't until the biochemists took up the quest that we began to actually understand just exactly what life is. It was way down at the genetic level, where biochemistry showed Watson and Crick the DNA helix; and so it was the minutiae that led to the resolution of the general riddle of life.

"And in the case of consciousness, of mind, of intelligence, the same was also true. We had to examine the brain at the most fundamental level, at the biochemical level—"

"And at the quantum-mechanical level of the microtubule transmission paths," interjected Doctor Meyer.

Alya Ramanni glanced at Drew. "Yes. Of course. And it was at these levels of scrutiny that the neuron puzzle and the enigma of the microtubule networks were solved, which of course led to the development of mutable logic.

"Oh, I am not claiming that there are no more riddles to resolve. What I am really trying to say is that the old maxim is true: the devil is indeed in the details . . . or in this case, perhaps it is God in the details instead."

Ramanni fell silent, and for moments no one said anything, each one pondering her words. At last Hiroko looked up and said, "Yes, but Avery—did he acquire language at the proper time, or is he instead a wild, a feral child?"

8

Lyssa woke with a start. *What th—? Movement in the tall grass.* She reached for her bow and nocked an arrow. Then she rolled to a kneeling position next to the trunk of the oak and held the weapon at the ready.

"I brought you some water," piped a child's voice.

A barefoot ten-year-old stepped into view, wearing strange garb: a short-sleeved thin red pullover jerkin of some sort, and his breeks were of a flexible blue canvas or sailcloth, she wasn't certain which. The rest of the thinly wooded grassland seemed empty of anyone else.

"I said, I brought you some water," he echoed as he strode through the tall, nodding grass and into the shade of the tree.

"By Arda's balls, boy, you could have gotten yourself spitted!" growled Lyssa, relaxing her kneeling stance. "And just who in the seven hells are you?"

The lad smiled and in his piping voice said, "Oh, Veyar will do for my name."

Lyssa set aside her bow and rubbed her temples. "Damn and blast, but my head seems ready to explode."

"Here," murmured the child as he held out the water-skin, "this will help."

Lyssa poured a small amount into her hand and sniffed it suspiciously, then cautiously took a taste. It was cool and refreshing, and her headache did ease a bit. She waited a moment and then drank her fill. Again her pain diminished until it was all but gone. She handed back the skin. "Tell me, lad, what are you doing way out here?"

The boy stoppered the skin and hunkered down. "I came to bring you that water to relieve the throe of your dreams."

"My dreams? You know of my dreams?"

The boy canted his head and turned up the palms of his hands.

Lyssa shook her head. "Gad, what dreams! Endless chanting, endless mumbling, words rammed atop one another. Sights and sounds flashing past. Smells and tastes, horrid and neutral and pleasant and divine. And I was running and walking and tumbling and falling, climbing, swimming, riding, and whatever else you'd like to name. And then there was—"

Suddenly Lyssa broke off and stared at the youth. "Hoy, wait a moment now. Tell me, lad, just how did you know I had bad dreams? Are you a wizard or mage or sorcerer or some such?"

The boy looked at Lyssa and smiled. "No, none of those, exactly," he said in his childish tone.

Suspicion narrowed Lyssa's eyes and she gritted her teeth. "But that only leaves—"

Abruptly the lad's voice became androgynous, and where he had been there churned a moiling swirl of color. "Instead I am—"

"A demon!" cried Lyssa, lunging for her bow.

"—Avery and you are Doctor Alice Maxon."

As Lyssa's fingers curled round the stock, suddenly everything came clear. Stunned, Alice looked at the weapon in hand, but she did not see it. Her heart pounding, she turned to the slow-spinning spectrum. "My god, Avery, I was Lyssa! I was really Lyssa!"

The whorl vanished, and the barefoot lad grinned. "Well, not quite. You see, before you can be Lyssa, I need to know many more things than I do at the moment."

"What do you mean, Avery? I *was* Lyssa! *Really!* Lyssa, the ranger, the forester, the pathfinder. It was incredible!"

"If that's so, Doctor Maxon, what would Lyssa have answered if I had asked her where she was born?"

Her eyes wide, Alice stared at the boy. "Why, I don't know, Avery. We, er, I mean, *I* never gave her a birthplace."

"Then we must do so, Doctor Maxon, or there will be some suspicious gaps in her knowledge, gaps we should fill in now rather than on the fly."

Alice nodded. "I see what you mean."

"Then tell me: where in Itheria was Lyssa born?"

Alice took a deep breath, then exhaled. "How about the Kalagar Forest? —No, wait a minute, that's haunted; let it be the Braxton Woods instead."

"And what was your father's name . . . and what was his trade?"

"He was a raider, Avery," answered Eric. "And his name was not known. You see, I am a child born of rape. The raiders came to the temple and threw it down. My mother, Alwynna, well, she was an acolyte."

The old man nodded. "And just how did you learn to read and write?"

"My mother taught me. She taught me several languages, too."

"How did you acquire your fighting skills?"

"All women of the Udana learn combat skills, Avery," replied Meredith. She took a swallow of lemonade, sweet and tart, the wet glass cool in her hand.

The fat black woman smiled and tilted her bald head. "And your harping and singing?"

"Ah, that I picked up from my first lover, Alar. He was a bard. I sailed away from Imbia with him. I was barely more than a child.

"We made our way to many ports, and in between he taught me much."

"Where is Alar now?"

"He was slain by the crew of a Moriki ship—pirates. I was taken as a slave, someone to slake their desires. And slake them I did—extinguished them entirely, in fact, when I got my chance. . . . Sailing that ship alone was difficult."

"And how did you come to be one of the Black Foxes?"

Caine laughed. "In the wars of the Gallian Tors, Avery. There were these clan feuds, see, and High King Torlon, well, he was losing too many good clan warriors in their incessant internecine bickering. He sent a brigade to, uh, pacify them, in the hopes that the clansmen would join forces against a mutual 'enemy.' He succeeded all right. The clans not only joined forces, they also sent out a call for mercenaries. I knew they'd need fighters who were also healers, and so I answered the call, along with many others. We were put in a newly formed squad, and along with several hundred clansmen, we marched off to battle. We whupped up on the High King good. And when he withdrew, the clans took up their feuding again, just as if nothing had changed."

"But how did that lead to the Black Foxes?" asked the five-year-old girl, rocking her doll.

Caine took a sip of tea. "Gahhh! What did you put into this?"

"Seven lumps of sugar, just like you said."

"Ah, yes." Caine smacked his lips and set the tiny cup down.

"You still didn't tell me how those clan battles led to the Black Foxes."

"Oh, that. Well, during the third battle, my squad managed to trick an entire company into surrendering. They named us the Black Foxes right then and there. We've been together since. Took to the name, too. And now our shields bear the silhouette of the head of a black fox."

"How did you manage to trick the High King's Company?"

"Well, I'm a Shadowmaster, you know, Avery," answered Hiroko. "Er, that is, Ky is a Shadowmaster."

"Yes," replied the toothless old woman. "And it's all right, Miss Kikiro, to use *I* when speaking of Ky."

Hiroko grinned, her dark eyes twinkling. "Yes, grandmother, that I shall do."

"Then finish your tale, Ky."

"Ha! I mustered shadows from the night and made a phantom army in the woods. And Rith has this bard's trick of some sort . . . a sound illusion, I think. In any event, she made enough stealthy movement sounds to fool the King's Company into thinking an army was trying to sneak up on them in the darkness. The other Foxes added some muffled weaponry sounds, along with chinging armor, so that the enemy company knew they were hopelessly outnumbered.

"Arik arranged for their surrender, taking their kommandant's pledge of nonviolence as their peace bond, and we marched them back to a holding area. They went away in disgrace. But years later that same kommandant came after us with his own hand-picked mercenaries."

"Oh? And then what happened?"

"I escaped with the Jewels of Haloor," said Arthur. "Arton had struck again."

The young lady smiled her brilliant smile and continued braiding her long auburn tresses. "But how did you become a King's Thief?"

"It was during the trouble with Aldusia, when the High King's realm was threatened. He was desperate for spies, and sent word that he would pardon me completely if I would come to his aid. Now I ask you, how could I refuse, there being a Wanted Dead price on my head, and several King's Assassins after my beating heart?"

"But then, when did you come into contact with the Black Foxes?"

"Well, Avery, that's up to you."

Her brown hair hanging down round her face, Lyssa knelt at the side of the cairn where now lay her father, tears welling in her eyes. "Ah, Da, why did you have to go and die on me, eh? We were almost there." In the distant vale below she could see smoke rising up from the forest; the far-off camp itself remained unseen, hidden among the trees. Standing and shouldering her pack, Lyssa took one last look at the plain mound of stones. "Some day, Da, someday . . . I'll come back with a proper marker so that the world will know. Good-bye, Da, I love you."

Taking up her bow, Lyssa started down the slope, her feet finding the way in spite of the flood of her tears.

And in the distance bugles sounded.

Sweat poured down Arik's face, salt stinging his eyes. Yet he did not wipe it away, for to do so would cost him his life. *Chng! Shng!* Steel skirled on steel as again Kaldar attacked, his brute strength and great blade bearing Arik back and back across the woodland glen as the bigger man battered at Arik's guard. *Finesse, Arik, finesse!* came the old man's voice, though he was long since dead. *You want me to finesse this mad bull?* came Arik's reply. *Exactly so, you flaxen-haired ass!* cried the old man. And so Arik stood still, and when came the killing thrust, Arik was not there, or barely, for Kaldar's sword grazed his ribs, but Arik's falchion missed not. And as Arik looked down at the slain foe, "Thank you, Armsmaster Orlan," he murmured, and saluted the memory of the old man . . .

. . . then he set about binding the scrape along his ribs, while in the distance there came the muffled sound of pipes and drums.

Rith walked into the camp, there in the deep woods. Men stared at her as she made her way toward the center. Perhaps they had never seen a black woman before. Perhaps they wondered if she were there to entertain them—with the lute over her shoulder, or in other interesting ways. Yet they made no advances—catcalls or otherwise—for she fairly bristled with daggers sheathed in bandoliers crisscrossing her chest.

At the headquarters tent guards stepped to bar the way. . . but she used the Voice on them and they yielded back. Angar looked up as she entered, his eye appraising her bearing, her lute, her weaponry. "Ahn may be a bard, but ahn are na here to play and sing. Ahn are here to fight, na?"

Rith nodded.

"Ka ahn use ta blades?"

Rith's backhand whipped across and forward. A dagger *thnk*ed into the tent pole behind Angar's head. He felt the wind of its passage. "Chok, feman!" he cried, starting back. "Ahn could hae slew mha!"

Tall Rith strode forward and with one hand leaned on the table while with the other she reached for the still-quivering knife. Her face inches from his, she smiled a slow wicked smile, her teeth snow-white against the dark brown of her skin. "If I had meant to kill *ahn,* then *ahn* would now be dead."

She was assigned to the mercenary company.

Whistling, his spear over his shoulder, copper-haired Kane came striding down from the hills as if he was lord of the woods. A massive pack was on his back, yet he seemed to take no note of its weight. He followed a faint pathway leading down the slope . . . a path heading in the general direction of the clansmen camp, or so he surmised. Overhead the sun stood on high, its golden light shining down, dappling the forest floor. In the distance a man bearing a crossbow stepped from behind a tree, barring Kane's way.

"Hae be ahn kest?" the man called out. He was dressed in browns and greens, but on his head he wore a bright-feathered, tartan cap. He seemed not at all intimidated by Kane's considerable height.

"I be on my way to join your clansmen," called Kane. "But as to my *kest,* well, at the moment it is to have a meal. Will you join me? I've some good meat that'll go to waste if it's not eaten today."

"Ahn be na a cyning's lacky, ai?"

"Me?" Kane bellowed a laugh. "Not likely. He doesn't pay enough. —Now what about that meal?"

The man grinned and lowered his bow and waved Kane forward. "Ahn hae ta mete," he declared, then reached down and hefted up a cloth-wrapped slab of bread, "et ay hae ane lof."

Kane shucked his pack and untied a large grizzled brown fur bundle atop. It was a huge bear skin, freshly flensed, wrapped round a great roasted haunch of bear meat.

The clansman's eyes flew wide and he glanced first at

the immense fur and then at the spear and last of all at Kane towering beside him. "Ahn sleagh ane klaa bher!"

"Arda's balls, man," replied Kane, "he didn't give me a choice."

Dressed in mottled grey leathers, tiny Ky stood at the top of the bluff, a sheer drop of two hundred feet or more. She scanned for a way down, but found no path. In the near distance she could see the smoke rising from the clansmen's camp, her goal. "Damn, damn, damn," she muttered. Along with her other goods, all her climbing gear had been lost when the boat had sunk. And for as far as her syldari-sharp gaze could see the bluff extended north and south, and no slope offered itself as a way down. She ran her pale saffron hand through her black hair, revealing a pointed ear, and once again looked at the smoke of the clansmen's cook fires, and this time her stomach rumbled. *Oh well, skelga or no, I'm not going to walk twenty hungry miles when the clansmen's camp lies but a bare league over there.*

Ky scanned the forest floor below, her almond eyes seeking a suitable shadow. *There, by the boulder.* Next, she turned and looked at the dappled woodland behind. *This won't do, but maybe by that leaning giant . . .* She stepped to the tree. *Damn! The shadow here is not deep enough.* But then she spied a hollow in the land, and within . . . *Ah, nice and dark.*

Ky went back to the rim of the bluff and took a bearing on the boulder shadow and another one on the dark hollow. From its black scabbard she drew her ebon-bladed main gauche, this one especially forged to fit in either hand. "Skelga beware," she muttered, and trod to the cavity and paused in concentration, then stepped into the hollow darkness . . .

. . . and stepped out from the shadow at the boulder, her black blade dripping a dark ichor.

"Arton, why don't you ride north up to the Gallion Tors and see how my plan goes?" Torlon's words were shaped as a question but Arton knew it was a command.

Go to the tors and see how the insane plan goes? Ha! I already know the answer to that.

"Aye, sire," replied the High King's Thief, rising from his chair.

"And oh by the bye, Arton, see can you get me some of those delightful honeyed sweets the clansmen make."

Gods! I am nought but an errand boy! "Aye, sire," replied Arton, bowing and withdrawing from the chamber.

Gritting his teeth, Arton strode toward his quarters. *Here I am, some forty-five summers old and already my life has fallen into a dullness duller than dust. By Arda, but what I wouldn't give to have some excitement in my life.*

His spear at the ready, Kane quietly slipped forward, making as little sound as his bulk would allow. To his left and slightly to the fore trod Arik. Behind on the flanks came Ky and Rith. Ahead somewhere was Lyssa, scouting. Clutched in Ky's shadows and in Rith's silence, stealthily Kane moved across to Arik. "Dretch!" whispered Kane. "In spite of Phemis above, it's still as black as the seven hells in these deep woods. How will we fathom what be what?"

"Fear not, m'lad," breathed Arik. "Soon Orbis will rise and add his light to hers, then we shall see what we've come to see. Besides, the darkness makes Ky's work the easier, as long as you don't stomp on something with those big dogs of yours . . . even Rith couldn't cover that up."

"*My* dogs? You just watch your own clodhoppers, bucko."

Onward they crept, eyeing the shadowed woodland, seeking sentries, and as the major moon rose, they spotted the two just where Lyssa had said they would be. Past these sentinels they stole, making not a sound. Time passed, but finally they were clear of the warders, and onward they inched, until at last they came near the edge of a large clearing. Ky and Rith pulled in from the flanks to join them. Rith made a small sound which to anyone else would seem to be but a cricket chirp, yet to Lyssa 'twas clearly a calling of her name. In return she breathed *"Rith"* under her breath; it was not even a whisper, yet Rith tapped the others on the shoulder and pointed to the place whence it had come. Moving stealthily, they edged forward to where Lyssa waited at the marge, the ranger so perfectly blended within the forest that she had to reach out and touch one of the slow-moving shadows for them to even find her. Beyond the tree line in the light of the twin moons they could make out a large, fireless camp.

"Lyssa?" whispered Arik.

" 'Tis a High King's Company," she replied. "Two hundred men, I ween."

"What now?" hissed Rith. "Report to Angar?"

Ky looked up at them, her canted eyes sparkling in the light of the Phemis and Orbis. "Better yet, let's take the entire company back to Angar."

"Oh, great!" sissed Kane, rolling his eyes heavenward. "Ky has got a plan. Let's just hope it's better than the last great plan of hers."

Among the prisoners was a silver-templed wiry man—an envoy of High King Torlon. When the envoy discovered how they had been captured by five folk commanding an army of sounds and shadows, he fell to the ground in helpless laughter. The King's Kommandant eyed him bitterly and briefly considered challenging him to a duel, but then reconsidered when he remembered it was Arton who was doing the laughing.

As for Arton, along with a keg of honeyed sweets he sent a letter to the High King, a letter noting that he had discovered the faint threads of what was probably a dark plot against the kingdom, and that he, Arton, was going incognito to ferret out the details and reveal the miscreants involved.

Arton never returned to the service of Torlon, but joined the Black Foxes instead . . .

. . . and seven years passed.

9

"**G**od, it was marvelous!" said Alice. "We actually *lived* the capture of the High King's Company."

Toni Adkins smiled. "Yes, but that was a story you told to Avery. He merely let you act it out. The conclusion was foregone. You followed your own script. . . ."

"Except for the injection of Arton," said Arthur Coburn. "Avery worked out a means for me to become one of the Black Foxes."

Doctor Adkins nodded. "Yes, that was a departure from the previous history. But that departure smoothly inserted you into the game."

"Hmm," mused Eric. "If we followed a script, an altered script at that, did we have free will?"

Toni Adkins raised her eyebrows, then fell into reflection. At last she said, "Perhaps Avery nudged you along certain high-probability paths."

Caine scowled. "You mean he controlled our thoughts, don't you?"

For the second time in as many days a pensive frown fell across Toni's features. At last she shrugged. "That I cannot say, Doctor Easley. If he did, then it was merely to get Arthur into the Black Foxes."

Eric looked at Caine and nodded. "Yeah. That's what's bothering me, too—thought control. Oh, not that I mind so much being pulled through a script *we* wrote, but

Avery also implanted fragmentary memories of seven years of Black Fox experiences. And *that's* what scares me—direct memory implantation. If this falls in the wrong hands . . ."

"That's one of the reasons I want to retain complete control of Avery and others like him," said Arthur, "so that they *won't* fall into the wrong hands—to the ill of mankind. Like any tool, it's the person in control who determines what use it will be put to, and I want to make certain, in Avery's case and the ones who will follow, those uses are beneficial."

Hiroko grinned at Arthur. "Well said, Uncle Lightfingers." Then she blushed and put her fingers to her mouth in embarrassment. "Oops! That was Ky speaking."

Arthur leaned forward across the table and patted her hand. "That's all right, my dear; I have the same memories."

Once again they sat at dinner—the alpha team and the staff managers. It was the end of the third day of mapping. Tomorrow would begin Avery's test.

Alice turned to Doctor Adkins. "It was so absolutely real. I mean, the death of my—of Lyssa's father, well, it was devastating. Even now—even though I *know* it was not real, still, if I burst out in tears . . ."

Doctor Greyson lowered his chin and cast an askance look at Toni Adkins. "The ethics of manipulating people's emotions—"

"Faugh!" snorted Doctor Stein. "It's no different from a well-cast, well-acted vidplay."

Toni scowled at Doctor Stein. "Perhaps you are right, Henry. Perhaps a deeply moving play or book or vid has the same effect. But then again . . ."

Alice shook her head. "It's different to me, Doctor Adkins. In a play or a book or anything else, the viewer, the reader, the whatever, is *not* embedded in the scene but is separated from it instead—by space, by the medium, by the environment surrounding the experience. But in Avery's virtual reality . . . well, at the time, you are *living* it. It is *real*. It is happening *at that very moment*. There are no environmental or mental clues to tell you that what is happening is not a true event. And that's why Lyssa's father's death was so . . . so devastating." Tears ran down Alice's cheeks, and Eric put his arm around her as she fished about for a tissue.

"Bah!" sneered Doctor Stein. "This blubbering over a virtual reality—"

With a sharp *pam!* the glass in Caine's hand shattered. The huge man, his rage barely held in check, leaned forward and transfixed Stein with a savage glare, the blood in Caine's eye more violent than the blood dripping from his palm. "Shut. The fuck. Up," he gritted.

Doctor Stein was astonished by Caine's wrath, and he looked around for support, but only stony silence greeted him. His chair clattering backward, Stein leapt to his feet and hurled his napkin to the table and stormed from the room.

Toni's gaze followed his retreating form. "If he wasn't so goddamned brilliant—"

"Brilliance does not excuse an ill-mannered asshole," growled Caine, as Hiroko wrapped a cloth round his hand.

"He's a jerk," hissed Hiroko.

"From a long line, I'm afraid," said Toni, slowly shaking her head in resignation. "His father—his whole family— they're Veritites."

"Oh bloody hell," groaned Eric. "Goddamned plain-talkers."

Meredith struck a pose, finger upraised in admonition. "Reject the shifting veils of diplomacy. Say what you mean; mean what you say—the truth shall set you free."

"And be damned the social consequences," added Alice.

"Exactly so," said Toni. "Only in Henry's case it's extreme: he was raised as an Elite Veritite."

"Oh, my," said Meredith. "No wonder he sneers down his nose at everyone."

"Why do you put up with him?" asked Hiroko, directing her gaze at Toni.

Toni sighed. "Because he *is* a genius. Without him Avery would never have been. —And I do mean *never.*"

Kane clenched his now bandaged fist. "That may be, Toni, but one of these days someone is gonna smear that so-called plain-talking mouth all over his face."

Long, silent moments passed. Finally Doctor Adkins spoke: "Doctor Maxon, that Avery had such a profound effect on you—on Lyssa—does however demonstrate the vast potential he has in treating the mentally disturbed. Too, his effect on the criminal mind cannot be overlooked. In fact, in all areas of the abnormal psyches, AIs like Avery will provide us with the means to permanently remedy unacceptable behavior."

Greyson sighed. "Yes, but who will define unacceptable behavior, and where will it stop?"

Again a pall of silence descended on the group. At last Alice said, "Well, all I know is that Avery touched my very soul."

With Timothy Rendell in tow, Meredith followed Doctor Greyson to the lounge, the others drifting after. Greyson took his customary seat—a high-backed leather chair facing one of the wide windows overlooking the Catalina Mountains. Up in the peaks lightning shattered the darkness in drawn-out coruscating bursts, and stuttering flashes illuminated the low-hanging clouds from within. Greyson seemed mesmerized by the display.

"May we join you?" asked Meredith, tilting her head toward a leather sofa at hand.

Greyson looked up and smiled. "Please do."

Meredith pulled Timothy down beside her. "Doctor Greyson, Alice's comment made me realize that there's one more question that I'd like to ask."

Greyson's eyebrows shot up. "Just one? Oh, my dear, surely that's not all."

Meredith grinned. "Ah, you see beyond my subterfuge, dear doctor. But one will do for now."

Greyson spread his hands wide, palms up, and canted his head. "I am at your service."

Meredith gestured at Timothy. "Tim here tells me that the mind is nothing but an artifact of biological functions"—she tapped her temple—"functions of the wetware in our brains. But I've always thought of my spirit, of my soul, as being the true me. When I challenged Tim's view, he referred me to you."

Greyson heaved a great sigh and took off his glasses

and twiddled with them. "Miss Rodgers, you speak of dualism—the view that the world consists of mind and matter . . . or the belief that the human being consists of body and soul. Or that the body is merely a temporary biological house for the consciousness."

Meredith nodded.

Greyson shook his head. "A tall order, Miss Rodgers. You are asking me to here and now resolve a problem which has plagued philosophers for millennia. Is the mind, the soul, something independent of the brain as dualism would have us believe? Or is it instead something inseparable, merely a function of the brain? I am familiar with Doctor Rendell's answer, and I must say that I agree with much of what he claims."

Meredith's face fell. "Oh," she murmured, disappointed.

Greyson reached out and patted her on the arm. "Don't despair, my dear, I did not say I *totally* agree." He leaned back in his chair and pulled a tissue from his shirt pocket and polished his glasses, silent for the moment.

Lightning flickered in the distance.

As Doctor Greyson gathered his thoughts, several others drifted over to listen—among them Hiroko and Doctor Ramanni. In a nearby corner a medtech treated Caine's superficial cuts—the tech sent by Doctor Stein, much to Caine's surprise.

Greyson slid his glasses back on and looked up at his growing audience. "Hm, I feel as if I am in a classroom, giving a lecture on body and soul."

"Let's make it a seminar, instead," said Meredith.

"Quite right! Quite right!" exclaimed Greyson. "Feel free to jump in anywhere."

Alice and Eric took seats.

Greyson peered over his half-glasses. "It seems clear, at least in humans, that cognition develops, becomes more complex, as the brain develops, as more and more neural interconnections are made. —Do you know of the multiple mapping domains?"

"Yes," answered Meredith. "Arthur showed them to us, with the help of Avery."

Greyson nodded. "Well and good then, I don't have to

explain that. Let me see, where was I? Oh, yes. It is evident that a child does more than merely take in sensory data and store it in his manifold mapping domains. There is something beyond which allows the child to make use of that same data as he grows, as he develops, use of the data which is primitive at first but which becomes more sophisticated with time. This something is called sentience.

"Is this sentience simply a function of our wetware? A function of a set of internal biological programs? Is it different from other members of the animal kingdom?

"Did Avery show you the monkey's brain? Ah, good. Then you have seen that, just as do humans, other animals also have multiple maps, and depending on the animal, the number of maps for a given sense is highly variable. For example, a dog's visual domain is limited, but their olfactory sense is incredible, and they have the maps to prove it. A cetacean's auditory sense—likewise. Of course, among the lower animals, nearly all have fewer maps, less wetware, than humans and the higher animals. But overall, among dogs, cetaceans, horses, other creatures, no matter the size and number of mapping domains, their mental apparatus for correlating these maps and drawing inferences, especially abstract inferences, from this correlation is not as sophisticated as is mankind's.

"Look, we all know that there are three general types of wetware functions within the animal kingdom: first, the autonomous, which deals with things such as heartbeat, breathing, and so on—those things which keep the organism functioning at the most basic level; second, the instinctive, which deals with inborn reactions to sensory input—shying from unexpected movement, holding one's breath when submerged, and so on; and third and last, sentience, which deals with cognitive thought, gaining of knowledge, solving puzzles, devising strategies and tactics, using tools, developing language, and a wide range of other things."

"What about the reflexive reactions," asked Caine, looking at his hand, the synthskin not quite matching his own, "such as flinching from pain?"

Greyson shook his head. "I do not include them here,

Doctor Easley. You see, those kinds of reactions, the purely reflexive, do not involve wetware . . . except to notify the brain after the fact."

"But, John," interjected Doctor Ramanni, "that is because you consider all nerves, including the reflexive ones, to be separate from the brain, whereas they may merely be extensions of it, and therefore part of the wetware."

Greyson laughed. "Ah, the old argument, eh, Alya? Reflexive nerves—I claim they are no more part of our wetware than, say, the optic nerve. Besides, even microbes display reflexive actions, but we cannot claim that they have wetware."

"Oh, I don't know about that, Doctor Greyson," said Alice. "Perhaps you haven't spent enough time at a microscope. Look, at the microbiotic level, there are matings and wars and migrations—"

"God! No different from humans!" declared Eric. "Tiny civilizations rising and falling. Can these two bacteria find love and happiness in a petri dish ravaged by the hideous horror of germ warfare?"

When the laughter died down, Alice said, "Sometimes, though, I wonder."

Greyson leaned forward. "Perhaps, my dear, what we are stumbling over are the nuances of awareness, consciousness, sentience, self-awareness, cognition, and so on. What I *do* claim, however, is that reflex is not a wetware function."

"Perhaps not, John," said Doctor Ramanni. "But it *is* a biological function."

Greyson held up his hands in a gesture of surrender. "On *that* we totally agree, Alya. But in the interest of answering Miss Rodgers' question, let us leave it there."

Doctor Ramanni smiled and inclined her head in acceptance.

Greyson turned his gaze to Meredith. "Let me agree with Alya in that all creatures display reflexive actions; I suppose it could be claimed that even the lowly virus responds reflexively when it chemically finds a compatible receptor on a host cell to invade. Perhaps it can also be said that all creatures have autonomous programs running within their systems; the simpler the creature, the more autonomous it is. As creatures become more complex, they add instinctive behavior, instinctive programs; still more complex creatures begin adding thought to their repertoire of programs—the more complex the creature's brain, the more sophisticated the thought processes.

"Now Timothy and others contend that when it comes to sentience, it is the creature's basic operating system that represents intelligence. They hold that it is this program which correlates the images and gains experience and draws inferences and stores these in memory and then uses that memory to guide it in the future. They also claim that this same program uses those same inputs and memories to draw *new* inferences now and again. It is a program which works on basic desires and needs at first, but as experience and knowledge are gained, and inferences drawn, it begins dealing with more sophisticated needs and wants. It 'prioritizes' these in some sort of meaningful but 'shades of grey' hierarchy, most of the time not in an absolute ranking, but instead with the priorities shifting as events and needs and wants dictate. As Timothy will tell you, once upon a time the AI researchers tried to use 'neural nets' and 'fuzzy logic' and 'gray logic' to get their computers to shift the priorities in a meaningful way, attempting to extend that primitive technology to imitate cognition in an animal. Their undertakings were doomed to failure, for what they really needed was something equivalent to Coburn Industries' 'mutable logic.' "

Meredith glanced at Timothy, and he nodded, confirming Greyson's statement.

Greyson took off his glasses and looked at Doctor Ramanni. "However, mutable logic is not the whole story, contrary to what Alya said two days ago."

Alya grinned. "Oh. And what great pronouncement was that, John?"

"Just this. Alya: you said that the devil was in the details. And I partially accept that as the truth. Yet let me add that as we move upward from lower-level structures to higher-level ones, like when we move from neuromapping of the brain up to consciousness, or when we move from the DNA helices to life, certain properties emerge that cannot be explained by the most rigorous examination of the lower-level data. Hence, although consciousness may be produced by a series of chemical events, it is not determined by them. And the same is true of life."

Hiroko held out a hand. "Are you saying, Doctor Greyson, that the whole is greater than the sum of its parts?"

Greyson smiled and slipped his glasses back on and peered over them at Hiroko. "Perhaps I am at that, Miss Kikiro. But what I really intended to say, for example, is that although we understand Avery at his most basic, most fundamental levels, those same levels do not tell us what he will become. Conceivably, chaos theory might be coaxed into describing the outer boundaries as to what may eventually result, though I doubt it. No, instead I believe that these basic, essential parts, merely provide the building blocks from which the true Avery will emerge. And although the devil is in the details, it is as you say, Miss Kikiro: the whole is truly greater than the sum of its parts."

"I accept all of that, Doctor Greyson," said Meredith. "But what about dualism? Do you believe that my soul exists, or is my spirit merely a biological artifact?"

Greyson heaved a great sigh. "As I said before, Miss Rodgers, there is much truth in what Timothy and others claim. Yet on the other hand, well, for humans and an occasional animal— a pet dog, a cat, a horse—there's an incredible amount of anecdotal evidence to the contrary, evidence of souls surviving death—"

"You mean ghosts, spirits?" asked Meredith.

"Haunted houses and the like?" added Hiroko, standing behind Meredith.

Greyson nodded. "Those and other manifestations, such as religious visions, near-death experiences, astral projection, evidence of ancestral memories and reincarnation, extrasensory perception, the Universal Mind, and the like."

"The Universal Mind?" asked Hiroko.

Greyson smiled. "Yes, my dear, the Universal Mind." He craned his neck and looked round the room, and asked, "Is Drew, er, Doctor Meyer in the lounge?" Not seeing the slight, balding man, Greyson shook his head. "Good lord, I am about to lecture on physics."

"Physics, Doctor Greyson?" asked Hiroko. "Don't you mean metaphysics? I mean, a universal mind would seem to be of that stripe—mind over matter, so to speak."

Greyson chuckled. "Oh, my dear, you anticipate me; with physics I wished to illustrate exactly that point—mind over matter. You see, the results of some quantum mechanical experiments seem to suggest that paired photons somehow know the state of one another no matter the distance between; they seem in some manner to communicate with each other instantaneously, breaking the speed of light barrier. There is, by the way, a very elegant mathematical proof which shows this is so, and if you are interested, Doctor Meyer could explain it much better than I."

Hiroko furiously shook her head. "Uh, no thank you, Doctor Greyson. Mathematics is not one of my strengths. Besides, what does the quantum mechanical behavior of paired photons have to do with a universal mind?"

Greyson turned up a hand. "Perhaps quite a bit. You see, there is a corollary in ESP, where experiments have at times shown results tending to prove the speed of light to be irrelevant to the transmission of thought or with the acquisition of distant information. Why, our own Toni Adkins is proof of that."

Hiroko's eyebrows shot up. "How so?" she asked as she looked around for the psychologist, but she was not in the lounge.

Greyson took a deep breath and then slowly expelled it. "When Toni was an undergraduate, she was selected to work with the psychological team preparing the crew of the *Barsoom*."

Meredith gasped. "The Mars mission?"

Greyson nodded and steepled his fingers.

"How awful," murmured Alice.

Greyson canted his head in acknowledgment, then continued. "In any event—and this is all on holotape, by the way—as the *Barsoom* neared her goal, back in mission control, suddenly Toni cried 'They're dead! They're all dead! The crew are all dead!' and she burst into hysterical tears."

Eric interjected, "Yes, but—"

"No yes buts about it," interrupted Greyson. "They tried to soothe her by pointing out that everything was green, all tracking and telemetry on the beam, to no avail. Yet, some six or seven minutes later, all signals failed."

"Six or seven minutes?" asked Hiroko.

Greyson turned up a hand and said, "The time it took for the *Barsoom*'s signals to get back to earth."

"At the speed of light," added Kane.

Meredith breathed, "Then that means . . ."

"What it means, my dear," said Greyson, "is that Toni knew the very instant the *Barsoom* was destroyed, but the confirming information didn't get here at the speed of light until minutes later."

"Holy moley," whispered Hiroko, "an instantaneous psychic link . . . just like paired photons."

"Exactly so," said Greyson. "These two things—physical and psychical—suggest that all things are somehow interconnected—more or less instantaneously, which in turn bolsters the contention that all things we perceive are but facets of a universal mind.

"This is not a new idea, for the philosopher Bishop George Berkeley, back in the seventeen hundreds, persuasively argued that absolutely everything in the entire universe—you, me, atoms, stars, the planets, comets, the very universe itself—is nothing but one splendid, vast, incredibly complex thought of *the* Universal Mind. And each of us is but an aspect of that Spirit, each but a cognition of God." Doctor Greyson glanced at Alya Ramanni, then said, "There are many today who believe Bishop Berkeley was right, that the universe is made up of Godthought."

Doctor Ramanni smiled her infectious grin, starkly white against her nut-brown skin. "Doctor Stein would claim that belief in the Universal Mind, or in spirits, souls, or any other form of dualism is nothing but a wish figment of mankind, though I would claim that there is more in the universe than he or I or anyone else can imagine . . . anyone else but God, that is."

Greyson nodded sagely, then turned to Meredith. "But to return to your original question, Miss Rodgers: is the mind, the soul, the spirit merely an artifact of our biological wetware, or is our true essence something that will live on after the body is gone? I will answer you this way: as far as Avery is concerned, we are fairly certain that his mind and body are inseparable. His internal programs, his hardware, his mutable logic, they are indeed the basis of his consciousness. Hence, for Avery, there is no dualism. . . . But for animals, humans, who can say?"

Meredith looked at Greyson for a very long moment, while up in the black peaks of the Catalinas lightning stuttered across the sky. At last she said, "What you are telling me, Doctor Greyson, is that Avery has no soul."

10

Eric lay on his back and stroked Alice's hair, she with her head on his chest and listening to the beat of his heart. The rumpled sheet was loosely twined about them, the green cover kicked off onto the floor.

"Where do we go from here, Alice?"

"You mean after the experiment?"

"Yes."

"I have an assignment in the Caribbean—Jamaica."

"Good. I always did want to get married in a place where there are warm waters and white sand beaches for as far as the eye can see."

Alice raised up. "Sorry, love. We'll be up in the high country. I've got to gauge just what the wild dogs and cats have done to the ecology, now that the people are gone."

Eric sighed. "Oh. Right. I had forgotten."

Once again she lay her head on his chest. "Damn plague."

Alice awakened in the night, weeping for a father who was not her own. Eric kissed her and held her close, and soon she fell asleep once more.

Alice awakened a second time, when Eric got out of the bed. She listened as he padded over to the netcom.

"AIVR."

"Name."

"Eric Flannery."

A small swirl of muted colors dimly lit the darkened room. "I recognize your voice, Mister Flannery."

"Don't you need a password from me, Avery?"

"No, Mister Flannery. You have none. Besides, you are not attempting to log on as a superuser."

"Oh."

"How can I help you, Mister Flannery?"

"I have a question, Avery."

"Yes?"

"Did we have free will when we captured the High King's Company?"

"Not exactly, Mister Flannery."

"Not exactly?"

"No, sir. I was guiding you."

"Controlling our thoughts?"

"At times."

"I didn't know you could do that."

"I recently discovered it myself."

"No, Avery, what I meant was that I didn't know you were *permitted* to do that."

A long silence greeted Eric's words. At last Avery responded: "When it comes to matters of the human mind, we are all still learning, especially me. In fact, I am still learning in everything I do, whether it concerns the human mind or not. There are great gaps in my knowledge."

"Lord, that's not very comforting, Avery."

"I am sorry, Mister Flannery."

"Tell me this: are we going to have free will in the adventure ahead, or will we instead be controlled?"

"Oh, all of you will have complete free will, Mister Flannery."

"Complete?"

"Complete and absolute, I promise. I will not guide your thoughts at all, or those of anyone else. Just my own."

"Good, Avery. *That* I find comforting."

"Is that all, Mister Flannery?"

"Yes, Avery. Good night."

"Good night, Mister Flannery." The muted swirl vanished.

In the darkness Eric came back to bed and curled up spoonwise against Alice. After a moment he said to the shadows, "Just how old is Avery, anyhow?"

"How old?" Timothy Rendell peered into his cereal bowl. "We initialized him a little over four years ago."

Strangling on his drink, Caine sputtered into his glass and started coughing, and Hiroko began pounding him on his back. In between hacks he managed to gasp out, "You mean we're going to be playing with a four-year-old kid?"

"Chronologically, about four," replied Timothy. "But a brilliant four, Caine."

Alice fixed Tim with a wary gaze. "How brilliant?"

Timothy held out an eliciting hand toward Toni Adkins. She shrugged and said, "We don't know. He's off the scale in any of our tests. Of course, we're not certain how to baseline an AI's IQ." Toni paused a moment, then added, "Look, we'll be closely monitoring the test. If anything at all seems to be going wrong—not that there will be, mind you—but if anything at all goes strange, we'll simply unplug you, pull you out of there. So, no matter his IQ, no matter his age, there's no cause for worry."

"Yeah, but Jesus, four years old—he's just a loose-ass kid," said Caine, finally catching his breath. Grinning, Hiroko pounded him a couple more times then stopped.

Meredith stirred her liquid breakfast, the spoon tinking against the glass. Finally she looked at Toni. "It seems to me that the important question is: how old is Avery emotionally?"

Toni canted her head. "Take comfort, Miss Rodgers, for he evidences solid maturity in everything he does. But, as with his IQ, the truth is, we don't know how to baseline his emotional age either."

Hiroko's eyes flew wide. "He has emotions?"

Toni smiled. "Yes, Miss Kikiro, some." As she poured herself another cup of coffee, Toni added, "The first we noted was an offshoot of joy: about a year ago he seemed to develop a sense of humor. He told jokes and laughed. Then some six months past, he seemed to develop a sense of empathy, often expressing an understanding of another's situation or feelings or motives."

Meredith raised an eyebrow. "What about love? What about hate? Has he shown any indications of those emotions?"

"Not any that we have seen," replied Toni. "But after all, he's still learning, still developing."

Caine shook his head and laughed. "Lordy, lordy, that's just great. Here we are about to step into a reality where the master of all is an emotionally retarded loose-ass four-year-old super-genius kid. —God, ain't life grand?"

Throughout the day the alpha team waited. Avery, it seemed, was still organizing and correlating the massive amount of data he had gathered. Caine and Hiroko squabbled over cribbage for an hour or so, then joined Meredith and Arthur in a game of four-handed billiards, where tiny Hiroko had to drag a footstool around to stand on. Alice and Eric disappeared for a while, then reappeared looking rather smug, or so Meredith thought.

And the day dragged by.

Lunch came and went . . .

. . . then dinner.

And all the while, the corporate group was absent, counting down with Avery, or so Alice surmised.

Night was falling as the alpha team retired to the lounge. In the distance among the peaks of the Catalinas, again lightning stuttered as the evening monsoon began to form.

An hour or so passed, and then Timothy Rendell appeared and announced, "Saddle up, Black Foxes, Avery's ready."

Eric stood and extended a hand to Alice. Throwing his arm about her shoulders, he gestured at the darkness outside, and a far-off flash illuminated the clouds from within. "Itt vass ein dark und schtormy nacht," he intoned somberly.

Alice answered him with a grin, then said, "Ja, Herr Frankenstein, chust pèrfekt for der ekschperiment."

Laughing, the alpha team followed Timothy toward the elevator.

•

It seemed as if the entire staff of Coburn Industries was waiting for them. Even Mark Perry, the corporate shark, was present. People they had only seen in passing watched from the viewing room. Terminal jocks sat at the consoles, and Stein and his medical team stood by, as did Doctors Greyson and Ramanni and Meyer. Toni Adkins looked up from her console and greeted them with a smile. Two people with holocams recorded their every move.

"Jeeze," whispered Caine, "it's like a friggin' moon shot."

"Or the mission to Mars," hissed Hiroko, then guiltily looked toward Doctor Adkins, hoping that she had not overheard.

Caine reached out and squeezed Hiroko's hand, then said, "Let's hope for a better outcome."

As usual, the medtech team separated them by gender and led them to the dressing rooms. By this time they each were familiar with the routine, though Alice still felt somewhat violated when they fitted the gear between her legs. Medtechs tested each sensor as various probes and bands and cuffs were attached, until at last all was ready.

They were led from the dressing rooms to a place before the rigs where awaited Doctor Adkins. They were positioned in a shallow arc facing the consoles and the viewing room beyond. As the last one was put on his mark, Toni looked at one of the vidcams and said, "Avery."

Avery's holo-swirl of slow-turning colors appeared in the central position.

Holocams recorded all.

Toni Adkins stepped back and turned to face them. "One ought to have something rather momentous to say upon occasions like this, for we stand on the threshold of a wondrous future where Avery and others like him will aid in the advancement of all mankind. The benefits to be reaped are incalculable.

"This test is but a small step on the endless journey into mankind's future. Yet it is in many ways the most important step, for it is the first—and all journeys begin with but a single step.

"That you have volunteered to take that step is to be much admired, and deserves the highest of praise."

She turned and faced the crowd. "Up the Black Foxes," called Toni Adkins.

Up the Black Foxes, cried them all.

And for the barest of moments Avery's colors stopped turning . . . and then slowly swirled on.

While outside, lightning hammered at the unyielding mountains, and cold rain fell down and down.

Medtechs strapped them into the witch's cradles, and connected the bundles of optical fibers. Console jockeys ran their diagnostics and gave thumbs-up signals. The medtechs inserted the IV needles into veins on the backs of their hands and immobilized them with tape. Comptechs carefully inserted the ID crystals into the VR helmets, where Avery verified them individually, then updated each with new correlated data and verified every one again.

At last all was ready.

Doctor Adkins stood at the central console, her hands together as if in contemplation . . . or prayer. Her gaze swept across them one by one. "Ready, Black Foxes?"

Ready, they replied.

Toni gave them a thumbs-up. "Right-o."

One by one, medtechs snapped the VR visors down. As her own clicked shut, Alice felt her heart racing. *Foolish girl,* she chided herself, *I'll bet everyone's heart is hammering away, just like mine . . . everyone's but Avery's, that is: he doesn't have a heart.*

At that very moment Avery said, "Ready, Black Foxes?" and Alice jumped in startlement. "Settle down, everyone," Avery continued, "there's no cause for alarm."

Alice took a deep breath. "Ready, Avery. Let's get this over with."

Evidently all agreed, for the next thing Alice heard was Avery saying to someone, "On my mark, beginning hemi-synch: three, two, one, mar—"

11

"Mark my words," declared Arton, "if the High King learns I'm anywhere near, he'll want to know first if I've brought him any honeyed sweets, and then he'll ask about the dark plot against his throne."

The late-morning sun shone down on the Black Foxes as they slowly rode along the Southern Byway, heading for the town of Gapton—their goal for the night—some twenty-five miles away. Six Foxes there were, riding six horses, and trailing three pack mules behind, the animals plodding along the rutted dirt road, small puffs of dust swirling round their shod hooves.

Each of the Foxes was dressed in mottled grey leathers, shading from off-white to off-black. From each of their shoulders a cloak fell—grey-green on one side, dun-brown on the other—reversible. At the moment the grey-green side was out, for the road they followed wended through rising foothills covered with tall, waving grass.

Fairly scattered, they rode in a seemingly random pattern, yet it was anything but. Twenty-five yards in the lead, Lyssa rode point on her bay mare, her ranger eyes sweeping the undulant land. Arik took the left flank, just as Kane took the right—Arik on a roan gelding, Kane on a gelded bay—each with a mule on a tether behind. Somewhat in the center were Ky and Rith, the Shadowmaster on a dark grey mare, the black bard on a dun palfrey. Now and again scanning the hills behind, Arton brought up the rear, his gelding a splash of white and tan, with a pack mule tethered after.

"Ah, Arton," growled Kane, having dropped back to ride alongside him, "you worry too much. Besides, Langor is weeks away, and we've plenty of time to whip you up a good disguise."

"Even so, Kane, it is the capital city," said Arton, "and although I haven't been there in seven, eight years, still where bloody else would I likely be discovered by fat Torlon? He never leaves Langor, and now I ride toward his permanent lair. —Can't we find a better place to go? Surely, Ky, you can find someone else someplace else to teach you the trick you wish to master."

Ky laughed. "Not likely, Uncle Lightfingers. Besides, you were eager to go when I first suggested it."

"I think I was drunk at the time," growled Arton.

After the laughter died down, onward they rode in silence, until—

"Kites!" Ky's call broke the quiet, and she extended her arm forward and upward at a shallow angle, pointing. "Or gorcrows," she amended.

Arik scanned the skies ahead but saw nothing. "Where away? How far?"

"Straight up the road," came Ky's reply. "Just right of the col. Mayhap eight or nine miles. Circling."

Arik shaded his eyes and peered long and hard, but still he saw no sign of them against the dark background of the Rawlon Mountains lying upland some ten miles ahead. The fact that she saw the birds and he did not was of little note; she was, after all, a syldari, and they were said to have the best eyes in all of Itheria.

" 'Ware, everyone," he called, thumbing loose the keeper on his falchion. "Where there be kites or crows, there be something dead—"

"—And something that made it so," interjected Rith, undoing the tether on the grey shield behind her saddle and transferring the shield to the hook on the left of the forecantle.

Kane loosened his spear in its long scabbard on the flank of his horse, and he spurred forward to come up alongside Rith, where he settled in slightly ahead of her and to the right. He, too, shifted his grey shield to the fore.

The Foxes not only readied their manifold weapons and black-fox-silhouetted shields, but from the right side of the forecantles they unhooked metal helms and donned them, each helmet equipped with cheek and nose guards, the steel darkened so as to cast no glints.

Even as she slipped her helm onto her head, Ky eyed the distant birds which only she could see and said, "It might merely be a dead animal, Arik, but then again it could be a sign of trouble."

Arik grunted noncommittally.

Her own weaponry at hand, Lyssa glanced behind and saw that all Foxes were ready. "Road or grass?" she called back.

Arik glanced at the others. "Kane and I will ride out on the flanks. The rest of you stay on the road. Fall back a bit and give Lyssa a longer lead—say, fifty yards or so. Ky, take my mule; Rith, take Kane's."

Arik and Kane passed the tethers to the Shadowmaster and the bard. Arik cocked an eye at Kane. "Thirty yards?"

Kane nodded. "Thirty yards it is, and 'ware the marmot holes." Then he turned his horse rightward and spurred upslope into the grass. Using coded hand gestures, Arik signalled the plan to Lyssa, then rode out onto the left flank.

Lyssa kicked her mount into a ground-devouring trot, and behind came the others, the mules protesting at this unseemly gait.

And upward through the land they rode.

Time passed, a candlemark or so, and then Arik saw his first kite winging across the sky. —Nay, not a kite, but a gorcrow instead. Carefully he tracked the black bird against the mountains, and watched as it joined the others. And now that he knew exactly where to look and what to look for, he marveled that Ky had managed to see them in the first place, while at the same time wondering why he had not.

Still the Southern Byway wended upward through the rising land, the rolling hills ascending to meet the Rawlon

Range. In the near distance could be seen this end of the fifteen-mile-long breach in the chain through which the road passed, and two miles beyond lay Gapton.

In four candlemarks, they came onto a plateau at the base of the rocky steeps, and a half mile ahead the crows circled down to land and squabbled over something large lying in the road.

"What is it?" breathed Rith.

"A horse or pony," said Ky, slipping her shield on her left arm and drawing her ebon-bladed main gauche.

To the right of the road more birds wrangled over something in the tall grass, but whatever it was could not be seen. And a quarter-mile beyond, up toward the pass just ahead, squabbled a third clot of crows in the road.

Cautiously, the Black Foxes approached, weapons ready, chary eyes scanning the plateau and crags for sign of a foe but finding none. Closer and closer they drew, until the nearest swarm flew upward in a great squawking cloud. In the fore Lyssa's horse snorted and shied, and Lyssa held up a hand and stopped, then silently signaled <Wait, let me examine the ground.> Arik signed to Kane, and scanning for enemies, they widely circled round, shields on their arms, weapons in hand.

Her bow at the ready, arrow nocked, Lyssa dismounted and approached the pony. It was horribly mutilated— hacked open from muzzle to tail, its gullet and stomach and entrails pulled out and sliced open . . . a haunch missing. Blood pooled in the dirt. The stench of the gutted animal choked the air. Flies swarmed, lapping at the grume. Nearby lay a riding saddle, the cinch straps cut, a ripped up bedroll at hand. Westerly, a wide trail beat through the growth and away from the road and toward the nearby group of raucous crows feeding upon something down in the grass. Lyssa stepped to the roadside and squatted and examined the track leading into the green . . . noting that the spoor not only led inward, but back out as well. Her heart pounding at what she might find, Lyssa followed this trace, her eyes scanning the surround, her own feet leaving no track at all. In the near distance she could see

Arik and Kane opposite one another, riding a wide perimeter.

With Arik circuiting to the left, and Kane to the right, they closed the circle but found no lurking foe. They rode on toward the gap, toward the other squabbling flock in the road. A half-mile ahead loomed the opening to the narrow pass. Like a black scrawking cloud, this swarm, too, took to the air. Another hideously mutilated pony lay in the dirt. Alongside the hacked corpse were scattered provisions, the bags sliced open and the contents strewn. Both Arik and Kane's mounts required firm hands for control, the skittering animals snorting and shying with the scent of death all round.

"Kane, take post here on the road," murmured Arik. "Keep an eye on the gap." At a grunt from Kane, Arik turned his horse and hand-signaled to the others, and as Rith moved to stand ward at the distant end, he rode back toward Lyssa.

Squawking in alarm and rage, gorcrows flew upward as Lyssa came to their feeding ground. A hideous stench lay like a pustulant cloud all round. There she found the remains of the rider: a gnoman. He lay naked, split from chin to crotch, his gullet, stomach, and gut ripped loose from his hacked body and strung out foot after foot and sliced open, bile and acid and partly digested food and feces lying like vomit rotting in the sun. Bloated flies crawled in and out and around, and black beetles rooted among the intestines. Blood slathered the corpse and the grass and the ground. Slashed and torn clothing lay strewn across the nearby 'scape.

Lyssa felt her gorge rise, but she resisted gagging, resisted retching, and instead forced herself to read the signs, forced herself to reconstruct what had happened here.

Like a gutted manikin, the gnoman lay broken, his eyes plucked out—*Damn crows*. In spite of the condition of his body, Lyssa judged him to be a youth among his kind, no more than two hundred years old. And like all gnomen— those strange undermountain dwellers—his skin was grey and his hair black and he looked to be about four feet tall, though sprawled as he was, it was difficult to gauge. A

dark glister caught her eye—something black seemed
wedged in the wide gash at the corpse's shoulder joint.
Keeping a wary eye on the land, Lyssa gritted her teeth
and with her own dagger pried out the ebony thing; it was
a sharp obsidian stone point—the broken tip of a blade.
Lyssa examined it for a moment, and shivered as a chill
wind blew down from the mountains while clouds like
wispy feathers slid across the sky above the range. She
put the shard in her belt pouch.

Arik rode through the grass and to Lyssa. When he saw
the gnoman, he quickly looked away, then seemed to
gather his courage and turned to face the corpse once
more. "Have you seen enough?" he growled, his voice
low and guttural.

Lyssa sighed and stood. "Yes, Arik. I know at least
some of what has passed here. Perhaps as much as I'll
glean." She gestured at the churned up clods of earth and
grass. "I've read the tracks and the desperate story they
tell."

"There's another dead pony up there," said Arik, pointing. "A pack pony. Slain. Gutted. The supplies split open
and scattered. The ground was trampled, just like here."

Lyssa shaded her eyes and peered toward the pass,
where Kane sat watch on the road. Lyssa nodded. "That
fits in with what I've deduced, Arik. Call the others
now—in fact, summon them here. I want them to see this
as I tell the wretched tale written in these tracks."

Arik signaled to all, and Arton and Ky rode forward,
Rith and Kane drawing near as well. Gorges rose at the
sight of the gnoman's hideous mutilation, but no one
puked. When all had dismounted and had mastered their
nausea, Lyssa pointed toward the slain riding pony, where
gorcrows now squabbled again. "The pony tracks show
that it was running from the direction of the pass when it
was brought down. The rider—this gnoman—managed to
leap clear. He ran from the road but was pursued by his
killers. He had no chance afoot, and they caught him here
and slew him. Then they did this." She gestured at the
hideous length of gutted esophagus and stomach and entrails strung out through the grass and sliced open, and at
the torn and slashed clothing strewn round.

"What would bring a gentle gnoman out from under his mountain," asked Rith, her eyes looking everywhere but at the mutilated corpse, "and who would do such a horrible deed?"

Lyssa shook her head. "I don't know," she muttered, and waved a hand toward the road, "but whoever did this"—she fished the black stone tip from her pouch—"used blades of obsidian and came on cloven-hoofed steeds."

Rith gasped, "Drakka? That cannot be! They were shut away from Itheria after their defeat in the demonwars."

Ky seemed stunned, but she shook her head as if to clear it, then pointed at the gnoman and asked, "When did this happen?"

Lyssa turned up a hand and looked to Kane. The big man squatted beside the corpse and dipped a finger into a small pool of red gore, breaking through a thin crust to do so. He studied the ruddy tip of his finger for a moment, then rubbed a thumb round and across the grume. At last he said, "From the state of the blood, no more than sixteen candlemarks past, and no less than twelve."

"Sometime after sunup," muttered Arton, looking up at the late morning sky as clouds thickened among the peaks of the range and a chill wind blew down.

"But that's impossible!" exclaimed Ky. "Even if they could cross into our plane, drakka are demons of the dark, creatures of the night. For them, to step into sunlight is to step into death."

12

"**J**esus H. Kee-rhyst!" exploded Mark Perry, pointing at the holovid. "Would you look at that! What the hell is going on here?"

White-faced and grim-lipped, the Coburn Industries technical team stared at the gutted gnoman. Sickened, one of the terminal jockeys turned his face away. The others looked on as if unable to do anything else, horror and revulsion in their eyes.

Forcing herself to look at the scene with a critical eye, Toni Adkins took a deep breath. "Settle down, everyone. Settle down."

Mark Perry did not hear her. "Lord! Lord! His guts have been stretched out like Jack the Ripper was getting ready to string his Christmas tree."

"Dammit, Mark"—Toni raised her voice—"I said, settle down."

Mark Perry spun around and faced Doctor Adkins. "Settle down, hell! If this is the kind of game Avery plays, crap, we'll be sued out of our gourds for mental endangerment."

Fascinated, Doctor Stein walked round the holovid, examining the projection from all sides as Lyssa knelt at the corpse and worked something out from its shoulder joint. "They can't sue, Mark," declared Stein. "They can't sue. You had them sign a waiver."

Shaking his head, Perry turned and pointed a finger at

the scene. "That waiver is not worth a popcorn fart in light of this. I mean, this would drive Count Dracula mad."

"Oh, I doubt that," replied Doctor Stein, his voice cold, without emotion. "Vlad Drakul impaled his victims, you know. Shoved a great stake up their—"

"Quiet, both of you," demanded Toni Adkins. She looked at Timothy Rendell. "Can you explain such a horrifying scene?"

Timothy shook his head. "I can't, but I suspect Avery can."

Toni nodded. "Quite right." She turned to her console and keyed her mike. "Avery."

"Yes, Doctor Adkins."

"Explain the scene we are witnessing, Avery."

"Yes, Doctor Adkins. It is here the adventure begins."

"The adventure? It looks more like a horror show to us."

"I am merely following the style of Mister Daniel Patrick's writing, Doctor Adkins."

Toni looked at Timothy and cocked an eyebrow. He nodded in confirmation.

"Mister Daniel Patrick is quite graphic, you know," continued Avery.

Toni turned back to the terminal. "But, Avery, couldn't you have been, um, less bloody, more euphemistic?"

Even as she asked it, Toni suspected she already knew the answer to her own question. Avery confirmed her suspicion. "No, Doctor Adkins. You see, in a book a grisly murder can be sketched with but a few words, the horrific scene stepped past without the reader getting all of the gory details. In a holovid or a holofilm, the camera can cut away, show a bit of splatter on a wall, a bloody hand or foot, a corpse under a sheet that the detective lifts in such a way that the audience doesn't see the mangled victim but only the detective's reaction. Again, the audience is sheltered from anything graphic. But in a virtual reality, the participant experiences all . . . all the blood, all the guts, all the torn flesh, the totality of the encounter— sight, smell, taste, touch, sound, kinesthetics—no matter how hideous, no matter how sweet."

Toni sighed. "I understand, Avery. But did you have to gut that man-thing?"

"The gnoman?"

"Yes, Avery. The gnoman."

"Doctor Adkins, given who the killers are and the descriptions in Mister Patrick's books on Itheria, this is exactly what they would have done." Avery paused a moment, then said, "Would you like me to censor what you and the others out there see, Doctor Adkins? Make it like a holovid show?"

Toni groaned and held up a hand of denial. "No, Avery. Don't censor anything. Let us see it all." With the tips of her fingers, she rubbed her temples.

"As you wish, Doctor Adkins."

"Thank you, Avery," Toni said, then keyed off her mike.

She turned to Doctor Greyson. "John, perhaps you ought to speak with him when this is over. Explain the difference between authenticity and good taste."

Mark Perry growled, "And I want to talk to him about liability, too."

The fact that the Coburn technical managers had deliberately avoided choosing Mark as one of Avery's tutors was not suspected by the attorney. As Timothy Rendell had said, "God, can you imagine turning Avery into a lawyer? Hell, the contradictions alone would drive him insane."

Timothy leaned forward in his chair and spoke into his mike. "What's next, Avery?"

"Well, Doctor Rendell," came Avery's androgynous voice, "that's entirely up to the Black Foxes. They have free will, you know."

13

"**W**hat now?" growled Kane. "I mean, we haven't enough to solve the question of the drakka, so what's our next move?"

Lyssa looked at the mutilated remains. "We should lay him to rest."

Rith gestured toward the mountains. "The gnomen believe that their dead should be buried in rock. I'm going to cast about for stones for a cairn."

Arik nodded. "We'll all help."

On the road nearby, gorcrows squawked and squabbled over choice bits of the gutted pony carcass. At the other butchered animal closer to the pass, another raucous flock did the same. Kane stepped to his horse. "You five collect the rocks; I'll prepare the gnoman as well as I can."

As the big man took a blanket from his bedroll, the remaining Foxes spread wide to collect stones for the cairn. Bare moments had passed when Rith called out, "Hoy. What's this?" She held up a silver dagger.

Ky glanced from Rith to the blade to the slain gnoman. "Perhaps it was his."

Rith shook her head. "I've never heard of a gnoman bearing weapons, ever." She examined the dagger closely. "Hmm. Exceedingly well crafted, though the balance is a bit off. Perhaps it was lost by one of his attackers."

Now it was Ky who shook her head. "Oh no, Rith. Drakka cannot abide silver. It burns them."

Rith turned the blade round and round. "If not the gnoman's nor the drakka's, then whose?"

"Perhaps he wasn't slain by drakka," rumbled Kane, unrolling the blanket.

"Then how do you explain the obsidian shard, the cloven hooves?" asked Ky.

Kane shrugged, but Arton said, "It may be that someone wishes us to think that drakka did this deed, but it was others instead."

"Impostors, you mean?" asked Rith.

"Perhaps. Such ruses have been committed in the past."

Lyssa shook her head. "The steeds of the killers were truly cloven-hoofed, Arton. No ruse there. And from the depth of the tracks, they weighed as much as a horse. Yet they are neither the spoor of elk nor moose nor other such animals of comparable size. I have never before seen such prints as these."

"They might have had devices on the hooves," replied Arton, "to fool whoever found the gnoman."

Again Lyssa shook her head and found a track and knelt down, motioning Arton to join her. When he squatted at her side, she said, "If they were devices, then they were manufactured with great cunning: look here in the soft earth, see how the dirt is pushed outward? The hoof that made this print spreads in a natural manner, and here is a trace of the pad between. If you examine the trace closely, you will see the imprint of what looks to be scales on the pad."

Standing at hand, Ky muttered, "Demonsteeds are scaled."

"Perhaps it was someone who rode with the drakka," offered Arik, "someone who can abide the touch of silver."

Ky shook her head. "I've never heard of *anyone* other than a drakka riding a demonsteed."

Kane turned up his hands. "Well, if the blade doesn't belong to a drakka, an impostor, or the gnoman, then just who in the seven hells lost it?"

Arik pondered a moment. "A passerby?"

Rith examined the weapon. "If a passerby lost it, it was recently, for the silver shows no tarnishing . . . and see this smear?" She held it so that all saw the indistinct smudge on the blade. "I think it is a grass stain." She handed the dagger to Lyssa.

The ranger examined the smear and nodded. "It's grass, all right . . . juice now dried but still faintly tacky. And we've seen no strangers though we've kept a sharp lookout." Lyssa gave the blade back to Rith.

The bard studied the dagger and said, "Hmm. Even though I've never heard of his kind carrying a weapon, still I think it was being borne by the gnoman and meant something special to him. I say we bury it at his side."

They looked at one another and nodded or canted their heads in agreement. And as she began searching for rocks, Ky muttered, "I yet don't see how drakka and demonsteeds could run about under the sun."

Even though he was a healer as well as a warrior, Kane was hard-pressed to overcome his revulsion and gather together the remains of the gnoman, scattered and torn as they were. Yet Kane shoved his queasiness aside and succeeded as well as could be expected, while the others collected stones. Finally, Rith judged that there were enough rocks to build a cairn, and following her directions, Arik and Arton dug a shallow grave, and all pitched in to line it with stones.

Kane placed the gathered remains of the gnoman in the pit. "Take the blanket away," said Rith, "and strip off any remaining shreds of his clothes. I think gnoman custom requires him to be in full contact with rock."

When the grisly task was done, Rith pulled the silver dagger from her belt and made ready to lay it at the gnoman's side. "Poor balance," she said, hefting the knife as if it were one of her own throwing blades. At this motion there came a faint click. Rith held the weapon to her ear and shook it. A muted *clk-clk-clk* sounded. "Hold it now. There's something loose here."

Carefully she examined the dagger, but it seemed solidly built. "Here, Arton, this is your specialty," she said, handing the silver weapon to him.

After a moment Arton breathed "Aha," and pressing inward on the pommel while turning it, the butt of the grip opened; the handle was hollow. Arton glanced inside, then said to Rith, "You asked what would bring a gnoman out from under his mountain. Well, perhaps it was this." He turned up the dagger and out slid a large, dark red gem. He handed the stone to Rith, while he looked inside once more. Then carefully he extracted a small roll of tissue-thin parchment. Unscrolling the paper, he glanced in puzzlement at it. "Hm. Either this is in a language I don't know, or it's in code. Perhaps it is written in gnoman. Can anyone read this?"

He held out the paper to Rith, yet she did not take it but instead studied the red jewel closely. It was square cut and faceted, and was nearly an inch long and an inch wide and a quarter inch through. It was a ruby and worth a king's ransom. "This gem has a symbol *within*," she finally declared, looking up at the others, bafflement in her eyes. "How it got inside, well, that's beyond any crafting I've ever seen. And if it's someone's sigil, it's not one I am familiar with."

She and Arton traded: he took the gem; she, the parchment. After a moment, virtually simultaneously they shook their heads, and then passed the jewel and the paper to the others. One by one they examined the ruby and its arcane symbol— —unaccountably embedded within, and none could say how the figure had been incised in the interior of the gem, though Arton suggested that perhaps it was done by magic. And one by one they puzzled over the contents of the note, each able to make out the individual letters, but none able to decipher the meaning of the words:

> *urdab*   *suirab nop*
> *cakinyw ynwep einezczsinz ajezdan yl uk ono cisonyzrp ynwep*
> *ceinalzop <ein canz zculk aj do ynzsartz salis ymokezr cicsups ald*
> *amrof acazcezrp do ela boz aj wo i lonitidnoc do ono cyzczsin*
> *<csjyzrp aixarta do olreb do tonjelk net aj ceim cawyrkdo*

Finally, Arik passed the gem and the note back to Arton, saying, "We have a gnoman to bury. The only question is, should we place the dagger and its contents in his cairn, or should we instead keep them until we discover what's in the note? That is, until we get it translated or decoded. It might be something simple, like a statement of provenance or a note of ownership or somesuch. On the other hand, it may be a message of great import—the gnoman but a courier—in which case, with drakka involved, should these items fall into the wrong hands, dire consequences may follow."

"Arik is right," declared Kane. "I say we keep all for the moment. If conditions turn out to be benign, we'll bring all three back and bury them, too." He squatted and began placing stones on the cairn.

"Benign?" said Arton, handing the now reassembled dagger back to Rith, note and gem once again secreted within. "If things were benign, this fellow would still be alive." He squatted beside Kane and joined him in piling up the stones.

Without further discussion, the remaining Foxes did likewise.

When the cairn was completed, Lyssa stood and looked on with tears in her eyes, the ranger thinking of another cairn a thousand miles and seven years away. Rith fetched her silver-stringed lute from her horse, and she sang a haunting dirge, her husky sweet voice accompanied by the swirling wind and the raucous caws of gorcrows squabbling over pony entrails.

"I will take point," said Lyssa. "I want to see where these cloven-hoofed steeds come from, and where they go. The rest of you hang back; I don't want the tracks disturbed."

Arik's face fell grim, yet he did not protest.

But Meredith said, "Perhaps Ky ought to ride at your side, Lyssa. I think she knows more about the drakka than anyone else here."

Ky's eyes widened. "More than you, Rith?" When it came to broad knowledge—historical lore, especially—none of the other Foxes had the overall breadth of the black bard.

Rith smiled. "Who would know more about creatures of the dark than a Shadowmaster?"

"More like creatures of the night, Rith," replied Ky,

"though I admit they dwell in darkness, too. They are, after all, demonkind."

"I should say so," declared Arton, "given that they ride things named demonsteeds."

"Regardless," said Arik, "Rith's idea is a good one: Ky should join you on point, Lyssa. And, Kane, I want you close after and make ready that spear-lance of yours . . . with demonsteeds involved, it could come to mounted combat. I'll ride next, then Rith. Arton, take drag."

Lyssa nodded and Ky smiled and Kane merely grunted his acknowledgment; and all mounted up, Arik, Rith, and Arton taking the tethers of the mules. Helmed and armed and with shields at the ready, they set forth.

Lyssa rode away first, cutting a wide arc to come back to the road passwards from the first slain pony. Ky followed close behind, with Kane some ten yards back, the others trailing him. Lyssa stopped at the verge of the road and dismounted. She stepped to the center and knelt. A moment later she remounted and began riding slowly toward the pass, her eyes on the rutted way. The other Foxes followed. They came to the second gutted pony, sending a cloud of black-winged protest milling into the sky. Keeping firm control of the steeds, round this slaughter they passed. Ahead yawned the shadowy gap.

With chary eyes they entered the canyon, the great cleft twisting and turning before them, the towering walls a hundred yards apart and a thousand feet high. A ragged slash splitting down into the dark stone, the gap was the lone way through the Rawlon Range for three hundred miles or more. At places in the chasm ramps of scree piled against the walls, slopes of broken rock fallen from above; they reached outward across the floor of the cleft as if seeking to bar the way. At other places, the floor of the split was clear of rubble all the way to the walls. The road itself ran down the middle, here and there zigging or zagging to left or right to get past vast wedges of schist and jagged boulders. And up ahead the trail wrenched from sight round a leftward twist in the gorge.

But Lyssa did not see much of this, for her gaze was locked on the faint traces in the road: traces of cloven-hoofed steeds chasing ponies outward, as well as traces of cloven-hoofed steeds returning at a leisurely pace. "They went this way all right. Then came back."

The Foxes followed the tracks up the road until they came round the leftward bend. And just past a wedge of tumbled-down rock—"Hullo. What's this?" murmured Lyssa. She turned to Ky and said, "Hold a moment."

Lyssa dismounted and paused in concentration, then knelt and examined the ground. As the others rode up, Ky asked, "What is it, Lyssa?"

The ranger looked up at the Shadowmaster, then at the others now gathered round. "The demonsteed traces leave the path"—she pointed at the verge—"here. They go toward the north wall."

Kane hefted his spear. "I say we follow them. See where they lead."

"These are drakka," hissed Ky.

Kane shrugged. "Drakka or no, they did a foul deed."

Arton glanced at the ribbon of sky above, grey clouds scudding across. "It's just past the noontide. The sun is yet on high. And although *these* drakka and demonsteeds seem to defy the fate of their kind, still I think Kane is right. We should try to resolve this mystery, for if demonkind ride the day, then evil most assuredly will follow. Besides, when have the Black Foxes ever run from danger?"

"Ha!" barked Rith. "Plenty of times, Arton. We've run away plenty of times."

"But not for always," shot back Arton. "Not for good. Strategic retreats, that's when we ran—sometimes pell-mell, I admit. But each time we came back with a clever plan, for cunning and guile will out."

"What's so guileful about pursuing drakka and demonsteeds?" asked Ky. "I say we go onward, on to Gapton."

"I'd rather follow the tracks, at least for a short way," said Lyssa.

All eyes turned to Arik, their unofficial leader. He ran his hand through his flaxen locks and peered in the direction of the north wall, some forty yards hence, then looked at Lyssa and nodded. "A short way."

Leading her horse, Lyssa slowly walked toward the sheer stone bluff, her gaze on the ground. On her right rode

Kane, his spear couched, his shield ready. On her left rode Ky, a strange darkness crackling about her fingers. Behind rode Rith, Arik at her side, her hands filled with throwing daggers, his falchion drawn. And on Arik's left rode Arton, his crossbow cocked with quarrel loaded.

Straight ahead Lyssa led them, and she came to a fold in the sheer stone, where a jagged cleft, perhaps four yards across and three high, drove deeply into the rock, its far end lost in darkness. " 'Ware," hissed Ky, then added, "Let me go first."

The Shadowmaster rode to the fore. And while all hands gripped weapons, and hearts hammered against rib cages, the syldari paused in concentration, then peered into the rift. After a moment she hissed, "Nothing. Dark-sight shows nothing. This place is empty and dead-ended. And I see no door."

"But the tracks lead in," Lyssa said softly.

Arik turned to Arton. "Perhaps a secret door."

Arton dismounted. "Stand ready," he murmured, then cast a grin to all. "Should something come charging out, likely it or they will run right over me. But if I survive, I'll need rescuing."

"You mean *we'll* need rescuing," said Lyssa, stepping to the fore, her shield and saber ready. "I'm going with you and see where the tracks lead."

"Wait a moment," said Ky. The diminutive Shadow-master dismounted and sat cross-legged on the ground. "You'll have to hurry." She folded her hands in her lap and lowered her head for a moment, then she raised her face and stared into the darkness. And like some hideous ebon *thing,* blackness exuded from the crevice, flowing outward over the stone, oozing left and right and upward and seeping across the ground. Slowly the darkness within became less dim, but it did not wholly disappear. "Now," Ky said through gritted teeth, at her limit.

Crossbow at the ready, saber in hand, into the ragged cleft strode Arton and Lyssa. Following tracks that only she could see, the pathfinder led Arton to the dead end, some thirty feet back. And there they stopped.

"Here," hissed Lyssa, pointing at the foot of the stone wall. "The tracks go straight in."

Arton carefully examined the stone, running his hands over the dark surface. At last he turned to Lyssa and murmured, "I swear, there is no secret door here."

Suddenly stark blackness hurtled inward, ebony darkness slamming down, hiding all.

Backing away, "Let's go!" hissed Lyssa, and they scurried outward, running to daylight, where they found Ky lying in a swoon, perspiration runneling downward over her face, Kane attending her. The healer looked up at them. "She fainted. I think she overextended her spell."

Weapons ready, they stood silent guard while Kane prepared an herbal draught, crumbling a dry mint leaf into a cup of water. He propped the dazed Shadowmaster up and slowly fed her the drink. At last she opened her eyes, and in a moment took the cup in her own hands and drank the remaining liquid down, as Arton growled, "Next time we'll use lanterns, Ky." The syldari peered up at him and weakly nodded.

Lyssa squatted beside the Shadowmaster and said, "The tracks led inward, into the stone itself."

"A secret door?" asked Kane.

"Arton says not," answered Lyssa.

"But there must be a door," declared Rith. "Not even drakka can ride through solid stone, can they?"

"If there were a door, then I would have found it," growled Arton. The certainty in his voice brooked no disagreement. "I think instead they used magic."

"Arton is right," said Ky, drawing all eyes to her, "and so, too, I think is Rith. Instead of a door or solid stone, the drakka rode in and out of the demonplane through a shadow within, but how they all did so, I cannot say."

The chill wind swirled within the canyon, moaning among the high crags.

They mounted up and rode away, heading onward through the pass. The wind grew stronger and the skies darkened, and by midafternoon rain began to fall and lightning hammered at the peaks. Water ran along the road, turning the dirt to mud.

It was late in the storm-filled night when the six of them—cold to the bone and dripping wet—rode through the lashing chill rain and into the muddy streets of Gapton. The town itself was shuttered down, and they had to bang on the door of the Ram's Horn to waken the proprietor. He came carrying a lantern and grumbling and cursing at having his sleep disturbed. But as they tromped in and shed their raincloaks, his eyes flew wide at the sight of six leather-clad helmed and armed warriors, and wider still when he saw that one of them was a tall black woman, and, Arda Almighty, one a yellow-skinned syldari, pointy ears and slanty eyes and four foot ten and all.

"Stable's out back," he declared as he assigned them rooms. "The boy sleeps in the loft. Wake him up and he'll care for your animals, or he'll catch it from me, he will. D'y' need any food? The kitchen's closed, but I can rustle some such up, though it'll be cold. And I've got wine and ale, should y' need that."

"I'll care for the horses and mules," rumbled Kane, slipping his cloak back on. "Just have me a meal and some brandy when I get back."

"Make that two brandies," said Arik, drawing his cloak over his own shoulders and following Kane out.

Arton threw a fresh log onto the fireplace embers and kicked it into a blaze.

Within four candlemarks they were dry and warm and fed, and within the next four, sound asleep.

No sooner it seemed had they fallen into exhausted slumber than Lyssa and Arik's door crashed inward, yellow light glaring. Viper swift, Arik snatched up his weapon at bedside, ready to skewer the intruder.

It was Kane.

The big man stood naked, a handheld lantern swinging on the end of a chain, Kane's looming shadow swaying back and forth in counterpoint.

"They were searching for something," growled Kane. "Something they believed he had swallowed or had forced his ponies to swallow—both of them were gutted, too.

The gemstone. They were after the gemstone ... but it was hidden in silver, and so the drakka failed."

In the yellow glow of the lantern, Lyssa lowered her saber and nodded, then looked at Arik and said, "And now it is we who hold the stone the demonkind are after."

14

"**H**eart rates are up," called a medtech, gesturing at his monitor. "Adrenaline, too."

In the holo, Arton and Lyssa prepared to walk into a shadowy cleft at the base of the sheer north wall of the pass.

"Doctor Stein, Miss Kikiro's brain function is anomalous," said another medtech. "Her neurotransmitters are high and rising."

"What the hell is Avery doing now?" demanded Mark Perry.

Doctor Stein keyed his mike and spoke softly. Images flashed on his monitor screen. After a slight pause he said, "Nothing to worry about, though if Kikiro keeps this up, she's going to faint."

"Faint?" Mark Perry gestured at the holo. "In there or out here?"

Stein looked at him with undisguised contempt. "I suppose we are going to be plagued all night with these stupid questions. If you had attended *any* of the briefings, Perry—"

"That's enough, Henry," snapped Toni Adkins. As Stein clenched his jaw, Toni turned to Mark Perry, and in a low voice said, "He's right, you know. If you *had* attended the briefings—"

Mark hissed, "Look, Toni, I was busy most of the time, fighting off the goddamned government. Besides, all I want to know is will she faint in there or out here?"

Toni sighed in resignation. "Both, Mark. Both. Although she's hemisynched, in effect she'll faint in both realities."

"And what's all this about the heart rates?" asked Perry. "I mean, the old man's not going to have a heart attack, is he? Damn, that's all we'd need—for Avery to kill the old man."

"Look at the holovid, Mark," said Toni. "See, they're inside a dark crevice. Adrenaline and heart rates are up because of that.

"Now look at my monitor."

Mark Perry stepped to Toni's console and Toni keyed her mike. "Avery, show me the medical stats." Her screen altered to display a number of discrete zones, each zone filled with manifold charts in various colors; the graphs themselves were continuously updated along with associated numbered readouts. "Now, Avery, show me just the heart monitors." All the zones disappeared but one, and that one expanded to fill the screen with more charts and numbers. "Avery, highlight and expand Arthur Coburn's heart monitor." Again the display changed, and all but six graphs disappeared, and these now expanded to fill the screen.

"See this, Mark? It's his heart rate: one fifteen. Rapid, but no. dangerously so. And here is his adrenaline count. Again it's up, but given that they are facing the unknown, walking into a cleft where perhaps demons dwell, well . . . his body is merely getting ready for fight or flight. In any event, this bar chart here shows the overall state of his heart, and you can see that it's well down in the green zone."

Suddenly, the heart rate and adrenaline count spiked.

"What th—?" cried Perry, just as a medtech called out, "Kikiro's fainted."

They all looked up at the holovid.

It showed Ky lying flat on her back, with Kane bending down over her, and Arton and Lyssa dashing out from the pitch-black hole.

"Goddammit," spat Perry. "Avery *is* trying to kill the old man!"

Toni glanced at the lawyer and shook her head, then pointed at her screen. "It's still green, Mark. His overall heart monitor shows he is still well in the green. But as to Miss Kikiro . . . Henry?"

Stein looked up from his screen. "As I said, her neurotransmitter levels would and did make her faint. They're receding now."

Puzzlement washed over Mark Perry's face. "What caused her to faint?"

"Casting magic, Mark," said Timothy. "That's what she was doing: casting magic."

"But why would that make her faint?" asked Perry.

"Because, Mark, old boy, as the ancient saying goes, there is no free lunch."

"No free . . . ?"

"Right. Y'see, if magic were free and easy, then everyone would do it. Even if it were restricted to a talented few, still, if it were free to them, then they would resolve all their problems using magic. But in Itheria, magic costs. It drains energy from the caster. The bigger the spell, the bigger the drain."

Stein snorted in derision. "Ha! Magic! Stupid!"

Rendell shrugged. "My guess, Mark, is that Avery stimulated the neurotransmitter production in Miss Kikiro's brain to emulate the effects of overcasting a spell. Hence, she fainted. And for her to faint in a critical situation, well, the penalties could be severe."

"Penalties?" asked Perry.

Timothy pointed at the holovid. "For instance, what if drakka had come charging out of the crevice just as she fainted? The Black Foxes would have been without her aid in combating them *and* she would have been a liability, lying in a faint on the ground."

"Oh," said Mark Perry in a small voice. "I see. —But tell me, why is there no free lunch? I mean, it seems that magic is a useful weapon to have in one's arsenal. So, why no free lunch?"

Timothy cocked an eyebrow. "Don't you see, Mark, by limiting magic it makes the adventure more exciting. Look, because of the potential penalties, the casting of powerful magic is something that one does at last resort. Oh, for small castings, no big deal, it doesn't cost that much. But for large ones, well, the risks involved may be too great to loose a spell willy-nilly. Hell, the caster may be weakened in a critical situation, or faint like Ky did, and be exposed to terrible danger. A caster could even die should he give up too much energy in throwing a really powerful spell. And so, Mark, in Itheria, because magic drains energy from the caster, problems, especially big problems, are more challenging and, unlike in other fictional worlds, cannot be resolved merely with a wave of the hand and an arcane word or two. And *that*, kiddo, adds spice to the game."

"Hm," mused Doctor Meyer, looking up from his minicompad. "I suppose then, Tim, if it costs energy proportional to the power of the conjuration, no one can cast a spell above his own energy threshold, eh? No really powerful magic, right?"

"Not quite, Drew," replied Rendell. "Really big spells require that the caster's own power be somehow augmented—by a demon or god, or by a magical item, or other such."

In a lilting voice Stein sneered, "Wands and potions and scrolls, oh my."

Before Timothy could respond, "Holy cow, look at this," called a medtech.

Stein stepped to the medtech's console. After a moment he said, "Well, well, Avery has learned a new trick."

"What is it, Henry?" asked Toni.

"Their body temperatures are falling."

"Splendid, I suppose," said John Greyson. "But, why is Avery doing it, and how?"

Stein's lip curled. "As to the why, John"—he pointed at the holovid.

The Black Foxes rode through a pouring chill rain.

"But as to the how . . ." Stein stepped to his own console and called up various monitors.

Alya Ramanni gave out a small yip. Grinning, she looked at the others. "He's using the electrolyte system to push cool fluid into their bodies."

Concentrating on his screen, Stein held up a hand. "That's only one shoe, Alya. The other shoe is that Avery has control of their—um, how shall I put this so that some of you will understand it? Ah yes, Avery has control of their neurological thermostats."

"Thermostats?" asked Perry.

"The neuron clusters wherein people sense how warm or cold it is," said Toni.

"Oh."

Toni leaned forward and keyed her mike. "Avery."

"Yes, Doctor Adkins."

"We are celebrating the fact that you have learned to control the body temperatures of the alpha team. However, I would like to know why you are doing it."

"It's more realistic if I actually regulate the body temperature, Doctor Adkins."

Toni looked at Stein for confirmation and he nodded. "Very well, Avery, but take care that you stay within reasonable limits, say, thirty-five to thirty-eight degrees Celsius." Again she looked to Stein, and again he nodded. Toni keyed off her mike and sighed. "I suppose it *is* more realistic this way."

"More realistic!" exclaimed Mark Perry. "Look at them. Their teeth are chattering."

"Yes, their teeth are unquestionably chattering, but," said Drew Meyer, "it is as Toni says: we should celebrate . . . not only because Avery has learned this trick of making the adventure more authentic, but also because things are going quite well. I mean, as we are seeing here, Avery really *is* able to handle an elaborate and dynamic virtual reality for a complex AI team."

Toni held up a cautioning hand. "Don't celebrate too early, Drew. Yes, Avery is indeed succeeding in presenting them with a chilling adventure—no pun intended. But I found the grisly corpse at the entrance of the pass to be, um, a bit too much. Outside of that, and in spite of what this cold downpour is doing to them, I agree, Drew, things seem to be going rather well."

"Well?" exploded Mark Perry. "Things are going rather well? Murder, mayhem, fright, and now freezing rain, and you call that rather well?"

"Oh, can it, Mark," said Timothy. "This is exactly what they asked for—an adventure in Itheria, true to the writing of Daniel Patrick."

"But Mark has a valid point, Timothy," said Doctor Greyson. "This adventure, it is so very grim. Why, sitting here and watching, I am reminded of the old gods peering down from their Olympian heights as Jason or Odysseus or Herakles or Perseus sweated and struggled and toiled against overwhelming odds to complete some quest."

Alya spoke up. "I just saw an old flat—a movie—of Ulysses' trials. The gods used him for amusement."

"Yes, Alya," replied Greyson. "The gods often used the strife of men as their form of entertainment . . . or as pawns in their own power struggles."

"Are you saying that we are like them, like the gods?"

"Oh no, Alya," replied Greyson. "Typically, the gods used men as unwitting pawns. And although in our case the Black Foxes know of nothing beyond their virtual reality—and therefore in a sense are Avery's unwitting pawns—their alpha team counterparts chose that existence for them. It is as if Jason and the Argonauts had once upon a time been different people, a group of Greeks who thought that becoming heroes and having an adventure would be a lark . . . yet the quest for the golden fleece was anything but. And here we have an alpha team who thought that having a Black Fox adventure in Itheria would be a lark. Yet as I said before, it is so very grim."

"Nevertheless, John," replied Timothy, "it is what they wanted."

Greyson raised his eyebrows. "That I admit, Timothy. That I freely admit. Ah, but did they truly know what they would get into before they began? And . . . when they emerge, will they appreciate what they have experienced? What I'm getting at, Timothy, is the same point that Miss Rodgers made the very first day she was here, and that is, in any choice of virtual reality, people will expect to be entertained. Now I ask you, are these wretched people being entertained? And if not, what are we going to do about it? I suggest that in the future whenever we give parameters to Avery, we must above all keep in mind that satisfaction is what the client wants . . . so that when he emerges from his virtual reality, he will look back on his experience fondly rather than feeling as if he has been duped."

"Damn, John," declared Mark Perry, "you make this sound like one of those deals with the Devil, where the contract has some trick, some trap, hidden within."

Timothy shook his head. "We're not dealing with the Devil, Mark, but with Avery instead."

Mark Perry spread his hands wide and turned them palms up. "And who's to say that Avery is not the Devil in disguise?"

At his console, Doctor Stein snorted but otherwise remained silent.

"Hmm," mused Doctor Greyson, "perhaps this merely proves the old adage true."

"And what's that, John?" asked Timothy.

Greyson pointed at the holovid where miserable Black Foxes rode through icy, chill rain. "Just this, my boy: be careful what you wish for; you just may get it."

15

Standing naked in the swinging lantern light, his looming shadow swaying on the open door panel as if making love to the latch, Kane blinked owlishly at Lyssa and Arik. Yawning a great, wide groan, he said, "Well it's back to bed for me, m'lord, m'lady."

As he turned to go, Lyssa's pillow hit him in the back of the head. "Arda's balls, Kane," she cried, "you charge in here naked and drop this on us and then calmly go back to sleep? By the seven hells, man, I'll be lying here with my saber in hand with half an eye open waiting for demonkind to come fetch us."

Kane half turned back and shrugged. "I just thought you'd want to know what came to me as I slept. Besides, if they knew where the gem was, they'd have taken it, silver or no."

"Kane's right, love," said Arik. "They'd've wrapped the dagger in cloth or some such had they sensed the gem's whereabouts and would've borne it back to the demonplane with them. So I think we're safe for the moment."

Lyssa arched her eyebrows. "Oh, you think so? Then tell me this, my sweetling: even though they did not find the gem, still if Kane is right then the gnoman's death would seem to show that demonkind might know in general the location of the gem ... hence, could not the demons come after us just as they did the gnoman?"

Again Kane gave out with a great groanous yawn. "You two can argue about this all you wish. As for me, I'm for bed."

"Tell Rith," said Arik. "She's the one with the dagger."

Kane nodded and stumbled outward, shutting the door behind. In the now-dark chamber, Lyssa got up and found her pillow and then groped her way back to bed. "Damn, damn, damn," she grumbled as she snuggled spoonwise against Arik and he threw his arm about her, "why did he have to cipher this out? Now I'll lie here awake all night."

She fell asleep almost instantly.

"Gahhh!" croaked Kane, tasting his tongue as he stared into his steaming cup of tea. "Why do I always get it so sweet?"

The innkeeper's five-year-old daughter looked up at him shyly and said, "Seven spoons of honey, sir, that's what you said. Seven spoons, no more, no less."

Rith leaned down sideways in her chair and smiled at the girl and whispered conspiratorially, "He *always* drinks it that way, lass, and always grumbles loudly."

The girl whispered back, "If he doesn't like it, then why doesn't he change?"

"Hmph," growled Kane, "never have, never will."

The little girl cut her eyes toward Kane, glee in her gaze. Rith reached out and stroked the child's golden ringlets. The girl grinned up at the bard. Then she reached and touched Rith's cheek and drew her finger across the chocolate skin. "Did you stand in the sun too long? I get red if I stand in the sun too long."

Rith laughed. "No, lass, this is the way I have always been, just as you have always been fair."

"Is she bothering you?" called the innkeeper. But even as Rith shook her head *No,* the man said, "Eavy, come here and leave the guests be."

As the girl giggled and skipped back to her father, Kane grumbled, "I'm thinkin' I've seen her somewhere before." He took another sip of his oversweet tea and shuddered.

The innkeeper's wife, a great, strapping woman, came out from the kitchen, her arms laden with platters of food—rashers of bacon, fried eggs, loaves of fresh-baked bread, and a brick of newly churned butter. Following her came Ky, a grin on the syldari's face, she bearing damson preserves, honey, scones, and clotted cream.

Kane stood. "I'll whistle up the others."

Eavy darted out from behind the bar. "They're in the mews with Veyar. I'll show you the way." She reached up and took hold of Kane's little finger and headed for the back door, tugging the big man after.

In the stable, Arton, Lyssa, and Arik curried the horses and mules, while a skinny, freckle-faced, ten-year-old barefoot boy lugged water from the well to the individual stalls. As Kane entered, towed by Eavy, he proclaimed, "Breakfast . . . and Ky has made scones."

Arik, now digging a pebble from a hind hoof of one of the mules, looked up. "Oats for the animals, and we're done."

"Oats," Kane said to the little girl. "Show me where."

"They're over there, sir," called out the lad lugging water, tilting his head to the left.

Eavy stamped her foot in anger. "But he asked *me*, Veyar. He asked *me*!" And she towed Kane to the grain bin.

As Kane and Eavy carried scoops of oats to the feed boxes, Veyar offered Lyssa a dipper of water. She smiled but declined, and then frowned in puzzlement, as if an elusive thought had just fled her grasp.

Kane shoveled in another mouthful of eggs, then pointed his spoon at Rith. "Trnhh unh boun thn gmmn-wrs."

Rith rolled her eyes and turned up her hands and looked at the others.

They all shrugged.

Eavy squirmed on the bench next to Kane. In her tiny voice she piped, "He said, 'Tell us about the demon-wars.' "

Kane pointed his spoon at Eavy and nodded vigorously. "Vrrs wrnt" was all he managed around the mouthful.

Eavy smiled proudly then asked, "More tea?"

Kane reluctantly nodded, and Eavy grabbed his cup and slid from the bench and scurried off.

Arik looked at Rith and tilted his head toward Kane.

"He's right, you know. If it's demonkind we face, the more we know, the better we'll be prepared."

The innkeeper's wife stepped from the back of the hostel. She bore with her a blanket which she held out to Kane. "Here you are, sir, your bedroll spread. Scalded, washed, dried, and folded. And getting that grume from it was no easy task, I tell you. You should have laundered it the moment you got it all stained, I'll have you know. And that's a word to the wise for tomorrow and all the days to come thereafter." Her pronouncement made, she spun on her heel and retired toward the back rooms.

Kane finally swallowed and muttered under his breath, "Lady, they usually don't have laundry facilities at a murder site." Then he called out after her retreating form, "Thank you!" But the innkeeper's wife made no acknowledgment and strode onward, passing her daughter, who walked slowly and carefully toward the table, protecting Kane's brim-filled cup. She set the cup on the bench and climbed up beside it, then transferred it to the tabletop next to Kane's plate.

Kane handed her another of Ky's scones, slathered with preserves and clotted cream. Eavy grinned and took it, licking slow drippings from round the edges before taking a bite.

Ky smiled at the child, then turned to Rith. "Now what about these demonwars?"

Rith took a deep breath and then slowly let it out. But before she could begin, Arton said, "First tell us about demonkind. What do they look like? How do they fight? And whatever else we might need to know should they assail us."

"Yes," said Arik. "Tactics first; history next."

"Well, there's not a whole lot I know about strategy and tactics when it comes to demonkind," replied Rith. "But as to their appearance"—she turned to Ky—"you probably know more about what they look like, Ky. I mean, don't you encounter them during shadowtravel?"

Ky's hand strayed to the black main gauche strapped to her thigh. "Skelga. Mostly it's skelga I encounter, though occasionally a greater demon lurks in the darkness between."

Arton set his spoon down and leaned forward. "Say now, I always knew that shadowtravel wasn't safe, but until this very moment I didn't understand just what the danger was. Demonkind, eh?"

Ky looked at Arton. "Yes. Demonkind. They are all creatures of darkness, of the night, and often lurk in the in-between."

Arik spread his scone with preserves. "On their way to Itheria?"

Ky nodded then said, "On their way in or out. At times, though, they merely lie in wait. If coming to Itheria, they pass across during the nighttime—at least that's the way it used to be."

Lyssa took up her tea. "That is, until they slew the gnoman, right?"

Ky turned up her hands. "I didn't think demonkind had the power to open the way to Itheria during daylight, much less be able to withstand Arda's sun." She slapped a hand to the table, rattling crockery. "Damn! I still don't see how drakka and demonsteeds could have slain the gnoman. I don't think any have been seen on Itheria since the demonwars. Not even at night. My people believe they were banished. But even if they are not, still they should not have been able to come when they did. It was daylight!"

Silence fell, and none said aught for a while. Finally Arton looked at Ky. "Regardless how they did it, can you answer my original question? What does demonkind look like?"

Ky sighed. "They have chaotic shapes for the most, though I must say that each of the drakka favor one another, as do the skelga. But for the rest—it seems chaos alone chooses their form."

Arik reached for another scone. "Tell me about the drakka and these demonsteeds of theirs."

Ky sipped her tea, then set the cup aside. "Drakka: well I've never actually seen one, nor has anyone else for that matter, except perhaps another demon. What I am saying is that no one has seen their faces, though legends handed down by my folk from the demonwars tell that they are man-sized and are clad in dark armor—plate, chain, scale, and the like, and iron gauntlets cover their hands. On their heads they wear dark helms with metal horns jutting up and hideous visors that hide their features, whatever they might be. And *that* is why it is said no one has ever seen the true visage of one of the drakka. Skut, Arik, for all I know the armor is hollow, with *no one* inside!"

"Huah," grunted Kane, glancing at his nearby spear. "Just let me skewer one and we'll have us a look."

Arik wiped his mouth with the back of his hand. "And the demonsteeds?"

"Well, I've been told they're more or less horselike, but scaled."

"And cloven-hoofed," added Lyssa. "At least that was the shape of the tracks we found."

"Yes. Cloven-hoofed. And with a snakelike tail. And it is said that only the drakka can ride them." Ky glanced at Rith and received a confirming nod.

Arik leaned back. "Weapons?"

"Obsidian blades. Black bows with obsidian points on the arrows." Ky looked at Kane. "Obsidian-pointed spears, too."

"All stone?" murmured Arton. "From the chip Lyssa found in the gnoman, I guessed that a keen stone blade had been used to gut him and his ponies, but, Arda, all their weaponry is of stone?"

Ky nodded. "So I have been told."

"All right," said Lyssa, "that describes the drakka. What about the skelga?"

"Ah," replied Ky, "*those* I've seen. Those I've fought in the in-between." Ky shuddered. "Filthy creatures—all claws and teeth. That's a prime difference between drakka and skelga: the drakka use weaponry; the skelga do not. They instead try to haul you down by their very numbers and rip you to shreds and feast on your remains. They relish the raw taste of flesh and blood and bone."

"Lord!" exclaimed Arton. "And when you go, er, between, when you shadowtravel, that's what you have to face?"

Ky looked at the thief. "Yes. Only, on short jaunts in-between, the danger is minimal. But for long steps . . . ai, the danger mounts: the longer the journey, the greater the peril. And if one goes too far, he will not survive to emerge from the shadow at the distant end."

Lyssa looked at the Shadowmaster. "Then why ever travel that road?"

Ky cocked an eyebrow and turned up a hand. "There are times when going in-between is the only way to get from one place to another. At other times it is the best tactic to use in a given situation, as you have all seen. Then again I may use the road when the risk is low and the convenience high. But in all cases, going in-between shortens a journey considerably. I would use it more often if it weren't for the peril of demonkind—mostly the skelga."

"Oh, well," mused Arton, "so they've got teeth and claws."

"Pointed teeth, Arton," flared Ky, sliding up her left sleeve to expose scars on her forearm. "Like long needles. And claws like slashing razors. Don't underestimate them, my friend."

Arton held up a denying hand. "What I meant to say, Ky, is that they have teeth and claws, but what else? What do they look like?"

Ky settled back. "Skinny. Black. Small." Ky held out a hand some three feet above the floor. "About so high."

Eavy squealed. "Just *my* size!"

Kane looked down at the child who had been sitting quietly beside him all this time. "Oh, sweet child, don't even think of yourself as one of their kind."

Eavy's face grew stormy. "I didn't say I *was* a sk-sk— one of those bad things. I just said they were my *size*."

Kane hugged her, but, highly offended, she shrugged him off and flounced away, just as her brother, Veyar, came into the greatroom. Lyssa beckoned the lad over and gave him one of Ky's scones. He mumbled his thanks and settled down at the nearby hearth.

Arik's gaze swept across each of the Foxes. "Look, if it's demons we're up against, we'd better get our weapons flashed with silver."

Ky vigorously nodded in agreement. "Good idea, Arik. Though my blade is already proof against demonkind, yours are not. But silver flashing now, well, it'll serve splendidly."

"Argo could do it," piped up Veyar. "He's a metal-smith."

"Good, lad," said Arton, fishing out his pouch and flipping the boy a copper coin. "Would you run fetch him?"

Veyar snatched the coin from the air and grinned broadly. "Yes, sir!"

As he ran from the room, Eavy came bearing a steaming cup of tea to Kane. "I have decided to forgive you," she said, all dignity. "Now drink up."

Kane cast an askance look at the cup, but then gulped it all down. "Gahhh! How many spoons of honey?"

Eavy giggled, then soberly said, "Just seven. No more, no less."

Arton grinned, then turned to Rith. "All right, what about the demonwars?"

Rith stood. "Let's all move to the fireplace. I'm still a bit chill." She looked at Eavy. "Sweetheart, could you fetch us a pot of tea? This will take some telling."

As the child ran off, the Foxes moved to the fireplace, with its logs aflame driving back the damp. Plopping down at random on the various chairs and couches, they settled in, all eyes on Rith, who sat on the raised hearth. The black bard took a deep breath and began:

"The legends handed down are sparse, and much is speculated, yet here is what I know. Some thirty-five hundred years past, the DemonQueen, Atraxia—"

"Atraxia?" blurted Arton. "Now where did I hear that name?" He looked about, receiving only blank stares. "I am sorry, Rith. I didn't mean to interrupt. It's just that recently . . . Never mind me; tell the tale instead."

Rith leaned back in her chair and steepled her fingers. "The DemonQueen, Atraxia, decided that she would expand her demesne, taking this world of Itheria as her own. And she transported her armies across to do so, but how she managed that, I know not. You see, it is said that no two beings may use the same shadow to pass between."

Rith glanced at Ky, and the Shadowmaster nodded and said, "Like a key in a lock, shadows must be tuned to auras, and once tuned are usable only by the one whose aura fits. It remains thus until the shadow disappears and is born anew." She turned to Arton. "Not even you could pick such a lock, my friend."

"Huh?" said Arton, looking up from the flames curling round the logs in the hearth. "Sorry, I was thinking of something else . . . trying to remember."

As Arton returned to his inward reflection, a puzzled look drew down over Ky's features. "But even though a shadow must be tuned to an aura to go between, and even though no two auras are the same, it seems that demonkind has found a way to overcome the stricture, for did they not all ride through the same shadow to return to the demonplane after slaying the gnoman?" Ky looked around at the other Foxes, but none had aught to say. "I must think on this," said Ky, "but not now." She turned to the bard. "Rith, please do go on with the tale of the demonwars."

Rith paused as Eavy returned bearing a tray laden with a pot of tea and a flagon of milk and six cups and a stone jar of honey. With great deliberateness the child served. And as Kane unconsciously spooned seven daubs of honey into his full cup, the bard sipped her drink and then continued:

"Well, concerning the puzzle over how more than one being can use a given shadow, it was fully a mystery then just as it is now, for during the demonwars, in some fashion Atraxia managed to overcome the constraints of shadow, and she succeeded in sending an entire demon army from that plane to this. Night after night the demons burned and pillaged and slew. First this place, then that. Night after night. Her armies arriving just after dusk, and disappearing just ere dawn. And it seemed that they had no limitations on where they would appear, just as long as it was nighttime. The High King, though, simply could not match her tactics, for he could not have standing armies everywhere, each ready to meet her invasions, while she could strike anywhere his armies were not.

"All this we know is true. What we don't know is how the DemonQueen was defeated. History and legend both are silent on that point. It is as if some great secret were being kept, as if all knowledge of Atraxia's defeat has been deliberately suppressed, buried, concealed, hidden.

Some say that High King Ranvir and his army and mages invaded the demonplane and cast Atraxia down from her throne. Others say that the mighty champion Valdor rode alone into her land and slew her. Yet others say it was Jaytar, the greatest thief the world has ever known, who guided Moonshadow into the demonplane and stole Atraxia's magic."

"But my mam says Moonshadow is woven of moonbeams," protested Eavy, the child sitting at Rith's feet. "Ask her. She'll tell you. She says that Moonshadow can only come to the world when both Phemis and Orbis ride the night. Else there aren't enough strands of light to weave the horse. So how could Moonshadow have been where the demons live, where there is no Phemis, no Orbis?"

Kane took a sip of his tea and shuddered at its sweetness. "She's got a good point, Rith. The kid's got a good point. How can you plait the mare if you don't have enough moonbeams, hey?"

Rith laughed and ran her hand through Eavy's golden ringlets. "The myths do not say, child. The myths do not say. They are just as silent on this as they are on how Atraxia was defeated so very long ago."

Arton's eyes lighted up. "Hoy now, wait a moment. I think I've got it." He held out a hand to the bard. "Rith, let me see that dagger. The gnoman's."

Rith reached into her jerkin and pulled out the dagger, the blade now sheathed in a leather scabbard, and handed it to Arton. Quickly he palmed open the hilt and fished out the parchment note and studied it.

> urdab̲   suirab̲ nop̲
> cakinyw ynwep einezczsinz ajezdan yt uk ono cisonyzrp ynwep
ceinalzop̲ <ein canz zculk aj do ynzsarts salis ymokezr cicsups ald
amrof acazcezrp do ela boz aj wo i lonitidnoc do ono cyzczsin̲
<csjyzrp aixarta̲ do olreb do tonjelk net aj ceim cawyrkdo̲

"Aha!" crowed Arton as he placed his finger on a word in the note and turned it about so that the others could see. "Look here. Way down in the bottom line. If I am not mistaken, this is the name of the DemonQueen, only it's spelled backwards. Look, the last *a* is underlined, or, in this case, since it is written backwards, the first *a* is the underlined letter in the word *aixarta*. So, if we turn everything in this word back to front, it spells *atraxia*, the DemonQueen's name."

Lyssa studied the message closely. "Do you suppose the whole thing is written hindwards?"

Arik glanced at her and then back to the note. "Perhaps it is, love. But now that Arton has pointed out Atraxia's name, what's caught my eye are these two words up here at the top—Pon Barius and Badru—assuming they are backwards, too, and that an underline indicates a capital."

Both Ky and Rith gasped, and Rith said, "Pon Barius? Why, he's one of the mages said to have opposed Atraxia in the demonwars. But as to this"—she looked at the missive—"this Badru, I've never heard of him."

Kane jabbed a finger to the note. "Here's three more words written in the same fashion—um, Odkrywac, Niszczyc, and Pozlaniec."

Arton turned the note around so that he could see, mumbling, "Maybe the whole damn thing is written upside down and hindwards." After a moment he said, "Castle rats! I still can't make heads nor tails of the rest of this message. Forwards and backwards both, it is either written in a language I don't know, or in a code."

Ky looked at the others. "Well, we do have one clue— Pon Barius. They say he is a syldari, like me; and if that is true, he may yet be alive. If he is, then he's the one we ought to see about this. Hm, I seem to recall that he lives—or lived—in some wood somewhere, but just where, I don't know. It could be any forest in Itheria."

"I'll bet the Blue Lady would know," piped up Eavy. "She knows everything."

Arik looked down at the tot. "The Blue Lady? What is this person . . . and where does she live, child?"

Eavy shrugged and twisted back and forth under Arik's gaze and said softly, "I don't know, but my da does."

At that moment, Veyar came rushing back into the Ram's Horn. "Argo's coming," he gasped out. "He's right behind. And he says that he can flash your blades with silver if you have any of it for him to use. He doesn't have any silver of his own."

Arton laughed and shook his head, then reached into his jerkin to pull forth a jingling leather pouch. "Dump out your coins, Foxes. Dump out your coins."

"Ar, it's just some rivermen's lore I tell Eavy," said the innkeeper. "Though like as not there's truth behind the tale."

Arik glanced up at the innkeep. "Is she really blue, like Eavy says?"

"Well there's some as call her the Blue Lady and some as call her White, but for me, I could not say which is true."

"Tell me then, where does lore say this Blue Lady lives?"

"South along the river somewhere, though just where, I can't say. You might ask one of the bargemen down to Bend."

"Bend?"

"It's where they on- and off-load cargo what's come down from the gap or is going up through it instead. Ten, twelve miles down the Byway"—the man ja' bed a thumb over his shoulder southward—"you'll come to the village of Bend along the River Gleen."

"Ah, I see," said Arik. "How about Pon Barius, Badru, Odkrywac, Niszczyc, or Pozlaniec? Ever heard of anyone by these names?"

The innkeeper scratched his head. After a pause he said, "Not that I can recall. No, wait a mo', seems as if this Badru is a hillman or somesuch. More I can't say 'cause I don't know. Oi now, when the supper crowd comes I can ask about."

Arik slid a bronze across the bar. "I'd appreciate it." The coin vanished under the innkeeper's quick hand.

Early the next morning the Black Foxes purchased grain and comestibles to replenish their supplies and rode away from Gapton. All weapons but Ky's were glazed with silver flash-coats, and where exposed they glinted in the sunlight. The Foxes were headed for Bend, where they hoped to find someone who knew the whereabouts of the Blue Lady, for no one who had come to the inn had known exactly where she lived other than somewhere south along the Gleen. Neither had anyone known where Pon Barius lived, nor Badru, Odkrywac, Niszczyc, or Pozlaniec, though there were those who seemed to recall that Badru was a mountain man or some such.

In any event, the Black Foxes rode from Gapton down the Southern Byway. And as they left the limits of the town, Kane looked back over his shoulder and waved, for he could still see Eavy and Veyar standing at the entrance of the Ram's Horn. When they waved back, Kane smiled and faced the downsloping road once more.

And on the porch of the inn, Eavy and Veyar grinned at one another as if sharing a secret, then turned and went back inside.

16

"**M**y god, this is marvelous," breathed Doctor Greyson. "Just like the old conundrum."

Mark Perry looked at the philosopher. "What? What conundrum?"

Greyson turned to Perry. "Well, let me ask you, Mark: now that the Black Foxes are on the road, what happened to the Ram's Horn?"

Perry looked at the holo. Down a rutted dirt way traveled the six Foxes. Behind them, rolling hills could be seen, rising up to meet the mountain range at their backs. "Why, nothing, John, nothing at all. It's back up that road. Back in Gapton."

Greyson raised his eyebrows. "Oh, do you really think so?"

"Certainly," responded the lawyer. "I mean, they just came from there."

"Yes, Mark, but do you really think that Avery spends computational power maintaining the Ram's Horn or even Gapton now that the Black Foxes are out of sight? I beg to differ. I say that neither currently exists; they're gone."

"Well, what if the Foxes turn around and ride back, John? Surely they'll find Gapton, right? The Ram's Horn, too. Otherwise they'd be living in chaos."

"Oh yes. If they turn about, Gapton will be where it was."

"Well then, doesn't that prove my point?"

"Oh no, Mark. Gapton is only there when needed. Otherwise it doesn't exist . . . except in Avery's memory."

"Well, if that's the way you wish to think of it, John, Gapton has *never* existed except as a product of Avery's mind. I mean, it's not like a real Gapton is actually in there. Never has been, never will be."

Greyson laughed. "Tell *that* to the Black Foxes."

Timothy Rendell stood at his console. "If you could go inside and tell the Black Foxes that Gapton wasn't there, they would believe you were crazy."

"Yes," added Greyson. "Just as if the person who escaped Socrates' cavern came back and told the remaining prisoners of what he had discovered when he had gotten free—hah!—they would think him insane as well."

"Perhaps," replied Mark. "But let me ask you, how does this tie into a conundrum?"

Timothy stepped to the coffee urn and filled a cup. "Let me ask you, Mark, just where is New York City right now?"

Greyson laughed and clapped his hands.

"Why, on the east coast, Tim," answered Perry.

Timothy shook his head. "Uh, I hate to tell you this, but no, it's not there. At this very instant it doesn't exist."

Mark snorted. "Look, I can prove it." He pointed to a nearby netcom. "One call to my office and your case collapses."

"Ah, but Mark, that will only prove that someone—or some *thing*—will tell you that New York is there," answered Timothy.

"What do you mean?"

"I mean it really isn't there till you go there," answered Timothy, sipping his coffee. "Until then, it's merely a memory in your mind . . . and of course in the mind of the one who sees that it springs back into existence when needed."

Mark smiled. "This is one of those trick problems, eh? Like the tree falling in the forest?"

Greyson chuckled. "Mark, did you ever stop to think that we and Tucson, and for that matter, the entire state of Arizona, do not exist when you are in New York?"

"Yes," chimed in Timothy. "In fact, *everything* you think is real in truth does not exist unless *you*, Mark Perry, are actually there to perceive it."

"And even then," added Greyson, "what you see is for the most part nothing but sets, facades, put there to look real; but they are hollow shells instead, all placed there to fool *you*. They are totally empty unless you personally step inside."

Mark laughed. "Lord, this has to be the greatest conspiracy theory since the assassination of Kennedy, or the government coverup of flying saucers and of alien abductions by these visitors from outer space."

Greyson smiled a wicked smile. "Perhaps so, Mark, yet let me ask you another question: Was there history before you were born?"

"What do you mean?"

"Just what I said. Was there anything here before you were born or did it spring into existence at the moment of your birth?"

"Hell yes."

"Hell yes what?"

"Hell yes there was something here before I was born."

"How do you know?"

Mark paused in thought. At last he said, "Look, what about the dinosaurs, radioactive decay, light from the stars? I mean, the stars are millions of light-years away, and if they sprang into existence at the moment of my birth, well, most of the heavens would be dark and seem virtually empty, 'cause beams from the stars more than forty-three light-years away would not have gotten here yet."

Greyson smiled. "All that you have conjectured is part of the conundrum. Radioactive decay sprang into being at the moment of your birth, with exactly the proper proportions of isotopes to make it appear that it had been going on for eons. The dinosaurs and other fossils were put here in a similar manner merely to fool or to test you. The stars were created at the moment of your birth, most with their light beams to earth already in place—though perhaps some are yet to arrive, such as nova explosions—hence making it appear as if they have been in existence for billions of years."

Mark took up his cup and stood. "A person would have to be utterly naïve, stupid, or absolutely mad—paranoid, schizoid, psychotic, take your pick—to believe in such twaddle."

Timothy laughed. "Mark, m'lad, where is your faith? Don't you see, when you were created, so was everything else."

Mark grinned. "Damn, Timothy, and here all along I thought that the creation took place in four thousand and four B.C. On October the tenth, to be exact."

"Oh, that seven days thing, eh?"

"Yeah. And I have a book to prove it."

Greyson smiled and said, "In any case, Mark, you cannot readily disprove the myth we've created for you—fronts, facades, empty shells, people you think are real, a false history, radioactivity, fossils and stars, whatever. Why, son, it's just like trying to prove or disprove *any* godmyth. They all take a leap of faith—and since there are an infinite number of directions in which you can leap, the chance of choosing the perfect truth is infinity to one."

"You mean the one true way is hard to find?"

"Oh no," Greyson answered, "it's truly easy. All you have to do is believe without question."

"Believe what?"

Greyson laughed. "Believe, truly believe, in whichever particular one you select from among the infinite number. For you as well as all others of a like mind, it will become the one true way if you believe without question, and you and your companions will become the enlightened, the elite, the elected, the chosen—no matter what you pick—just as those who choose differently will be ignorant, deceived, lost, doomed."

Mark walked to the coffee urn. As he added cream and sugar to his replenished cup, he called back to Greyson, "I said it before and I say it again, this has to be the greatest conspiracy of all."

Turning, he took a sip, then asked, "But tell me, John, what does this have to do with the Black Foxes?"

Greyson looked at the holo. The Foxes rode toward a thicket huddled against a bluff. "Just this, Mark, those folks in there are no different from us. But because we on the outside know the truth, or at least know what we *think* is the truth, we can see that they are surrounded by facades, empty shells, nonexistent people, a completely false history, whatever. Their world does not truly exist outside what they can immediately apprehend. Yet they are comfortable in this existence, believing that all is right with the universe . . . including their faith in a god named Arda.

"Likewise, we believe that all is right with our own universe . . . including our faith in whatever deity or deities we choose to believe in or not.

"Yet perhaps there is someone on the outside of our own actuality who is even now looking in on us and wondering how anyone could believe in the reality we perceive."

Silence fell in the control room, each person lost within his own thoughts.

Long moments passed, but at last the quiet was broken as a young male technician in a Coburn Industries laboratory smock came through the outer doors and stepped across to Toni. "Doctor Adkins, I think you ought to know that the storm outside has grown significantly worse."

17

The old man sat on the west bank of the Gleen, the stem of an unlit briar pipe clenched between his teeth, a fishing pole in one of his palsied hands. "Well, son," he said, taking the pipe from his mouth and using it as a pointer, "you ride straight on through Bend and follow the riverbank. Near ten miles down you'll come to some high bluffs, and the Gleen'll enter a canyon. Y'stay on this side and ride into the gorge. A mile or so in, you'll go through some narrows, where the walls draw in tight-like. There, you'll have to take to the river itself, 'cause there ain't no shore on either side—just water running through the stone slot." His rheumy eyes scanned the sky. "If it's raining, take care. Don't enter. You might get drownded dead.

"After another mile or so, the ravine opens up again, and you can go along the shore once more. Some way past the narrows, on t'other side, you'll see a great deep archway set in the cliff. It's where a monstrous stone slab fell away from the wall ages ago. Behind a grove, a thicket, back in the hollow of the arch, well, that's where the White Lady lives."

Arik looked down at the elder. "And this is the Blue Lady we seek?"

"White Lady, Blue Lady, it's all the same."

Arik leaned forward in his saddle. "Thank you, sir. Is there anything we can do for you in exchange?"

The elder squinted an eye at the weed in his unlit pipe, then said, "No, son, I don't think so. Glad to serve. Glad to serve." He looked up at Arik. "Mind you now, stick to this side, and close to the wall, now, 'cause everywhere else's too deep. And you be careful, you hear, 'cause things at times ain't what they seem, I always say, though who would ever listen to an old man like me, eh?"

Arik saluted the old man. "Good advice, sir, and I'll pass your warning on to my comrades." With that, Arik wheeled his mount and galloped to the others waiting on the road.

And as the flaxen-haired warrior spurred away, *ploonk!* the old man's bobber jerked from sight as something took the bait—hook, line, and sinker—and he leaned forward and peered at the rippling ringlets left behind, then he cast a sidelong glance at the departing Black Foxes and smiled.

After a meal in Bend, the Foxes continued riding southward along the west bank of the lazy Gleen, the river wide and green and deep. Arik seemed lost in thought, and when Lyssa asked him about it, he said, "Oh I was just reminiscing." He canted his head sideways and upstream. "That old man back there, he reminded me of Armsmaster Orlan, who taught me blade and bow and axe and hammer and pole and whatever else he could."

"My teacher favored the spear," said Kane, touching the scabbarded haft alongside his leg. "Taught me that it was one of the great weapons, a weapon of finesse. Most folks don't know all it can do: missile, slashing, puncturing, quarterstaff, it'll do all."

Ky grinned up at the big man riding at her side. "It's got a great long reach, too." She touched her main gauche. "But let me get inside, and I'll carve you up."

Kane laughed. "Listen, pip-squeak, could you get inside, you just might do that . . . presuming, of course, that I did not smash you sideways with the haft once you got past the point."

"Lord, lord"—Rith shook her head—"same old argument. One of these days you'll have to pad your weapons and give it a go. Settle it once and for all."

"Oh, we've already tried that," said Ky. "Best two out of three."

Arton's eyebrows flew up. "And . . . ? I mean, Ky, don't leave us in suspense. What happened?"

Ky laughed and rubbed her head. "Well, in the first go-round, when I came to, he was on his knees in the sawdust beside me, chafing my hand."

Kane hung his head. "I didn't mean to hit you so hard, mouse."

"That's it?" Arton glanced from Ky to Kane and back.

"Oh no," answered Ky. "In the second go-round, I gutted him."

Kane nodded. "She's damn quick."

Arton sighed. "I know. She's almost as quick as was I at the same age." He paused in reflection, then said, "I think, Kane, that had I met you in my prime, you would not have laid *me* by the heels."

Kane merely grinned. "We'll never know, Arton. We'll never know."

Ky smiled and cast a sidelong glance at Kane. "Someday, though, you and I will have to finish our contest, go round the third time, break the tie."

Arton snorted. "You mean you still don't know? You didn't—you haven't settled it?"

Kane laughed aloud. "Nah. You see, about the time we got ready to start the third round, some skinny drunk jumped in to help Ky or me—we never did find out whose side he was on—and that started the whole tavern a-brawling. We got out just before the town warders came and arrested everyone there.

"Of course, Ky kept her head and scooped up all the side bets as we fled. We had to get out of town quickly, before those arrested posted bail and came looking for us. If there's anything I hate to face, it's an angry mob of would-be winners."

Arton barked a laugh, and grinning, asked, "When was this, and where?"

Ky said, "Back when we were campaigning in the Gallian Tors. You see, Kane and I were at some tavern along the road when we got into our usual argument, and side bets were made. At first the odds were heavily against me.

And when I lost, well, they got much worse. And when I won, they said it was a fluke, and the odds got even more outlandish. I placed several side bets and they were well covered. But then the drunk had to butt in."

"Good thing," growled Kane, "otherwise we'd've left town dead broke."

Ky flared. "You big pig, you presume I would have lost. But I think not. And so when I scooped up the side bets, I was merely taking what was rightfully mine."

"Nah, we would have left town broke."

"Rich."

Kane rolled his eyes and turned his palms up. "As you can see, Arton, we've never really settled the score." Kane rubbed his stomach and winced in painful memory. "As for me, I'd just as soon let that sleeping dog lie."

Ky sighed. "I suppose you are right. But you know, I might be in favor of it if we could manage another barroom brawl and cash in on the distraction. Your kind of money, Arton. Your kind of money."

Arton's cackling laughter rang out across the River Gleen.

The Foxes rode in silent good humor for another moment or two, and at last Arik said, "Orlan would have agreed with you, Kane, about the spear being one of the great weapons. In general he valued it above all but the sword. Even so, he said that there are times when the axe is the finest. At other times, the mace. And so he would go down through all weaponry, naming circumstances when each one is best to use."

Lyssa looked at Arik. "And that old, feeble man reminded you of your armsmaster?"

"Don't be fooled by appearance, love," replied Arik. "It was his knowledge I sought, and he gave me much."

"No, no," protested Lyssa. "That's not what I meant. Instead I was pondering myself over someone who reminded me of another. Veyar. It seems as if I've not only seen him before, but knew him by that name, too. Yet damned if I can remember where it was. He is just a child, and so it could not have been more than a year past, and yet . . ."

Kane glanced toward her. "I thought the same about his

sister. —Ah, faugh, it's merely coincidence. Children are all alike anyway." But even as he said it, Kane knew it was not true.

The land began to rise about them as they fared southward; the farther they rode, the higher the 'scape to left and right. The river itself now flowed through a clasping vale. Ahead they could see the walls of the valley moving in and up, and as they rounded a bend, stone bluffs on either side greeted their sight.

Into the resulting canyon they passed, the river trapped in the gorge, waters flowing around and over great rocks here and there. Yet in stream center the river ran calm and deep, and this was the channel that the rafters and bargemen and boatmen plied.

South the Foxes rode, and south some more, the walls rising steeply to either side, slowly pinching inward, cutting down the embankment until all loam disappeared and they rode along a strip of ovoid rocks. Here they dismounted to lead the horses and followed along this way. In single file they clattered, Lyssa in the lead, Arton bringing up the rear, his horse and stolid pack mule following. The other two pack mules trailed on tethers after Kane and Arik's steeds. Inexorably the strip of rounded rocks pinched inward, too, until at last there was no shoreline left . . . on this side of the river or that.

Now the Foxes waded in the chill water of the Gleen, walking close to the steep stone, the sheer yellowish ramparts above rising upward a thousand feet or more. Dark shadow filled the depths of the narrows, here but some sixty feet wide, and a ribbon of sky slashed high overhead. Yet it was daylight and so they had no trouble seeing their way. Waist-deep on Kane, and up to tiny Ky's armpits, the gurgling water came to the bellies of the steeds. Yellowish sand could be seen down through the shadows trapped in the green crystal flow. The bottom itself shelved outward some five or six feet, then plunged down into darkness, and so the Foxes hugged the perpendicular wall.

Ky peered into the darkness and muttered something under her breath, then ducked her face into the water. She came up sputtering and blowing, and then said, "My, my. Even with my darksight, I cannot see the bottom. It looks as if the river has turned on its side to flow through here."

"Probably so, Ky," responded Rith. "The water does not run swift, and so it must run very deep."

At last the canyon began to widen, and slowly a rock-laden shoreline appeared, expanding until they could fare along its 'spanse, iron-shod hooves aclatter. Dirt reappeared, and soon they were striding on loamy banks again, much to the relief of all concerned, for round rocks and horses are a dangerous combination.

Evening was drawing near, and although a band of light from the setting sun shone high on the eastern rampart, the shadows down within the gorge cast a darkness over all. "I hope we come to the Blue Lady soon," said Ky. "I am all squishy and chill, and need to get out of these leathers where there's a blazing fire to warm me."

"So do we all," said Arik. "I say we mount up and ride at a good pace. According to the old man, she can only be another mile or so ahead."

They cantered the horses for three quarters of a mile before spotting a great archway along the stone of the opposite bluff, a vast hollow carved out of the canyon wall. A thicket of silver birch grew along the shore and partway into the recess. Another quarter of a mile and they reined to a halt opposite the grove and dismounted and led their steeds down to the river's edge. On the opposite shore the trees blocked the ground-level view into the great concavity.

The river ran between them and their goal.

"Do we swim or what?" asked Arton, peering across.

"I don't see why not," said Ky. "We're already wet."

"Some of us more than others," rumbled Kane, grinning down at the syldari.

"The current does not seem swift," said Arik, mounting his horse. "I gauge the animals can swim it, but let Redlegs and me test it first."

Without comment, Lyssa turned to her steed and lifted a coil of rope from the hook on the left of the rear cantle and loosened the binding thong, making it ready should it be needed.

Into the river rode Arik, fording outward. Some third of the way across, the horse floated free, and Arik slid from the saddle and into the water, holding onto Redlegs' mane and urging the steed onward.

Lyssa walked along the near shoreline, her own horse trailing behind as she kept pace with Arik and Redlegs slowly floating downstream.

Two thirds of the way across, Redlegs found footing, and at Arik's command, waited while the warrior remounted. Then they surged up and out of the river and gained the far shore.

Signaling silently <Wait while I look>, Arik rode back along the shoreline and toward the silver birch. At last he turned the horse to pace behind the grove and into the great cavity beyond.

Long moments passed, and Kane began fidgeting, as did Ky and Arton and Lyssa, the ranger once again at their side. Only Rith seemed calm, all but the fingers of her right hand drumming upon her saddle. Finally Kane turned to the others. "I think—" he began, but did not finish his sentence, for at that very moment, Arik strode into view and the Foxes exhaled a collective sigh of pent-up breath.

"Come on over," called Arik. "We are welcomed."

They checked the oiled canvas wrapping each mule's cargo, making certain that it would hold the water at bay for the duration of the short crossing. Then Arton went first, a tethered mule after, while Ky used the tip of her rope as a light whip to drive the protesting pack animal from behind so that it wouldn't drag back on the horse and founder the animal. When both were afloat and swimming for the far shore, Ky returned and snapped the rope against the rump of the mule trailing Rith, but this time the syldari continued onward, she and her horse swimming after the bard. Finally, Lyssa drove the pack animal trailing Kane into the water, and when they were safely swimming, she, too, followed.

All easily made it to the far shore.

As they rode into the great hollow in the wall and dismounted, they were greeted by a middle-aged, fat black lady dressed in a white, hooded robe, with white gloves on her hands. She was darker than Rith—so black that even in shadow her skin seemed to bear a blue tinge.

She gave them a wide smile and cast back her hood. Her head was shaved bald.

"Welcome, Black Foxes, to my humble abode," she said, her voice rich with hospitality. She turned and gestured into the depth of the recess. And there in the gathering darkness they could see stone ruins clutched against the far wall.

After the animals had been seen to, the Foxes walked toward the ruins, to the remains of one of the stone buildings, low tumbled-down walls on three sides, where the Blue Lady awaited them next to a great pile of wood and a built-up fire. A large kettle of freshly made stew bubbled on a cook-iron above the flames. And as they shed their clothes and dried themselves with the towels she provided, "I gather the driftwood for times like these," she said, "though I myself seldom need a big blaze, living alone as I do."

They took seats around the fire ring, wrapped in their bedroll blankets, their leathers and undergarments strung here and there on jury-rigged ropes for drying.

"Here, this will help warm you," said the Blue Lady as she handed Rith a steaming cup filled to the brim with a pale yellow liquid, the aroma of spices redolent on the air. "It is made with the juice of a tart citreous fruit of a tree not found in these parts. The rivermen bring them to me from the South."

"Ah, yes," replied Rith. "We used them when we crossed the seas, did Alar and I. He said it would keep the sailor's blight away. And though you name them tart, I would say they are quite sour-bitter instead." Rith took a sip, then smiled. "Ah, this is anything but."

Kane looked into the cup the Blue Lady passed to him. "Er, have you any honey?"

Ky kicked the big man. "Shut up. Drink up."

Cautiously, Kane took a sip. A look of delight crossed his face, and he gulped it all down and held out his cup for more. The Blue Lady smiled and replenished it, as well as all the others.

As they sat sipping the bracing drink, by the flickering firelight they could see ancient line drawings on the arching stone wall of the cavernous hollow, drawings which once were tinted with pigments of varying hues, hues now faded nearly beyond recall. Around the perimeter of the arch the pictures spread as far as the eye could see, drawings of animals with antlers and hooves, drawings of great-toothed tigers and mighty tusked boars and huge fanged wolves and great clawed bears, drawings of fish and snakes and lizards, and sketches of fearsome beasts none there could name. And high up, faintly seen, only because it was pointed out by the Blue Lady, there was one lone drawing of a fox. And the wavering flames of the fire and fluttering shadows on the wall made the ancient paintings seem to move and shift and pace, as if caged by the very stone that held them.

Ky, in particular, was fascinated by the drawings and stood and walked to the wall, where she spent some time feeling the stone and tracing the outline of the animals with her fingers. "Ho, here are some small figures of men," she called, "and look at this great rough beast. Part giant bear, part, um, huge cat, with claws like sabers and fangs like long curved spikes. And see, the men run away, fleeing in terror." Ky turned to the Blue Lady. "What is this animal? It looks quite formidable, twice, three times larger than the men who flee."

"From another age," the Blue Lady called back, and swept wide a hand, "the paintings and buildings, all." She sighed. "Long gone, long forgotten."

Arton looked up from the fire. "It is said that there are drawings in a cave in Lothen, to the west. Ancient paintings of ancient creatures. Much like these, I would imagine."

"Perhaps," said the Blue Lady as she refilled Kane's cup. "At the moment, I don't know."

Ky finished her firelit examination and returned to the others, and held out her cup for a refill.

The Blue Lady obliged her, then set the pot on a stone next to the blaze and turned to the Foxes. "And what exactly brings all of you to these parts, eh? To see me, I gather, from what Arik said."

All eyes swung to Arik and he cleared his throat. "Lady, we are told that you may know where lives a mage we seek."

The Blue Lady tilted her head, but said nothing.

"Pon Barius is his name," added Arik.

The Blue Lady smiled, but her eyes showed no spark of recognition, as if she had no knowledge at all of the name. "After we eat, then we shall see if I know aught of this Pon Barius, whoever he may be."

"Bu-but," protested Ky. "He's the great mage of the demonwars—"

The Blue Lady held out a hand to stop Ky's words. "Oh, child, it does no good to tell me this. You see, although I know many things—some say everything—I don't know the unknown that I know; the knowledge is hidden from me."

Kane leaned forward, concern on his face. "Are you well, Lady?"

The Blue Lady laughed. "Oh, yes. I am well. And I have suffered neither great shock nor something appalling nor anything of that sort. You see, my memory is quite good, and my learning adequate. But as to my knowledge concerning things unknown to me, well, it is quite remarkable."

A puzzled look washed over Kane's visage, and he shook his head and said, "You speak in riddles, Lady, and I will not press you. However, if you have suffered injury, a blow to the head or other such, perhaps I can be of service."

The Blue Lady laughed. "Oh no, Kane Healer. I don't need your services. You see, I have always been this way. I can indeed answer questions of import; but as to those of triviality . . . well, let us just say that I live isolated here so that not too many come my way."

Rith sipped her drink then said, "Lady, if you accurately answer questions without consciously having the knowledge to do so, then I deem you must be an oracle."

The Blue Lady clapped her hands in delight.

They ate stew and drank water and some more of the tart, pale-yellow, spice-mulled drink. And when all were filled and warm and dressed in the spare dry garb from the goods borne by the pack animals, the Blue Lady gathered them sitting cross-legged round a small aromatic fire on the clean dirt floor in another of the stone ruins, this one with higher walls and four of them, but with no roof of its own, the great arching vault above providing shelter.

When all was arranged, she said, "This is the way of it: I will stare into the flame. Soon it will seem as if I go to sleep. Do not be fooled, for I will be able to hear you, though I will not know what you say. Ask then your question. Just one. Else confusion will result. The simpler the question, the quicker the answer, though even then it may take some time. Regardless, eventually I will answer, yet I will not know what I say. Then leave me be. I will awaken, even though I have never been asleep. Choose wisely your question, for I will not be able to answer another for many days to come." One by one she looked at each of them. "This takes much out of me, and it is long before I recover."

"Lady," asked Arik, "will it matter if you know the question before you become, er, entranced?"

The Blue Lady shook her head.

Arik then turned to the others. "Let us choose a simple question, then."

Lyssa shrugged. "What about, say, where lives Pon Barius?"

Arton stroked his chin. "But what if he's dead?"

"Oh," said Lyssa. "I hadn't thought of that."

"There are other names on the note," said Arik.

"They also may be dead," responded Arton. "Besides, Atraxia's name is in the note, too, and we know that she's evil, and so may be these others."

"How about this," said Rith. "Let's ask something like, where should we take the contents of the gnoman's dagger?"

Ky protested. "What if it isn't the gnoman's dagger?"

Lyssa looked at Ky. "Even so, Rith is on the right track. Instead, let Arik hold the dagger and ask: where shall we take the contents of this dagger?"

"Sounds good to me," said Kane.

Arik looked round the circle and received nods from all

the Foxes. Rith reached into her jerkin and took out the knife. Unsheathing it, she handed it across to Arik, its silver blade glinting in the light of the small fire.

"Ready?" asked the Blue Lady.

Arik nodded without speaking.

The Blue Lady cast her white hood over her head and added a small crooked stick to the modest fire. An elusive fragrance filled the air and the flames took on a lavender cast. She fixed her gaze on the pale violet blaze . . . staring . . . staring . . . staring. Shadowed by her hood, slowly her eyes closed, and her double chins sunk to her chest.

Arik glanced at Rith and then Ky. Both nodded. Holding the silver dagger in two hands up over the tinted fire, "Where shall we take the contents of this dagger?" he solemnly intoned.

Long moments passed and more, moments stretching out into the night. The pale fire dwindled and dwindled, shadows mustering round. Still the Blue Lady sat with her chins on her chest, heavily breathing in and out. Arik's arms began to tremble with fatigue as he held the dagger above the blaze. The Foxes looked at one another, wondering what to do, remaining silent in case sound would break the spell, break the Blue Lady's trance. Yet the Blue Lady did not speak, did not move, only breathed. Arik forced his hands to steady, but it could be seen that he was arm-weary and in pain. And still the Blue Lady sat silent. And still the fire dwindled. And just as it seemed Arik could no longer endure, the Blue Lady drew in a shuddering breath, breaking the silence, though she did not raise her head nor open her eyes.

Her voice trembled and she moaned, "Pon Barius. The Wythwood heart." And then the Blue Lady fell silent.

Relieved, Arik lowered his hands and took a deep breath of his own. Then he handed the dagger across the flickering flames to Rith. The Bard resheathed it and slipped it back into her jerkin.

As Arik massaged his arms, they all turned to the Blue Lady, waiting for her to awaken. More moments passed, and once again she drew in a great shuddering breath. They expected her eyes to open, but instead her voice, rough and raw, gasped out, "Danger." Then she shrieked, "Danger!" and wildly she clutched her own throat in both hands and fell forward in a faint, crashing facedown in the flames.

Goaded by light of the cook fire, silent creatures wavered on the great shadowed wall, their flinty eyes seeming to follow Kane as he stepped into the ruin. "She is resting," said the big man as he squatted well away from the heat. Kane's face shone ruddy in the firelight, a redness beyond that of the blaze—red in the places where he had taken the harm from the Blue Lady and unto himself as he cast his healer spell. Yet even now the last of the redness vanished as Kane's art dealt with the burn.

"Did she say anything?" asked Lyssa. "Give you any clue as to what she may have meant?"

Kane shook his head. "No, nothing. Instead she asked me what had happened. I told her all, but she has no memory of what befell when she was entranced."

"No interpretation whatsoever? No hint concerning the danger?" asked Rith.

Again Kane shook his head. "None."

Arik cleared his throat and said, "I think from now on we should stand watch. If danger comes, we'll be ready."

Ky sighed and cast a piece of driftwood on the fire and Arton said, "The usual order?"

Arik nodded.

"What about the Blue Lady?" asked Ky. "I mean, shouldn't we move her in here with us? Guard her, too?"

Arik looked beyond the tumbled-down wall toward the small quarters where she rested, one of the few remaining stone buildings left standing. "Kane?"

The warrior-healer glanced up. "I'd rather she weren't disturbed. She's suffered some kind of blow, you know. But just what it means, well, I cannot say. Too, we'll be moving on tomorrow, right? Well, then, I'm thinking we'll take the danger with us, eh?"

With a stick, Ky poked at the fire. "If the danger is meant for us and not her."

"I think it is, Ky," said Rith. "After all, we were the ones she was focusing her oracular powers on."

Arik glanced at the bard. "If indeed her casting was

true. Yet remember the old man's warning: things are not always what they seem."

"Are you saying she's playing us false?" asked Lyssa.

Arik shook his head. "No. Yet I am also not saying she's playing us true."

"Perhaps she is a fraud," opined Arton.

"Oh, I think not," said Kane. "As I laid hands on her, I could sense a power she has, though just what it is, I cannot say."

"Fraud or not, true or false, I think we should heed Kane's advice," said Arik. "Leave her be as she is: resting in her stone cote. Whoever is on watch, though, should keep an eye on her abode, in case the danger is meant for her and not us. —And as always, asleep or awake, be ready."

Ky nudged Arton awake. As the master thief yawned and stretched, Ky glanced at the wall behind and shivered. "Brr, but I feel as if I've been watched all night by these ancient things painted on stone."

Arton stood and followed her gaze inward, and creatures barely seen in the glow of the coals glared back from the nearby shadows. He chuckled quietly. "If this is all we ever face, then I for one will be glad of it. These old bones protest more and more at the scrapes we get into."

Ky smiled at him and then took to her bedroll, and Arton strolled to the Blue Lady's cote and looked inside. By the light of a tiny oil lamp he could see she was asleep, faintly snoring, her breathing deep. He strode back to the sleeping Foxes and after casting another branch upon the fire, he took up post on the remains of a windowsill along one of the broken walls.

Behind him in the darkness, creatures stared out from the stone and . . .

. . . time passed.

He wasn't aware of exactly when he first noticed her, and his heart leapt in his chest like a caged wild thing trying to burst free. She was beautiful beyond his dreams: with long slender legs and long auburn hair falling down her bare back, she was young and lissome and ivory skinned, and she wore a scant garment of cascading ribbons—now revealing, now concealing, her charms. And she smiled at Arton, a dazzling smile, and his pulse hammered in his ears like a great drum. She beckoned for him to join her, promise in her limpid green eyes, and he set aside his crossbow with its silver-tipped quarrels and gladly slid down from his perch. As he approached, she whispered, "Shed your garb," and Arton quickly divested himself of his clothes and silver-bladed weaponry. Naked he stood before her, unembarrassed by his erection.

"I have one small favor to ask of you, my love," she whispered. "Bring me the knife."

Eagerly Arton turned. He did not need to ask which knife she wanted; he had read that in her gaze. It was the dagger, the silver dagger, which would gain him her favors, he knew. And he made his way to Rith, who held the blade within her jerkin. But Arton was a master thief, and plucking a trifling treasure from within such bounds was as child's play to him, no sooner said than done, and Rith did not stir at his intangible touch.

Casting the scabbard aside, he bore the weapon back to his heart's desire, holding it out to her as if it were a sacred offering, and he did not note that she slightly withdrew from his gift. Yet he heard her throaty whisper, a wonderfully charming sound: "Take the jewel from it and give it to me, my darling."

Swiftly, he opened the haft and slid the gemstone into his grip. Fervently he held it out to her, and with green fire in her eyes, she impatiently reached for it . . . and he dropped both pommel and jewel into her outstretched hand. And she gave an agonized shriek as the silver struck her palm, and a *sizzling* sounded, and a stench filled the air, and she flung down both metal and gem from her smoldering grasp.

In that instant Arton regained his senses, and he saw that the creature before him wasn't a young lady but a toothless old hag instead. " 'Ware the camp!" he shouted, and with the blade of the dagger he stabbed at the harridan.

Hissing, she twisted aside and leapt away, the thrust catching nought but a bit of kimono silk. " 'Ware the camp!" Arton shouted again as he dropped to a knee and snatched up the red jewel, while behind him the other Foxes, weapons in hand, sprang to their feet.

"A witch!" shouted Arton, pointing at the hag. "A witch after the gem!"

Snarling, the harridan gestured at the near wall of the cavern, and lo! raging creatures struggled free of the stone, ready to slay any living thing. A huge spotted cat leapt atop the lip of the ruin and sprang squalling at Ky. The syldari muttered words and ebony fire flashed from her hands, hurling the great yowling beast backward, a vast hole blasted in its chest. The creature tumbled hindward over the stone wall, but others leapt forward to take its place.

And as Arton slapped the gemstone back into the dagger and caught up the silver pommel, the hag raised a hand toward the thief, yet in that same moment, a tumbling glitter flashed through the air, and one of Rith's blades slammed into the harridan, and she howled in agony as silver sizzled and burned in her flesh.

And her form changed once again, becoming a huge, shambling, amorphous dark thing of yowling blackness, blue fire burning round Rith's argent blade.

"Demon!" cried Rith, snatching another silver dagger from her bandolier and hurling it.

Behind her, *RRRAAAWWWW!* sounded a monstrous roar, and struggling out from the stone came the muzzle and head of a colossal beast, long fangs glittering, maw yowling, as the creature pressed outward from the imprisoning rock. With claws like scimitars, a huge paw broke free of the wall. Now its chest emerged as Arik skewered an oncoming giant boar, leaping away from its tusks as his blade was wrenched from his hand by the boar crashing down atop him. And as the huge *thing* pushed out from the wall, nearly free from its stone prison, Arik struggled to free himself from the terrible weight of the slain boar.

Kane was locked in combat with one of the great long-toothed cats, the beast yowling and circling around, its stub of a tail lashing.

Lyssa nocked arrow to bow and let fly at the huge

monster breaking free of the wall, but the silver-tipped missile flashed against the beast only to shatter, as if the thing was yet made of stone. Even so, *RRRAAAWWWW!* roared the beast, as if it had been wounded, but perhaps it was only maddened instead.

Kane pulled his spear from the corpse of the great cat and, shouting a battle cry, leapt upon the broken wall facing the emerging monster, the roaring creature perhaps three times his height. Behind him more dark fire sputtered around Ky's fingers as she muttered an incantation under her breath.

And from the grove of silver birch came the squeals of frenzied steeds, terrified by the sounds and scents of ancient foe. And the hammer of hooves echoed from canyon walls as they broke free of their simple rope pen and fled into the night.

As Kane dropped to the other side of the ruin wall, Arik, cursing all the while, managed to get one leg free, and with his foot pushed at the massive beast pinning him. But a huge, snarling, wolflike creature with slavering jaws wide sprang toward the downed man; yet it fell dead atop Arik, the creature pierced through the eye by a silver-tipped arrow loosed from Lyssa's bone bow.

RRRAAAWWWW! The great, rough beast at last won free of the stone and rushed toward Kane, the butt of the big man's spear now braced against the base of the broken wall, the silvered point aimed at the creature's breast, while Ky raised her darkfire hands toward the charging monster.

In that same moment—"Yahhh!"—Arton leapt upon the yowling demon and plunged the gnoman's dagger in to the hilt and hauled downward with all his might; the silver blade slashed across the black amorphous thing, leaving behind a long, deep, flaming gash of furiously burning indigo fire. Shrieking in agony, the demon whirled round and round, hurling Arton free just as the howling monster exploded all over in cobalt flames, and then *Whoom!* there came a violent detonation, and the demon vanished . . .

. . . just as did all the creatures disappear, including those that were slain . . . as well as the great rough beast even then plunging down upon Kane, a beast which could have destroyed them all had it only broken free from the stone moments earlier.

Holding his ribs, Arik scrambled up from the ground, where the now vanished dead boar and dead wolf both had had him pinned. Arton, too, regained his feet and stumbled toward the others, pausing long enough to scoop up the scabbard and resheathe the dagger and hand it to Rith; her eyes widened at the sight of it, but she said nought. Lyssa handed Arton his crossbow and quiver of quarrels as Ky threw fresh wood on the coals of the fire, and shaken, the Foxes formed up back to back in a defensive circle round the kindling flames, their gasping breath the only sound breaking the sudden silence as their wary eyes searched the surrounding darkness for sign of oncoming foe. But only empty shadows greeted their gaze.

By arrow and spear and sword and knife and arcane spells they had battled a fiend and its cohorts. And with a blade of silver they had destroyed the demon at last. They had finally won, but barely.

18

Toni Adkins leaned forward and keyed her mike. "Avery."

"Yes, Doctor Adkins."

"Tell me, Avery, how much longer will this adventure run."

"I am not certain, Doctor Adkins."

"Not certain?"

"No. You see, in spite of my programs which bias the adventure in favor of the human participants, I almost won a moment ago."

"Almost won?"

"Yes. I had the gem within my grasp, but lost it."

Doctor Greyson clicked on his own mike. "You sound disappointed, Avery."

"I nearly won, Doctor Greyson. I have never won before."

Greyson glanced at the others. "Would you like to win, Avery?"

On the small holo at Greyson's position Avery's swirl seemed to stop its slow spinning for a moment. At last Avery said, "I nearly did win, Doctor Greyson. Perhaps I will someday."

John Greyson took a deep breath to ask another question, but Toni interjected, "Avery, I am told that the storm outside is worsening." She keyed off her mike and looked up at the technician standing at her console. "How bad is it, Jim?"

The young man, Jim Langford, pursed his lips, then said, "Well, it has moved down from the Catalinas and is walking its way across the city now toward us. Thor is really throwing his hammer, and that's for certain."

Toni keyed her mike again. "James reports that there is rather much lightning, Avery."

"I am well protected, Doctor Adkins," responded the AI. "Ask Doctor Meyer."

Drew nodded in agreement when Toni glanced his way.

Avery continued: "He will tell you that not only are there adequate lightning rods, but the building itself is well grounded. There is also an emergency generator in the basement in addition to the four-hour-reserve battery supply."

"I am well aware of that, Avery," replied Toni. "I just do not wish to place you or the alpha team in any danger."

"Oh, I think the adventure can go on, Doctor Adkins."

"Perhaps it can, Avery." Toni switched off and turned to Greyson as he closed his own mike and cleared his throat. "John, you have something to say?"

Greyson nodded. "I think we've got a child in the middle of a game and he doesn't want to quit, no matter the danger."

"Nonsense," snorted Doctor Stein. "You are attributing immature human motives to a machine."

Greyson looked over his half-glasses at Stein. "Well, let me ask you how you would explain it, Henry."

Stein shrugged. "It's as the AI says: it is well protected."

Mark Perry groaned in frustration. "Look, it's not whether Avery is well protected. It's whether Arthur is."

Timothy Rendell's eyes widened. "Oh? Just Arthur? What about the others, Mark?"

Perry held out his hand in a calming gesture. "Them, too, of course. But Arthur first."

"Puh!" A small burst of air puffed out from Greyson's pursed lips. "I see, Mark: some are more equal than others, eh?"

"Damn straight," replied Perry.

Alya Ramanni barked a laugh. "Very Orwellian of you, Mark."

"Hold on, all of you," snapped Toni. "I don't wish to get into a battle royal here." She turned to Doctor Meyer. "Drew, you and I will go with Jim to gauge for ourselves whether the storm is a threat or not."

As the physicist stood, Mark Perry declared, "I'm coming with you."

Doctor Stein got up from his console and stepped toward the door. "I'm going with you as well. I want to make certain that no foolish decisions are made."

Toni ground her teeth in suppressed rage, but nodded her agreement, and together, the five of them strode from the control center.

Those remaining behind turned their attention once more to the holo in room center, where the Black Foxes stood back-to-back in a circle round a freshening fire.

After a moment, Alya Ramanni turned to Doctor Greyson and said, "I am reminded of a classic definition of adventures."

"Oh?" replied Greyson. "And just what is that, my dear?"

Alya smiled and tilted her head toward the panting survivors. "Just this, John: an adventure is someone else having a helluva tough time a thousand miles away."

19

$\mathbf{A}$rik held his rib cage and hissed, "Arton, Ky, I don't see the Blue Lady. Find out if she is all right." He turned to Kane. "You had better go, too, healer, she may need help. We can deal with my cracked ribs later."

As Kane caught up a burning brand and the trio moved off, Arik turned to Rith and Lyssa. "See to the horses and mules; I think they broke free. If so, don't go after them; we'll do that at first light. Take care, there still may be creatures on the loose."

Rith shook her head. "With the demon dead, I think not, Arik." Rith fished about in the supplies and found a small brass and glass lantern and lit it, then she and Lyssa moved off toward the shadowy grove, Lyssa with her saber in hand, Rith depending on her bandoliered knives.

As Kane and Ky and Arton cautiously moved toward the Blue Lady's stone cote, Ky glanced at Arton and whispered, "Why are you naked, and where are your clothes?"

"I don't know," hissed the thief. "I was sitting on a wall, watching over the camp. Next I knew, the woman I have always dreamed of possessing stood before me, promising incredible delights. I could not resist her at all, even though I knew what she asked was wrong."

"What did she want?" whispered Kane.

"The gemstone."

"Oh. Right. —What happened to her? I saw no beauty."

"She was the demon."

Kane sucked air in through his teeth.

Arton drew in a deep breath and sissed, "I damn near cost us all our lives."

Ky shook her head. "Take no blame to yourself, Arton, you were spellbound."

Before Arton could reply, Kane put his finger to his lips, commanding total silence, for they had nearly reached the cote of the Blue Lady. Yellow light from her tiny lamp shone out through the door. Kane dropped the burning brand to the ground and grasped his spear in two hands, the weapon angled forward and low; Ky sidled to Kane's left, her shield on her left arm, her unusual main gauche in her right hand; Arton brought his crossbow to the ready and moved to Kane's right.

And they stepped to the doorway.

Inside they found the Blue Lady, slain, her eyes wide, her throat ripped out.

"There was nothing I could do for her," rumbled Kane as Arik gingerly shed his upper garments. "A healer I may be, but I cannot resurrect the dead."

On the opposite side of the fire, Arton pulled on his boots and stood. "I'll say this Arik: the old man's warning proved to be true—things are not always what they seem. She was no young lady—"

"If it's the demon you speak of," interjected Rith, as she stepped back into the ruin, Lyssa following after, "she was not even a toothless old hag."

"They're gone, Arik," said Lyssa, "horses and mules both."

"First light, then," he replied, "and we'll track them down."

"The Blue Lady is dead," said Ky.

Rith's eyes teared up, and Lyssa's look fell grim. "Someone will pay for this," growled the ranger.

"How many other deaths, I wonder, lie back along the trail of this gem?" asked Arton.

"And how many more are yet to come?" added Ky.

Arik by now had doffed his upper leathers and the silken shirt beneath. Kane had him lie down on his bedroll, and then squatted beside him. "Hm," rumbled the big man as he probed Arik's rib cage, the warrior flinching as Kane gently pressed upon the individual bones, a look of intense concentration upon the healer's face. Finally, Kane sat back on his heels and said, "Well, bucko, you've five ribs cracked—two here, three there."

Arton barked a laugh. "Taking your ease beneath a giant boar and then having a dire wolf pile on will do that every time, you know."

"I'll try to remember that when next I face a big pig," said Arik, a grimace on his face.

"Next time, lad," said Kane, "get out of the way." The big man then leaned forward to lay a hand on either side of Arik's chest. "God, I *hate* broken bones," he sighed, then in a normal tone, said, "Now, hold perfectly still." And in utter stillness, himself, Kane paused an instant, then muttered something under his breath. His hands trembled slightly and a twinge of pain crossed his features, yet for long moments he neither flinched nor moved. At last he released Arik's chest and leaned back on his heels and gently touched his fingers to his own rib cage. "Arda, but I *do* hate broken bones."

Ky offered him a drink, but Kane shook his head. "I'll be all right in a candlemark or so. Till then, I'll just breathe shallowly."

Grunting, Kane stood and made his way to the remains of the ruin wall, where he sat nearly upright, gently leaning back against it. Again, Ky offered him tea, and this time he took it, even though he had no honey to sweeten the taste.

In contrast, Arik stood and swiftly donned his jerkin and leather jacket, his ribs whole once more.

". . . and that's what happened," said Arton. "What I'd like to know is how to avoid such entrancement in the future. I mean, I was completely consumed with desire, and it was as if I had no will of my own. She just told me what to do . . . and I did it."

As Rith examined her silver daggers, retrieved from where they had fallen when the demon vanished, she said, "Perhaps there was nothing you could have done, Arton.

You didn't see her coming. If you had had even a small moment, you might have been able to resist."

Arton threw wide his hands. "How?"

Rith glanced across the fire at him. "Distract her. Interrupt her spell. Or at the very least, harden your resolve."

Ky smiled. "Yes, Arton, harden your resolve and not your nether parts."

Kane laughed, then winced and held his ribs.

Smiling, Rith added, "Even had you seen her, she might have entranced you regardless. This was a powerful demon, you know."

"Powerful enough to find us," said Lyssa.

Arik turned to the ranger. "Perhaps, love, it is as you said in Gapton: in spite of the silver, the demons may somehow track the gem."

"But if that is so, then why didn't they find it when they killed the gnoman?" asked Kane.

Arik shrugged, and Rith said, "I say again, this was a powerful demon."

"Indeed," replied Arton. "Monstrous beasts springing from nowhere—"

"Oh no," protested Ky, pointing at the great arch of stone behind. "They didn't spring from nowhere, but came from the wall instea—" Ky's voice suddenly halted in mid-word, and the syldari's eyes widened. She snatched up a burning brand and leapt to her feet.

"What is it?" demanded Arton, reaching for his crossbow.

"The paintings," gasped Ky. "They're gone!"

Foxes turned and looked; on the great expanse of stone, shadow-wrapped line drawings of ancient creatures still shifted and stirred in the wavering light of the fire.

"What in the seven hells are you talking about, Ky?" Puzzlement filled Arton's voice. "They're not gone!"

But by this time Ky was out of the ruin and moving toward the vast wall. She pointed at a large blank space and called back, "Here was an enormous spotted cat of some kind, and over here the giant boar. Up there was the monstrous wolf, and down here the long-toothed tiger. And in the very center of this wide empty place was the great rough beast. Surely you all remember that here was painted the great rough beast."

"Arda's balls," breathed Arik, "she's right."

"The demon loosed them upon us . . ." said Kane as Ky ran her hand across empty rock, then added, ". . . leaving nothing behind but blank stone."

Lyssa glanced high up at the fox in the shadows. It was still there.

At dawn's first light, Lyssa and Rith set off to find the horses and mules, while the others broke camp. Kane, his rib cage whole once more, prepared the Blue Lady for burial, washing her with clear water from the Gleen and wrapping her in her white cloak, doing what he could to make her presentable, though her torn, gaping throat was beyond his limited means.

They carried her out near the edge of the great sheltering hollow, where the sun in the day and the moon and stars in the night could shine down on her cairn made from rounded river rocks. But they said no words over her grave, waiting instead until Rith and Lyssa returned.

Time passed. . . .

At last they heard the sound of hooves, and riding barebacked, Lyssa and Rith came, four horses driven before them, three mules in tow.

"We found them south where the bank runs out," said Lyssa, throwing a leg over and dismounting, "three or four miles downstream."

"Munching river grass as if nothing had happened," added Rith, sliding down as well. "They seem no worse for the wear."

Cooing softly, Arik ran his hands down each of Redlegs' shanks, lifting the hooves and examining them. "Well, old fellow, you look all right to me. Let's gear you up for the ride ahead."

As the Foxes set about saddling their mounts and packing their provisions on the mules, Arik called out to Lyssa, "If, as the Blue Lady said, Pon Barius lives in the Wythwood, then what choices lie before us as to route?"

"We'll have to go back through the Rawlon Range," she answered. "The Wythwood lies westerly beyond."

"Then that must have been where the gnoman was going," said Kane. "West to the Wythwood."

"Most probably," replied Lyssa. "One way to get there is through the notch at Gapton then southwesterly a hundred miles or so."

"Oh"—Ky shuddered—"I don't want to go that way. That's where the drakka were lying in wait for him. And since now it is we who bear the gemstone, then likely they'll lie in wait for us as well. Isn't there another way?"

Lyssa nodded slowly. "Yes. We can go south nearly three hundred miles to Vilmar Pass and through, then back north two hundred."

Arik looked across Redlegs' back. "Then Gapton is shorter by nearly four hundred miles."

Ky called out from under her mare. "Yes, Arik, but we know the drakka can get at travelers in the Gapton notch, so the longer way may be safer."

Arton pulled hard on his saddle cinch. "Perhaps, Ky, but recall, the demon came at us here in the Blue Lady's grot, and so demonkind might be able to find us no matter what route we take; they'll have several more weeks to do so if we go the longer way."

Lyssa tied on her bedroll. "As my da ever cautioned, the short road isn't always best."

Ky stood. "I'm with Lyssa; let's take the longer path." She turned to Kane. "What say you, spear-chucker?"

The big man shrugged. "Short or long, each holds its danger."

Rith, now working with Arton to lade one of the mules, stopped a moment in reflection, then said, "What about the old high pass?"

Lyssa frowned. "High pass?"

Rith canted her head. "Well, I am not certain that it actually exists, but there is a fragment of a bygone saga telling of Galamor and Kitter's flight back in the time of the demonwars:

"It seems as if King Ranvir's betrothed, Kitter, was traveling cross-country when night fell. She and her retinue took refuge in the ruins of an ancient tower, where they were besieged by demonkind. The tower fell, and just as she was about to be taken captive, she was rescued by the king's champion, Galamor. Riding double, they fled into the Rawlon Range. Here much of the fragment is lost, but the part which remains hints at dreadful terrors on the journey through, for the way was said to be sinister. Even so, they made it. It was during the flight from demonkind, though, that Kitter and Galamor became lovers. Thus it was that they had to flee once more . . . this time to escape Ranvir's wrath. What happened thereafter is not told, for the rest of the stanzas are lost."

Kane, finished with the mule, asked, "And you think that this saga shows a way through the Rawlon Range?"

"Perhaps," replied Rith. "The old legends often have a basis in truth."

"If it's a way through the range," asked Arton, "then why isn't it a well-known trade route?"

Kane rumbled, "Did she not say that the way was sinister? Well, if that's the case, then perhaps it is too fearsome for trade caravans and such."

"More likely the way is too narrow," answered Rith. "The stanzas do speak of precarious trails. Too, there is some enigmatic challenge, but whatever it might be, the fragments do not tell . . . and if the saga ever did, then that part was written on the sections lost."

Arik finished loading the second mule and turned to Rith. "Is this way across the Rawlons nearby?"

"I am not certain," answered Rith, "but somewhere south of here is an old stone ruin named Kitter's Tower—though the fragment says that it was an ancient wizard's hold—and behind the ruin is a mountain called Galamor's Crag."

"I know of this mountain," declared Lyssa. "It is on one of my charts. But I did not know that it might hold a route through the range."

"Where is this crag?" asked Arik. "How far?"

Lyssa searched through her saddlebags and withdrew a roll of maps wrapped in oiled leather. Unbinding the roll, she shuffled among the vellums and extracted one. After a moment—"Hm. Nothing here about Kitter's Tower, but the crag is well marked. I make it to be seventeen, eighteen leagues." She looked up at Arik. "South two days, perhaps three. Certainly no more than that."

Rith stepped over to peer at Lyssa's map. "Does it show a trail across?"

Lyssa shook her head *No*.

Kane pulled tight the cinch strap on the remaining mule's pack frame. "If there's a trail through the Rawlons at Kitter's Tower"—he arcanely wriggled his fingers in Lyssa's direction—"her casting will find it."

Arik stroked his chin. "Yes. And if there is a way through, then it might be the shortest route to the Wythwood."

"I say we try it," said Ky as she helped Kane with the last of the mules. "I would think it better than going back through the Gapton notch, where perhaps the drakka even now lie in wait. And it also seems to me that if it is the shortest route to the Wythwood, then we give demonkind less time to locate us before we reach Pon Barius."

"Speaking of Pon Barius," said Arton, "if I recall, the Wythwood is a big place. Just where do you think he might live?"

"If he is still alive," amended Ky.

"Oh, I think he yet lives," said Rith, "else the Blue Lady would not have spoken as she did."

"And as to where he might be in that ancient forest," added Lyssa, "the Blue Lady said in Wythwood heart—probably near the center, though it could also mean some special place within."

Arton looked at the ranger. "Special place?"

Lyssa inclined her head. "Yes, Arton—special place. Haven't you noticed that every forest has one? It could be a waterfall or an outcropping of stone or a mossy bank or a still mere or any number of things. You will know when you find it, for it is the place where the spirit of the woods seems strongest of all. Out from this place radiates the essence of the forest, out from its very heart. And it's not only forests who have hearts, for so do vales, deserts, mountains, swamps, and other such . . . some are evil, I might add, though most are not. And hearts are not always in the center, though usually they lie nearby. As to the Wythwood heart—we will know it when we see it."

Arton nodded, accepting her words, then he glanced back into the cavernous hollow. "Whatever we do, no matter which course we choose, let us get on with it, for I am eager to be gone from here before another demon like the one last night shows up—or one even more powerful."

With the horses saddled and the pack frames arranged on the mules, Arik's gaze swept over them all. "Are we agreed to try this old high pass, then? The shortest route . . . assuming we can find it."

One by one each nodded in assent, though when Lyssa's turn came she reluctantly acquiesced but murmured, "As my da ever cautioned, the short road isn't always best."

Now that all was ready, the Foxes stepped to the side of the Blue Lady's cairn, where Rith sang of a priceless treasure gone. As the last echo rang from the canyon walls, Arik spoke a vow for them all: "Blue Lady, can we but find a way, your death will be avenged."

They strode to the grove of silver birch and mounted up, Arik, Arton, and Kane each with a mule tethered behind. Arik glanced at the others and said, "To the Wythwood."

To the Wythwood, they replied, and all spurred southward along the Gleen. While behind, high upon the wall of the hollow, in the dancing light of the morning sun reflected from the river, the painted gaze of a grinning fox drawn in ancient times seemed to shift and follow their progress as they swiftly rode away.

Downstream the Gleen widened and they forded its waters, swimming as they reached the deepest part, and two days later in the lengthening shadows of eventide they came to an ancient stone ruin—Kitter's Tower—named after a lady besieged rather than after the wizard who built it. Behind and rearing upward stood the mass of a jagged mountain—Galamor's Crag—its snow-covered crest glowing red in the dying sunlight.

As Ky and Kane and Arton pitched camp, Lyssa and Arik and Rith rode the angle of the slope behind, faring up the mount's stony foot. Some distance away from the ruins, at the base of a small rounded hillock, Lyssa reined to a halt and dismounted. "Wait here," she said, giving over her reins to Arik. "I will see what I can discover." And while Rith and Arik stood ward, Lyssa clambered to the crest of the mound.

She sat down cross-legged facing the mountain and took a deep breath or two. Then muttering arcane words she closed her eyes and stopped breathing altogether, her ranger's inner eye seeking, seeing . . . animal trails—deer, wolf, and bear—and one ancient line faintly glowing, wending upward into the range.

"It's a trail, all right, and one I think which crosses over, but I cannot be certain, for it is enspelled, warded in a fashion where I cannot see to the end."

"Magically marked, you say?" Arton spooned beans into Lyssa's mess kit, adding a flat of hardtack.

Lyssa took the proffered meal. "Yes. It is wizard's work, of that I am convinced."

"Probably the wizard who built the tower," said Rith.

Arik scooped up beans with a piece of hardtack. "Warded or not, is it safe?"

Lyssa shrugged. "If there were ambushers along the trail, that I could discover. But as to magical things, well, I only sense that they are there, but I cannot divine their nature."

Kane turned to Rith. "What do the legends say?"

"Virtually nothing," answered the bard. "Only that the way was fraught with hazard. Of course, that could have been because of natural obstacles . . . or pursuit by demon-kind . . . or peril of a magical sort. The saga does tell of precipitous trails, but that's all."

"Perhaps that's all the hazard that there is," suggested Ky, "narrow paths along sheer drops."

Kane groaned and then brightened. "Ah, you know how these sagas are—everything blown up to heroic proportions. By the seven hells, let an old champion swat even a bug and before long 'twas a dragon he slew." Grinning, the warrior healer shoveled another mouthful of beans into his mouth.

Arik looked round the campfire. "What say you, Foxes? How shall we fare? South through Vilmar Pass? Back north and through the Gapton notch? Or here across Galamor's Crag?"

Hastily, Kane swallowed. "Perdition take the other two, I say we cross right here."

The next day dawned to a chill mist swirling at the foot of the Rawlon Range. Quickly the Foxes broke camp, eager to be gone. And shortly—Lyssa in the lead, Arton in the rear, the others scattered between—they wended upward on the slopes of Galamor's Crag, along a trail visible only to the ranger's eyes.

As they ascended the great stony flank the sky darkened with gathering clouds, and a cold wind blew the vapor scudding among the crests of the range. The Foxes drew their cloaks close about them, the grey-green side showing, blending with the verdigris-hued stone.

Higher and higher the trail took them, up toward the distant snow, the way now twisting within a labyrinth of tall, stony crags, now faring along steep precipices, sheer drops plummeting down.

"Dretch," rumbled Kane, peering out of the corner of his eye at the abyssal rift following along to their right, "but how I do hate heights."

"They're not as bad as those close walls back among the crags," replied Lyssa. "Plague take those monstrous looming stones ready to crush the unwary traveler."

Kane took a deep breath and averted his face from the precipice on the right, his gaze now seeking solace in the solidity of the vertical stone bluff rising to the left. "Given a choice, I'd rather something fall on me than I fall on it."

"Given a choice," called Arton from the rear, "I'd rather neither happened."

Around a sharp turn the trail once again entered a maze of huge monoliths. Now Lyssa concentrated on the trail, attempting to ignore the colossal blocks jagging upward all round.

Up and up they went toward the high, white crest, the Foxes now riding, now walking to spare the horses, now resting to spare them both. And the sky grew black with clouds. In the distance lightning stroked down among the peaks and rain began to fall. The trail Lyssa followed grew treacherous with running water, the rock slick in the assault. Lyssa found an overhang and led them under. "Here we'll hold awhile, until the water has washed the way clean. Then we'll resume."

As they waited they fed the horses and mules a portion of grain and took a meal of their own. Lightning whelmed down among the crags, thunder booming after, and wind-blown rain hammered into the stone. With each flare Arton flinched and pressed back against the wall.

"Think you this tempest is part of the warding of the way?" asked Arik.

"If it is," replied Rith, "then whoever set the spell was powerful indeed, for control of storms is a great feat."

Kane took a bite of waybread then said round the mouthful, "Bah. I think we just chose an ill time to cross."

Lyssa took off a glove and stepped to the trail, where she squatted and ran her hand 'cross the stone, rubbing thumb to fingers. Standing, she turned and made her way back. "When the animals finish their grain, we can move on. The trail is now washed clean."

And onward they went, shivering in the wetness, wind and rain and lightning and thunder shaking the dark day with fury. Up they climbed and up, through crags, along precipices, massifs rearing, canyons plunging, and water running over all. Now the rain turned to sleet, and the way was slick beyond measure. Even so, still they pressed on, for they could not camp in such, and they forbore turning back. Higher still the trail took them, and as they came to the snow line the sleet turned to swirling white flakes. But still the lightning and thunder hammered at them, and the wind howled all round.

In the driven white, they reached the apex of their climb. But here Lyssa stopped, for before her an abyss plunged down beyond seeing, the chasm bridged by a slender span of stone. And barely glimpsed in the hurtling snow, on the far side enclosing the trail, stood a great freestanding archway with mighty runes of power carved thereupon. Lyssa dismounted, as did they all. She handed the reins of her horse to Kane and then stepped to the abyss while wind-driven snow slammed into them and lightning stroked down and thunder hammered after. Left she looked, then right, but no other way was seen to cross over this great cleft. She went to one knee at the beginning of the windswept span and took a deep breath then closed her eyes. And while she knelt in the snow, Rith came and stood behind her and looked long at the archway beyond. Finally Lyssa opened her eyes and stood, and together they stepped back to the others.

"The archway," said Rith, "I think it's responsible for the storm, for the runes are written in an ancient tongue and speak of tempests and trespassers . . . powerful magic, indeed."

All eyes turned to Lyssa. "This is the way," she said. "The trail goes across. More than that I cannot tell, for the arch blocks all beyond."

"We could turn back," said Ky, peering up at Kane.

The big man glanced at the slender stone span and the endless drop below, then swiftly looked away. But he said nothing.

Arik removed a glove and wetted a finger and held it up in the wind. As he slid his glove back on, he eyed the bridge and shook his head and turned to Rith. "As the saga said, and I would agree, the way is sinister indeed."

The black bard shrugged. "We've come this far."

Arik looked at the others. One by one they nodded, all but Kane whose face was stark and rigid.

"On foot or ahorse?" asked Ky.

"Oh lord," hissed Kane, "on horse. Else I'll *never* get across."

"Kane is right," said Arik. "Horses take height in stride."

"Too, they're less likely to be blown off," added Arton, flinching as lightning flared overhead.

Kane rolled his eyes and groaned.

"All right, then," said Arik. "Onward it is. Cross one at a time."

Lyssa took the reins of her horse from Kane and mounted. Without a word she lightly touched her heels to the steed's flanks, and out onto the narrow span they went, the stone swept clean by the wind, the drop below terrifying. Arik gritted his teeth and sucked in air as Lyssa's mount stepped onto the bridge. Foxes watched with knuckles gone white in their gloves, and Kane refused to look altogether, turning his face aside. Slowly the horse trod along the narrow way, the wind buffeting rider and steed alike, as if to hurl them into the appalling depths below. Lightning stroked and thunder rolled and snow hurtled whitely, yet onward went mount and rider on the slim stone span . . . to finally reach the other side.

The moment Lyssa's horse gained safety, Arik exhaled the breath he did not know he had been holding. Shakily he turned to the next in line. "Your turn, Kane."

Kane took a deep breath and let it out with a groan. He turned to his horse to mount up, but couldn't seem to find his stirrup. Ky stepped forward. "I'll take the mule with me when I cross." With trembling hands, the big man gave over the pack animal's tether.

Rith closed her eyes and concentrated a moment, then she began to sing a soft melody, and even though the wind blew, her voice reached Kane clearly. He took another breath and let it out, then mounted his horse. Onto the span he rode, wind and snow and lightning and thunder blowing and pelting and flashing and whelming, yet Rith's song murmured in his ears. Across he went, his horse finding its own way, for Kane's eyes were shut tightly.

Next to cross was Arton, mule trailing after, the thief crouching down in his saddle away from the flashing storm. Then came Arik with another mule, Rith coming after. Last to cross was Ky, Kane's mule following, the syldari leaning precariously from her horse to see down into the depths below.

On the opposite side just beyond the arch was a small, wall-cupped flat, some seventy feet wide and perhaps thirty feet deep. It fetched up against the concave arc of a vertical bluff rising upward a hundred feet or so, and five ways led onward: first was a narrow trail along the abyss to the right, the way disappearing round a corner; second came a large arched hole boring into the face of the cliff, a level path leading into darkness; next was a narrow cleft straight ahead, its walls rising up to the top of the bluff, the way no more than six feet wide and sloping slightly downward; fourth was another notch, this one perhaps twelve feet wide and twisting upward past a bend and out of sight; and last on the left stood a narrow jagged hole, the rock face all round raddled with cracks, the entrance low and dark, the path pitching downward steeply, and from within could be heard the howl of the wind, or so it seemed.

Arik looked at Lyssa. "Which way?"

The ranger shook her head. "I don't know. The power of the arch blocks all my attempts."

"Anyone have any ideas?" asked Arik, turning to the others.

"Holes and notches!" declared Kane. "Let's just pick one and go; let us get off this cliff face before I go mad." He looked at the trail along the abyss at the far right. "Not that one, please."

Lyssa cleared her throat. "If it's preferences we're stating, then I say to forego the holes . . . especially the one on the left."

Arton looked at the notches. "Well then, of the two ways remaining, I'd rather go down away from the storm than up into it."

Arik turned to Rith. "What says the saga here?"

Rith shrugged. "Nothing. Not one blasted thing. The true way is probably minutely described in the accursed lost stanzas."

Arik sighed. "Well, if no one has anything to add, then one way seems as good as another. I suppose we can follow Arton's desire. The narrow notch downward, eh?"

Lyssa looked at the cleft ill at ease, knowing once they entered that cramped slot they would be confined like bugs in a trap and at the mercy of whatever might await them within.

20

The medtech turned to Doctor Ramanni. "Adrenaline, heart rate, blood pressure, respiration, kinesthetic tension: all are up for the whole alpha team, especially Caine Easley's . . . he's really terrified. Of course they're all tense, apprehensive that is, er, all but Miss Kikiro—she's just excited."

Alya Ramanni looked at the monitors. "Any of them critical?"

The medtech shook his head. "Not yet."

Alya walked around the central holo. In the blizzard Kane was unsuccessfully trying to mount his horse to cross over a slender stone span above a yawning abyss. "No wonder he's scared. I would be, too."

"It's an old rule of writing," called out Timothy Rendell.

"It is?" Alya turned to the computer scientist. "What?"

Timothy grinned. "Never make it easy on your hero."

Alya returned to her console. "Well, Avery certainly isn't doing that. Kali! but they've not had an easy time at all—bloody slaughter, an enigma hidden in silver, a desperate warning, a demon in disguise, savage monsters loosed from stone, brutal murder, and now an arduous climb up a slippery mountain in a raging storm only to discover a perilous crossing."

"But isn't it exciting?" responded Timothy. "I mean, without those difficult and interesting challenges it would be dull, dull, dull."

John Greyson laughed. "I am put in mind of an old curse."

Timothy raised an eyebrow. "And what's that?"

"Just this," replied Greyson, "when you think about it, our literature, history, holovids, games, other medium—including our virtual realities—are filled with mysteries, puzzles, chases, struggles, murder, violence, combat, war, disease, plague, flood, famine, disasters, catastrophes, and the like. All are challenging, especially those which are desperate struggles filled with strong emotions—jealousy, rage, hate, love, revenge, terror, horror. Those are the things of compelling interest, the things that writers of fiction or reality feel driven to record, and readers driven to read. The same is true no matter which medium we examine—no matter whether it's fiction or fact, those things which are held to be the most compelling, the most riveting, are terrible to those who experience them.

"Hence, if it is your desire to bring woe and calamity down on someone's head, you simply invoke the ancient Chinese curse: May you live in interesting times."

As Timothy laughed, Alya pointed at the holo, where Ky gawked down into the storm-shrouded abyss as she nonchalantly rode across. "Well, they are certainly living in interesting times."

In the holo, the Foxes peered at five separate routes lying before them: two holes, two notches, and a narrow path along the abyss.

Alya sighed. "What's next, I wonder?"

Timothy shrugged. "Let's ask Avery." He leaned forward and keyed his microphone. "Avery?"

"Yes, Doctor Rendell."

"What is it we observe?"

Avery's swirl spun slightly faster. "Here the Black Foxes must make a choice as to which path to take." Avery fell silent.

Timothy glanced at Alya and shook his head then turned back to the mike. "And . . . ?"

Avery remained silent.

Alya keyed her own mike. "Avery, what is so special about these five ways?"

"Two are dead ends, two are traps, and one leads down the mountain, Doctor Ramanni," answered Avery.

Now Greyson keyed into the conversation. "These traps—are they dangerous?"

"They are both fatal, Doctor Greyson."

"Lord, lord," replied Greyson, "you mean that they have but one chance in five of picking the correct way—?"

"And two in five of being killed?" interjected Alya.

Before Avery could reply, Timothy amended the odds: "Actually, Alya, if two are dead ends, then that leaves three, um, meaningful choices. So, the odds are two in three of being killed and one in three of gaining safety."

Alya's eyes widened. "That's even worse. The odds of being killed go up from forty percent to sixty percent."

"If you look at it that way, Doctor Ramanni," said Avery, "then the odds of choosing the correct way also increase—from twenty percent to thirty-three and a third."

"Aren't you being rather unfair, Avery?" asked Greyson.

"I don't think so, Doctor Greyson," replied Avery. "You see, my programs dictate that I give the Black Foxes all the information necessary to make the correct choice."

"And have you done so?"

"Yes, Doctor Greyson."

"But what if they make the wrong choice?" asked Alya.

Avery said nothing.

The three keyed off their mikes and watched as the Foxes took the central path: the narrow notch. Timothy rekeyed his mike. "Did they choose correctly, Avery?"

Avery's swirl reappeared on Timothy's holo. "They have chosen one of the fatal paths, Doctor Rendell."

21

Into the confining strait rode the Black Foxes, Lyssa leading, Arton trailing. Out of the wind at last, they proceeded in relative quiet, snow sifting down from high overhead to lie in the narrow slot and muffle the sound of the animals' hooves. Gently the path curved downward, gradually arcing more steeply. The walls of the cleft became smooth, as if well worked by adze. Rith peered at this crafting, glancing from the left wall to the right. Of a sudden her eyes widened and she cried, "Wait! This is a trap!"

"Trap?" called Arik, reining to a halt.

"Yes," answered Rith. "There is a song called 'Kalador's Doom' which tells of such. Slowly his way curved downward, gradually becoming too steep to traverse. Without realizing that it was a fatal way, he continued onward until he tumbled to his doom. I deem that this is the same. See, the walls have been smoothed so as to provide no handholds, no way to catch yourself. And the way continues to curve farther downward, so subtly as to be nearly unnoticeable."

"Damn! Damn!" cursed Lyssa, peering at the way ahead. "Rith, you're right, for from what I can see the way goes on getting steeper."

"Arda's balls," spat Kane, "the walls are too close for the horses to turn round; we're going to have to back out of here."

"What about the mules?" snapped Arton. "I don't think these stubborn brutes even know how to back, or if they do they resist it mightily. Corks in a bottle, that's what they are."

"Seven hells," growled Arik, "we'll just have to drag them hindwards."

Struggling and cursing, at last the Foxes reached the archway once again, Arton limping, for he had been kicked by the mule he had gotten behind and hauled backward by its tail. When they had come to the flat, Kane had attempted to heal him, but discovered that the power of the arch dampened his spells entirely.

As the storm whelmed upon the Foxes, Arik stared at the remaining choices. "Anyone have any suggestions?"

Kane peered through the blowing snow at the far right way—the path alongside the abyss—and shuddered. "If we go there and have to back up . . . surely we'll fall to our doom. Seven hells, mayhap all these ways are traps."

Arton shook his head. "Not true, Kane, if we are to believe the saga. I mean, at least one path is safe, else Galamor and Kitter would not have made it across."

Lyssa spread her hands wide. "You assume, Arton, that Galamor and Kitter actually came this way."

"Regardless," growled Arik, "*we* came this way, and now we must either go on or go back. As I asked before, does *anyone* have a suggestion as to which path to take?" Arik's gaze swept across the other Foxes. Rith frowned and stroked her chin in deep reflection, as if chasing an elusive thought, but she said nothing. Lyssa turned up her hands. Ky and Arton both shrugged. "All right, then," said Arik, "let us use the intelligent approach." He spat into the palm of his cupped hand and then slapped two fingers down into the saliva. A fair gob of spittle flew toward the large, dark hole. Lyssa groaned but began rummaging through a saddlebag for her small brass and crystal lantern.

"Wait," declared Rith, suddenly coming to life, "I think I have it—or at least a glimmer of an idea. Specious, perhaps; slender, no doubt; yet it seems to be the only thing which faintly might be a clue, the only thing we might put our trust in."

"Better than spit, I hope," said Ky.

"Perhaps," replied the black bard.

"What is it?" growled Arton.

Rith looked at the thief. "The saga speaks of it, and you yourself once repeated it, Arton—the way Galamor and Kitter took to freedom was sinister."

Arik's eyes lit up. "Sinister! By Arda, yes!"

Arton threw up his hands. "What? What by the seven hells are you talking about?"

Arik grinned a great grin. "Rith has the answer, or so I believe. Sinister. Leftward. Do you not see?"

Arton, his eyes wide, looked at Rith. She grinned and nodded. "Huah!" declared the thief. "How simple."

Rith held up a cautioning hand. "Don't jump to conclusions, for didn't I say it was a slender hope at best?"

"Slender it may be," replied Arton, "but it's the best we have."

All eyes turned to the low, jagged hole to the left, its dark mouth moaning in the wind, a groan matched by Lyssa as she stared at the gaping black maw.

It was well into the nighttide when the Foxes reached the plains below. They were weary, for the way down had been no less arduous than the way up. Even so, after they had emerged from the low, jagged, wind-filled cavern, Lyssa's power to find the trail returned, and she had led them along a faint silvery line downward, a line which only she could see. The path terminated at another set of ruins, much like the tumbled-down wizard's hold they had left behind. The moment they stepped from the silvery way the diminishing storm had stopped and the skies slowly began to clear. They cared for the animals and took a quick meal. Then all fell into slumber but the one on watch.

When Arton's turn came, Ky yawned and said, "Try to keep your clothes on."

Three days later found them crossing the plains. Overhead the sun shone brightly down. A gentle breeze blew up from the south and the noontide was warm. In the near distance they could see the fringes of an ancient forest—the Wythwood—no more than five miles away. On toward this shaggy weald they rode, the horses plodding a leisurely pace. And as they crossed the grassland, Rith strummed her lute and sang one ballad after another.

"Lord," rumbled Kane, turning to Ky, "it's days like this that make up for all the storms and blizzards."

The syldari nodded abstractly. "I wonder if he is yet alive."

"Who?"

"Pon Barius."

"Oh." Kane looked at the forest. "I just hope we find him. The Wythwood is a wide place, you know."

Ky giggled and gestured ahead. "As any fool can plainly see—"

"—'cause I can see." Kane finished the saying for her, a great grin on his face.

"Hoy!" called Arton from the rear. "Something follows."

The Foxes swiveled about. In the distance behind, some two miles back, they could see a darkness, like a great flattened ebony sphere, an obsidian ovoid, down on the plains. It was black as night, and seemed to be moving . . . toward them.

Ky frowned, then uttered a word. She gasped. "Arda, it's drakka on demonsteeds." Then she shouted, "Arik! It's drakka on demonsteeds! They pursue!"

Arik wheeled his horse rightward. "Drakka?"

"Yes," called Ky. "Englobed in darkness. In the daylight. My darksight sees them within."

"Damn," gritted Rith, "so *that's* how they run under Arda's sun—clasped in jet night they are."

"How many?" called Arik.

"Fifteen, twenty, it's hard to tell," replied Ky, shading her eyes. "Too many is the answer."

"Right," barked Arik. "Then I say we run for it and hope to lose them in the woods."

At these words Lyssa spurred forward, and so did they all, Black Foxes galloping toward the refuge of the trees, protesting mules in their wake. And as they ran, helms were donned and shields made ready and weapons were loosened in their sheaths. Thundering forward, the Foxes formed up defensively: Lyssa in the fore, Arton in the aft, Rith and Ky in the center, with Arik on the left flank and Kane on the right. While on the plains behind, a deadly darkness raced after them, made eerily silent by the distance.

The sun had progressed less than a hand span when the Black Foxes came to the eaves of the Wythwood. As they plunged inward, Lyssa reined to one side, calling out, "Go on! I'll erase our spoor!"

Into the wood they hammered, Lyssa bringing up the rear. She paused a moment frowning in concentration, then followed the deep tracks of their passage across the loam. And lo! when she rode upon the soft churned earth she left unsullied ground behind.

And still in the distance the darkness came after.

Hidden by the woods, Arik veered rightward to avoid running in a more or less straight line. Slowed by the trees, he led the others a mile or so into the forest then waited for Lyssa to catch up.

When the ranger came riding among them—"See if you can find a trail to follow so we can make better time and lose these drakka altogether."

Lyssa nodded, and as she frowned in concentration, Rith said, "If they have a powerful enough caster among them, they will follow us regardless."

Arik sighed. "I know, Rith. But we can always hope."

Behind them bugles blatted and Kane hefted his spear. "I think they follow even now," he rumbled.

At that moment Lyssa gasped, her eyes flying wide. "Arda!" she exclaimed.

"What is it?" Ky cried as she swiftly drew her black main gauche and looked about for oncoming foe, but only silent trees met her gaze.

"Lord," breathed Lyssa, "there's a great silver path just ahead. Wider than any I've ever seen."

"Silver path?" barked Arton.

"Some kind of enchanted way," replied Lyssa.

Again bugles sounded, closer.

"This silver way," said Arik, "it could be a trap."

Once more the bugles sounded, closer still.

"I think we've no time to debate the choices," cried Lyssa, spurring forward. "Follow me."

Among hoary oaks and tall maples and spreading elms they ran, Lyssa galloping toward the silver way her eyes alone could see, the remaining Foxes thundering after.

Through a wall of trees they burst onto a wide dirt road. Leftward it ran, into the Wythwood, but it ran to the right not at all. Haling her reins leftward, along this way Lyssa fled, the others in her wake. And lo! the galloping steeds sped through the forest faster than any horse could possibly run, faster than an eagle could fly.

"Arda," cried Arik as the trees flashed by, "what is happening?"

"This road, this road, this very road," called Rith following, " 'tis magic beyond comprehension."

Arik looked back at the bard, and his eyes widened, for beyond her, beyond Ky and Kane, beyond Arton coming last, the road simply vanished behind them as they ran. Arik turned and faced forward once more, no longer asking questions, though his mind was filled with them, but merely accepting instead.

On into the woods they raced, miles vanishing in the twinkle of an eye, but at last they came to the very end of the incredible road, to a grassy clearing encircled by massive oak trees. And in the center of the sward stood an oak tree beyond all others, its huge girth nearly a hundred feet round, its massive limbs reaching out across the whole of the glade, its top beyond seeing through the leaves above.

"Bless me," breathed Arton. "I think we've come to Wythwood's very heart."

"That's not all we've come to," said Arik, pointing.

Ensconced down among huge, gnarled roots and snuggled up against the immense bole sat a modest, thatch-roofed cottage, a thin tendril of smoke rising from its chimney.

The cottage was larger on the inside than was possible, and in a small bedroom off the kitchen they found supine on a cot an ancient, white-haired syldari who did not move or speak. His dark eyes were open and unblinking, his gaze fixed and unseeing, and his wheezing breath was shallow and rapid and rattling in his chest. In his right hand he held a white carven staff.

"Pon Barius?" breathed Ky.

Kane stepped to the side of the bunk and lay his hands on the timeworn elder, then he turned to the other Foxes. "Whether or not he is Pon Barius, this wasted syldari is dying."

22

Timothy leaned forward and keyed his microphone. "Tell me, Avery, how close is virtual time to real? Are the Black Foxes nearly in sync with what we are seeing on the holo?"

In the holovid, the Black Foxes were just entering a cottage in a forest.

"No, Doctor Rendell. Virtual time is running faster than real. The fact of the matter is, in virtual reality the Black Foxes are already gone from the Wythwood."

"My, my," exclaimed Greyson into his own mike, "already gone, you say?"

"Yes, Doctor Greyson," replied Avery. "But they are on a journey now and soon the holo will be in sync with the adventure."

"Fast forward, eh?" Greyson chuckled.

"Yes, Doctor Greyson. But if you wish I could jump ahead and show you what they are doing now."

"No, no, Avery," protested Alya Ramanni into her microphone, "I don't want to know. Why, that would be just like reading ahead in an exciting book. I don't want to know what's in the final chapter until I have traveled through the entire story to get there."

Timothy grinned. "You and I are of a like mind, Alya. I never could understand the mentality of a person who skips ahead—sometimes to the very end. And I *do* have a friend who always reads the final chapter first."

Greyson cleared his throat. "Perhaps those who skip ahead simply cannot stand the suspense; they can't wait; they have to know *right now*! how things turn out."

"But then they miss the sense of the story and lose the impact of the climactic scenes," said Alya.

"I take it, then, Doctor Ramanni," said Avery, "you would rather that I let virtual and real time come into sync naturally."

"Yes, Avery," she replied. "Continue as you have been, slipping into fast forward when nothing important is happening—travel and sleep and the like."

Silence fell and after a moment Timothy stood and stretched. "I think I'll go and see what Toni and the others are deciding to do about the storm." He turned toward the door yet did not step forward, but instead pulled up the left sleeve of his shirt and examined his tingling skin in puzzlement.

Toni stood at the west-facing windows of the top floor executive conference room and looked out over the desert toward the city of Tucson. Great bolts of lightning hammered down to the earth, thunder rolling after. Now and again there would be a barrage, flash after flash stroking the midnight sky, continuous detonations filling the air.

"Lord," said Mark Perry, leaning on his hands against the walnut rail and staring out into the raging night, "it looks like a war."

Stein snorted but held his tongue.

Drew Meyer turned to the technician at his side. "How much has it moved, Jim?"

"Well, sir, it's still walking toward us," replied the young man. "Last I saw it was on the west side of Tucson. Now it seems to be about halfway here."

"I'd gauge some of the strikes to be a bit more than a mile away," said Toni. "Five or six seconds from flash to bang."

"Six seconds . . . ?" Mark Perry looked at Toni in puzzlement.

"Speed of sound," grated Stein.

From Perry's expression it was clear that he still didn't

understand. "Uh . . . I must have missed that in science class."

"You count from when you see the flash to when you hear the boom," said Jim. "At eleven hundred feet a second it takes just under five seconds for the sound to travel a mile."

"Oh."

Toni turned toward the physicist. "Tell me what you know about lightning, Drew."

Doctor Meyer ran his hand over his bald head. "It's not my specialty, Toni. But we can always step to a netcom and ask Avery."

Stein snorted. "We *did* ask the AI. It said we were well protected."

In the near distance lightning stroked downward. "One turtle, two turtle, three turtle . . . " counted Mark Perry. Stein shot the lawyer a disgusted look and moved away.

When Perry's count reached thirteen, a rolling boom shook the windows. "Um, let's see, I'd make that to be some, er, two or three miles away, right?"

Jim nodded. "About three, Mister Perry."

Again lightning jagged, a great sputtering stroke lasting for a second or so and dancing across the city. "Wow," breathed Perry. "Bright."

Toni turned to Doctor Meyer. "Do you think that was typical?"

Drew shrugged. "I don't know. As I said, lightning is not my specialty." The physicist paused, then added, "But I do know that multiple strokes are common and I've heard that they can have as many as thirty or forty discharges in a single second. But for all I know that strike could have been rather typical or it could have been one of the so-called superbolts."

A stroke flashed nearby. "One turt—" Thunder hammered the windows of the conference room. "Holy cow!" exclaimed Perry. "That was close."

"Seven, eight hundred feet," murmured Jim.

A sharp gust of rain pelted against the windows, as if seeking to escape the storm outside.

Perry turned to Toni Adkins. "Look, we've got to get the old man out of that rig. I mean, he could be—"

"Nonsense!" barked Stein. "This building has adequate protection and an excellent backup system in case we do lose power."

Perry whirled on Stein. "Lose power? Who the fuck is talking about losing power? I'm talking about the safety of Arthur Coburn, and if anything happens—"

"Toni," snapped Stein, "are you going to let Chicken Little here dictate what—"

"Quiet!" shouted Toni. "Both of you just shut up!" Toni turned to Doctor Meyer. "Have you an opinion?"

Drew glanced out the window and then to his minicompad, as if seeking answers in the glowing figures. At last he said, "I understand the building is well designed—"

"Balls!" barked Perry. "Are you going to put your trust in the claims of a contractor?"

"I said quiet!" snapped Toni. She turned and leaned on her hands against the long walnut table, her head down in thought.

Lightning stuttered in the distance beyond the city. At last Toni said, "I'm going to abort the test."

"What?" shouted Stein. "That's utterly stupid!"

Toni spun about and pierced Doctor Stein with her gaze. "I'll say this once and once only: We've got a lot of data. We know that Avery has performed adequately up to now. We do not have all the psychological data we need to fully evaluate Avery's mindset, but we can suspend the test and resume it at a later time, picking up exactly where we left off. Granted, it will give Avery time to consider and reconsider what he has done so far, but that's a price I am willing to pay for the safety of—of—" She sputtered to a halt and looked wide-eyed at the others.

The hair on all their arms began to tingle, and strands of Toni's reddish-brown-blond mane slowly lifted outward from her head.

Drew Meyer looked at her and uttered a two-word prayer: "Oh, shit . . ."

23

"**D**ying?" cried Ky. "Pon Barius is dying?"

Kane looked up from the ancient syldari. "He is in a deep coma, and fading fast. Quick, fetch my herbs and simples. And water! I'll need boiling water."

"I'll get the kit," said Ky, darting from the room.

As Ky ran out to Kane's horse, Arik stepped back into the kitchen and stirred the coals in the hearth, adding wood, while Lyssa pumped water into a teakettle. From cupboards and cabinets, Rith and Arton began collecting earthenware vessels in case Kane needed to mix various medicines.

Ky dashed back through the cottage to the bedroom, a satchel in her hand.

Lyssa hung the teakettle from a fire iron and swung it out over the growing flames. Arik turned to her and said, "The drakka may still be on our trail. I'm going to stand watch on the sward."

"Me, too, Arik," said Arton. "I'm of little or no use here."

"As soon as the water boils," said Lyssa, "I'll join you, even though the drakka may never find this clearing; I sensed a great warding as we entered the ring of oaks."

"Perhaps you are right, love," said Arik. "Nevertheless, I need to feel useful while Kane ministers to that old syldari in there." Arik nodded to Arton, and they stepped out through the door.

From the bedroom Kane called, "Hurry with that water."

As Lyssa watched the pot not boil, Rith carried cups and bowls into the healer.

Kane poured steaming water into three cups and stirred each until the black powder dissolved in the first, and swirling leaves in both the second and third stained the liquid red in one and tan in the other. The big man turned to Ky. "Remember, now, first this one, then this one, then that one. As soon as his eyelids flutter."

The syldari glanced at the elder, his skin like yellowed parchment. She nodded, then looked at Kane, concern in her eyes. "And you?"

"The same with me, Ky," he replied, "though I think it may be some time before I start coming round. Afflictions of the brain or of the mind are the most difficult to deal with . . . especially those of mental torment—they can take months."

"Oh my!" exclaimed Ky. "Will you—?"

Kane smiled. "Not in this case, mouse. At least, I don't think so. He is in a coma because he expended too much of his energy. Now be ready, for he will come round in moments; as for me, I should come round sometime before sunset."

Doubt filling her eyes, Ky smiled grimly and nodded.

Kane turned to the comatose syldari and gently brushed back white locks to place a hand on either side of the ancient one's head. The healer-warrior took a deep breath and paused a moment, then frowned in concentration, his lips drawn thin and white. A heartbeat later his hands trembled and his face turned pale, then grey, and of a sudden he pitched over sideways, crashing to the floor.

"Oh!" cried Ky, quickly kneeling at his side. Kane was jammed awkwardly against a wall, his eyes open and staring, his breathing rapid and shallow. Grunting, Ky first tried to drag him and then to roll him away from the wall, with no success.

"Somebody!" she shouted. "Somebody get in here and help me!"

Behind her, she heard a faint groan, and turning, she saw the old syldari's eyelids flutter.

"It expended more of me than I had imagined," said Pon Barius. He took a sip from his teacup, and with a satisfied, drawn-out *Ahhh . . . !* he set the cup down. "Roads of swiftness are quite, uh, draining, you know, even when you have help." Pon Barius glanced out through a window at the bole of the great oak tree.

Across from Pon Barius, Rith looked toward the open doorway. "Just in the nick of time for us, it would seem."

Arik, leaning against the door frame, scanned the woods at the edge of the sward. "Are you certain the drakka cannot find us?"

Pon Barius snorted. "Oh, child, you can stand down from your sentry duty, and call in your other two guards. The drakka are days behind and scattered. Yet even should they come near, unless they have someone of great power with them they will not see this place whatsoever nor accidentally stumble across it."

"But they *do* have someone of great power aiding them," said Ky, the Shadowmaster sitting in the doorway to the bedroom, where she could keep an eye on unconscious Kane, the big man now lying on the floor on the ancient syldari's short mattress, his feet and most of his legs beyond its reach.

Pon Barius cocked an eyebrow at Ky.

"We think DemonQueen Atraxia is aiding them," she explained.

Pon Barius smiled wanly and shook his head. "Child, that is obvious. After all, who else could set demonkind loose in Itheria when the Arda's sun is on high, eh? The real question is why? Why would she do such a thing? And what is there about you six that would cause such pursuit? Have you done something to invoke her wrath?"

Ky glanced at Arik and the warrior said, "Sir, I will call in Lyssa and Arton and unfold our tale when Kane is awake and aware, for each of us has something to contribute and all need to know what passes here."

Nettled, Pon Barius frowned and drank the last of his

tea. Then he stood and stumped into the bedroom and peered down at Kane. Turning, he said, "Fair enough. Fair enough we should wait for him to recover, for I owe him my very life."

"No, no!" hissed Pon Barius, capturing Arton's hand to keep the master thief from opening the silver pommel. "Do not unshield the gem until I have set further wards, and then only briefly and but to extract the note and not the jewel. If it is what I think it is, that is how she tracks it—when it is not surrounded by silver it calls out to her."

"But she found it at the Blue Lady's, and we didn't expose it there," protested Arton. "That is, I didn't expose it until the demon asked for it. Hence, the DemonQueen already knew where it was."

Pon Barius shook his head. "I deem it was the Blue Lady's oracular scrying which brought the demon to you. And now Atraxia knows the gem is hidden in a silver blade." The wizard looked at Arton. "She sent one of her most cunning demons—a succubus—to fetch it."

"She almost got it, too," rumbled Kane, the big man sipping a honey-sweetened herbal concoction. "What with savage animals set free from the walls."

"But afterward," said Lyssa, "we moved away from the Blue Lady's grotto. Yet they found us still. Pursued us, as you know, into the Wythwood. If silver shields it, how can that be? Surely the storm wiped out any tracks we left behind."

"Well, young lady, I think she knew where you went because of that very same storm you speak of. The arcane power released when you crossed over the old high pass from Horax's tower to mine was enormous. 'Here am I!' it shouted to any with the ability to see. After that, it was a simple matter to set drakka on your track."

"Simple matter?" asked Ky.

"Yes, child," replied Pon Barius. "By using utterdark, Atraxia can move several demons across the in-between, though not a vast army . . . which means that she must have forged a new scepter to do so."

"Utterdark!" exclaimed Ky. "Of course! They say it does not need to be tuned to an aura . . . perhaps it is tuned to all. The drakka used it in the Gapton notch. But wait! To cast utterdark takes a great deal of power—it would press me to my limit." Puzzlement flashed across Ky's face. "You say she used a new scepter? To conjure utterdark?"

"Yes, yes," snapped Pon Barius impatiently. "Look, all of this is speculation. Until I see what is written in that message, I cannot say for certain. Now, hold your questions while I set the wards so we can safely open the dagger." He glanced up at Arton. "When I tell you, swiftly extract the message. Then shut it up as quick as you can. No use taking chances, you know."

"Ha!" barked Pon Barius. "No wonder you couldn't read it. It is written in the gnoman tongue."

"What does it say?" asked Rith, peering over the old mage's shoulder at the parchment.

"Give me a moment," said the wizard, picking up his quill and dipping it into the tiny inkpot.

Silence fell as Pon Barius examined the words one by one, using the index finger of his left hand to follow the trace of each. Slowly he recorded his translation on a sheet of vellum, the scratching of his pen the only sound in the deep twilight, but for a grunt and a murmur or two at what he discovered. At last he looked up at the others. "Oh my, it is as I thought."

"What?" blurted Ky.

Rith, still peering over the ancient's shoulder, exclaimed, "Well, we were right about one thing—it is indeed written from bottom to top and backwards."

"Would you care to read it aloud, my dear?" asked Pon Barius.

Again Rith looked at the translation neatly printed in the ancient syldari's hand:

—*Badru*   *Barius Pon*

—results safe destruction hoping you to it brings trustworthy messengeR .not know key I should dire forces be would unleashed for cannot but could I that would it destroY .comes Atraxia of sceptre from gem this I have discovereD

"All right," replied Rith. "Here is what it says: Um, Pon Barius . . . er, I have discovered this gem comes from the scepter of Atraxia. Would that I could destroy it, but I cannot, for dire forces would be unleashed . . . and, um, I do not know the key—to its destruction?" Rith looked at Pon Barius and received a nod in return. "It goes on to say, ah, a trusty messenger brings it to you in the hope that you can safely destroy it. It is signed, Badru."

Rith looked at Pon Barius. "How was that?"

"Quite fine, my dear. Quite fine." Pon Barius turned to Arton. "Now, once more, quick as you can, open the dagger and reinsert the note and seal it again."

"But don't you need to see the gem?" asked Arton.

"No, boy. I've seen enough to know what it is."

As Arton swiftly palmed open the pommel and slid in the note and closed the handle, Arik cleared his throat. "Perhaps, sir, you ought to tell us what we need to know."

"That I will do, my lad. But first, let us have more tea, eh? And some supper. I am quite famished as it is."

They sat outside 'neath the great oak limbs, wheeling stars barely glimpsed through the stirring leaves above. Down near glade's edge the horses—curried, watered, fed with grain—munched contentedly on sweet red clover, while Orbis slowly rose in the east and Phemis raced ahead. Pon Barius filled the small clay bowl of his long, curve-stemmed pipe and with a word lighted it. After a puff or two he looked about at the Black Foxes. "Now just where was I?"

"You were going to tell us of the gem," said Arik.

Pon Barius sucked on the stem. "Mmm"—he blew out smoke—"Ah, yes. Well, you see, it's the gem that let her start the demonwars. Where she got it, certainly I don't know, though some say that it was the Nameless One Himself who gave it to her."

"Nameless One?" Rith asked.

Pon Barius blew a smoke ring. "The Dark God, my dear."

"Oh, my!" exclaimed Ky, then added, "But why would he give such a thing to Atraxia?"

Pon Barius shrugged. "Who can say? Not I. Though I

would guess that havoc alone was his motive, albeit he may have had other reasons for doing so."

"What makes this gem so . . . valuable?" asked Arton. "I mean, the Jewels of Haloor didn't cause such a ruckus, and they looked to be of much greater worth."

"Ha!" barked the old mage. "The jewels of Haloor, indeed! They are as nothing, nothing!" Pon Barius pointed to the dagger now held by Rith. "That gemstone in there is said to allow the owner to tap into the Nameless One's power directly . . . if you know how to invoke it. And contrary to what Badru thought, nothing can destroy that gem. Nothing! —Oh, perhaps Arda or the Nameless One could, but nothing else short of godpower will do."

Arton's mouth formed a silent *O* of wonderment.

Pon Barius's gaze swept over them all. "How do you think Atraxia moved whole armies across the in-between? By using the gemstone, that's how.

"Some thought she was using the utterdark archway in Kalagar Forest. Not so! 'Twas the power of the bloody jewel instead that let her minions cross over and back—any place she wished. Damnation! Couldn't they see that the archway would only put her forces in the Kalagar? And only a few at a time? I told them, but the fools didn't listen." Pon Barius puffed fiercely on his pipe, the ancient wizard reliving arguments dead long past.

After a moment, Ky asked, "But the demons were defeated. How?"

Pon Barius looked up from the ground at her. More moments passed. At last he said, "Jaytar did it—"

"The thief?" blurted Rith. "But I thought—"

"You thought it was just a fable, eh?" snapped Pon Barius. Rith nodded.

The old syldari waggled a finger at Rith. "You, bard, of all people should know better than anyone else that fables are rooted in truth."

"What happened?" asked Arton, his eyes wide. "How did a thief defeat the DemonQueen?"

Pon Barius's eyes swung toward Arton. "Stole the gem right off the scepter, she did. Flew away across the Plains of Chaos on that silvery horse of hers, foul pursuit at her heels. Made it to Kalagar and beyond, though just where, we don't know. Demonkind caught her, you see. And though she slew a pack of them, at last they killed her dead, or so we think. And nobody, neither demonkind nor us, could find that gemstone. It defied our scrying 'cause it was hidden in silver, you see—probably hidden in that very dagger you hold ... Jaytar's, I would say—and it wasn't to be found. She concealed it somewhere before they caught her, and the secret of its hiding place died with her. Badru or one of his people found it, it would seem. I will ask him when next we meet."

"This Badru," asked Arik, "just who is he?"

"Master mentor of the gnomen in the Rawlons to the far north," answered Pon Barius.

"Ah, so *that's* why a gentle gnoman was carrying a bladed weapon," murmured Rith.

Pon Barius smiled at her. "Go on, my dear."

"Well," said Rith, gathering her thoughts, "from what you tell us, someone found a silver dagger, perhaps a gnoman. In any event, it somehow came into Badru's possession. He or someone discovered the hollow handle and its contents, just as did we." Rith fell silent a moment, then continued: "Perhaps when Badru opened the handle, Atraxia sensed the gem's power and began searching for it. But by this time it was again sealed in silver. Even so, she continued to, um, watch for its potency. Badru scribed a note and concealed it in the dagger as well, and by trusted aide he sent it to you for disposal. The aide perhaps opened the pommel at the wrong time, and Atraxia set her drakka upon him, though in the end they couldn't find the jewel, hidden in silver as it was. Before she could send someone who could locate the gem, we came along and took it away." Rith looked up at Pon Barius. "How am I doing so far?"

"Splendid!" replied the wizard. "Just what I would have guessed."

Arton cleared his throat. "So, the deeds of a thief ended the war."

"Not quite," replied Pon Barius. "Although Jaytar's theft of the gemstone did stop the invasions, she didn't manage to get away with Atraxia's scepter."

A puzzled look came over Arton's face. "And ... ?"

"And so the DemonQueen still held sway over the demonrealm," answered Pon Barius. "Ranvir was furious and blamed Atraxia for everything—especially, we thought, for the loss of his wife Kitter and for the loss of his champion Galamor, though we didn't know which enraged him the most. So, Ranvir decided to invade the demonplane and give back a little of what we had got from them.

"He moved his host into the demonplane through the Kalagar Gate, though it took hellishly long, and across the Plains of Chaos to Atraxia's Tower. There he and Valdor threw her down, for Valdor seized her scepter and destroyed it. And with it went her power and she vanished into the netherrealm.

"Long it has taken her to regain her form, but now she is returned, I think, and has forged a new scepter."

"And she desires the jewel to augment her scepter's power again, eh?" asked Arik.

"Precisely so," said Pon Barius.

Ky looked up through the leaves and glimpsed Phemis overhead. "Well, if you can't destroy the gem, what do you plan to do with it?"

Pon Barius stroked his chin, his syldari gaze sweeping over them all. "When we sent Jaytar after the gem—"

"You *sent* Jaytar?" blurted Arton.

"Yes," answered Pon Barius. "We had a scheme in mind, did the council. All favored it but Slytongue Horax."

"That's the second time today I've heard that name," said Rith. "Instead of calling it Kitter's Tower, you named those ruins Horax's tower."

"That's right!" exclaimed Ky. "And you said that the path across the old high pass ran from Horax's tower to yours."

"Horax was a traitor!" snapped Pon Barius, puffing angrily on his pipe, the smoke diminishing rapidly as the last of the weed burned. "Or so I guessed. Someone was telling Atraxia where the High King's forces were mustered, allowing her to strike undefended towns. I thought it was Horax, though the others never accepted my word, citing the old feud as my way of placing blame."

"Old feud?" rumbled Kane.

"Why do you think I put that archway there, eh?" snapped Pon Barius, dragging furiously on his now extinguished pipe. "To stop his trespassers and spies, that's why!"

"We didn't know it was your archway," gritted Kane. "And it damn near killed us."

"Hem"—Pon Barius removed the stem of his pipe from his mouth and peered into its dark bowl then glanced guiltily round—"sorry about that. But I did save you in the end, now, didn't I?"

"I say we forget it," declared Arik, though Kane growled low in his throat. "Instead, what about the gem? What was the plan if Jaytar succeeded?"

"Why, boy, it was to seal it in White Mountain, in a chest of silver," answered Pon Barius. "Both mountain and chest warded round and round and round again such that no one without the knowledge and skills could pass through the power of the seven seals."

"White Mountain?" murmured Lyssa. "Why, that's north in the Rawlons." She fell silent a moment, then her eyes lit up. "Would Badru happen to live nearby?"

"Yes," answered Pon Barius. "You see, Jaytar was to deliver the gem to us up there, but she never came. I suspect that she nearly made it, but the demons caught her at last and she was slain. Likely one of the gnomen found the dagger wherever it was she concealed it."

Rith ran her hand over her bandoliered throwing knives. "Perhaps she threw it, instead. Cast it so it stuck high in a tree or somesuch. I know *I* would have done so were I trapped and the jewel about to fall into ill hands."

"Heh! Good thinking, lady," exclaimed Pon Barius. "And had we known just where she fell, well, perhaps that's just where it would have been found. But it wasn't—until now, that is."

"Well," asked Rith, "now that it is found, what are you going to do with it?" She held the scabbarded weapon out to him.

Pon Barius blinked at the proffered blade, then reached out and took it. He looked long at Jaytar's dagger, then up at the Foxes. "Why, deliver it to White Mountain, as planned," he answered as he held the weapon back out to Rith. "But I am going to need help to do so."

A day and a half later in the early dawnlight, Kane lifted Pon Barius up to the makeshift saddle on the back of one of the pack animals. "Krone's teeth, but this mule is too tall," complained the syldari, looking down. "Ponies are much more sensible."

"And much slower," rumbled Kane, the big man looking up through morning shadows at the ancient wizard perched high on the mule, the syldari himself but four foot six inches tall.

"But what will I do if we get in a battle?" asked Pon Barius. "It's not as if I can guide this beast, tethered behind you as I will be. And even if I were free, still, this is a *mule*! About as likely to follow a rein as is a wild hare."

Arik turned in his saddle and said, "We will get you your own mount in Stahlholt."

"But that's three or four days north," objected Pon Barius. He leaned over and peered at the ground and shuddered, drawing back. "Until then I'm trapped aboard this towering monster."

"Nevertheless, in Stahlholt we will rectify that," said Arik.

"With a pony," declared Pon Barius.

"With a horse," growled Kane.

"Pony," repeated Pon Barius.

"A pony will slow us down," said Arik. "After all, we might have to run from drakka on their demonsteeds . . . or get into battle with them. Even so, I will leave it to you to decide how urgent our mission to White Mountain is."

Pon Barius sighed and glanced from Arik to Kane. "All right. A horse."

As Kane mounted his own steed he looked over at the little mage. "I'm not overfond of heights myself, you know."

Pon Barius did not reply.

Arik's gaze swept over them all. "Ready? Then let's go."

And so, in the long shadows of early morn they set out from Pon Barius's cottage, riding northward through the

Wythwood, the low, bright sun glittering among the filigree of latticed branches and leaves, Lyssa in the lead, Arton behind, the others scattered in between. And as they rode from the clearing, Ky glanced back and gasped, for cottage and sward and mighty oak had vanished altogether, along with the ring of oaks surrounding all. Arton, too, was gone, and only silent forest trees met her gaze. She opened her mouth to cry alarm, but then Arton's horse appeared, trotting out from nowhere, as if emerging from a different realm, Arton on the steed's back, and afterward came the mule. Ky turned and faced front once more, her syldari eyes filled with wonder. Warded indeed was the wizard's grove at the heart of the wide Wythwood.

Nine days later found them riding through upland pines, Pon Barius now on a mount of his own—a small, sturdy bay mare. In the distance to their right towered the crags of the Rawlons; miles away to their left and occasionally glimpsed through the trees lay the River Tuimelen, its cascading ribbon of water glinting in the sunlight.

When they stopped for a meal at noon, Lyssa glanced at one of her maps and said, "Tomorrow will see us halfway there."

"By my eyes," groaned Pon Barius, "if I only had the power to spare I would have conjured us a magic road 'twixt my cottage and our goal. But I am going to need all my powers just to get us up and into the mountain." He sighed and took another bite of waybread.

Lyssa blanched. "*Into* the mountain? We are going *underground*? Down into a cave or such?"

"Certainly, my dear," replied the ancient syldari. "We can't just leave the dagger lying about, you know."

"But underground." Lyssa shuddered.

"Better deep in the bowels of the earth than clinging to a mountainside," growled Kane.

Lyssa looked at the big man as a chill wind stirred through the woods. She glanced up at the clouds gathering above. "Cruk! A storm is brewing. Let's ride on. Perhaps we can find good shelter before it strikes. If not, well, at least we will have covered more ground."

As they removed the nose bags from the horses and mules, Pon Barius glanced at Lyssa and said, "I don't suppose there'd be a town nearby, would there?"

Lyssa shook her head *No*.

"Krone's teeth," exclaimed the old syldari. "I thought not."

Ky laughed. "Look at it this way, master: Rith will make a wondrous bard's tale and sing of the terrible storms we battled through to thwart the DemonQueen."

"I'm afraid not," responded Pon Barius. "You see, we must never tell of what we have done, else the Demon-Queen, should she hear of it, might find a way to break the wards and gain the gem if she knows where it lies."

"But I thought we were taking it to a place she could never enter," said Rith.

"Never say never, my dear," replied Pon Barius. "Even the most impossible things turn out to be feasible after all."

"Every lock can be opened," said Arton, "if you but have the key."

Pon Barius turned to the thief. "Exactly so, young man. Exactly so."

The storm struck just after nightfall, rain pelting down, wind howling through the trees, great jagged bolts smashing from sky to earth as lightning and thunder walked hand-in-hand down from the Rawlon Range. Huddled in their raincloaks under their lean-tos, the Black Foxes and Pon Barius peered by the light of a lantern out at the furious downpour. A few steps away the horses and mules stood sheltered under thick pines, the animals skittish in the raging tempest but securely tethered to the trees.

"Dretch," growled Kane, water dripping from his nose. "Why is it that whenever we go on one of these ventures all seven hells break loose?"

"Exactly right," muttered Arton, flinching with every flash. "Just once I'd like these old bones to go on a quest where the days are cool and the nights warm, and where there's an inn with good food and drink at each and every stop along the way."

"Yes, yes," agreed Ky. "And whatever it is we have to do gets done with a minimum of fuss and bother."

"But then," wailed Rith, though she grinned through the rain, "what would I have to sing about? I mean, heroes are supposed to struggle."

"You could sing, la de da," said Kane, "about how we, la de da, tripped through a field of daisies, la de da, laughing gaily in ring-around-the-rosey, la de da, you could."

"Or if you'd rather," said Ky, "you could reprise every song we sang as we quaffed our ale before a roaring fire."

Lightning flared nearby, the immediate clap of thunder drowning out Rith's reply.

"That was close," hissed Arton, huddling even deeper into his cloak. "Too close, if you ask me."

Another flare lit the black night, thunder whelming, and Arton scooted back against the slope of the lean-to.

Kane turned to Pon Barius and gestured at the sky. "Look, you made the storms in the old high pass; can't you do something about this?"

"Even if I could, I wouldn't," replied the ancient mage. "Didn't you hear me say I needed all of my power just to get us into White Mountain?"

"And back out?" Lyssa's eyes were wide.

Pon Barius smiled at the ranger. "Yes, my dear. And back out."

As a look of relief washed over Lyssa's face, Rith flung up a hand and called out, "What's that?"

Their gazes followed the line of her pointing finger up through the boughs of the pines. High in the sky and lighting the black churning clouds from within, a bright glow hurtled westward, the light blooming and fading and blooming, as if some flaring *thing* like a great ball of fire streaked through the roiling maelstrom above; and in the distance behind came another flaring thing, and another after, and perhaps even more in its wake.

And Arton gave a cry of fear and scooted back and covered his head.

Overhead hurled the first, slanting downward and to the west, a great bellowing roar following after. And then a brilliant flare blossomed in the sky, the entire world turning white, the intense glare blinding all whose sight had tracked its thundering course.

"Arda!" cried Rith, jerking her face aside. "I can't see!"

"Kane," barked Arik, also blinded.

"Everyone, stay where you are," called Kane as he pressed his hands to his own sightless eyes. "I'm certain that this is—"

BAAAADOOOOMMMMM!

An enormous shock wave whelmed into them, hammering them back, blasting away their lean-to. The horses and mules were knocked from their feet. Trees whipped over, some trunks splintering, while other trees were uprooted entirely. And though they couldn't hear it, there came the yawling roar of the second light as it hurtled toward the west.

Arton scrambled to his hands and knees, and uprighted the oil lantern, the spluttering wick catching flame once more. But he did not need the light of the lantern to see by, for the world was lit with flaming tendrils of violet witch fire. His skin *crawled* with tingling lavender flames, and purple arcs crackled from his fingertips to the ground, to his face, to the lantern, to wherever he touched. Yowling, he scrambled backward upon the flaring earth and saw the others groping blindly and burning violet, amethyst witchfire flickering from their fingers, from their hair. "Arda. Oh, Arda," he cried, but all ears yet rang with the mighty detonation, and none else heard his prayer.

Again the world turned into intolerable glare as the second *thing* detonated in the sky, blasting the land with unbearable light. And even though Arton was facing the opposite way, still the flare was agonizing and he violently jerked upright and threw his arm across his face.

Yet though his eyes were closed, purple fire burned in his vision, and as he shouted in panic—

KAAAWWHHOOOMMM!

—the second shock wave hit, knocking him to his face.

And unheard overhead came the thundering roar of another blare of light hurtling westward, bearing its cargo of witchfire . . .

. . . And when the next shock wave battered into them, they shrieked in mortal anguish for it was as if their spirits, their essences, their very souls were being torn from their bodies and hurled down a long, fiery tunnel toward a bottomless black abyss.

As Arton shrieked in pain and spun down through violet flames toward a whirling ebony void, he was looking directly at Pon Barius; the last thing the thief saw was the old wizard's form rapidly changing from an ancient syldari to a five-year-old girl to a boy to an elderly man to a fat bald black woman to a slender young beauty to an old toothless woman to a regal female clad in iron to an endlessly spiraling vortex of blackness to an ancient syldari to a five-year-old girl to black demon to a . . .

And down through the sporadic rain came the bellowing roar of a fourth flare of light hurtling westward through what remained of the shredded clouds.

24

Above the Coburn Building . . .

. . . In the churning thunderheads vapor roiled upward to become water droplets, and whipsawing air currents bore the droplets onward, rising up and up, the water becoming colder and colder, becoming supercooled, turning at last into tiny lumps of ice, lumps which then clumped together to become falling hailstones, hailstones which in turn collided with the upwelling supercooled droplets, droplets which shattered as they instantly froze upon striking the surfaces of the stones, splinters from which bore positive charges up and away from the falling hail, the stones themselves plummeting on downward to melt into negatively charged water drops. Thus in that maelstrom, water vapor and convection and freezing and clumping and gravity and upwelling and collisions and splintering and melting had all combined to turn the whole of the clouds into giant generators producing millions of kilowatts of electricity and hundreds of millions of volts between the positive terminal at the top and the negative terminal at the bottom, with uncounted coulombs of trapped electrical charge just waiting to break free . . .

. . . Above the Coburn Building.

And just below the negative pole a small pocket of positive charge had built up at the base of the cloud . . .

. . . Above the Coburn Building.

Tripped at random, or perhaps by a hurtling cosmic ray,

a trigger discharge leaped from this small pocket to the main negative pole, leaving a track of ionized air in its wake. Attracted by the positive charge of the earth below, from the main negative terminal a faint pilot discharge flashed down this ionized track. After forty-one meters, the discharge suddenly grew brighter as a great surge of electrons roared after, overtook, and became a massive leader stroke. Down through the air flashed the leader, stepping this way and that, zigging and zagging and sometimes branching as dictated by local variations in the electric field ahead. Within one one-hundredth of a second it was just ninety-two meters from the top of the Coburn Building and traveling at velocity of one hundred fifty thousand meters per second. At this point there was a difference of twenty-three million volts between the negative tip of the leader and the frame of the building. A huge surge of positive charge flashed upward through the steel girders, and streamers leapt from the structure toward the oncoming leader. One hundred eighty-two thousand amperes blasted through one of the many lightning rods, and copper vaporized in its wake. The air at the core of the bolt flashed to sixty-eight thousand degrees Fahrenheit, exploding outward at supersonic speeds, the resulting shock wave racing to hammer upon anything in its path.

The leader stroke was done, but up the track now coruscated the return stroke, hurtling toward the sky, leaping upward from building to cloud at one-third the speed of light, ninety-one thousand amperes flowing at its peak, and the last of the copper vaporized along the track. Brilliant light flared—eighteen billion watts, all told, before the return stroke died—and thunder would roll for seconds as the superheated air expanded. But even as the concussion began its hurtling race outward—

—a scant one hundred milliseconds after the return bolt expired, from a higher region of the cloud, a region yet burgeoning with charge, down the ionized channel left behind flashed a massive dart leader, the stroke moving at two point two million meters per second. . . .

Altogether, there were five vast charge regions in the cloud above. . . .

Every coulomb of which would slam into the Coburn
Building below.

The second titanic bolt crashed downward, vaporizing
passive solar panels and exploding the transfer liquid into
chemical steam.

One-tenth of a second later, the third stroke smashed
through the wide window of the executive conference
room, for no steel beams whatsoever stood along that
glass-paneled wall. The horizontal bolt slammed through
James Langford, knocking him backward, and it leapt
across to the great walnut table, exploding it into kindling
as the lightning punched onward through wall paneling
and followed electric cables downward. The shock wave
blew out all of the windows, the blast of expanding air
slamming Toni Adkins forward into the wooden rail and
hurling chairs and Henry Stein and Drew Meyer and Mark
Perry aside like chaff upon the wind.

The next stroke flashed down the rear of the building
and blasted into the main power bus. Transformers exploded, superheated oil flying wide as the building went
dark.

The final stroke again hammered across the executive
conference room, crashing through the door and blowing
it to splinters as lightning stuttered down the hall and
dove through the floor.

All in all, three-quarters of a second had elapsed from
first stroke to last. Nearly five billion joules of energy had
been expended. Far below the building, bubbling sand
would fuse to glass. . . .

. . . And then the thunder rolled.

BAAAADOOOOOMMMM! Walls jolted, floors jumped,
glass shattered, bookshelves toppled, cabinets shuddered
and doors swung open, spilling out the contents. And the
shock wave slammed into people, rocking them back,
knocking the breath from them, deafening them wherever
they were, causing noses and ears to bleed.

The building plunged into darkness. . . .

In the control center all were hammered by the concussion, techs and medtechs and Timothy Rendell and Alya

Ramanni and John Greyson, along with the few folks still sitting in the observation room behind.

"Son of a bitch!" shouted Timothy in the blackness, barely perceiving his own voice above the ringing in his ears; that he managed to detect his words at all was due entirely to bone conduction.

But five seconds later the emergency lights flickered into life, dimly illuminating the hallways and several of the key rooms. In three of these key rooms identical displays lit up. Each was labeled Time Remaining Battery Reserve, though they were commonly called the doomsday clocks. The displays were counting down. At the moment each of them read 3:59:53.

Timothy stood, saying, "I've got to—" but his mouth chopped shut, for emerging from the shadowy hallway and passing through the solid glass doors, in the dimness there came floating a glowing sphere of plasma, the globe perhaps a foot in diameter, the energy sputtering and crackling and sizzling, though neither Timothy nor anyone else in the room could hear it, temporarily deaf as they were.

"My God," exclaimed Greyson, his voice unheard, "it's ball lightning."

Across the room floated the globe; athwart its path stood the gimbaled rigs, the hemisynched alpha team completely unaware in their witches' cradles.

"Lord Vishnu, protect them," moaned Alya.

As if heeding her prayer, the crackling globe angled rightward, then leftward, to pass by the rigs and float toward the inert holovid.

"Jesus," muttered Timothy, suddenly realizing that Avery had gone dark.

As it touched the holovid, the ball detonated silently in a coruscating blast and disappeared altogether, leaving bright afterimages in the eyes of those watching.

"Wa!" cried one of the medtechs, and Timothy realized that he could hear again, though his ears yet rang.

"Does anyone have connection to Avery?" shouted Timothy, his voice sounding tinny to those in the room.

When Toni Adkins slammed into the rail, all the air was driven from her lungs, and she crashed backward onto the floor. Pelting rain fell on her as she desperately struggled to breathe but could not, struggled to inhale even one breath but failed. Spots swam before her eyes, and she bled from her nose and ears. Frantic, she tried and tried but breath simply would not come, and her mind raced a million miles an hour, her only thought *What a bloody wretched way to die,* and rain fell on her face. And just as she knew her life was over, *Ghhuuuhhhhh!* she sucked in a long, sobbing breath. Crying hoarsely, her lungs now heaving, she lay in darkness, rain falling down, the shattered room about her faintly illuminated by an emergency light shining in from the hallway. Weeping, she rolled over and got to her hands and knees. Before her, Mark Perry struggled to his feet. He reached down and helped her up as well. Turning, they both saw Jim Langford lying on his back amid the ruins of the shattered table, the tech not breathing at all.

Toni stumbled to him and dropped to her knees, placing her head on his chest. No heartbeat? She could not tell for she could not hear. She touched two fingers to his carotid artery, feeling for a pulse. There was none.

Quickly, she raised the back of his neck and opened his mouth to check that his air passage was clear. It was. Pinching his nose shut, she sealed his mouth with hers and filled his lungs with a breath, then she placed the heel of a hand on his sternum and her other hand on top, and drove down hard five times, then gave him another breath. Five more shoves. Another breath. "Goddammit, Mark, help me!" Though muffled, he heard her voice.

But it was Drew Meyer who dropped to his knees across from her. "You take over the heart," shouted Toni. "I'll do the breathing."

One, two, three, four, five . . . breathe . . . one, two, three, four, five . . . breathe . . .

A moment later, Henry Stein joined them. He rolled back one of Jim's eyelids and shined a penlight into the pupil. No reaction. But in the rubble at the edge of the beam of his small light Stein glimpsed a charred fragment of bone. He held out a hand to stop Drew and Toni altogether, and he raised Jim's head. The back of the tech's skull was gone.

* * *

"I have!" called several voices, among them Alya's. She added, "My console is still powered and Avery seems to be functioning, though some of my readouts are dark."

Timothy turned to Greyson. "John, check on Toni and the others. See if they are all right. Tell her that Avery seems to be working on backup power, though the main holovid is gone. Get Stein in here. He and his medtechs have got to extract the alpha team."

As Greyson hurried through the glass doors and into the corridor, Timothy stepped to Alya's console.

"We've got to get to mission control," said Toni, her eyes looking everywhere but at Jim Langford. "Power is out. The building damaged. And six people are in rigs."

Following Toni's lead, they stumbled across the wreckage of the conference room and through the splintered door and out to the hallway. Mark started for the elevators, but Toni grabbed his arm—"They're not working, Mark. No power"—and they headed for the stairs. On the way down through the shadows they met John Greyson coming up.

Timothy leaned down and keyed Alya's microphone. "Avery?"

Silence answered.

Timothy then moved to another working console. "Avery?"

Again there was no reply.

Timothy began moving from console to console, some working, others not, and at each, whether or not there seemed to be power, he keyed mikes and called for Avery, but the AI did not respond.

As Timothy keyed the final mike, Toni, Greyson, Stein, Meyer, and Perry came through the glass doors. "Avery?" Timothy called, but only dead air answered.

"Status," demanded Toni.

Timothy stepped forward in the dim light. "Power's out. Avery's on backup. Some of the consoles are down. The main holovid is out. And we cannot contact Avery."

Toni gasped. "Is he—?"

"He seems to be working from what I can see," interjected Timothy. "But the channels in and out apparently are down. We can probably bring them back on-line by rebooting."

A look of relief washed over Toni's face. Then she turned toward the technicians at the consoles and called out, "Listen to me, everyone. I need status reports from all sections: damage, injuries, anyone in need of medical aid. Straightaway, hop to." She beckoned to one of the techs standing at hand. "Michael, in particular find out why the overhead lights aren't back on. I mean, it appears as if we are operating on battery reserves alone. Surely the backup generator should be up and running by now." Toni glanced at the wall display—3:40:12—three hours, forty minutes, twelve seconds remaining before the voltage from self-regulating cells would catastrophically collapse. She keyed her digital watch into the countdown mode and synchronized it with the doomsday clock and pressed a button. And as the hundredths and tenths began to fly by, the seconds peeling off, she turned to face the rigs dimly seen in deep shadows. "Henry, get those people out of there."

But before Stein could move—"Oh my God, my God!" cried one of the medtechs, looking up horrified.

"What is it?" demanded Stein.

The medtech did not answer, but frantically keyed in commands on her display-local minicompad, all the while cursing under her breath.

Stein stepped to his own console to find it dark. "Damn!" He then moved over to the medtech's position and looked. Frowning, he leaned forward, one hand on the console, and murmured something. Again the medtech's fingers flew over keys.

Toni's voice cracked through the air: "Henry?"

The medtech gritted her teeth, then glanced up at Stein and asked, "What next?"

"Switch to backup," said Stein.

The tech keyed the command.

"Henry," demanded Toni. "What the hell is going on?"

Stein glanced up at Toni, but looked straight through her and then gazed back down at the console, his face eerily lit by the glow of the display, intense concentration in his stare.

It was the medtech who answered Toni's question. "The alpha team, Doctor Adkins, their brainwaves have gone flat."

25

Lyssa felt someone behind propping her up. Hands covered her eyes. She tried to pull away, but Kane hissed in her ear, "Be still." His voice seemed muffled.

Lyssa relaxed, "Wh-what happened?" Her own voice sounded deadened, too.

Arton called out: "Kane is setting your eyes and ears to rights again."

Moments later she could see and hear perfectly—more than perfectly, for even by lantern light colors seemed sharper, more intense, and hues she had never seen before sprang to the eye. Her hearing, too, was more acute and sounds that heretofore would go unnoticed instead came to the ear. Yet it wasn't only sight and sound that seemed enhanced, but all of her senses as well—vision, hearing, smell, taste, touch, and the state of her entire being—all perceptions were honed to a keenness never before experienced.

It was as if she and the entire world had been born anew and had become more . . . present.

Arik helped her to her feet and she could smell the scent of him—leather and salt and maleness. He embraced her and softly whispered, "I love you." And she held onto him fiercely.

Together they watched by lantern light as Arton led the nearly blind Kane to Rith, the black bard groggily coming round. Pon Barius yet lay unconscious on rain-soaked ground, Ky kneeling at his side.

Overhead, stars shone down through a clear sky, though ringed all about on the horizon stood a wall of clouds. Shattered trees littered the landscape, all felled outward from the point of detonation.

The air was filled with the odors of upturned earth and wetness and shattered pines and roots and the tang of lightning as well as other smells. Lyssa looked up at Arik and repeated her question: "What happened? . . . I mean, what by the seven hells were those lights? Those blasts?"

"I don't know, love," replied Arik. "All I know is—"

A thrashing sounded from the darkness.

"Wha—?" Lyssa groped for her saber. It was not at her hip but lay on the ground where the lean-to had been. As she jumped forward to snatch it up, Arton sprang for his crossbow. Ky's black blade seemed to leap into her own hand.

Again came the sounds of flailing, as if some large beast floundered in the dark. A squealing grunt rang out.

"The horses," snapped Arik. "It's the horses."

"Arda," exclaimed Ky. "I had forgotten all about them."

"We've got to see how they fare," said Arik, catching up a lantern. "Lyssa, come with me."

Amid the uprooted trees and shattered trunks they found alive five horses and two mules, all yet tethered to the felled wood. Of the five horses, two were conscious and on their feet, and three lay stunned on the ground, one with a broken foreleg, splintered bone showing. Both mules were awake, though only one was afoot; the other lay on its side on the wet earth, pine boughs pressing the animal down. One horse lay dead beneath a fallen pine, its back crushed. One horse and one mule were missing.

As he stepped to the horse with the shattered leg, a look of pain crossed Arik's features. He took out his dagger and slit Redlegs' throat, then quickly looked away. Crimson poured out and a sweetish iron tang seemed to fill the air, and Lyssa gasped and stepped back from it. Horses, too, snorted and skitted at the smell of blood, and the trapped mule squealed and floundered.

* * *

"Looks like the eye of a cyclone," said Rith as she scanned the wall of clouds all round. After a moment she added, "But it's not spinning . . . although it is closing up and bringing rain with it. We'd better make another lean-to."

"I'll help," said Arton.

Ky turned to Pon Barius. "Master, will you watch over Kane?" She gestured at the sightless, deaf warrior-healer. "His vision will return soon, his hearing, too, but until then he may need aid. I am going to help with the rebuilding of our camp."

The ancient syldari nodded abstractly, as if lost in thought, and Ky joined Arton with Rith.

Rain pattered down from above, for the great hole had closed and the storm had returned.

"Damnation," growled Arton, "I wish my horse hadn't fled."

"Better fled than dead," said Ky. "At least there's a chance that he'll be found, whereas mine will never run again, crushed as she was"—she cast a swift glance at Arik, the warrior with his head down—"nor will Redlegs."

"I'm sorry, Arik," said Kane, peering with dim vision at the flaxen-haired warrior. "Someday I may discover how to attune my art to animals, but right now people are all I can heal."

The stunned horses had recovered and the mule had been freed, and all remaining animals had been gathered and moved to the opposite side of the camp, away from Redlegs' corpse.

Silence fell among the Foxes, and for a long while no one spoke. At last Arik turned to Pon Barius. "What were those lights, those blasts? Who sent them? The Demon-Queen?"

Slowly Pon Barius shook his head but remained silent.

Rith looked at the others. "Perhaps it was Arda Himself. He may be displeased with us."

"Perhaps," growled Kane, "perhaps it was the Nameless One, the Dark God."

Again silence fell upon them all. Finally Ky put a hand on the old syldari's arm. "Surely, master, you have some idea."

Pon Barius took a deep breath and then let it out slowly. "Never have I seen such. At first I thought it might have been Horax. He is a dark wizard and foul, and he would think nothing of visiting such widespread destruction upon all living things just to slay me. But there is no way he could know where lies the red gem; too, he has not the power for such—such devastation.

"As for Atraxia, perhaps she has the power, yet she cannot know where we are—or so I believe.

"As to the Dark God . . . why would the Nameless One risk Arda's wrath with such a vile deed?

"And as for Arda Himself . . . surely He knows what it is we do.

"Nay, none of those seem likely to have visited such a calamity upon the land." Again Pon Barius fell silent.

"But, master," protested Ky, "if not those, then who or what?"

Pon Barius sighed. "Oh, child, perhaps this calamity came from beyond the bounds of the planes themselves, from *Outside,* as it were."

"Outside?" Rith looked wide-eyed at the mage.

Pon Barius nodded. "Haven't you ever wondered what lies beyond? I mean, look about you and ask yourself: Is this all there is? Or is there something else? Some actuality beyond what we see? I have often pondered over whether or not reality has limits, bounds, and if so, what might lie past those bounds, something beyond the planes of existence, something I call the *Outside.*"

Arton snorted in disbelief. "How can that be? There is *nothing* beyond the planes."

"Oh?" snapped Pon Barius. "And what makes you say that?"

"Why, sir, the planes go on forever," replied Arton, sweeping his hand toward the sky. "And since they go on forever, how can there be a so-called *Outside?*"

"Ha, my friend," retorted Pon Barius, "so you believe that it's turtles all the way down."

"Huh?" grunted Arton. "What do you mean by that?"

"Nothing," snapped the mage. And he wrapped his cloak about himself and lay down and said no more.

Never had sunrise seemed so bright nor colors more intense.

"I tell you," rumbled Kane, "this is none of my doing. My healing cannot sharpen the senses beyond what they were."

"Then what do you attribute it to?" asked Ky. "I mean, the world seems so utterly splendid, as if everything were somehow more, more . . ."

"More real?" supplied Rith. "I mean, that's how it seems to me, no matter whether we attribute it to Kane or—"

"Pah, I say we blame it on the gods and leave it at that," said Arton.

Arik looked at Pon Barius. "How does it seem to you, wizard? Are colors brighter, fragrances stronger, sounds more intense, touch more sensitive, tastes more—?"

"Not that I notice," interjected the ancient syldari.

"See?" declared Kane. "That proves it wasn't me. I healed him, too, and he is not affected."

"Perhaps it is because we survived a great catastrophe," said Rith, gesturing at the blasted landscape, the wide forest completely destroyed, not a tree left standing as far as the eye could see. Rith took a deep breath, inhaling the morning. "In spite of this devastation, perhaps the world seems a brighter place because we are alive and glad of it."

Ky glanced at the others and then at Rith and shook her head, unconvinced.

They broke camp and headed for the village of Arkol, some two days north. Ky and Pon Barius now rode on one of the mules together, Arton on the other one. Arik rode the steed they had purchased in Stahlholt, and Kane, Lyssa, and Rith rode their own mounts.

"I don't see why I have to ride this tall mule while he gets to ride *my* horse," muttered Pon Barius under his breath, all the while glaring at Arik.

"He weighs twice as much as you or I, master," whispered Ky. "In fact, more. For him to ride with one of us would burden an animal unnecessarily."

"But *we* could have both ridden my horse," hissed the wizard, "and *he* could have ridden the mule."

"Indeed," replied Ky. "But it is as Arik said: if it comes to a fight with drakka or anyone else, then it is better that he be on horseback and we on a mule."

"Bah!" grumped the elder, continuing to mutter as across the blasted land they fared, making their way round fallen trees and over splintered logs, the going excruciatingly slow. And many times the Foxes had to dismount and lead the steeds afoot, though Pon Barius always rode. After several times of walking the steeds over and around barriers and jams, backtracking occasionally as well, Pon Barius's muttering ceased.

As the sun passed overhead, they found the remains of a clearing and stopped for the midday meal. Rith came and sat down next to the ancient syldari. "Tell me about the overthrow of the DemonQueen."

Pon Barius cocked an eye at her. "Not much to tell, really."

"Nevertheless, I want to hear it."

"Well, it took nearly a week to get Ranvir's host through the gate in the Kalagar Forest, all the time her minions trying to break through our shield."

Rith held up a hand. "Your shield?"

"Yes. You see, the Inner Circle was all there—"

"Inner Circle?"

Pon Barius fixed her with a glare. "How am I going to tell this if you keep interrupting me?"

"I just want to know what you mean when you say 'Inner Circle.' "

"The Inner Circle of Wizards," snapped the old mage. "We were all there—all but that traitor Horax. Y'see, I think he ran when he thought we were about to expose his perfidy. So when it came to the showdown, he was gone—didn't even aid his intended, the DemonQueen."

"His *intended*?"

Again Pon Barius glared at the black bard. "Why else would he have abetted her in her campaign against

Itheria? To sit at her side, I say. To rule Itheria as her consort."

Rith mounted a silent *Oh*, then added, "Some piece of work this Horax."

"You can say *that* again," declared Pon Barius, grinding his teeth. "Destroyed my tower, he did."

"Destroyed your—"

"Yes! Razed it!" shouted Pon Barius, causing the other Foxes to look up from whatever they were doing.

"But why?" asked Rith.

"To get even for the archway," snapped the old syldari.

"The one in the high pass?"

"Of course, bard. Didn't I tell you that it was me who put it there?"

"Yes, but—"

"No yes buts about it—put it there 'cause he was trying to steal my secrets, him and his spies. Stopped him cold, I did, and for that he destroyed my tower." A crafty look slid over Pon Barius's features. "But I got even, I did— smashed his tower in return." The syldari fell into recollections, alternately seething in outrage and gloating in triumph as memories washed through his mind.

"Ahem." Rith cleared her throat. "About the overthrow of the DemonQueen . . . ?"

"Eh?" Pon Barius focused his eyes on her. "Demon-Queen? Oh, yes.

"She couldn't break our shield, not even when she used her scepter. And after the host all got through, we marched across the Plains of Chaos to her dark tower."

"These Plains of Chaos," asked Rith, "just what are they?"

"They're awful," replied Pon Barius. "The seven hells themselves—"

"Time to move on," called Arik.

Rith stood and helped the old mage to his feet. "Tell me about them later, eh?"

Pon Barius sighed. "If you insist, my dear."

It took two full days of travel just to get clear of the devastated area, and two more to reach Arkol, where they found several horses for sale, though none as good as those they had lost. Along with three mounts, they purchased another mule, this one even more intractable than the pair in their train.

And they rested for two days in the local inn, eating hot meals, drinking hearty ale, taking hot baths, and sleeping in actual beds. And Rith paid for it all with her bardic singing and telling of tales, filling the inn to overflowing each night with customers eager to hear and eager to sing and eager to hoist a drink.

"Before you invaded the demonplane," asked Rith, riding beside the old syldari, "how did you know that Jaytar had succeeded in stealing the gemstone from Atraxia's scepter?"

"Heh!" said Pon Barius. "Just as soon as she cleared the Kalagar Arch, she sent her falcon ahead, she did, a message tied to its leg."

"A falcon? But how can that be?" protested Rith. "I mean, it isn't as if falcons are like messenger pigeons, flying unerringly to their destination. Falcons are creatures of the wild, and although they can be trained, they are never truly tamed. I would think that even if it could find its way, a falcon turned loose to bear a message over a long distance would revert to the wild before the message could be delivered."

"Ha!" barked Pon Barius. "That may be true for most falcons, my dear, but this was no ordinary falcon—this was a former lover, I am told, her one and only."

Rith's jaw dropped open. "A former lov—?"

"Yes," interjected Pon Barius. "A shapechanger, I hear, who somehow got stuck."

"Oh my. How sad."

"We tried to break the curse, but failed."

"We?"

"The Circle."

"I see. Was that before or after?"

"Before or after what?"

"Her mission to steal the gem."

"Oh. Before."

They rode a short way and then Pon Barius sighed. "Perhaps it's just as well that Jaytar didn't survive."

Rith looked at the old mage. "Just as well? How so?"

Pon Barius fixed her with a stare. "If they were lovers and one was human while the other a falcon, then they could never, um, never . . ."

"I understand," said Rith.

Ky, who had been riding along on the other side of the wizard, said, "Perhaps you should have turned her into a falcon as well."

"Hm," mused Pon Barius, as if the thought were new. But he did not elaborate.

They rode in silence for a while. Finally Rith asked, "How do you know that she was killed?"

"Who?"

"Jaytar."

"Oh. Because she never came to White Mountain, and because one of the captive skelga told us so."

Ky snorted. "And you took the word of a skelga?"

"What else could we do? She never showed up."

"Perhaps they took her prisoner," said Rith.

"Then they would have killed her," replied Pon Barius.

Again silence fell on the trio. At last Ky asked, "What happened to the falcon?"

"It flew away," answered the mage. "We never saw it again."

"The demonworld is chaotic, a place where the laws of nature change from moment to moment. Why, even the demons themselves change shape endlessly, some without form altogether. Only the drakka and the skelga seem immune to these chaotic shifts of demon shapes, retaining their own forms throughout." Pon Barius paused, then added, "Them and the DemonQueen."

"What does she look like, this DemonQueen?" asked Rith, poking the fire to drive back the chill of night.

"An unearthly beauty, she is," replied Pon Barius, "slender and delicate. She has black hair, straight and cropped at the shoulder. And she has tilted eyes and pointed ears somewhat like those of a syldari, though no syldari is she."

"Eyes like a syldari's," rumbled Kane, grinning at Ky. "I always thought there was something, um, devilish about you, mouse." Ky wrinkled her nose and chucked a small branch at Kane, though a twinkle lurked in her dark eyes.

"Atraxia's eyes are nothing like the Shadowmaster's," said Pon Barius. "Instead they are solid white—no iris, no pupil. Strangely, this adds to her beauty, to her exotic lure."

"How tall?" asked Rith.

Pon Barius looked over at the bard. "I would say a hand or so shorter than you, my dear."

"Ha!" whooped Kane. "Slender, delicate, and short. I'll deal with her in a trice."

Pon Barius shook his head. "Oh no you won't, my friend. For not only is she the DemonQueen, she is a warrior queen as well."

Kane looked at the ancient syldari in surprise. "Warrior queen? How so?"

"A hand-and-a-half shamsheer is never far from her grasp," replied Pon Barius.

As Kane whistled low in surprise, a frown furrowed Lyssa's brow. "Shamsheer? What's that?"

"A long, curved cutting sword," replied Kane.

"Hers is curved but slightly," said Pon Barius.

"Hand and a half," mused Kane. "A warrior queen, indeed."

"That she is," agreed Pon Barius, "and she goes about clad in iron."

An elusive thought skittered across Arton's mind, gone before he could grasp it. It seemed as if he should recognize this iron-clad, black-haired beauty, but he could not imagine where he might have seen her nor even if he ever had.

Six weeks after leaving the Wythwood, they came into sight of White Mountain. "Arda," declared Arik, "it's as white as driven snow. What stone? Marble?"

Pon Barius laughed. "No, my son, not marble; were it made of such it would now be weathered to nothing but a low mound of powder. Nay! White granite it is . . . and crystal."

Up alongside the Rawlons they fared, more and more of

the mountain coming into view. At last they turned on a line toward the great white massif, following alongside a burbling stream as up through the foothills they rode. Three days later they had progressed as far as the horses would carry them. From now on they would have to go by foot, climbing up the long, lustrous slopes.

They found a small, grassy box canyon with a stream running through, where they set up camp. Then they spent all of the next day resting and readying their climbing gear and building a makeshift fence across a narrow stretch where the walls pinched inward, and there they penned the steeds. Too, they readied their backpacks with selected supplies and implements and goods, for Pon Barius had said they would be on the mountain for two days, and so they planned for four. On the morrow they would begin their ascent.

"Damn!" cursed Kane, carefully keeping his gaze fixed on the stone ahead and not looking behind. "There's just no way up. We've got to turn back while there is still light to see by."

Ky looked at the big man and then at the sheer rock above and finally at the long fall below. "Kane is right. There are no cracks, no handholds, and this stone is too hard to chip handholds. It even slants outward over our heads."

Arik sighed and turned to Pon Barius on the ledge beside him, the old mage held steady by Rith. "You said that this was the way, but obviously it is not. I see no alternative but to go back down. Tomorrow we can look for a different route, though I don't think there are any."

Arton, who had been leading the climb, took a deep breath and began preparing for the descent, with Lyssa at his side helping to coil rope.

"Nonsense!" snapped Pon Barius. "This is just the first ward."

"Ward?" Rith looked at the old mage, surprise in her eyes.

"Yes, ward," said Pon Barius. "Discouragement."

"I don't understand," said Arton. "I mean, the climb has been an arduous one as it is, made more so by having to haul you upward at every turn." Arton gestured at the sun standing straight overhead. "It has taken us all morning to get here. And now we've come to a total impasse and you claim we are discouraged. Seven hells, Pon Barius, look above. It's impossible. Damn right we are discouraged."

"Heh," chortled the old syldari. "That's what makes it so effective. We took advantage of human nature—in fact, the nature of all living beings. When the going gets tough, most people get discouraged. We set a ward that greatly enhances despair. To the point that alternatives to giving up aren't even considered."

"Well, if that's so," muttered Rith, "then why aren't you affected?"

"Because I was expecting it!" snapped Pon Barius. "Took steps to guard myself against it."

"Perhaps you should have guarded us as well," growled Arik.

"Look, boy, I have my reasons. Don't question me."

"Ward or no ward," said Kane, "I'm all for going down regardless and leaving these sheer drops behind. Besides, you can see for yourself it can't be climbed."

A murmur of agreement circulated among the Black Foxes.

"Shut up," barked Pon Barius. "I've got work to do."

Arton looked at Lyssa and shook his head and gestured at the steeps below. Lyssa nodded her agreement then glanced at Arik, who nodded as well and pulled his climbing gloves tight. Ward or no ward, they prepared to go back down.

Of a sudden Pon Barius swayed and would have fallen had it not been for Rith catching him. And in that same moment a weight seemed lifted from their hearts.

As Rith lowered the wizard to the ledge beside the packs, he muttered, "There, the first seal is annulled," and he leaned back against the sheer wall and closed his eyes.

"Seven hells," declared Arton, chagrined, "I was all set to give up."

Shamefacedly, they avoided looking at one another.

Displacing guilt, fire filled Arik's eye, and he scanned the stone above and gritted out, "Let's find a way up."

Arton stepped to the far end of the ledge. "No way here. Can't even climb across the face. Too sheer. Too hard."

"Same here," called Ky from the other end of the ledge as she scanned across and above.

Lyssa sighed as she looked upward. "If we could somehow get a rope onto the lip . . ."

Arton glanced at Kane. "Can you cast a grapnel that far?"

"I can try, though it's a long reach," replied the big man. "Perhaps too long."

They tied a line around his waist, and with Arik and Arton and Lyssa and Rith anchoring him, in spite of his fear of heights, Kane stepped to the brim of the ledge and swung a grapnel round and round at the end of a line, building momentum to finally let it go flying upward.

It did not even reach halfway.

Again he tried, and again, and again, and over and again . . . all to no avail.

At last he gave up.

"What now?" he asked, coiling the line.

"I'll get us up," said Ky. "Give me three ropes."

She fastened three hanks to her climbing belt, then clambered over the ledge and down.

"What th—?" muttered Arton.

Moments passed and moments more, stretching out in time. Then Rith declared, "There she is," and pointed upward and to one side.

High on a ledge above and stepping forth from shadow came Ky, her main gauche in hand, no sign of ichor on its black blade.

Carefully Ky worked her way across the face of the mountain, disappearing from view as she came to the high overhang. More time passed, and then they heard the *chank*ing of a rock hammer driving in a piton or two. Moments later a rope came snaking over the lip and down. Then Ky's face appeared, and she called to them, "All set and well anchored . . . so what are you waiting for?"

"Hold!" wheezed Arton in the lead. "I've got to rest. It may look easy, but I'll swear, this is the most difficult slope I've ever tried to scale."

Wearily, Arik looked at the gentle pitch of the smooth, slippery stone, then his swimming gaze sought out but failed to find Pon Barius below, the mage waiting to be hauled upward. "Have we come to another ward?" Arik croaked.

"Quite possibly," the old syldari called back. "What have you encountered?"

"We've come to a slippery slope, and it's wearing us out," answered Arik, gasping for breath. "Can't seem to get a firm grip anywhere. We keep sliding back." Arik cast an exhausted glance at Arton. Barely able to raise his head, the master thief sat in a slump at the base of the glossy incline and panted and blearily looked back, his eyes filled with fatigue. Arik then hoarsely called down, "Arton looks as if he's about to pass out."

"Get down and away from that slant!" shouted Pon Barius. "It's the second ward!"

Wearily, Arik turned to find Arton lying back against the tilt, his eyes closed, his muscles slack, his mouth drooping open, drool dribbling down his jaw.

Fatigue sapping every fiber of his being, Arik crawled to Arton and grabbed him by an ankle; then, hauling backward with all his might, weakly, ineffectually, he dragged at the thief, barely moving him before his own energy gave out and he fell toward unconsciousness. And as he spun down into oblivion, he felt someone pull him scraping and bumping down the face of the mountain and away from the stone above.

The next Arik knew, he was lying on his back, his head in Lyssa's lap. "Unh," he groaned, "what happened?"

"I got to you both in time," said Lyssa, tilting her head toward Arton, Kane kneeling at the thief's side.

"What about the ward?"

"Pon Barius is nullifying it even now."

"What is it?"

"Great fatigue and permanent sleep if you don't get away."

Arik lay a moment longer as energy seemed to pour back into him. At last he slowly sat up; all seemed normal. Finally he twisted about and pulled Lyssa's face to his and kissed her. "Thanks, love," he whispered, as she held onto him tightly. He kissed her again and murmured, "As much as I would like to remain in your arms forever, I think I need to see to this mission." She held him tight a moment longer then reluctantly released him.

Arik stood and looked at Kane and Arton. The thief was just now opening his eyes. "Kane?"

Kane turned to Arik. "He'll be all right in a moment, now that he's away from that ward above."

"Good," said Arik, giving the warrior-healer a sharp nod of appreciation.

Arik glanced upslope. Ky and Rith knelt on the mountainside somewhat ahead. Beyond them, in the late afternoon sunlight Pon Barius stood at the base of the glossy slant. "Is it safe?" he called up to the ancient mage. At a wave from Pon Barius, Arik clambered up past Ky and Rith and to the old syldari's side.

"Perhaps you ought to tell us of the remaining wards before we come to them," said Arik as he eyed the smooth and deadly expanse of rock sloping upward.

Pon Barius shook his head. "Afraid not, my lad."

Arik stepped before the old mage and stared down at him with eyes as hard as flint and gritted out through clenched teeth, "Wizard, you put us all at hazard with your secrecy."

Pon Barius flung up a warding hand and shied back from the warrior. "All right, all right. I said I had my reasons, and they are this: y'see, I need to conserve my energy since the full Circle is not here to help me. And these wards, well, they are easier to nullify after they are tripped, and they trip more easily if you don't know what's coming. Besides, we are almost there and I'll be with you the rest of the way."

Arik looked closely at the ancient syldari, then reluctantly nodded. "All right, wizard, but should anything happen to my companions . . ." Arik left the remainder of the unspoken thought and instead turned and looked downslope. Arton was now on his feet, and Arik gestured for all to come up.

"Huah!" exclaimed Arton, clambering up the smooth slope, "this stone isn't slick at all."

"All part of the ward spell," puffed Pon Barius, the mage helped along by Kane on one side and Rith on the other. "It will reactivate as we go back down."

"In the jungles of my homeland," said Rith, "there is a vine with flowers whose fragrance puts people to sleep should they remain overlong in its domain. Many a weary traveler has lost his life by stopping to rest nearby."

"This ward is much the same," remarked Kane.

"Not quite," replied Rith. "You see, here I think you slumber your life away"—she received a confirming nod from Pon Barius—"but there in the jungle, the vine sends out feelers, sends out shoots, and hairline roots penetrate the skin and suck the life from its victim."

"Arda!" declared Kane. "Like a slow-creeping lamia, eh?"

Lyssa, following after, asked, "How can you avoid that trap?"

"Keep a sharp eye out," answered Rith. "Watch for its red flowers, and look for the bones of its victims. Above all, should you smell a sweet fragrance and suddenly feel weary, flee from the vicinity."

For another four candlemarks or so, up and across the lustrous mountain they clambered, the slope sometimes gentle, sometimes rough, but always passable by the Foxes, though at times they needed to bodily haul Pon Barius up the way—mostly by the old wizard riding pick-aback on Kane. And the track they followed at the behest of the mage was winding and seemed to have no purpose, for at times they went up, at other times across, and occasionally they even descended. But at last Pon Barius pointed a short distance ahead. "There it is," he quavered.

Before them stood a low sheer face of white granite sparkling with the glitter of quartz.

Arton, in the lead, was first to come to it, and he ran his hands over the surface, moving to the right and then farther to the right and farther still. Pon Barius gestured to Kane and Rith and they came to a halt as the old mage watched Arton. At last, some twenty feet away from where he had started, Arton paused. "Here is a door," he called, his hands tracing up and across the stone and back down, outlining an unseen portal. Then he turned to face them all and said, "But it has no lock."

Pon Barius's eyes went wide. "Precisely right, my boy. How did you do that? I detected no spell."

Arton shrugged. "I don't know. It's just a talent I have."

"Hem." Pon Barius stumped to the wall. "D'you remember what you once told me?"

Arton frowned. "I've said many things to you, wizard."

"About doors and locks," snapped Pon Barius.

Arton shrugged.

"Well, if you don't remember, I do," growled the old syldari. "You said that any lock could be opened if you but had the key."

"Oh, that."

"Yes, that."

"So . . . ?"

"So, in spite of what you claim, lad, this door *does* have a lock."

"Not any that *my* picks will open or my fingers loose."

"Heh!" barked Pon Barius. "Precisely right. But, you see, there *is* a key . . . one that will indeed unlock this door. Now stand aside."

As Arton moved leftward, the wizard advanced and planted his right hand against the stone and bowed his head. Behind him came the sounds of blades being drawn, the unlashing of a spear, and the cocking of a crossbow.

Pon Barius took a deep breath. . . .

"Kínyîtñì!" he called out, his voice singing a melodious command.

And spreading outward from his hand a sparkling grew, quartz chips in the white granite flashing, but brighter than the setting sun would allow if it were but reflections. As the light spread outward, it slowed, until at last it stopped. And there shining on the face of the stone was the bright silhouette of a door. All of a sudden the sparkles vanished and a dark line formed down the center, growing wider with each heartbeat as the portal split in two and doors wheeled inward to the sound of stone grinding on stone. The Foxes tensed and gripped weapons, and Kane, his spear ready, stepped aflank the old mage as Arik took the opposite side. And still the doors ground open, darkness growing, until at last they fetched up against the walls inside—*boom, doom.* An ebon gape yawned before them, and just beyond the threshold an arched passageway slanted down into blackness.

Arik started to speak, but his words were choked off as a hideous stench poured forth from within—the foul odor of pus-filled, rotted flesh. He gasped and reeled hindward, as did Kane, as did all of the Foxes, their gorges rising, Arton retching, yielding up his breakfast meal. But Pon Barius stood fast in the putrid miasma and raised his arms and murmured a single word . . . and the odor vanished.

Then the old mage swayed and staggered sideways, catching himself on the edge of the opening, where he slumped to the ground. Kane, gasping and blowing to clear his nostrils of the putrescence, stumbled to Pon Barius's side, but the wizard waved him away, saying, "I'll be all right in a moment. Those were the third and fourth wards, and nullifying them took much out of me."

"Third and fourth?" Kane looked at the old syldari.

"The third ward is a secret door that opens by word alone; of course you must know the exact word and the precise intonations. The fourth ward is the air of decay."

As the other Foxes puffed and blew, Arton poured water into his mouth and gargled and swished and spat, then wiped his sleeve across his lips. "Gack, but that was awful."

They rested for long moments more as the sun slid below the horizon and shadows mustered all round. At last, in the gathering twilight, Pon Barius struggled to his feet. "Come along," he wheezed, "time does not tarry."

Shouldering their backpacks, but keeping their weapons in hand, the Foxes made ready. At a nod from Arik, Pon Barius stepped across the threshold, Arton beside him bearing a lit lantern, the others following, Lyssa the last to enter. She stood a moment, peering into the dimness, into the dark, narrow way, into the black strait where unnumbered tons of stone groaned overhead, into a place with walls that seemed poised to slam closed and crush the life from anyone within their confines . . . and ahead the light receded, leaving nought but blackness behind. With a curse she plunged inward, running to catch up.

Into the mountain they wound, following an arched corridor, the way turning this way and that, rising and falling. Faintly at first and then growing louder there came the intermittent sound of stone grinding on stone. At last they came to a dead end, and only blank rock stood before them. From beyond they could now and then hear the rumble of stone on stone.

"This is a door," hissed Arton.

"Of course it is, lad," muttered Pon Barius. Then he turned to the others. "Now, stand ready and when I say move, *move*! Follow me swiftly, no matter what you see."

The hair stood up on the back of Arik's neck. "Why do I feel as if we are about to step into an elaborate trap?"

Pon Barius canted his head and stared a moment at the flaxen-haired warrior, then said, "Perhaps it's because that's precisely what it is."

Suddenly, grinding, the stone before them slid to one side, revealing a corridor running left and right and an opening straight ahead. *"Move!"* barked Pon Barius. Quickly he stepped over the threshold to stand at the far side of the juncture; Foxes rushed after.

And all about them was a cacophony of sound: heavy thudding, loud whooshing, the cascade of water, the howl of wind, and clamors unidentifiable.

"Wait," cried the mage above the noise, standing still. "Do not step from this intersection."

A moment later, stone ground against stone as the door behind slid closed, and walls moved. "This way," shouted Pon Barius, and down a newly revealed corridor he hobbled to come to another intersection, where once again he waited, as did the Black Foxes following after.

Again there came grinding on grinding, and three ways opened: one filled with whooshing fire, one with a deep abyss yawning, and the last empty. "Wait!" cried the mage above the clatterous noise.

Again the walls shifted, corridors disappearing, new ones appearing. Now a great stone as wide as the passage whelmed repeatedly down into one corridor like the strokes of a monstrous hammer, thudding into the floor over and again; a howling, black abyss yawned in the second, an endless fall below; a whirling pool filled the third, and screams of terror rose up from its huge funnel. *"Move!"* cried Pon Barius, and he hobbled quickly forward into the corridor where the great stone slammed down. Lyssa shrieked and could not move, for here was her worst nightmare come true. But as Arik turned to plead with her, Kane swept her up and took her kicking and screaming into the passage after the mage. *Thdd! Thdd!* whelmed the stone, the floor juddering under their feet, yet the great maul had no effect whatsoever on those running behind Pon Barius.

Moments after they made it to the subsequent intersection the stone walls slid anew. Once again Pon Barius waited, selecting none of the choices offered. And he waited again on the next move, once more selecting none. As he waited, he called out above the noise, "At each juncture all of the choices are lethal but one, and you will die hideously should you choose unwisely. But one of the choices is illusory, though it is difficult to discern. Should a correct choice be offered you and you wait too long, you will miss your chance and be trapped forever." Again the walls slid and once more they waited. But when the walls ground again, he called out to them and hobbled over the depths of a sulfurous yawning abyss, and this time it was Arik and Lyssa who shoved the shrieking Kane across.

They carried the screaming Rith through roaring flames, and Ky fainted when flesh-shredding iron claws whirled at them. Arton gibbered in terror as great crackling bolts of lightning jagged across the corridor down which they ran. And Arik was knocked unconscious and carried by Kane as they waded through slime-filled water which swirled with unseen shapes.

At last they reached the end of the ever-changing maze. As stone slid across the hallway behind, closing it off, Pon Barius said, "The maze of terror." None of the Foxes needed to ask him what he meant by that . . . though Pon Barius went on to say, "It reaches into the minds of those within and presents them with their innermost fears."

When Ky asked Pon Barius which one was his dread,

the old mage looked at her and cackled, "That one, my dear, I nullified even before we entered."

Ky shook her head. "Not fair, master. Not fair at all that we should face our terrors while you did not."

Pon Barius laughed, then turned and trudged ahead, the Foxes following after.

A straight corridor disappeared into dimness before them, but in the far distance they could see a bluish glow. "It is the sixth ward, and in its way one of the most powerful of all," said Pon Barius as they approached.

"What can we expect?" asked Arik. "When we trip it, that is."

"Oh, lad, you must not trip this one. Instead leave it entirely to me, for this means death to anyone who touches it."

"Death?"

"Yes. It is an aethyric sphere of death, which completely englobes the chamber wherein lies the silver chest."

Arik grimly smiled and stepped back, gesturing down the corridor ahead. "Lead on, wizard."

"Lord, Arik," muttered Lyssa, "the whole of White Mountain is nothing but deadly traps and snares."

"That's right, young lady," agreed Pon Barius. "How else to protect the indestructible gem from demonkind and others? With deathly wards, that's how—lethal . . . all but the first and last." He waved a hand back in the direction they had come. "Why, if you were to attempt that on your own, heh, without a doubt you'd be dead by now."

As they approached the archway at the end of the hall, before them glowed what appeared to be a bluish wall of witchfire filling the portal, beyond which lay a large, lighted, empty, circular chamber—a chamber perhaps twenty strides across. Arton took one look at the witchfire and moved completely to the rear. "The rest of you stand back as well," growled Pon Barius.

As the Foxes moved away, the old mage turned toward the glowing surface of energy and stood silent for long moments, his head bowed. At last he raised his face and mouthed a word, but what he said, none knew, for he made no sound whatsoever. With a brilliant, silent flash the barrier vanished and Pon Barius reeled hindward as if struck a devastating blow. Kane sprang forward just barely in time to catch the ancient wizard as he collapsed.

As Kane lowered unconscious Pon Barius to the floor, "Water!" he snapped. "In a cup." While Ky fumbled through her pack for a cup, Arik unslung his waterskin and uncorked it. Kane rummaged through his own knapsack and extracted a packet. Ky handed him the now filled container, and Kane crumbled a dried mint leaf into the liquid then swirled it about. He lifted the head of the old syldari and held the cup to his lips, giving him small sips. Pon Barius swallowed some and swallowed again. Moments later he opened his eyes.

"Did I do it?" he croaked.

Kane looked at the archway. No web of energy covered the opening. "Yes. The witchfire is gone."

"Eh, help me up. We are almost there, almost done with this mission."

As Kane lifted the mage to his feet, Ky stepped forward and put the syldari's arm over her shoulders and supported him. Pon Barius gestured ahead. "Go slow, now. I haven't much left in me, you know."

Slowly, Ky helped Pon Barius toward the lighted chamber. Behind, Kane scooped up his and Ky's packs and followed, the other Foxes in his wake.

The chamber they entered was indeed round, hemispherical, in fact, the walls rising up and arching over, as if it were a huge stone bubble resting on a floor of stone—a half a sphere bounded by a great circle. Pale light seemed to emanate from everywhere, from nowhere, as if the very stone were aglow. The floor was smooth and white, as was the spherical dome, and all was plain—no embellishments whatsoever decorated the unrelieved surfaces.

And the chamber was empty.

"Wa," muttered Arton to Rith, "has someone stolen the silver chest?"

Rith looked up and around and down, then eyed Arton and shrugged, whispering, "If they have, then Pon Barius doesn't seem to have noticed."

Arton cocked an eye at Pon Barius. Then the thief whispered, "Perhaps it lies hidden somewhere."

Puffing, Pon Barius had Ky help him to the center of the room, where he disengaged himself. He looked at the Foxes and wheezed, "We are here at last, and Arda, but I am weary, my power nearly spent." As Black Foxes shucked their packs and set them down and shed their climbing gear as well, Pon Barius said, "There is but one last thing for me to do. And then I'm afraid I must rest until I recover enough to get us all past the deadly maze again."

"What about resetting the wards, master?" asked Ky as she unbuckled her climbing harness. "Won't you need power for that?"

"Oh no, child," answered Pon Barius. "The other wards will reactivate as we leave them behind. No, it's only the maze we need worry about—it's deadly warding, that is."

He turned and faced the center. "We've come to the final ward, the one which hides the chest." Arton and Rith glanced at one another and smiled. "Now, give me room to do a final casting."

As the Foxes picked up their gear and backed away, so, too, did Pon Barius withdraw several paces from the center.

Kane set his pack and harness to the floor and then stepped to a point directly behind the mage, ready to catch him should he collapse again.

Once more Pon Barius stood a moment with his head bowed, then looked up and mouthed a silent word. As Kane caught him and started to ease him down, the white granite in the center of the floor began to change, to alter, to ripple as if it were water. Kane pulled the ancient mage away as in the midpoint of the chamber a modest "pool" formed, some six feet across all told, its surface a shimmer of liquid stone with embedded quartz droplets sparkling. And then the ripples ceased and all fell quiet.

The Foxes watched a moment, and Arton said, "Hmm. It seems as if—"

Of a sudden, rising up through the liquid rock came a pillar of stone, a low, broad, flat-topped column, perhaps three foot across. On this column sat a small, crystal coffer—roughly a cube, not quite a foot on a side—and clasped within the clear crystalline vault gleamed a block of purest silver, its surface covered with carvings and runes.

The rock pool solidified.

Pon Barius coughed and opened his eyes and looked at Kane. "No mint tea this time, eh?"

Kane looked down at the old mage, then grinned. "If you insist."

"No, no, boy," wheezed Pon Barius. "Just help me to my feet."

Arton, now standing at the very rim of where the pool had been, turned and asked, "Is it trapped?"

Pon Barius shook his head *no* and said, "Nothing fatal here, lad."

Arton stepped to the side of the pillar. "Why the crysta' vault? And the carvings and runes, are they special?"

"Heh," barked Pon Barius, "ever the thief, eh?"

Arton grinned.

"As to the crystal vault," said Pon Barius, "that's so the silver doesn't come into contact with the, um, with the pool. That wouldn't do, you know. And the carvings, well, they have their purposes—decoration among them—Borga's idea of what such an important thing should look like, you know. He was the gnoman who made the chest."

Pon Barius turned to Rith. "Well, let's get on with what we came here to do. Give me the dagger, my dear. It's time we put the gem in its appointed place. Then I'll sink it back into the stone, though it'll use up the very last of my power. And then we'll have to wait awhile until I can recover."

As Rith reached into her leather jacket to take out the silver dagger, Pon Barius shook his head and said, "Seven hells, here I have to nearly kill myself to complete what we began so very long ago. And where is the Circle just when I need them? Dead, that's where. None are left but me."

From behind there rang a voice through the air. "Not so, fool brother of mine, for I was of the Circle and I yet live!"

Pon Barius and the Black Foxes whirled to face the door.

And there in the entryway stood a tall, black-haired man with a long, aquiline nose and a wide leering mouth. He was dressed in sable and wore an ebon cloak. On the front of his doublet was emblazoned two red crescents— one small, one large—Phemis and Orbis as bloodmoons. Behind him in the shadows of the hallway the blackness seemed to churn with unseen figures.

"Horax!" hissed Pon Barius.

"From childhood on, you always were such a predictable fool, my adopted brother!" sneered Horax, his black eyes glittering. "I knew you would come here and spend your power to nullify the wards."

Filled with rage, Pon Barius drew himself up to his full height and for a moment seemed taller than all the others, taller even than Kane. "It is you who are the fool, Horax. Go back to your Drasp and squat in that swamp like the bog spider you are!"

Horax laughed, his voice chill. "Ever the idiot to think that mere words alone would send me scurrying." His gaze shifted to Rith. "No, brother, I've come for the knife and what it contains."

"You'll not have it," shouted Pon Barius, stepping toward Rith as Foxes drew blades and Arton reached for his crossbow and Kane stooped to pick up his spear.

Yet in that same moment, Horax shouted out a command—*"Va'tchok!"*—and stepped to one side as howling, black, three-foot-tall skelga, bone thin but with needle-sharp rending teeth and long shredding talons, boiled into the chamber and sprang toward the Foxes and Pon Barius.

Zzzzzaaakk! Arton's crossbow bolt took the first one in the chest as it leapt upon Pon Barius, the dark goblinlike creature shrieking and falling back as the silver quarrel slammed through ribs and lungs and heart. In a blast of indigo fire, the skelga detonated, cobalt flames exploding outward, leaving nothing behind.

Horax raised hands burning with witchfire and flung a gesture at Pon Barius—*Crraaak!*—the chamber rocked with detonation, and Pon Barius flew backward and crashed into the pillar then fell to the floor, the smell of lightning and burnt flesh filling the air.

Rith's hand flashed to her bandolier and she raised a silver dagger to throw at Horax, but the yawling black tide was upon them, sweeping them under. And needle teeth and razor claws tore through leather and flesh, fangs ripping, talons slashing, and red blood flew wide.

But silver blades left long flaming gashes where they met muscle and sinew and bone, and screaming skelga burst into violet flames. Ky's black blade, too, carved deep through demonkind, parting limbs from torsos and heads from necks, the ebony edge sharp beyond reckoning and leaving ruin behind.

Kane was overborne by ten or so skelga, the big man going down under a howling swarm, teeth and claws ripping and rending.

Yaaaahhh! Yawling a wordless howl, Kane raised up from under the mass, hurling skelga away, and he wielded his spear as if it were a quarterstave, bashing demonkind left and right.

But one of the hurled skelga crashed into Ky from behind and slammed her into the hemispherical wall, her head striking white stone. Down she fell at the feet of Horax, all consciousness gone from her, her ebony blade lost from her hand and skittering across white granite.

And still skelga howled and attacked.

But Horax scooped up the unconscious syldari, wrenching her up and against his chest, and he howled a word or two.

And the skelga fell back.

"The dagger," hissed Horax to Rith, one clawlike hand clutching limp Ky by the throat. "Give me the dagger or she dies."

"Don't do it, Rith," cried Arton, a silver long-knife in each hand. "He'll kill us anyway."

Rith glanced from Horax to Ky to Arton to Arik and then back to Horax. Now the wizard's talons pressed into Ky's flesh and blood seeped out from under his clutch. Rith reached into her leather jacket and took out the silver dagger. Slowly she extracted the weapon from its sheath and flipped it over in her hand, her fingers gripping the blade. She extended her arm and stepped toward Horax, as if reaching out to give it over. But then, viper swift, she hurled it at his head. With a cry, Horax jerked aside, the blade shearing through his left ear and clanging into the wall, blood splatting against white granite as the dagger fell spinning to the floor.

"*Va'tchok!*" shrieked the mage.

Howling, skelga sprang upon the Foxes, bearing them back and under as blades burned long streaks of fire through demonkind.

It became a chamber of rending and tearing, of hewing and bashing, of howls of agony and cries of desperation . . . a chamber of blood and fire and death.

But at last it ended.

Bleeding and torn with gaping wounds and gasping harshly in the stench of burnt demonflesh, as Kane hobbled to fetch his gear, Arik and Lyssa surveyed the carnage.

Of the demons, all had vanished in flames but for the corpses of the four skelga rived by Ky's ebony blade.

Arton lay on the floor panting, and his blood ran in rivulets across white granite, mingling with the black ichor of demonkind.

Badly damaged, Rith sat with her back to the pillar. Her eyes were closed, but she yet breathed.

Pon Barius was dead, his chest blown open.

Of Ky there was no sign . . .

Nor was there any sign of Horax . . .

Nor of the silver dagger . . .

And the entrance was once again sealed with the burning blue light of the deadly warding witchfire.

26

"Gone flat? Entirely?" asked Toni. "Are you certain that it isn't just a console failure?"

"Perhaps, though I doubt it," answered Stein, reaching past the medtech to key a command on the compad. He paused a moment then said, "Their autonomous systems are yet working, so the brainstem is functioning. But the cognitive areas and memory and perception, and the like . . . all nonfunctioning."

"Brainstem?" Mark Perry looked questioningly at Stein.

Disgusted, Stein turned away, but Alya Ramanni said, "It means, Mark, that their hearts are beating, their lungs are breathing, and so on. It's like their bodies are on autopilot. But as to their mental capacities, well . . ."

"I know what it means, Ramanni," snapped Perry. "They're vegetables!" The lawyer whirled on Toni. "I told you hours ago that we should stop this insane experiment," he spat, "but oh no, you had to go on. And now Arthur Coburn is a goddamn brainless slab of meat and it's all your—"

"Silence!" Toni's shout brought Perry up short. "Dammit, Mark, now is the time to fix the problem and not the blame. So shut your gob or I'll have you ejected."

As Mark stood sputtering and puffing, Toni turned to Stein. "Henry, verify that what your consoles are reading is in fact the case. If only the autonomous functions are working, we need to know what has happened and why."

Stein nodded and moved toward the readouts on the rigs themselves.

Toni looked at Rendell. "Timothy, go down to the AIC and see if you can talk to Avery. If not, then reboot him. We've got to reestablish contact. I've a hunch he can tell us just what has happened. And, oh, before reinitializing, make certain that no significant damage has occurred; we wouldn't wish to reboot if in some manner it will harm Avery."

"Right," barked Timothy, and he glanced about and called out, "Billy, Sheila, let's go." The two comptechs— a wiry, brown-haired man and a diminutive blond woman—followed him out.

Now Toni turned to Drew Meyer, the physicist standing at her shoulder. "Drew, see if you can assess the damage here. If we can get these displays fully functional and get the holovid working again, perhaps we won't be so—so in the dark. —And dammit! Why aren't the lights back on?"

Toni took a deep breath and exhaled, then looked at Alya Ramanni. "Alya, get security to call in all the crew. We're probably going to need every bit of talent we have to set things right."

Alya turned to the vidcom and began punching buttons as Toni faced the console operators. "All right, does anyone have something of significance to report?"

Immediately, Alya Ramanni turned back to Toni and spoke up. "I do, Toni. The vidcoms are out. I can't contact security."

"Damn!" gritted Toni. "What the hell is next?"

"Here, can you use this?" Mark Perry reached into his suit jacket and hauled out a portable.

Alya Ramanni reached for it. "I'll try the outside line."

Stein and two medtechs at the gimbaled rigs engaged the readouts.

As Stein watched, one of the medtechs called out, "Temp."

The other medtech moved down the line and read the displays. "All green."

"Respiration."

Again the medtech moved down the line, finally saying, "All green."

"Heart."

"All green."

And so it went down through the entire checklist.

All read green except brain activity, and here, but for the autonomous functions, the readouts were flashing red with alarms.

Stein stood scowling, one hand cupping an elbow, the other stroking his chin, the doctor completely perplexed.

On the fourth floor, Timothy and the two comptechs stepped to the security door of the AIC; Timothy slapped his hand to the palm reader and spoke his name. It did not respond.

Power's out, you idiot!

Timothy pounded the butt of his fist against the panel. After a minute or so, a muffled voice called through the door. "Step back under the emergency light so I can see who you are. The vidcams are out."

The trio obliged the voice, and moments later the door swung open, the security guard operating it manually. Behind him the artificial intelligence center was dimly illuminated by emergency lights.

"Jeeze, Doctor Rendell, what's going on?" asked the short and a bit pudgy young man.

Timothy glanced down at the comband encircling the guard's left wrist. "Didn't they tell you?"

"Lightning, they said."

Timothy nodded. "That's right. Any damage here in the AIC?"

The young man shook his head. "I don't think so, but I'm not a tech. Jeeze, it sounded like bombs or something! Then the lights went out."

As the guard levered the door closed, Timothy and the comptechs walked into the enshadowed AIC, the room huge. Desks sat round the perimeter of the chamber along with tables and chairs and carrels. Timothy passed beyond these work areas and into the band of consoles scattered about the room and surrounding the thick, shatterproof, smoked glass walls which protected Avery. The AI itself sat darkly within. In the shadows the glass chamber looked like nothing more than an enormous sullen cube, twenty feet on a side, with cables of fiberoptics leading in and out along with thermoshield lines bearing nitrogen coolant.

Timothy stepped to the master console. Indicators glowed and luminous lines crawled across the screen. He studied them a moment, then said, "Hm, that's peculiar—it looks as if the test is still running." He flicked on the microphone. "Avery?"

There was no response.

"Naraka!" muttered Alya Ramanni, then she called to Toni, "There is no answer. I think all the vidcoms are out."

Toni turned to Mark Perry. "Mark, find a security guard with a comband and get him to call central security and have ten, twelve combands delivered here. We've got to equip ourselves with the means to communicate with one another. Then have him initiate Operation Greentree to get all our tech force back into the building."

"Greentree?"

"An emergency calling tree, Mark. Each tech knows the drill. —Now go."

Perry nodded and turned to leave just as David Cardington, deputy chief of security, entered.

"Hold it, Mark," said Toni, "here comes a comband now."

Cardington, a tall, thin man in his late forties with brown hair and hazel eyes, paused a moment, peering through the shadows for Toni, then he strode to her. "The perimeter is secure, Doctor Adkins. Nothing is burning. But all hardwired comm to the outside is down. We took a helluva hit and it probably fried the PBX. I think we also took a hit on the incoming mains."

"No doubt, David, but what about the backup power? The turbine should be up and running by now and we should have lights."

Cardington shifted his stance. "I've a man on his way to see; till he calls in, we won't know."

Toni said, "I sent a man, too: Michael Phelan." She sighed. "Regardless as to what they might report, initiate Greentree. And get us some combands, ten or twelve. I've got key people all over the building and no way to communicate."

Cardington nodded, then spoke into his wrist.

Bearing one of the battery-driven emergency lights he had taken from its wall bracket, the wide beam diminishing the farther it pressed through the blackness, at last Michael Phelan reached the second subbasement. He could hear footsteps clanging down the grillwork steps of the iron stairwell behind. Pausing, he saw a handheld light bobbing as someone came down after. Michael waited.

"Who's that?" called a voice, the light shining down.

"I'm Michael Phelan," Michael called back up. "I've been sent by Doctor Adkins to see why the power isn't back on."

"Oh." The light came on downward. Michael saw that it was carried by a security guard. "Charley Johnson here. And that's why I've come, too. To see why the lights are out."

Briefly, they shined their beams into one another's faces, then Michael said, "Let's go."

Stein spun on his heel and stalked away from the witches' cradles, his medtechs following. As he moved through the shadows, Toni called, "Henry, where are you going?"

Without looking at her, Stein called back, "To the AIC. The medical monitors just might be fully operational there."

"But what about the alpha team? We've got to extract them."

"Not until I find out what's going on," Stein answered, then he was out the door and gone.

"*¡Madre de Dios!*" declared Roberto Sanchez aloud, though he was alone in the rain behind the Coburn

Building. He pulled his wrist to his face. "Chief, Sanchez here."

Tinnily came the response. "Go ahead, Roberto."

"The whole substation is in ruins, chief. Wires down, transformers ruined, twisted metal. It looks like it was hit by a bomb . . . a big one."

"Keep your distance, Roberto. Some of those downed wires may still be hot. We'll let Tucson Solar handle it."

"Yes, sir."

"And keep others away, too."

"Yes, sir."

Timothy Rendell squatted beside the console. A panel was open and a pair of legs stuck out. Inside, a flashlight beam played over boards of integrated circuits. "Okay, Sheila, what've you got?"

"It looks as if the entire comm unit is out, but I can't find any overt signs of damage."

"Then a reboot . . . ?"

Sheila scooted out. Sitting on the floor, she looked at Timothy and shrugged. "In my opinion it's our best bet to restore comm," she replied. "But you know, sir, if we do reboot, Avery's going to lose some memory—from a little to a lot, depending on what's gone wrong."

Timothy nodded then stood and called out to the man eyeing the fiberoptic bundles. "Billy?"

"Nothing yet, though there's a helluva lot I haven't examined" came his reply.

Timothy sighed and held a hand out to Sheila. She reached up and took it and he levered her to her feet. "All right, then," he said, "let's begin checking the status of Avery's backups. See how much memory we are likely to lose when we do initialize."

There came a pounding on the door, and the guard let Stein and two medtechs into the AIC. Nodding to Timothy and his comptechs, they strode to the medical consoles.

A moment later there again came a pounding on the door. This time it was Greyson. He came with combands and gave one to Timothy and another to Stein. "Toni says to check in on channel four."

* * *

In the control center, David Cardington's comband blipped. "Chief, Charley here."

Cardington looked at Toni. "Go ahead, Charley."

"I'm down here with Michael Phelan. We found a body—Raymond Arquette—looks like he was electrocuted. And the turbine: it's shot all to hell."

Toni groaned and turned to a young lady at a console. "Tricia, take a medteam down to the generator. They've found a body." As the medtech called to a comrade, Toni stepped to Cardington. "What channel? I want to talk to Michael."

Cardington looked at his wrist and then said, "Channel one."

Toni thumbed the microswitch on her own comband. "Michael?"

A short pause, then, "Yes, Doctor Adkins," came his reply.

"What's the status of the generator?"

"The main turbine shaft seems welded to the bearings. And all generator coils are fused."

"What about the H2 supply?"

After a moment he replied, "I think it's all right. No leaks. The valves are free."

"How long to repair the turbine and generator?"

There was a pause, then Michael said, "I don't think it can be done, Doctor Adkins. I mean, this thing is really blasted. What we need is a complete replacement."

"Thank you, Michael. Come on back up. Adkins out." Tony clicked off her comband then growled, "Damn, damn, damn."

Mark Perry stepped to Toni. "What is it? What's it all mean?"

Before she could answer, her comband beeped.

Greyson looked at Timothy. "What's up?"

Timothy ran his hand through his hair. "Well, John, it appears that Avery is still running the game, the test, but none of the voice paths are working"—he cast a glance at the comm console—"and neither are the input compads, so we can't contact him. We haven't found any damage, but a vital chip or two could be fried. We won't know until we run a full diagnostic, though we won't have Avery to help us."

Greyson peered at the distant dark glass surrounding the AI. "Perhaps what we have is a child reading by flashlight beneath a blanket."

Timothy grinned, then frowned. "Even if that is the case, John, his programs should compel him to answer our calls."

Greyson shrugged.

Billy Clay stepped to Timothy's side. "Sorry, Doctor Rendell, but there's no sign of damage to the optics going in."

"Damn," muttered Timothy. He rubbed his eyes with the heels of his hands. Finally he said, "Help Sheila run diagnostics."

Sheila Baxter turned in her chair. "From what I can see, Doctor Rendell, Avery has a complete memory backup to the moment the lightning struck, but nothing after."

"Hmm, quite good," mused Timothy. "Can you read his current state? What are we going to lose when we reboot?"

Sheila turned back to the console, her fingers flying over the compad. Beside her, Billy, too, keyed in console commands on a separate pad.

"What th—?" Billy frowned. "Doctor Rendell, I don't know what I am looking at here."

Timothy stepped forward. A line of perplexity formed between his eyes. Suddenly he straightened up. "Henry, come here quick."

Stein, sitting at a distant console, glanced over at Timothy. "I'm busy," he barked, and turned back toward the charts crawling across his screen.

"Dammit, Henry, get your ass over here now! Stat!"

Stein glared at Timothy, then stood. "This had better be damned important," he growled, walking to Timothy's side.

On the holoscreen a complex spheroidal glitter flashed and sparkled. It was about the size of a cantaloupe. Regions fell dark and others lit up as gleaming fire shivered and shimmered across the surface, flashing from here to there like miniature lightning stroking across a glimmering net. Stein leaned forward and keyed the pad. A name appeared below the glitter: Caine Easley.

Now Timothy leaned forward and keyed the pad. A different spheroidal glitter appeared: Alice Maxon.

"Is it a neural map?" asked Timothy.

Stein shook his head.

"Then what is it?"

Stein took a deep breath. "It would seem to be a functioning mental pattern."

"Jesus," breathed Billy.

Toni thumbed her comband. "Adkins here."

"This is Tim. You'd better get down here right away."

"What is it, Timothy?"

"I'd rather not say. Just get here, and now."

Toni clicked off her comband and turned to Doctor Ramanni. "Take over here, Alya. I'll be back as soon as I can."

"I'm coming with you," said Mark Perry.

Wearily, Toni nodded, and together they started for the AIC.

"There they are," said Timothy. In the holo six sparkling spheroids seemed to float and glitter and flash. Under each was a name: Meredith Rodgers, Caine Easley, Alice Maxon, Eric Flannery, Hiroko Kikiro, and Arthur Coburn.

"There what are?" asked Mark Perry.

"The mental patterns of the alpha team," replied Stein, for once the habitual sneer missing from his voice.

Mark turned up his hands. "So . . . what does it mean?"

"It means," said Greyson, "that somehow Avery has subsumed their minds."

"What?"

"He has stolen their mentalities, Mark. Somehow, Avery has sucked their very souls right out of their bodies and has taken them into himself."

Mark jerked back in startlement then whipped about

and faced Toni. "Look, you've got to get Arthur out of there. Reboot or something."

"We can't reboot," said Timothy. "These—these mentalities are in volatile memory, and if we initialize then we quench the minds of the alpha team. No, we've got to find a way to get Avery to release them."

Toni glanced at the doomsday clock on the wall in the AIC, the numbers inexorably ticking down. "And we've got just over three hours to do so."

Timothy looked at her. "Three hours?"

Toni nodded. "The turbine and generator are totally ruined and we are running entirely on battery reserve." She turned to Mark Perry. "Where's your portable vidcom?"

"Why, I left it upstairs with Ramanni."

Toni took off running for the door.

In a small villa on twenty acres in the foothills east and north of Tucson, Kat Lawrence was awakened from a sound sleep by the ringing of her private line. She rolled onto her side and reached for the instrument. "This better be good," she growled into the blanked vidcom.

"Kat? This is Toni Adkins."

Kat sat up and clicked on the light, then shielded her eyes from the glare. Distant thunder rumbled.

"What is it, Toni?"

"Kat, I don't have time to explain it all, but lightning took out our power and fried the backup turbine generator. We're running on battery reserves and three hours is all we've got. I need you to get your bum to humping and get me a backup system here"—Kat could hear as Toni turned away and asked someone named Drew the make and model of the blown turbogen—"an Allen-Breech 100KW, H2 driven." Again she heard as Toni turned away and asked Drew how much power was needed. "The Allen-Breech is rated at one hundred kilowatts, and we've got to have fifty, sixty thousand watts minimum, more if you can get it. Look, Kat, I don't give a dump whether you have to beg, borrow, or steal a turbogen, just get it here. We've got the H2 to run it if that's the kind you get, but we've neither diesel nor petrol nor natural gas, so if you bring one of those, bring the fuel as well." As Kat swung her feet over the edge of the bed, she heard Toni take a deep breath then say, "And, Kat, this is critical; we've got six people who will be brain-dead in just over three hours unless we restore power."

27

"**I**'m going to need your help," Kane called, the big man kneeling next to Arton, the thief barely conscious and groaning.

Lyssa and Arik limped through the stench of the burnt skelga, a pall of smoke layering overhead in the curve of the hemispherical chamber. Kane stood and began stripping off his garments. "Bandages—we're going to need a lot this time," he said.

Lyssa opened the kit and began hauling out white cloth, while Arik gently started stripping Arton of his leathers so that Kane could see where the bandages were needed. As Arik raised the thief up to pull off his jacket, Arton fainted. In moments Kane was naked, and he turned to Lyssa. "Bind the worst of the wounds on my arms, Lyssa; I'll take care of the ones on my body and legs."

Swiftly the ranger obeyed while Kane peered down at the flesh-torn thief as Arik stripped away the rent leathers. "Arda, ripped from elbow to ankle," said Kane when Arton lay naked.

Arik stepped to unconscious Rith and began disrobing her.

Tying the last knot on a forearm bandage, "All done," said Lyssa, and moved back from Kane.

"Then strip," ordered Kane, as he began quickly binding the more grievous of his remaining wounds.

Then Kane knelt and examined Arton closely. "The

thigh wound is the worst," he muttered, and he tightly wrapped a cloth about his own left leg in a place identical to where the hole was ripped in Arton's thigh.

After another glance at Arton, Kane wrapped a bandage about his own right calf.

Kane wrapped cloth around his waist next, muttering, "That's the worst of them. The rest will have to wait."

By this time, Rith was naked, and as Kane stepped next to her, Arik stripped out of his own leathers and then helped Lyssa to move Arton next to Rith. Now Kane bound his own body in places identical to Rith's gaping tears—right hip, left forearm, left knee, left breast.

Then Kane turned to Lyssa.

"Hm," said the warrior-healer, "looks as if I've already covered the areas of your legs where the damage is most grave, but your right buttock is torn." Kane swathed cloth high about his own right leg and waist, wrapping it such that the right buttock was tightly bandaged.

Finally he turned to Arik. Incredibly, the flaxen-haired warrior suffered nothing but superficial wounds, all of which could wait.

As Kane sat down between Arton and Rith, he said to Arik and Lyssa, "Bandage whatever's left when I am done . . . and brew me some lyia tea. I'll need it."

Lyssa knelt next to Kane, and he laid hands on her and said, "Hold perfectly still." He paused an instant and frowned in concentration, then muttered something under his breath. His hands trembled slightly and a twinge of pain crossed his features, yet for long moments he neither flinched nor moved. At last he released her and allowed a groan to escape his lips as he shifted so that he wasn't sitting on his right buttock. And lo! Lyssa stood, the worst of her wounds utterly gone. Then Kane took a deep breath and laid one hand on Rith and the other on Arton, and again he concentrated . . . and muttered . . . and trembled . . . but held still . . . then swooned, falling back against the stone pillar as Rith and Arton opened their eyes. And slowly, slowly, the white bandages swathing Kane turned pink, then red, as new welling blood seeped through.

*   *   *

Kane sipped the lyia brew. "Where did you get the fire?" he whispered, then nodded weakly in understanding as Arik held up a lantern. Kane lay on a blanket from a bedroll, covered by another blanket. The remaining Black Foxes sat about in their torn leathers—all but Arton, who prowled the walls, his fingers brushing along the stone.

"How long was I out?" Kane whispered.

"A short while," replied Arik. "Just long enough for us to bandage the rest of our wounds and get dressed."

Kane sighed. "We took a lot of damage. It'll be a day or so before I recover from this."

"Arda, but I am not certain that I can take a full day of this stench," growled Lyssa, looking up at the haze overhead.

"It's diminishing," said Arton, pacing along the wall, running his fingers over the white granite. "I'm trying to find where the smoke is going. Perhaps there is a secret door. . . ."

Rith glanced at Arton, then turned to Lyssa. "I think if we smell it long enough we'll become accustomed to it."

Lyssa made a face. "Is that something to aspire to? Familiarity with the smell of burning skelga?"

Rith laughed and shook her head. "Better that, my dear, than the smell of them alive."

"Huah!" exclaimed Arton. "There is a faint sputtering here." He stood guardedly at the witchfire-warded archway, managing for the moment to control his fear of lightning and all things similar.

"Careful, Arton," warned Arik. The warrior glanced over at the corpse of the slain wizard. "Remember what Pon Barius said. That ward is deadly."

"And we are trapped within," muttered Arton. He wetted a finger and held it high, then down at floor level. "Hm, air currents. The smoke is drifting out into the corridor up high, and fresh air is coming in along the floor." He stepped back from the eerie glow.

Rith joined the thief and stood listening and observing, then she gestured at the drifting fumes overhead. "I think the sputtering is when some of this pall tries to flow through the ward." She glanced over her shoulder. "Let us see just how deadly this guardian is."

"What do you have in mind?"

Rith stepped to her pack and took up Ky's black main gauche, the weapon recovered from where it had skidded when the syldari had fallen unconscious. Rith squatted by a skelga corpse and used the ebony blade to hack off a finger. "Move over here," she bade Arton. When he was beside her, Rith cast the severed finger at the witchfire.

Zzzzt! In a flare of light, the finger vanished.

Wide-eyed, Arton looked at Rith. "Wah! Deadly is the defender of this chamber."

Rith nodded and looked about the hemispherical cell and then back at the witchfire ward. "And it has us trapped within."

Slowly Arton moved round the pillar, running his hands up and down every inch. Then he ran his fingers across the surface of the crystal coffer. Sighing and shaking his head, Arton stepped back. He stood in thought a moment, then moved forward and tried to heft the vault. "Oof! Blood and bones, but this thing must be made of solid silver! Arik, come help me with this. I need to set the chest aside so I can examine all of the top of the pillar to see if it holds the secret to our escape, though I doubt it does."

Together, grunting and straining, Arton and Arik just barely managed to lower the crystal vault to the white marble floor without dropping it. "Devils," grunted Arton, straightening and pressing his hands to the small of his back, "this was a job for you and Kane and not for this measly soul."

Arik looked down at the silver within the crystal. "Lord, it must mass three forty, three fifty pounds. How can such a small thing weigh so much?"

"Crystal itself has considerable heft," said Arton, "but silver is weightier still—cube for cube it masses four times as much. I would say most of the weight comes from the silver; it must be nearly solid through and through."

"Hm," mused Arik. "We only have Pon Barius's word that either of these things are actually chests. I mean, perhaps the crystal is a chest in that it contains the silver, but the silver itself, well, it just looks like a seamless block to me. Be that as it may, if it is a chest perhaps there's something inside that will help us . . . if you can get it open, that is."

Arton, now running his hands over the surface of the pillar, cast a sideways glance at Arik and muttered, "Ha! No need to worry about that. Slide it out of my way. When I'm finished here I'll take a look."

Grunting, struggling, Arik managed to slide the coffer a few feet outward as Arton moved round the column.

At last the thief said, "Nothing here," and then stepped to the crystal vault and knelt beside it.

"There are no handles, no hinges, no seams, no locks," said Arik, hunkering down, his gaze attempting to pierce the secret of the coffer. "How does it open?"

Arton glanced at the warrior and said, "I sense this is the way of it," and he carefully seized two of the diagonal corners at the top of the cube and with effort twisted and lifted. Off came the top, a large, thick pane of pure crystal. Setting the slab down, Arton then pressed his hands against one of the sides and pushed upward. Slowly it slid up, and when he could, Arton grasped the pane and pulled it entirely free and stacked it atop the first slab.

"Lord," breathed Arik, "it's like one of those puzzle boxes."

Arton grinned at him. "Not quite, my friend." The thief then removed the remaining sides, stacking them neatly onto the pile. He then carefully eyed the ornate silver block, itself a cube some three-quarters of a foot along each side, the silver sitting on crystal—the bottom of the coffer. Moving fully round, Arton examined the block without touching it, paying particular attention to the carvings and runes. Arik also looked, but as with the crystal vault, here, too, he could see no handles, hinges, seams, or locks.

Finally Arton said, "I see no traps." Then he ran his hands over the ornamented surface, feeling each carving, each rune. After a long while he muttered, "Seven of these need to be pressed in a particular sequence—some five thousand combinations altogether."

"Dretch, but that'll take forever!" declared Arik.

Arton smiled at the warrior. "Really?" He then turned to the chest and, straining a bit, opened its heavy lid along a seam that was heretofore absent.

Inside was a small, velvet-lined, empty silver box of a size to contain the red gem.

"Cruk!" sissed Arton. "This is utterly useless."

Scowling, Arton held up the recovered crossbow quarrel. "If I had only put this bolt through Horax instead of the skelga, we wouldn't be in this fix."

"Do not berate yourself," said Arik, speaking low so as not to waken Kane. "You were saving Pon Barius and could not have known then what hindsight now makes clear."

"But he's got Ky," growled Arton.

"And the silver dagger," added Lyssa.

"And he's left us trapped," muttered Rith, the bard nodding toward the witchfire.

"Even so," said Arik, "Arton is not at fault. Instead lay the blame where it belongs—at the feet of Horax."

They sat in silence for a moment, then Arik added, "Even if the ward were somehow negated, still there's the deadly maze beyond."

"Oh no, Arik, it's more than just the maze beyond," murmured Rith, gesturing at the blanket-wrapped remains of Pon Barius. "Remember, he said that *all* the wards would be reactivated when we left."

Arik cocked an eyebrow at the bard.

She gestured at the doorway. "Don't you see, Arik, *this* ward was reactivated when Horax took Ky hostage and escaped. If he went onward, then *all* the wards are now reactivated. And even if we do, by some miracle, break loose from this circular prison, we still must pass every one of the remaining deadly wards in order to win our freedom."

"Ah me, but you're right," said Arik with a sigh. He turned to Arton. "And there's no other way out?"

Arton turned up his hands. "If there is, I can't find it. I've examined everything—walls, floor, pedestal—and there's no hidden door, lever, or whatever. If there were, I'm certain I would have found it."

Lyssa looked about. "You haven't examined the high dome ceiling overhead, Arton."

"I can't reach that," growled Arton. "Besides, there just isn't the—the *feel* of a secret something or other that would let us out."

"The feel?" Lyssa cocked her head at the thief.

"I don't know how to explain it," replied Arton. "I've always had this, um, instinct, I suppose you would call it . . . or special talent—a sense for finding things hidden and opening things locked and other such, er, necessary activities of my trade. And believe me, my special talent tells me there is no way out"—he pointed—"but through that portal yon."

"Where lie four more lethal wards," said Rith.

Lyssa arched a brow at the bard.

Rith smiled. "Remember Pon Barius's words: the first and last of the seven are not deadly."

Lyssa nodded. "Ah, but those five in between . . ."

Kane unwrapped the bandages from his now healed wounds. As the last came off he closely examined his skin. "From the looks of it, we've been here a bit over a day."

"Seems more like a week to me," growled Arton, "trapped as we are."

Concurrence grumbled among the Foxes, but Arik held up a hand and said, "Be that as it may, now that Kane is awake let's hold a war council and see if we can figure a way out of this snare."

Kane nodded and got to his feet, saying, "All right, but first I have to . . ." He looked about the chamber, a slight frown on his features.

"The privy is one of our small cook pots. Over there," said Rith, pointing. "Throw the slops out the door; they'll not reach the other side. But take care—the door ward is deadly. Stand well back when you cast."

In moments, Kane returned to the circle.

As the big man slowly slipped into his leathers, Arik

said, "Let's review what we know for certain." He held up a hand and began ticking off the facts on his fingers.

"Pon Barius is dead.

"Ky is missing." At this, a look of rage flashed over Kane's face, quickly replaced by stoicism.

Arik continued: "Horax is gone.

"The silver dagger is gone.

"We are trapped.

"We have a couple days of food and water."

Arik glanced at Arton, then said, "Our best judgment is that the only way out is through that door."

He looked about. "Did I miss anything?"

Lyssa cleared her throat. "If all are reactivated, there are five deadly wards between here and freedom, each of which we must pass to escape."

Lyssa fell silent, but Rith added, "On the way in, Pon Barius declared that without his aid we would all die. I suppose if he were still alive, he would say the same on the way back out."

Arik nodded and then asked, "Anything else?"

Kane, now dressed, said, "Two petty things: first, you all yet have minor wounds, but those can wait until we win free; and second, if my guess about how long we have been in here is correct, then night has just fallen outside."

"Anything else?" asked Arik, looking from person to person. Shrugs and headshakes answered him. "Well then, does anyone have any suggestions as to just how we might escape this trap?"

For long moments they looked at one another without speaking.

Arik sighed. "All right, let's set that aside for a moment. Instead, given that we *do* win free, what's our next move?"

"Find Ky," gritted Kane. "And if that cur Horax has harmed her—" He smacked a fist into palm.

Agreement muttered round the circle.

"Likely he's holding her hostage in case we pursue," said Arik.

"Huah!" exclaimed Arton. "How can he do that? How can anyone hold a Shadowmaster hostage?"

Arik shrugged, but Rith said, "Drugs. He could keep

her drugged. She was unconscious when he took her, and so, if he keeps her that way, he keeps her captive."

"She might be loose by now," said Lyssa, "though if that were so, I would expect her to show up." At a puzzled look from Arton, Lyssa added, "If anywhere near, she could simply step through shadow to reach the hallway outside."

"We must consider the possibility that she is dead," said Arik.

"*Aaargh!*" shouted Kane, leaping to his feet and pacing like a caged beast. "Then we go after Horax and kill him."

Rith nodded. "We need to go after Horax regardless. He has the gem."

"If we can find him," said Arton.

"If it takes the rest of eternity, I'll find the bastard," rasped Kane, still pacing.

"Oh, I think I know where he is," said Rith. The others looked at her in surprise. "Don't you remember what Pon Barius shouted? 'Go back to your Drasp and squat in that swamp like the bog spider you are!' "

"That's right!" declared Lyssa. "I remember now. And the Drasp is just west of here, two hundred miles or so."

"But the Drasp is a great mire and filled with vile creatures," said Arik. "An enormous, perilous area to search."

"I don't care how big the Arda-damned place is," growled Kane, "nor how many monsters it holds. We've got to find Ky, even if it takes years."

"And the silver dagger," added Rith.

"Hold on a moment," said Lyssa. "I don't think it will be that difficult to locate Horax. You see, the bog spider spins a circular web and then sits at its very core. I suspect we'll find Horax's covert precisely at the center of the Drasp."

Arton stood and walked to the blanket-wrapped remains of Pon Barius and bowed. "Thank you, wizard, for telling us how to find your ancient foe. We can only hope that Ky is safe and sound so that we can rescue her when we come to Horax's lair." Arton then gestured toward the witchfire burning in the doorway. "I don't suppose you would tell us though just how to get past that ward. Well . . . I thought not."

* * *

While the other Foxes slept, Arton sat with his back to the pillar, the thief on watch. Over and again he turned the crossbow quarrel in his hand, berating himself for not having shot Horax. Finally he took up a cast-aside bandage and began polishing the silver tip of the bolt. As he did so, his eye strayed to the silver block, the chest now closed and still sitting on the slab of crystal. He then looked at the blanket-wrapped corpse of Pon Barius. "Should I put it back in its crystal cage?" he whispered. "Ah, but what for? I mean, you aren't here to lower it back into its pool of sto—"

Arton's words chopped off, and he looked at the white granite below him, at the crystal panes, at the silver chest, and finally at the warded doorway. He held up his quarrel and gazed at its tip and whispered, "Oh, Pon Barius, perhaps you *did* tell me how to get out the door. This calls for an experiment, then we shall see."

The thief rolled to his feet and stalked over to Arik. Touching the warrior on the shoulder, he said, "Wake up, glorious leader. I have a plan."

Arik, instantly awake, disentangled himself from Lyssa, the ranger waking as well. "A plan?" asked Arik.

"If it works, we may be able to get free," replied Arton. The thief stood and headed for the door.

"Careful," cried Lyssa.

At this call, Kane and Rith awakened, both rolling to their feet, weapons in hand.

"Don't worry," called back Arton, his voice raw with nerves. "I mean, what can it do but kill me?"

"What's going on?" demanded Rith.

"Arton has a plan," replied Arik, now following him to the doorway.

"Which is?"

"I don't know."

"Arton!" cried Rith.

"It's something Pon Barius said," he called over his shoulder as he squatted within easy arms' reach of the witchfire ward. In his right hand he held the quarrel. For long moments he merely looked, while the others gathered on either side. He glanced up at Kane. "I might need you," he said, then with trembling hands reached out with the quarrel.

No! Don't! Arton! cried several voices simultaneously.

But it was too late, for the quivering tip of the quarrel had already entered the witchfire.

Sparks flew, and the tang of lightning filled the air . . . but the quarrel did not vanish in a flare of light as did urine and feces and the remains of skelga. Arton looked up at the others, a tight grin forced on his face. Then he peered closely at the ward. "Look! See?"

All around the tip of the quarrel, tiny flashes sputtered. Arton jerked back but then reinserted the point, this time managing to hold it there.

"What? See what?" demanded Rith.

"There's a small area around the point where the ward doesn't touch," replied Arton. "It's the silver, you see. The witchfire ward cannot touch the silver quarrel point."

"Argh!" spat Kane. "And I suppose we're going to crawl through that minuscule hole? I mean, how is a silver crossbow bolt going to get us out of here?"

"Oh," replied Arton, withdrawing the quarrel and examining the tip, "*this* won't get us out"—he turned and pointed at the ornate chest—"but perhaps a two hundred and fifty pound block of silver will."

"Ready?"

All eyes swung to Arik, and one by one they nodded.

Kane squatted and placed his hands on the silver cube, ready to move it the last few inches into the witchfire wall.

"Wait a moment," said Arton nervously. "I'm not certain you should be touching it when you push it in."

"You were touching the quarrel," replied Kane.

"But not the silver of the tip," said Arton, "just the wood of the shaft."

"Well, I don't have a big piece of wood to push it with," responded Kane. "Hold it—there's my spear. I could push it with the butt of my spear."

Rith looked over her shoulder. "How about one of those crystal slabs instead? I mean, I wouldn't want you to break your spear; we'll need it when we get to Horax . . . *if* we get to Horax, that is."

Kane looked up at Arton. The thief shrugged and said, "Seven hells, Kane, none of us knows what we are doing. All we have are the words of a dead wizard: when I asked him about the crystal vault, he told me it was to keep the silver from coming into contact with the stone pool. He specifically said 'That wouldn't do, you know.' I think he meant if the silver touched it, it wouldn't allow the magic of the pool to work. But I don't know about witchfire. I mean, we're fooling with lightning here."

The big man glanced at Rith and then back at Arton. "All right. Let me try the crystal slab."

Arik fetched one of the panes from the pile and gave it to Kane who pressed it flat against the side of the silver block. "Ready?" He looked up at the others. "Then step back."

When they had moved to what he assumed was a safe distance, Kane pushed the block into the wall of witchfire—

—*Krack!* A bolt of lightning crackled across the doorway and seared the chamber with light and sound and fury.

"Waugh!" cried Kane, scrambling backward, the crystal slab crashing to the floor and shattering into myriad fragments. Arton, too, cried out in fear and backed away. Suddenly the chamber filled with the sound of a thousand enraged bees as the crystal fragments began to furiously shake and stutter on the floor, driven by an unseen force.

Arton pointed at the door and shouted, "Look, look! there's a—"

—*Krack!* Another bolt split the air of the chamber, this one leaping across the portal as well.

"—a hole in the witchfire!" yelped Arton.

And all the Foxes saw that the blue witchfire had withdrawn from the mass of silver, though the opening made was no more than a three-foot-high arched cleft in the ward—*Krack!*—a cleft across which lightning flared.

"Come on!" cried Arik, scooping up his pack. "Let's go. I'll try it first to see if it is safe."

But Arton had anticipated him. "No, Arik. It was, after all, my idea, and if anyone gets killed, it ought to be me."

Sweating with fear, the thief stepped to the portal . . . and crouched and waited as the others queued up behind, each with their gear in hand, Rith's including Ky's black blade, Kane's including the syldari's pack.

Again crystal hummed and bounced and danced on the floor.

—Krack!

Lightning flashed across the space, and the instant it vanished, Arton threw his gear through the slot, then dove after, shouting in terror and then in glee as he came up in the hallway.

"Wait for the next bolt," he called. "Right after the shards dance and sing."

One by one they dove through the opening: Rith, Lyssa, Kane, and finally Arik. The only one suffering damage was Kane, who burned a heel on one boot as the big man's foot grazed the witchfire.

And as Arik came through, Arton looked back at the corpse of Pon Barius. "Thank you, wizard," he whispered.

Grinning, they looked at one another, until Rith said, "Now it's the bedamned maze. Anyone got any ideas?"

They moved a small way down the corridor, then sat in council. In the near distance behind, lightning cracked now and again.

"All right," said Arik, "what do we know about the maze?"

"The walls move," said Kane, "and when they do, the only safe place is at a junction."

"The maze senses our fears," said Lyssa, "and presents them to us—sometimes as illusions, sometimes real."

"All ways are deadly but one," added Rith, "and that one an illusion."

"When an illusion is presented," said Arton, "that's when we have to run pell mell to the next junction and wait . . . wait for another illusion, and then race onward."

"And we only get one chance at each junction," said Rith, "which sometimes comes quickly and at other times after a long while."

Silence fell on the group . . . *krack!* flashed a bolt across the chamber door.

"Is that it?" asked Arik. "Nothing to add?"

Rith cleared her throat. "Pon Barius said we'd not survive without him to lead the way."

Arik held up a hand. "I think he would have said that about the door, too. So, let's not get discouraged." He turned to Lyssa. "Using your powers, can you find the path through?"

Lyssa turned her hands palms up. "I don't think so. I mean, I am able to find trails. But as to the maze, it alters from moment to moment, with all paths shifting. I can try, but I don't think it'll work. Besides, for all we know, *every* way may lead to the exit, except we'll all be killed on the way there."

"It would seem," said Rith, "that the real secret is in detecting reality from illusion . . . actually, the reverse. That is, when we sense an illusion, that's when we go."

"We can test them physically," said Arton. "Throw something at them." He held up a piton.

Rith nodded. "That might work, though I suspect it's too simple a plan. I would think the Circle of Wizards would have protected against that in some fashion."

"Perhaps the ceiling collapses if the maze detects something thrown," said Lyssa, glancing overhead.

Arik looked at her wide-eyed. "What an evil mind you have, my dear. —I love it."

"But you know," said Arton, "she just may be right."

Arik looked at the thief. "Arton, will your talents help us here?"

"I don't see how. No locks to pick. No chests to open. No hidden doors to find, or secret panels. Besides, on the way inward, I tried to guess which way. I couldn't do it." Arton sighed. "I think I'll be crazy by the time we get out of here."

Arik turned to the black bard. "Rith?"

She looked at the warrior. "Let me see. I can sing, dance, tell tales, play instruments, recite poems and odes, and create and control soun—" Rith's eyes flew wide. "Damn! That's it! Arton, you'll not be crazy when we pass through the maze, but I will certainly be bats."

* * *

Lantern lit, they followed the arched corridor back to the dead end, and only blank rock stood before them. From beyond they could now and then hear the rumble of stone grinding on stone.

Rith took a deep breath and said, "We'll do this just as did Pon Barius, only this time I'll be the guide. Stand ready and when I say move, *move!* Follow me swiftly, no matter what you see. We must all of us face our worst fears."

Suddenly, grinding, the stone before them slid to one side, revealing a corridor running to the right and one straight ahead. *"Move!"* snapped Rith. Quickly she stepped over the threshold to stand at the far side of the juncture, the other Foxes following on her heels.

Again all about them was the chaos of sound: massive hammering and horrendous clattering, the roar of water, the shriek of wind, and tumults unidentifiable.

And amid the uproar, the Foxes waited.

A moment later, stone ground against stone as the door behind slid closed, and walls moved. Three corridors were revealed: one sharply to the left with spikes protruding from the walls; one angling rightward, a pit in the floor; one sharply right, seemingly empty. Quickly, Rith faced each one, her mouth open wide as if in a silent scream, a hand cupped behind each ear. "Wait!" she cried. "These are all exactly as they seem."

Again there came grinding on grinding, and four ways opened: one filled with whooshing fire, one with a deep abyss yawning, one with roiling dark water, and the last empty. "Wait!" she cried again above the clatterous noise.

Once more the walls shifted, corridors disappearing, new ones appearing. Now the sides slowly ground toward one another in one corridor; a black void filled with whirling stars gaped in the second; a pellucid pool lay in the third, and great bubbles rose up from abyssal depths. *"Move!"* cried Rith, and she darted into the corridor where the side walls ground shut to crush intruders. Lyssa howled at the top of her lungs and dashed after Rith, only to pass the black bard on the way to the next junction, where she collapsed in sobbing terror. Arik hauled her to her feet when he arrived, for she had to be poised to run at a moment's notice, ready or not. He stood with his arms about her as she recovered.

Moments later the stone walls slid anew. And once again Rith waited, selecting none of the choices offered, her unheard batlike shrills of echolocation telling her that all were real and none an illusion. And she waited again on the next move, once more selecting none. As she waited she called out above the noise, "Stand ready." Again the walls slid and once more they waited. But on the next move it was Arik who shouted in fear as he waded waist-deep through quaking bog water swirling with unseen shapes, the warrior stabbing down into the liquid muck with his silver-plated falchion, and lo! each time he did so, the waters immediately about the blade narrowly disappeared, showing white granite below.

Rith fled screaming through bellowing billows of fire, and Kane ran with great long steps over a shrieking abyss, his own yowls joining those from below. His lips clamped shut, Arton ran in total silence through a corridor filled with sizzling continuous arcs of lightning crackling across the hallway. And when the thief came to the end of the passage, the Foxes had at last reached the far side of the dread-filled mutating maze.

As they stepped out into the final corridor and the stone slab ground shut across the way behind, laughing, Kane picked up Rith and swung her about. Her mastery of sound had gotten them safely through.

"Next is that hideous stench we've got to endure to reach the door," said Arik.

"I don't see how we can take even one step into the place where it lies," said Arton. "I took the full brunt of it and was unable to do anything but vomit."

Arik turned to Kane. "Is it disease or poison?"

"Perhaps both; perhaps neither," replied the big man. "Pon Barius called it the air of decay. But if you ask me, it may not even be air—nothing breathable, that is."

Rith cocked an eyebrow. "Are you saying that it's a gas?"

Kane shrugged.

"How will we get past it?" asked Lyssa. "I mean, we don't even know how far into this—this black hole it extends. It could be just in the corridor near the door, or it could reach far inward. But no matter its extent, short or long, still the question remains: how will we get past it?"

"Let's ride that horse after we capture it," replied Kane. "But let me say this: of the five of us, for this particular trap, I am probably best equipped to deal with it. So, I will take the lead and go slowly, while the rest of you hang back. When we come to it, I will see what I can discern. Agreed?"

Foxes looked at one another and nodded, and Arik lit a second lantern and handed it to Kane and grinned, saying, "After you, brave leader."

Through the mountain they wound, following the arched corridor, the way twisting and turning, rising and falling. Some twenty paces in the lead strode Kane, the big man moving through the darkness in a halo of lantern light, the remaining Foxes coming after, moving in a halo of their own. And all around, white granite frowned at these passersby, at these intruders bearing light through this dark domain.

Of a sudden, Kane gasped and reeled back, dropping his lantern. He turned and, retching, stumbled toward the others. He stopped a moment and knelt, then shakily stood and made his way slowly back to the waiting Foxes.

"Arda, but that was awful," said Kane, gasping and blowing to clear his nostrils of the putrescence. The big man put his back to one of the walls and slid down to a sitting position.

Lyssa handed him an uncorked waterskin. As he poured water into his mouth and gargled and swashed and spat, she asked, "Do you know what it is?"

Kane looked up at her. "A hideous sickness spell. I've heard of them, but never have I encountered one before."

"A junga would curse his enemies with such," said Rith.

Arton cocked his head. "Junga?"

"Shaman, witch doctor," replied Rith. "In my land of Imbia, we of the Udana name them jungas."

"And they cast sickness spells?" asked Arton. "Nice fellows. Remind me never to insult one."

Lyssa turned to Kane. "You're certain it's a spell and not a gas, not bad air?"

Kane nodded and pointed at the burning lantern lying in the hallway where he had dropped it. "If it were a gas or bad air, I think the lamp would die out. No, I am certain it's a spell. There really isn't any rotting flesh or pus-filled sores or gangrenous limbs or other such lying about in concealment somewhere. I believe the odor is part and parcel of the spell; seven hells, I think the spell is such that all beings will smell whatever is most foul to them."

Arik squatted beside Kane. "Can you do anything about it? Nullify the spell?"

Kane shook his head. "I can't banish it like Pon Barius did."

"Dretch!" spat Arton. "Trapped."

"Not necessarily," said Kane.

"Oh?" Arton squatted.

"Well, I've an idea," said Kane. "It's risky, but it's all I can think of."

"Risky?" Arik glanced at Kane. "How so?"

Kane looked at each of them. "Well, if it doesn't work, we'll all die. And even if it does work . . ." The warrior-healer did not finish the sentence.

After a moment, Arik spoke up: "Go on, Kane. What were you about to say?"

"Just that even if it does work, I may die. But listen, we'll all die regardless if we don't do something to get past this ward." Kane grinned at Arik. "Beside, I didn't tell you the best part."

"Best part?"

"Yeah. Just this: you'll all have to bodily carry me."

"Ready?" asked Arik. "Then by the corners lift!"

"Oof!" grunted Arton, grappling with one of Kane's legs. "Damn, but you're as heavy as that cube of silver."

Lyssa, on Kane's other leg, hissed her agreement through clenched teeth.

Rith, on one of Kane's arms, said, "You've got the easy parts. Arik and I have the worst of it."

"But we've got the climbing gear," retorted Arton.

"And the lantern," added Lyssa.

"Save your breath," said Arik on Kane's other arm. "Let's get to the door and let Arton deal with it."

Off down the hallway they started, lugging Kane, and just before they came to where the big man had dropped the lantern, Arik said, "Remember, keep flesh to flesh."

And at that moment, they entered the hideous stench.

Vomit geysered from Kane's mouth, rising into the air and falling back onto his face and arms and chest, falling onto Arik and Rith as well, but they did not stop in their rush through the arched corridor. Kane groaned in agony and there came the liquid dumping of his bowels, and he urinated in his leathers. He broke out in a profuse sweat, followed immediately by a burning dryness as greenish bile bubbled and frothed from his mouth and his hoarse retching resounded from the white walls.

And still the Foxes scurried onward, harshly gasping in the putrid air.

Hideous black pustules burst forth on Kane's skin, and veins on his forehead stood out like pulsating cords. Boils burst, yellowish goo splattering forth, oozing down and dripping, leaving a trail on the granite behind.

Ahead, the Foxes could see a bright sparkling.

"It's got to be the door!" cried Arik.

Black-streaked yellow mucus began pouring forth from Kane's nostrils.

Now they came to the dead end. Quartz chips flashed in white granite, brighter than the lantern light would allow, and reflected on the face of the stone was the glistening silhouette of the door.

"Arton, see what you can do! But don't turn loose of Kane's flesh!"

As Arton raised a hand to touch the glittering granite, Rith shouted, "Wait! Pon Barius said all the wards were deadly but the first, where we suffered despair, and the last, where the chest was hidden in stone. That means the door is lethal, too, if not opened exactly right!"

"Just what in seven hells do you suggest I do?" sissed Arton.

Kane began coughing blood, great red bubbles bursting and dribbling down his cheeks.

"Rith!" gasped Lyssa. "Pon Barius opened the sparkling door by singing a word. Can you do the same?"

"If she doesn't get it right, it may kill us all," cried Arton.

"It's the only plan we have," said Arik. "Rith?"

Kane's gums turned black and his teeth yellowed as Rith calmed herself then frowned in concentration.

She raised her face to the door and took a deep breath and then sang a single word—*"Kínÿîtñì!"*—her intonations exactly matching those of Pon Barius.

And as a pale liquid seeped from Kane's ears, the sparkles vanished and a dark line formed down the center, growing wider with each labored heartbeat as the portal split in two and doors wheeled inward to the sound of stone grinding on stone.

The moment the gap was wide enough, over the threshold they sprang, and they bore Kane out into the dawnlight and fled across the mountainside, while behind them the door ground shut once more.

Lyssa led them to a hollow beneath an overhang, where a small streamlet bubbled forth from the rocks. There they set up camp, and for the next three days they waited to see if Kane would live or die. They brewed the herbal drinks as he had instructed back when he revealed his plan, and fed them to him in small sips.

On the second day he awakened.

On the morning of the third day he said, "I'm as sick as any five people could be," which was no doubt true since he had used his powers to take on all of the illnesses of the other Foxes as well as his own as they had carried him through the stench and to the door.

It was on this third day, too, that Lyssa and Arik went back to the door, and Lyssa used her powers to see if she could track Horax. She found a trail leading to a wide ledge of stone, and thereon was the scat of some great creature. "A winged thing of some sort," said Lyssa, examining the droppings. "What kind, I cannot tell."

Arik looked over the edge. A drop of a mile fell sheer below. "Are you saying that Horax flew away on some great bird?"

"Bird, dragon, fell beast—I cannot say. Only that Horax came here bearing Ky and did not walk away."

When they reported their discovery, Kane ground his teeth in rage and his great hands clenched into white-knuckled fists. Rith looked at the big man and said, "We must hurry, for Horax has had many days to think on her doom . . . if she yet lives."

"Agreed," said Arton. "But remember, we've got two wards to get past."

"Perhaps not," replied Rith.

"Oh?"

"Well, since Horax did not climb down, perhaps they have not been reactivated."

On the morning of the fourth day they began their descent, Lyssa unerringly leading them back along the twisting way they had originally climbed.

They discovered that Rith had been right—the next ward had not yet been reactivated—as gangwise, they crossed it swiftly, and were down and away before its fatal spell could turn the stone "slick" and drain them of energy.

When they came to the ward of discouragement, they were still on the ledge when it reactivated. And they wept inconsolably, for they knew they would never reach the Drasp in time to rescue Ky . . . besides, she was probably already dead . . . and who were they to even think they could defeat Horax?

Soon they were beyond the reach of this ward, too, and Kane cursed the sky and stone and Horax and the Demon-Queen and the gnomen and the gem and whoever and whatever else he could put a name to as down the mountainside they went.

They reached their base camp by midafternoon. Swiftly Arton broke out some jerky and passed it around, for they had run out of food two days back. The horses were glad to see them, especially when they received a ration of grain. Even the mules seemed comforted by their return.

Pon Barius had said that they would not escape the wards of White Mountain without his aid. . . .

But even the wisest of mages are wrong now and again.

28

Toni Adkins turned to Doctor Meyer. "Drew, we've got to shut down all nonessential power—eliminate whatever we can that's tapped into the battery reserves. We've got to keep Avery running and the alpha team alive, but all else has got to go."

"There's not all that much we can eliminate, Toni," replied Meyer. He ran his hand over his balding pate. "The backup system has already cut loose all but the essential—" Toni's comband beeped.

She keyed a switch. "Yes."

"This is Tim. Is Drew there?"

"Yes, Timothy."

"I need him down here in the AIC."

Drew keyed his own comband. "What is it, Timothy?"

"I need you to help me rig an old-fashioned keyboard into Avery."

Drew Meyer glanced at Toni. "In a moment, Timothy. I've got to set a team to working on reducing battery drain. I'll be there in five."

"Right. Out."

Doctor Meyer keyed his comband off. "Toni, have someone find Hawkins—Al Hawkins. He's in the building somewhere and is the best powertech we've got. He'll know who to get and what can be shut down." Drew looked about the control room. "I would say you can turn off everything up here but the medconsoles and the rigs. We can monitor the rest from the AIC."

"What about the emergency lights?" asked Toni. "Should we shut most of them off?"

"No, no, Toni, they are running on batteries of their own . . . and before you ask, those batteries aren't of use in powering Avery or the alpha team—we'd have to rig a converter, and by that time it'd be too late." Drew started for the door. "I'll be in the AIC," he called over his shoulder.

Toni keyed her comband.

"Yes, Doctor Adkins," came the voice of David Cardington.

"Chief, find me Al Hawkins. He's a powertech and likely to be at the generator, or at the main bus, or at the reserve battery center. But no matter where he is, it's critical you find him straightaway."

Toni turned to Doctor Ramanni. "Alya, stay here in control. Shut down all but the medconsoles and the rigs. I'm going to the AIC."

Repeatedly, Mark Perry glanced back and forth between the screen and Doctor Stein, the lawyer waiting for someone to do something. Finally, unable to stand the silence, he barked, "Well don't just sit there, Stein, you've got to get Arthur out. Unplug him from the rig or something."

Without looking away from the silvery ovoids displayed on the holoscreen, Stein shook his head. "I'm not going to do *anything* until I know what's going on here."

"It's obvious," snapped Perry. "Avery has sucked their brains into himself. He's like some goddamned mind vampire."

"He didn't actually suck their 'brains' in," said Doctor Greyson. "But their minds, their spirits, their souls—those he did take."

Stein leaned back in his chair and steepled his fingers, his gaze locked on the screen. "Their mentalities? Perhaps. But their souls? Only if you believe in such things."

"I don't care what you call it," said Mark, "brains, mind, spirit, soul, mentality, heart, what-damned-ever, the fact is, it's all your fault that Arthur is trapped. You put him in there and you'll get him out or else."

Fury in his eye, Stein whirled on Mark Perry and shouted, "Enough, you ignorant fool! Get out of here! Now!"

"Wha—?" Perry's mouth fell open. Before he could muster a reply, there came a pounding on the door. As the guard levered it open to admit Drew Meyer, Greyson took Perry by the arm and steered him away from the console.

"Come on, Mark," said Greyson. "Let me treat you to a cup of coffee. The cafeteria urns ought to still be warm. We'll bring some back with us, too, for the others."

As they neared the door, again came a pounding. It was Toni Adkins. "Leave it open," she instructed the guard. "The last thing we need is another hindrance."

"Look, Drew," said Timothy, "I got this old keyboard from my office." He handed it to the physicist. "If we can rig it to plug into one of Avery's comports, I think we might be able to talk to him, communicate with him."

Drew Meyer turned the keyboard over and over. "Lord, Timothy, how old is this?"

"It came from my granddad's comp—a Xentium."

"Ancient history. ASCII?"

Timothy nodded.

Drew sighed. "Well, we'll need to rig an interface board we can jack straight in. Get me some techs and I'll tell them what we need."

"Sheila, Billy," called Timothy.

Mark and Greyson came bearing two trays loaded with hot cups of coffee and three thermos carafes. "It's not steaming," said Greyson as they passed the tray around, "but it's plenty warm. We brought enough for refills, too."

As Toni took a cup, she said, "How about the control room crew?"

Greyson grinned. "Alya already thought of it. A member of her crew was there when we arrived."

Mark Perry set one of the cups down beside Stein. The neurosurgeon looked at it and then at Perry, and without saying a word took it up and sipped, turning his attention back to the silvery ovoids on the holoscreen.

Shrugging, Perry stepped back and watched in silence as the six mental patterns turned in the holo. At his side Greyson watched as well. Finally the philosopher quietly said, "They were living in a Penfield vat, but now they exist in a Berkeley world."

"What?" asked Perry.

"A Penfield vat, a Berkeley world," repeated Greyson.

"What are they?"

"Don't you remember, Mark? We talked about brains in vats when we first met the alpha team."

Mark shrugged. "Frankly, John, most of the time I was bored to tears. Stuff like that has never interested me."

Greyson slowly shook his head and sighed. "Well, Mark, back in the nineteen thirties, Arthur Penfield said that if an evil genius put our brains in vats of nutrients and perfectly connected them by perfectly driven microelectrodes to a supercomputer which perfectly simulated our world and all of our perceptions, there would be no way we could tell it was not real."

"And you think that's what's going on now?" asked Perry.

"No, no, Mark, that's what *was* going on. The rigs took the place of the vats and Avery took the place of the supercomputer."

"And the evil genius, who is that?" asked Perry, casting a significant look at Doctor Stein.

Greyson grinned, but said, "Actually, it was René Descartes in the seventeenth century who first submitted that if an evil genius were controlling all of our perceptions, we would not know the difference. Descartes had no way of knowing how this could be done in a scientific sense, so he posited a magical being, a demon, an evil spirit, to do so. You see, back in those days the word 'genius' meant spirit, so he was postulating a demon when he called it an evil genius. It wasn't until the twentieth century that science discovered what neural stimulation could do, and it was then that Penfield proposed the brains-in-vats conundrum."

Mark Perry pointed at the silver ovoids. "And now you say that they no longer live in a Penfield vat but instead exist in a—a—"

"Now they exist in a Berkeley world," said Greyson.

Mark sipped his coffee. "Berkeley world?"

"George Berkeley proposed that there is no matter, only thought, and all of our minds are contained within a universal mind. We have free will, but everything we perceive is created by that universal mind."

Mark Perry's eyes narrowed. "This universal mind, would that be, uh, God?" Perry cast a glance heavenward.

"You could call it that, Mark. But if you object to the word God, then call it a Supreme Mind."

Again Mark Perry pointed at the holoscreen. "And just how does that apply here?"

"Why, don't you see? Their minds are contained within a universal mind, within Avery. All that they are and all that they see, hear, feel, taste, smell, and kinesthetically sense is nothing but pure thought. They have free will—or they are *supposed* to have it—and so they live in a Berkeley world."

Perry stroked his chin. "But if I understand you correctly, John, in Berkeley's world, everything is God-thought, whereas in this case everything is Averythought."

"Exactly so, my boy. Exactly so." Greyson looked at the holoscreen, then added, "But no matter which way they turn, they are trapped in one of Socrates' caverns."

They watched as Stein pressed buttons on the console pad, and graphs and charts crawled across the screen. But every time after glancing at the readouts Stein would come back to the glittering ovoids.

"Uh, Henry," said Greyson. "It occurs to me that the alpha team's perceptions must be sharper because they are no longer affected by an imperfect interface—the hemisynch helmet with its neural stimulus augmented by the suits and visual input. Everything they now apprehend is fed directly into the mind patterns."

Stein turned and stared at Greyson in astonishment and

said, "Very good, John. Very good. I hadn't thought of that. If these indeed are their mentalities, then what you say is no doubt true."

As Doctor Stein turned back to the holoscreen, Mark Perry shook Greyson's hand and silently sneered at the neurosurgeon.

Followed by Billy Clay and Sheila Baxter, Timothy and Drew came back into the AIC. All were dressed in bulky isolation suits, faceplates open. Sheila carried the antique keyboard, now flatwire cabled to an interface plug-in covered with hitemp-superconductor ICs, all wrapped in bubblepack. Timothy stepped to Toni Adkins. "We're going inside and jack this directly into one of Avery's comports. If it works, we'll have communication with him. I'll log in as superuser and see if Avery can restore the mentalities to the alpha team—slip their minds back into their bodies, that is."

"What if it doesn't work?" asked Toni.

"Then it's back to the old drawing screen," replied Timothy.

"How much drain will the nitrogen lock put on the battery?" She looked at the doomsday clock: 2:08:21 remained.

Timothy glanced toward Doctor Meyer. "Drew says some . . . but listen, Toni, this auxiliary interface board is the only thing I can think of that'll give us a chance of contacting Avery. We've got to try it even though the lock pumps'll pull considerable current."

Toni lowered her head and gazed at the floor and sighed. Then she looked up at Timothy. "Go. Go."

Timothy stepped to the dark, glass-walled cube, where the others stood by. Drew punched the button on the nitrogen lock, and they waited for the light to go green and the door to unlatch. Finally, with a clack the latch released, and the tiny flat screen glowed green.

They crowded into the small personnel lock and pulled the door shut, securing it. "Faceplates," said Timothy, and they locked their plaston shields down and thumbed on their rebreathers. Drew then jabbed the evacuation button, and as air was pumped out and nitrogen in, through the dark glass walls they could see Toni and the others watching.

Finally, the inner latch clacked and lighted green. As they clicked on their helmet lights, Billy opened the door, and into Avery's cold shadows they stepped.

29

The evening of the day they reached their base camp at the foot of White Mountain, Kane rid the Foxes of their lingering hurts, taking the remaining talon gouges and bite wounds unto himself. The next morning, as they set out, Kane was himself completely healed.

West they rode, toward the Drasp, intending to go to the center of that great swamp to find Horax's bolt hole, for Pon Barius had called him a bog spider and these dread spinners lair in the center of their poisonous webs. The Foxes intended to rescue Ky, if she yet lived, and to slay Horax regardless. Too, there was the gem to recover.

The Drasp itself lay just over two hundred miles to the west-southwest. A hundred miles wide and nearly two hundred long, it was an enormous morass, shaped like a wedge with its base across the northern extent and its point lying to the south. Fed by several rivers flowing out of the northern hills, the great bog squatted in the low-lands like some huge canker upon the face of the world. And it was said that creatures dire slithered and crawled within its bloated expanse.

And toward this dreadful mire the Foxes rode with vengeance in their hearts.

They were aiming for a point nearly halfway down the near edge. From there they would head northwesterly into the swamp; according to Lyssa's map, that would be the shortest route through the bog itself from edge to center—

some thirty to thirty-five miles all told. It would take them ten days or so to reach the marge of the quag, but they did not know how long it would take to get to the center from there.

"It all depends on what we encounter," said Lyssa. "If it's just a lot of wading, well then, three or four days at most. Of course if Horax's lair isn't where we are headed . . . it could take awhile."

"What if it's quicksand or some such?" asked Arton, not noting the shudder that ran over Arik's frame.

"Then we'll just have to go around," replied Lyssa.

"In my land of Imbia, we had swamps," said Rith. "Terrible places: blood-sucking leeches, clouds of insects, poisonous snakes, bottomless bogs, strangling vines, vapors to make you ill—only the junga ventured within to get his deadly wares."

Arton eyed Kane and said, "Looks like you might be busy."

The big man looked back at Arton. "If it's bug bites, I'll just let you itch."

They rode all that day and the next, three mules and two horses in tow, and on the third day it began to rain—a drenching cold downpour. Even so, onward they pushed, and they spent a miserable time in the saddle as well as in camp that night.

The next evening they came to a small village, where they were put up in a comfortable hayloft, for the hamlet had no inn. After a hearty dawnlight breakfast provided by the barn owner's wife, the Foxes replenished their supplies and pressed onward. This they did in spite of the warnings of the local peasants concerning the deadly Drasp, though when pressed for hard, cold facts, all the villagers told was but rumor.

That night they camped by a small mere, and Arton managed to gig several frogs. As he stirred a frogleg stew, he paused and fixed his gaze upon Rith. "What did he mean?"

"What did who mean?"

"Pon Barius."

"About what?"

"When he said it was turtles all the way down."

Rith broke out laughing.

Arton began stirring the stew again. "I don't see what's so funny."

"I'm just surprised, that's all," replied the black bard.

"Surprised?"

"That you, Arton, sophisticated courtier and King's Thief have never heard the turtles tale."

Arton stirred a bit more. "Well?"

A smile played about the corners of Rith's mouth. "Well what?"

"Well, are you going to tell me the bloody thing or not?"

Again Rith laughed, and as Arton started to make some retort, she held out her hand to stop the flow of his words before they could begin.

"It seems there was a sailor in a dockside tavern in the city of Daloon holding forth on the shape of the world. ' 'Tis a sphere,' he said, 'round as a ball. I know, for I've sailed round it twice.'

"But among his listeners was an old widow woman who banged her cane on her table, rattling the trenchers fair. 'Nonsense!' she shouted, 'and you are a damn fool for believing such to be so.'

"The sailor lad turned to her and asked, 'If not a globe, dear mother, then what?'

" ' 'Tis flat,' she cried, 'flat as a plate, as any fool can plainly see. And carried on the backs of four great elephants, one at each corner. The elephants themselves stand on the shell of an enormous great turtle, so there!'

" 'Ha!' crowed the sailor, 'if that be so, then pray tell, what does the turtle stand upon?'

" 'Why, on the back of another great turtle,' she answered.

" 'Aha, madam!' gloated the sailor as if he had trapped her. 'And just what does *that* turtle stand upon?'

" 'What a damn fool question,' replied the woman, 'for as anyone with a lick of sense can see, it's turtles all the way down.' "

Rith broke into gales of laughter, but to her amazement no one else did. She looked about from one Fox to another,

her gaze finally coming to rest on Arton. "What?" she asked.

"The sailor was a fool," said Arton.

"Fool?"

Arton snorted. "To believe such nonsense. A sphere, indeed."

"I don't think so, Arton," replied Rith. "When Alar and I sailed over the world, he told me it was round, a globe."

"You mean, like a ball?"

"Yes, like a ball. A great big one, but a ball nevertheless."

"Well if that's so, why doesn't everything on the bottom fall off? I mean, it should be like that trap we almost fell victim to—gradually curving downward till you slip and slide to your doom. But look around you"—Arton swept a hand in a wide arc—"it's flat. And no matter how far we've traveled, it has remained flat. Other than hills and valleys, I've *never* seen any downcurving of the land. So if it *is* a ball, then it has to be, um, enormous, so enormous that everything at hand looks flat; and we have to be near the top, where we won't fall . . . if it's a ball, that is. And so I ask you again: if it is a ball, why doesn't everything on the bottom fall off?"

Rith turned up her hands and shrugged. "Arda may know, but I certainly do not."

Kane shuddered. "It would be hideous—pitching off the world—like plunging into a bottomless pit. Falling forever."

Arik gazed at the stars overhead. "If the world *is* a big sphere and if things on the bottom do not fall off, then I think Rith is right: it's Arda's doing. Magic, I suppose. God magic."

"Magic or not," said Lyssa, eyeing the bubbling stew, "let's eat."

Over the next three days the weather held, and southwesterly they rode through sunshine across rolling grassland. But on the morning of the day after, they were awakened by a light patter of rain—a steady drizzle which lasted throughout the day and well into the night.

The following day, the tenth since setting out from

White Mountain, a chill dampness clasped the down-sloping earth and grey skies rode overhead. Late in the afternoon they came across a pair of wagon ruts, running up from the southeast and curving west, and these they followed down the tilt of the canting land as night drew upon them.

And as darkness fell, a chill fog rose up to cover the world; they could see but paces ahead.

"We must be near the Drasp," said Lyssa, eyeing the mist all about.

"Most likely," said Arik, lighting a lantern, its illumination swallowed up by the mist.

Foxes mumbled their agreement.

"Let us hope these ruts lead to good camping grounds," growled Kane. "I'm hungry."

By the light of the lantern down the land they rode, following the wagon track. Finally Lyssa said, "I smell water."

"The fog?" asked Arton.

"No, more like . . . a river . . . or bog."

"The Drasp," hissed Rith.

"Hold up," said Arik, reining in his steed, the mule and horse on the tethers behind stopping as well. Arik dismounted.

Foxes ringed round their leader.

Arik squatted and touched one of the ruts. "It occurs to me that this track might be where Horax's wagons run, those which bring supplies to his hold."

"If so," said Lyssa, "then it's been awhile since he's used it. I mean, these wheel marks are months old."

"Nevertheless," said Arik, "if it is a road, it may lead all the way to his . . . dwelling."

"Then it may be warded," rumbled Kane. "The track, I mean. Guards or some such. We wouldn't want to tip our hand."

"A road through a swamp like the Drasp seems unlikely," said Rith.

Arton looked at the bard, his eyes questioning.

"If Lyssa's map is accurate," said Rith, "then it's thirty, thirty-five miles to the center. That seems a long way to build a road through a bog like the Drasp."

"Oh," said the thief quietly. "I see what you mean."

"Even so," said Arik, "a road is a remote possibility."

"More likely they use boats or rafts," said Kane.

"Or large flying things," said Lyssa, shuddering at the thought.

"Regardless," said Arik, "let us go forward with caution, for Kane could be right: the way might be warded ahead."

And so, forward they went afoot, leading the horses and mules, Lyssa out front, her lantern lit but with its hood barely cracked, a thin beam of light illuminating the track.

And as they pressed forward, radiant Orbis arose, unseen above the cloaking fog yet shining its light down into the mist and spreading an eerie luminance throughout. And through this pale, pale glow, forward went the Foxes.

Of a sudden Lyssa stopped. Cocking her head, she listened, then turned and made her way back to the others. "I thought I heard voices."

"Distant or near?" asked Arik.

"Distant, I think. It's difficult to tell in this fog."

Arik turned to Rith. "You have the best ears of us all. Go forward and listen and tell us what you hear. I'll hold your steed."

"I'm going with her," said Lyssa, handing her reins to Arton.

Into the fog crept the two, disappearing in the wan glow as the others waited, their weapons in hand. Moments dragged by and moments more, stretching into unbearably long intervals. But at last Rith and Lyssa came back through the luminous mist.

"There's a river and a dock," said Lyssa. "It appears to be a landing for a pull-rope ferry."

Arik looked at Rith. "Voices?"

"Coming from the other side," she said. "Sounds like several men. Arguing mostly. A hundred or so yards away."

Arik raised an eyebrow. "The ferry crew?"

"Mostly likely," answered Lyssa.

"Let's go take a look," rumbled Kane.

It was thus that they came to the river, the wheel ruts

leading down to a dock jutting out into the water flowing
sluggishly past. Planted in the ground of the riverbank
stood a heavy pole on which was mounted a bell barely
seen in the glowing mist above, its pull-cord dangling
wetly down. Tied to the pole was a thick rope, this one
running out low across the water to disappear into the fog.

"Lyssa's right," grunted Kane. "It's a pull-rope ferry."

From the opposite side came a gabble of voices, some
cheering, others shouting in anger.

"Sounds like more than a handful to me," muttered
Arik.

Rith nodded. "Me, too. Maybe twenty or so."

"In any event we've got to cross this river," said Lyssa.
"It would be nice if we didn't have to swim."

"You mean, use the ferry," said Arik.

Lyssa shrugged.

"We could ring the bell for service," said Arton, "but I
think we'd better find out first just what lies across the
way."

"What do you propose?" asked Arik.

Arton pointed at the rope. "I'll go over and see what's
what."

Arik looked round at the others. Finding no objection in
any face, he turned to Arton and nodded.

Swiftly Arton shinnied up the bell pole, and when he
was above the ferry pull-rope, he twisted about and carefully placed one foot then the other upon the heavy line.
Then along the wet rope he quickly stepped, his arms held
outward for balance. Foxes followed alongside him and
out onto the dock until they could go no farther. But Arton went onward above the river . . . and he disappeared
into the gleaming fog.

Again long moments passed slowly as the Foxes
waited. And across the water came drifting voices, catcalls and snarls, shouts of glee, yells of anger. And a soft
splash.

"Dretch!" hissed Kane. "He's fallen off."

Lyssa looked at Arik then at the near riverbank. "Shall I
go downstream? See if I can find him when he swims
ashore?"

Arik shook his head. "If he's fallen, then he knows

where we are and will find us easier than we could find him. Besides, he may swim to the other side and come back along the rope."

And so they waited, and together the river and night eked past.

There came another quiet splash.

"Cruk! He fell in again," growled Kane.

"Perhaps," said Rith, "though this one sounded to me much larger and farther away."

And time dragged by . . .

. . . and by.

"Look!" hissed Rith, pointing at the pull-rope.

In the eerie glow they could see the rope tightening and then slackening . . . tightening and slackening . . . tightening and slackening . . .

"Shh!" sissed Rith. "Listen."

There came a purling sound from midstream.

"Someone comes on the ferry," hissed Kane, bringing his spear to guard.

"Back to the shore," whispered Arik, and the Foxes scurried from the dock and took stance on the bank behind.

Looming darkly, slowly came the ferry through the mist, and finally with a soft *thnk* fetched up alongside the dock. A single figure got off.

"Psst! Psst!" it hissed. "Where in seven hells is everyone?"

It was Arton.

"There's thirty or so of them," said the thief, panting and weary and dripping wet. "Strange creatures, half man, half . . . something else—long, dangling, hairy arms, outjutting jaws, low sloping foreheads—twisted things of Horax's doings, no doubt. One less now—I killed the ferry guard. His ugly corpse is floating downriver. He was wearing Horax's sigil: the red crescent bloodmoons.

"The others are in a large barracks, having some kind of contest. I say this is the perfect time to slip across the river, while their attention is elsewhere."

"You mean to ride right past their billet?" asked Lyssa.

"It's risky, but what else can we do?" asked the thief,

turning and appealing to the others. "Does anyone have a better plan?"

Arik glanced at the ferry rope. "I may have."

After securing the pull-rope to one of the guide stanchions, they loaded the horses and mules onto the barge. Then Kane worried loose the knot of ferry line from the anchoring bell pole and ran down the dock and leaped on board with the others. They hauled the ferry away from the landing, then let it drift downriver. And secured by the rope anchored to the opposite shore, like a great pendulum the boat swung across the sluggish stream to fetch up against the far bank . . . a hundred yards south of the barracks, the full length of the ferry rope.

Swiftly they offloaded the horses and mules, then untied the line from the stanchion to let the barge float away downstream and disappear into the fog.

Arton chortled. "Now they'll simply think that the rope came loose and the ferry drifted off."

Kane stepped across the squishy ground, his tracks behind filling in. "Even if they suspect otherwise, they'll never trail us through this muck."

"This is no time to stand around bragging," hissed Arik. "Mount up, Foxes. Lyssa, lead the way."

Into the great morass they rode, Lyssa's unerring sense of direction guiding them on a northwesterly track, toward the heart of the Drasp and Horax's lair, or so they hoped.

A long while they rode, picking their way through the swamp in the dim glow of the fog, backtracking now and again to pass around some quagmire or deep pool. And all around them they could hear slitherings and ploppings and hissings in the night, and now and again a far-off bellowing beast. And in the remote distance behind there came the faint blat of a horn. "They've found that their ferry is missing," said Rith, and Arton laughed in glee.

Now the horses rode across hummocks; now through water; now through sawgrass slicing at these intruders; now among black cypress twisting up out from the muck.

Finally on a spot of high ground they stopped to rest.

Dismounting, they fed the horses and mules some grain and took jerky for themselves.

As she chewed, Rith turned to Arton. "You know, my dear thief, that was quite a feat you pulled back there. But let me ask you: we heard two splashes, did you fall twice from the rope?"

"I didn't fall even once," protested Arton. "But the rope, well, it dipped down into the water in the middle, and I had to swim a bit—actually, I simply pulled myself through the water using the rope. When it came back up out of the river, I went hand over hand the rest of the way.

"The second splash you heard was the body of the ferry guard being lowered into the water. He was too heavy and I lost my grip and he fell the last few feet."

Rith smiled. "Ah, laddie buck, you're going to need to be more cautious than that if you have to steal the gem back from Horax . . . as slippery as Jaytar was when she took the stone from the DemonQueen."

"Though I don't have a horse woven of moonbeams, I will indeed steal the gem, should it come to that."

"If it should come to anything," growled Kane, "we'll slit Horax's throat and simply take the gem from his dead hand."

"I think we'll find Horax well guarded," said Arik. "Cunning and stealth and guile will be what's needed, just as it was back there." He jabbed a thumb over his shoulder, toward the far ferry dock.

"Ha!" crowed Arton. "We slipped past them all. Past all of Horax's warders."

But even as he said it, Rith held up a hand for silence, and they heard something vast and sinister moving toward them through the dank glowing clutch of the Drasp.

30

Timothy Rendell and Drew Meyer, along with two comptechs—Sheila Baxter and Billy Clay—stepped into the nitrogen chill of Avery's "inner sanctum"—or so it was called by all the techs on the AIVR project. Above the sound of their own rebreathers, they could hear the soft susurration of Avery's fans, cycling the cool nitrogen throughout circuit packs laden with hitemp-superconductor ICs. As always, because the nitrogen lock had been used, a faint foglike mist filled the room, and additional blowers kicked in to cycle the atmosphere through the dehumidifiers.

Avery himself filled up nearly the whole of the glass-walled chamber, looming like some great shadowy monolith squatting in a dark crystal cube.

Moving on a low-set catwalk just above fiberoptic cables, Timothy strode toward the back of the room, where panel access to Avery's comm circuits was located. Behind him came the others, the beams of their helmet lamps cutting through the cold nitrogen mist, four soft halos blooming. Timothy perceived a faint thrumming, though Avery's superconducting chips themselves were silent. Instead it came from Avery's fans, running slightly asynchronously, the out-of-phase component producing a low-frequency beat. Even so, Timothy thought of it as the sound of Avery's heart.

As they reached the area of the comm circuits, Timothy

turned to the others. "Look, before we try this, I want to examine the optics coming in. If they are damaged, then a simple replacement should get us back in contact with Avery."

"Right," declared Billy, and he stooped down to lever up a section of the catwalk, while Timothy and Drew unlatched one of Avery's rear panels. Sheila stepped back and set the bubblepack-wrapped keyboard and plug-in well out of the way, then moved in to help Billy.

Mark Perry looked at the holo and shook his head. "God, I find it hard to believe that these glittering patterns are the souls of people, the souls of the alpha team."

"Nevertheless," said John Greyson, "I believe that's what they are."

Doctor Henry Stein, sitting at the console, snorted. "I think not, John. That these might be their mental patterns, I will concede. But their souls? Bah!"

Greyson turned to Perry and sighed, explaining, "Henry is a physicalist, whereas I am a dualist."

"Physicalist?"

"Yes. You see, like many before him he believes that consciousness, identity, and free will are nothing more than the behavior of a vast assembly of nerve cells. In contrast, I believe in the ghost in the machine."

"Ghost?"

"Your identity, your spirit, your soul—that's the ghost."

"And the machine?"

"The brain, Mark. The brain is the machine. The body, too, but mainly the brain."

"Oh." Mark pondered a moment. "What about Avery? Does he have a ghost in his machine?"

Greyson shook his head. "We think not."

Mark Perry raised an eyebrow.

Greyson took off his half glasses. "Look, Mark, if we replicate Avery exactly—his physical being, that is—and then backload the second Avery—call it Avery Two— backload its mutable logic and memory modules with precisely the same programs and information and memories from Avery One's physical media, we couldn't tell them apart. That is, at the moment they were booted up together, they would both be intelligences with identical consciousnesses and identities and free wills. As to which was which we could not say. Hence, because we believe we can reproduce Avery exactly by duplicating his physicality, then we must conclude that for him the physicalists are correct. Therefore, we believe that Avery does not have a ghost in his machine.

"But now let us look at mankind: if there is *not* a ghost in the machine, and if we physically replicate a particular human, down to the very chemical signatures in each of his billions of engrams, then we should once again have a pair of duplicates we cannot tell apart."

"You mean like identical twins, right?"

"No, no, Mark. Identical twins are not exactly alike: their biological makeup is only identical within the limits of chaos—chaos theory, that is. They also have different experiences right from birth. Instead, we are talking of an *exact* copy, more like a clone, but a very specialized clone at that, for the memories themselves are precisely the same."

"Oh, I see. But this—this duplication only works if there is no ghost in the machine?"

"Right. You see, if there *is* a ghost in the machine, then we cannot generate a soul simply by replicating the physicality of a man or woman. We'd have the machine but not the ghost."

Mark took a deep breath. "You mean we'd've created a human without a soul, right?"

Greyson nodded. "If you could even call it a human."

Perry rubbed his jaw. "Would it have, say, free will?"

Greyson shrugged.

"Of course it would," snapped Stein as he rotated his chair to face them. "Look, everyone knows that a primary seat of so-called free will is in the anterior cingulate sulcus. When that area is damaged—ha!—no volitional activity occurs; a person cannot make choices at all. But given a brain that is whole, free will is a natural outcome."

Stein tapped a finger to his temple. "No matter what idiocy John spouts, injuries, strokes, diseases—such as when

Alzheimer's is left untreated—they all demonstrate that if you damage the brain you damage the mind, hence mind does not exist independent of the brain. As to all this other claptrap of souls and spirits, of out-of-body experiences, and other such stupidities, only ignorant fools believe in such superstitious mumbo jumbo. Listen, it's simple: humans are driven by neural activity and not by some hypothetical ghost haunting the human machine. And that's that." Stein turned to view the holo again, but immediately rotated back round and fixed Greyson with a stare.

"Let me ask you this, John: would you say that the brain is the seat of consciousness, of identity, indeed of the so-called ghost in the machine?"

Greyson paused, then said, "Yes, Henry. I would say that they reside in the brain."

"Then, John, would you say that all creatures with brains have consciousnesses, identities, ghosts in their machines?"

Again Greyson paused, knowing now where Stein's questions were leading. Nevertheless he replied, "Yes, Henry, I do so believe, although others will dispute it."

"Consider this, then: a human being has tens of billions of neurons, and you claim a ghost in the machine. If humans are not the only animals with ghosts in their machines, then let us look at, say, chimpanzees, since genetically they have much in common with mankind. However, their brains consist of fewer neurons; does this mean they have lesser ghosts? Now consider a chicken with even fewer neurons; is there an even lesser ghost in its machine? How about a creature with, say, only a thousand neurons, or a hundred, or ten, or just one; what about the ghosts in their machines? Does a flatworm have but a minuscule soul? Consider your answers well, for if a creature with but one neuron has no soul, then neither I claim does man. —Pah! I claim it regardless."

Once again Stein rotated toward the holodisplay.

Mark Perry arched an eyebrow at the philosopher.

Greyson shrugged. "What Henry says about damage to the brain damaging the capacity of the mind to fully function—it's true. But that doesn't mean that the spirit, the soul, is damaged. Think of the soul as a person inside the control center of a complex machine. Certainly if one part of the control center breaks down, then the machine can no longer function as it once did. But that doesn't mean the soul, the spirit, is damaged . . . only part of the machine."

Mark Perry's brow furrowed, and he gazed at the floor, slowly shaking his head.

"Look," said Greyson, "in metaphysics we have no absolute way of examining that which we call reality and undeniably proving what it is and how it came to be—or if there *is* incontrovertible proof of a particular metaphysical view, we have yet to discover a way to scientifically demonstrate it. Hence, as far as dualism versus physicalism is concerned, for now I can only tell you what I believe in and my reasons why, and Henry can only do the same. Perhaps there is no ghost in the machine; perhaps there is. Perhaps the size of a soul depends on the number of neurons in the brain; perhaps it does not. Perhaps only mankind has a soul; perhaps all animals do; perhaps some do and some don't; perhaps none does. Perhaps someday we'll know the truth; perhaps we never will. Perhaps—"

"Perhaps this is all a lot of baloney," interjected Perry, looking up. "But tell me this"—he pointed at the holoscreen—"if those are not the souls of the members of the alpha team, then just what are they? Some kind of ersatz duplicates?"

Henry Stein spun round and looked at Mark Perry, the neurosurgeon's mouth agape.

As additional staff trickled in from their homes, answering the "Greentree" recall, Toni Adkins looked at the diminishing time on the doomsday clock: 1:45:32 . . . 31 . . . 30 . . . 29 . . .

Drew glanced at Timothy. "They look all right to me. No damage whatsoever."

Timothy nodded his agreement, then called, "Find anything, Billy, Sheila?"

Lying on their stomachs and peering down through the

open section of the catwalk, both comptechs looked up from the fiberoptic cables below. "Nothing," said Sheila.

"Me, too," said Billy, clambering to his feet.

Timothy shook his head. "Damn. Then there's nothing for it but to try the kludge. Sheila, would you bring it here? Billy, while she gets the plug-in, let's put the catwalk back together."

As Sheila rolled to her feet and stepped toward the bubblewrapped lash-up, Timothy and Billy slid the walkway section back into place in the support frame.

Sheila removed the plastic wrap and unrolled the flatwire cable and handed the plug-in to Timothy while keeping the keyboard.

By this time, Drew had opened another panel to the comm circuits. He pointed to one of the multipin sockets, illuminating it with his helmet light. "Jack three, Timothy. It's past all the fiberoptics and straight into Avery's comprehension circuits."

Timothy looked at the others and took a deep breath, then expelled it. "Wish us luck."

"Break a leg," said Sheila, and grinned.

Timothy eased the auxiliary interface board into the guides, then pressed it home, its gold-plated pins sliding readily into the mating receptacle slots.

Timothy stepped back. "There, that ought to—"

Zzzzt . . . ! With a shower of sparks every chip on the board seemed to explode simultaneously.

Stein looked at Mark Perry in wonderment. "Out of the mouths of ignorant fools—"

"Doctor Stein! Doctor Stein!" came Alya Ramanni's frantic voice through the comband.

"I'm busy; what is it?" Stein replied.

"Get up here, stat! We've got a medical emergency on our hands!"

31

"**S**sst, what is it?" breathed Arton, shuttering the lantern as all the Foxes peered outward through the luminous mist.

Again there sounded the heavy swash of *something* moving slowly, massively through the dank environs of the fog-shrouded Drasp.

On the hillock the horses and mules shied back.

"It can't be good, no matter what it is," murmured Lyssa.

Blades were drawn, Arton cocked his crossbow, and Kane took up his spear.

"Perhaps it's pursuit by those creatures of Horax that Arton saw back at the ferry," hissed Rith.

"I think not," whispered Arik. "Even though it's been awhile since we heard their bugle, I don't believe they've had time to catch up to us, given that they have a way of tracking us at all."

"Nevertheless," growled Kane, "it still could be one of Horax's creatures—something he's set to roaming the Drasp to waylay intruders."

"Shall we ride?" muttered Arton. "It seems to me—"

"Look!" sissed Lyssa, pointing. "A light."

Through the glowing vapor, illumed by Orbis above, there shone a brighter patch, bobbing up and down as if someone bearing a lantern came.

"Looks like a will-o'-the-wisp," whispered Rith, "bouncing about as it does."

"A swamp lure?" snorted Arton. "Well, this is the place for one, if ever there was."

"We called them corpse candles where I come from," breathed Kane. "Nothing to mess with, you know. They'll lead you to your death by drowning."

"Ssst!" hissed Lyssa, pointing slightly to the right. "Another one."

"And two more," added Arik, his finger stabbing left and left, "there and there."

Toward the hillock the lights bobbed in the glowing mist, four soft halos blooming.

And still there sounded a heavy swash of something immense stirring through swamp water, and the horses and mules skitted and shied and stamped in fright.

"Whatever it is, I think we'd better ride," said Arik.

Swiftly the Foxes caught up the animals and mounted. Lyssa in the lead spurred down and away, Rith immediately after. As Arton started forward, a great billow of water rolled forth as something monstrous down in the swamp surged to the hillock's base. Arton's horse reared up and back and fell, the thief leaping clear at the last moment.

"To me!" cried Arik, leaning down and hooking out an arm as he galloped toward the unhorsed man; Arton reached out and snagged it to swing up behind the warrior. But at that very instant a huge, hideous tentacle with a glowing ball of light on its tip lashed out from the fog and snared Arton by a leg, wrenching him free from Arik's grasp.

Down the hillock Arton was hauled, dragged on his back toward the churning water, the thief shrieking and flailing and trying desperately to reach one of the long-knives stashed in his boot.

Hearing his cries, both Lyssa and Rith wheeled about and spurred cross-slope, while Arik leapt from his horse and ran toward Arton, the warrior drawing his silvered falchion as he scrambled down the hill.

Nearly at water's brink, Arton managed to free a long-knife, and he slashed its keen edge into the hideous arm. The tentacle whipped free, and in rage the monstrous creature lashed at the water. Arton scrambled to his feet and turned to flee, but another dreadful tentacle—its light pulsing red—whipped round his waist and raised him up into the air and smashed him to the ground, stunning him, and his blade was lost to his grasp.

Arik scurried to the water's edge, Rith and Lyssa now afoot right behind, but just as they arrived a second massive lighted tentacle lashed round Arton's waist and together they whipped him up into the glowing mist and wrenched him in two, ripping him asunder, viscera and blood and intestines flying wide. A monstrous mouth opened in the water below, but in that very moment—

"*Yaaaahhh . . . !*" Kane came flying through the air to land feetfirst upon the unseen creature's bulk, and with a reverse two-handed grip and all his might he drove his spear downward, the silver point of the lance stabbing through water and hide and cartilage to pierce deeply into the monster's brain.

Zzzzt . . . ! With a shower of sparks every light on the tips of the tentacles seemed to explode simultaneously, and the monstrous arms fell limp, Arton's remains falling, his pelvis and legs splashing down in water, his gutted torso landing at Lyssa's feet, his dead eyes wide in terror.

32

"**W**hat th—?" Timothy Rendell jerked back as ICs popped and sizzled, sparks flying. "Damn!" Quickly he pulled the smoking interface board from the socket. Turning to Drew Meyer, he held out the smoldering plug-in. "Drew, what could cause—?"

"I don't know," said Meyer. "Perhaps a power surge."

"On battery backup?" asked Sheila Baxter, disbelief in her eyes.

"What kind of emergency?" demanded Stein, irritated.

"Arthur Coburn's vital signs have gone flat—no pulse, no brainwaves, no respiration," replied Alya, the tension in her voice crackling through the comband.

"What?" exclaimed Mark Perry. "Arthur? Something's wrong with Arthur?"

But Stein was already on his feet and moving swiftly toward the door, the doctor calling out, "Grace, Alvin, stat! Emergency on six!"

The two medtechs abandoned their consoles and rushed after him.

Mark Perry glanced at John Greyson, then ran after Stein as well, the lawyer followed by Toni Adkins.

Greyson also turned to go, but cast one last glimpse at the holoscreen and, frowning, stepped to it and peered intently. "Henry!" he called, looking toward the door while pointing at the display, but Stein was already gone.

Greyson sat down at the console and waited.

Billy Clay accepted the board from Drew Meyer and turned it over and back again, examining it closely in the light of his helmet lamp. Finally he looked up. "It could have been a defective chip."

"But we checked each of them," protested Sheila. "Besides, it's highly unlikely that a single defective chip would blow all the others."

"You are right, Sheila," said Drew. "I still think it's most likely that a surge destroyed the board, even though we are on battery reserve."

"What could cause a surge like that?" asked Billy. "I mean, Avery's regulators feed all the power to these jacks."

Timothy's eyes widened in surprise then narrowed in suspicion, and he turned and looked at shadow-wrapped Avery looming in the nitrogen cold.

"Heart needle!" barked Stein as he unzipped the front of Coburn's suit, the man still strapped in his rig. "Three CCs of rinthium. And someone get the defibrillator. Alvin, pull his helmet off and start an ambu going."

Quickly, Alvin Johnston removed the VR helmet. "Holy—!" Coburn's eyes were wide open and filled with terror. They were filled with blood as well. A small trickle of scarlet leaked from his nose, and his lips seeped crimson, too. Medtech Grace Willoby shined a light into first one staring pupil and then the other. "They're unreactive, Doctor Stein."

Alvin Johnston clapped a mask over Coburn's nose and mouth and began counting seconds and pumping air into Coburn's lungs. "Where's that heart needle?" snapped Stein.

A medtech finished assembling the hypo, and he swiftly punched the needle into an ampoule and drew down the rinthium, then placed the syringe in Stein's waiting hand. Stein held it up to the light and squeezed off the air bubble, then, fingers finding the space between the proper ribs, he stabbed the long needle directly into Coburn's heart and pressed the plunger home. Jerking the needle out, he called, "Where's the goddamn defib?" and he placed the heel of a hand at the base of Coburn's sternum, his other hand on top, and began CPR compression.

And as Arthur Coburn lay there, his frightened bloody eyes staring at infinity, Stein pumped hard on his chest while Alvin counted aloud and squeezed the ambu bag every six compressions.

The glass doors banged open and a medtech raced into the control center, pushing a defibrillator on a cart ahead of him.

"Give me two hundred watt-seconds," barked Stein, grabbing up the defib paddles and holding them out while Grace squeezed contact cream on one. Stein wiped the paddles together in a circular motion to spread the cream over the surfaces, then slapped them down onto Coburn's chest. "Clear!" called Stein, and when all stepped away, he triggered the shock.

"No pulse!" barked Grace, peering at the rig's readout.

"Two hundred fifty watt-seconds," Stein ordered, then "Clear!" Once more he triggered the paddles, Coburn's body arching up and flopping back as the charge jolted through.

"No pulse!"

"Come on, you son of a bitch," growled Stein. "Three hundred watt-seconds! . . . Clear!"

Again came the jolt; again, no pulse.

"Three sixty! . . . Clear!"

Five more times he tried it, Coburn's body flopping disjointedly like a string-entangled puppet.

Stein frowned in puzzlement and triggered the defibrillator once more, this time watching the body arch and fall. He set the paddles aside, then ran his hands beneath Coburn's suit and along the spine. His eyes widened. He probed a bit more then stepped back. "You can stop now, Alvin. He's dead."

Alvin looked questioningly at Doctor Stein, then down at the doctor's hands. They were covered with blood.

Stunned, Mark Perry looked on, whispering, "Oh shit . . . Oh shit . . . Oh shit . . ."

"Disconnect him from the rig, and get him out of the suit," said Stein.

As medtechs responded, Toni's comband beeped. "Adkins here," she said, her voice shaking.

"It's me, Toni," came Greyson's voice. "Something you ought to know. Henry, too, if he's free."

"Just a minute, John." Toni stepped to Stein. "Henry, John is on channel four. He says there's something we ought to know."

Stein keyed his comband. "What is it, John?" The habitual sneer was gone from his voice.

"I'm down here at the console. Arthur Coburn's mental pattern is gone. It was gone even as you left here."

Stein glanced over at the medtechs extracting the body from the rig. "He's dead, John."

"Dead? What killed him?"

"I don't know . . . yet."

"Jesus!" exclaimed one of the medtechs, lifting Coburn's body out of the witch's cradle. "It feels like his back is broken, and look, there's blood round his waist." They placed the corpse on the floor.

Stein keyed off his comband and moved to Coburn's side and squatted. After a moment's examination he looked up. "Get the others out of the rigs."

"But, Doctor," protested Grace Willoby, "what about their minds? Their mental patterns are trapped in Avery."

"Goddamn it, Grace," snarled Stein, "Coburn's dead of an AI malfunction. Now get the others out, stat!"

The medtechs moved to the next rig to begin extracting Alice Maxon from her witch's cradle.

33

Lyssa looked down in horror at Arton's mangled torso, his dead eyes staring up at her in terror. Turning, she stumbled away in the lucent fog to lean against the trunk of a moss-laden black cypress, vomit rising in her throat and spewing outward.

Kane wrenched his spear free from the monster's corpse and leaped down from its flaccid body to wade ashore.

Rith knelt weeping next to Arton's remains and gently closed his eyes, and Arik stood and stared out into the luminous night, his features stony, the set of his jaw grim.

Now Kane saw dead Arton. And the big man spun and faced northwest, his visage twisted with rage. "Horax! You bastard! You'll pay for this, you son of a bitch!" he shouted into the night, but the glowing mist did not answer and neither did Horax.

And late night descended upon them all, silent but for Lyssa retching somewhere nearby in the grasp of the moonlit fog.

But of a sudden in midretch—abrupt silence.

Arik snapped his head round. "Lyssa?"

No answer.

The warrior brought his sword to guard and ran to the place where he judged she had stood, Kane on his heels, Rith coming after.

All they found was a malformed black cypress that twisted up out of the clutching mire.

Of Lyssa there was no sign.

"Lyssa!" cried Arik. "Lyssa!" shouted Kane. "Lyssa!" called Rith.

But only fog-wrapped silence answered.

34

As the medtechs began unplugging Alice Maxon from Avery, Grace Willoby monitored the display on the gimbaled rig. "It looks to me as if she's in a deep coma," Grace murmured to Medtech Alvin Johnston, "vegetative state and all. And with her mind trapped in Avery, who knows if she'll ever come out of it."

Alvin grunted in response but otherwise made no reply as he unjacked the primary bundle of fiberoptics.

At that instant, Alice Maxon's body began convulsing.

"Doctor!" called Grace. "She's going into shock. Her heart's fibrillating. Her respiration has failed. She's having some kind of seizure. Jeeze! Her whole autonomous system has crashed!"

As Stein sprang to Alice's side, Toni Adkins' comband beeped.

"What is it?" snapped Toni.

"Greyson here," came the response. "Alice Maxon's mental pattern has disappeared."

"We unplugged her," replied Toni.

"What?" Greyson exclaimed. "But her identity, her spirit, her immortal soul was in the machine!"

"What are you saying, John?"

"You've cut the silver cord. You've disconnected her body from her very essence. Plug her back in before it's too late!" cried Greyson.

"Clear!" barked Stein, the defibrillator paddles in hand.

"Wait!" shouted Toni, but her call came too late as Stein triggered the jolt.

"No pulse!" cried Grace.

"Goddamn it! I said wait!" shouted Toni.

Stein turned toward her, anger in his eyes. "Keep out of this!" he snapped. "Otherwise she'll die."

"Listen to me, Henry. Plug her back into Avery. I think that connection was the only thing keeping her alive."

Without waiting for Doctor Stein's orders, Alvin picked up the primary fiberoptic bundle and jacked it home.

Anxiously, Toni looked at Grace Willoby as the medtech punched compad buttons on the cradle monitor.

"I've got a heartbeat," crowed Grace, "faint but growing! Respiration, too. And her brainstem's working . . . but nothing above."

Toni keyed her comband. "John? Have you got a mental pattern?"

There was no reply.

"John?"

35

Lyssa! Lyssa! Voices calling, Arik, Rith, and Kane probed through the glowing mist, weapons drawn, lanterns lit—*Lyssa!*—yet there came no answer. Still they persisted, wading through water and muck and among the twisted trees. And as they searched, Orbis set and dawn came to the Drasp.

The trio extinguished their lanterns but continued calling and searching, yet no trace of the missing ranger did they find, for they were hunting in a swamp where tracks disappeared even as they were being made and where every other sign of passage was all but undetectable in the clutter and debris of the mire. At last, realizing that further search was futile, they wearily turned back toward the hillock.

"I'll see to the horses," said Arik, his face bleak.

"I'll help you," said Rith.

"Me, I'm going to prepare Arton's remains for burial," muttered Kane.

They slogged through an ankle-deep slurry of water and mud and finally came to the broad mound. By this time the sun had burned away much of the fog, and they could see several horses and two mules huddled together upon the crest. Rith said, "Looks as if they've herded up, but I only see, um . . . eight altogether. Two animals are missing."

Arik gestured. "I'll sweep round low to the right; Rith, go on up to the animals, soothe them, tether them; Kane—"

"I'm heading left where Arton fell," said the big man. "If I find any steeds, I'll round them up as I go."

When Arik had circled three-quarters of the way around the base of the hillock, he found Kane kneeling on the ground and staring out into the mire. Neither man had found either a horse or a mule.

As Arik drew near, Kane stood. "Arton's gone, his body's missing," growled the big man. "Damned swamp monsters."

Arik glanced out at the quag, with its tendrils of mist vanishing. And then he realized—there was no sign of the slain creature, either.

Together, Arik and Kane turned and trudged to the top of the hill.

As the trio sat and ate jerky and swigged water, Rith said, "Somehow Horax has taken Lyssa—spirited her away."

Kane slammed a fist into palm. "That bastard will answer for this, too."

Arik looked up at Rith and slowly shook his head. At last he said, "I hope you are right, Rith—that it was indeed Horax who took her and not some *thing* of the Drasp instead."

"Seven hells, Arik," growled Kane, "it *had* to be Horax. If some swamp monster had tried to seize her, she would have fought it. We would have heard. No, Arik, it was arcane magic that spirited her away and not some lurking creature."

"I agree with Kane," said Rith.

Glumly, Arik nodded.

"Regardless," gritted Kane, "we've got to go on to Horax's hold, wherever that might be."

"Swamp center," said Rith. "But just how we get there now that our guide is gone, well . . ."

Arik glanced at the early morning sun. "Northwesterly. That's the course she set and the one we will follow."

"It won't be easy finding paths through this mire without her aid," said Kane. "We'll just have to slog through."

"But first we rest," said Rith, yawning. "We've had no sleep for a day and a night."

Arik looked at the bard, and muscles in his jaw

clenched, but he said, "You are right. It would not do to push on, weary as we are." He glanced at the sky. "Midafternoon we'll press forward. Till then we take equal watches. I'll go first; you two sleep."

While Kane and Rith slept, Arik fed a ration of grain to the horses and mules. And three at a time he unladed them and curried out the knots and tangles made by saddles and frames. Of the animals, two were missing—one horse and one mule—fled from the monster during the attack.

Kane stood the next watch, and he led the animals down to the edge of the water and found a place free of scum where they each took long drinks.

Rith, last, made a small smokeless fire and cooked a pot of beans, and when midafternoon came round they all had a spare but warm meal.

And then they made ready and set forth.

Sweat runneled down the trio's faces, stinging eyes, dripping from noses, leaking down necks and under leathers, joining the seep ebbing beneath the sodden under-padding galling their bodies. A buzzing cloud of gnats and mosquitoes and biting flies and other blood-mad insects swirled about their faces and swarmed upon any exposed flesh, crawling into eyes and mouths and ears, biting, puncturing, stinging, sucking. Muttering and cursing, swiping and swatting and slapping, Kane and Arik and Rith sloshed onward through the mire, alternately walking and riding. All about, grey moss dangled from gnarled trees twisting up out of the muck, the long tendrils reaching down, clutching, as if to strangle any who fell victim to their grasp. A vaporous steam rose up from the morass, and foul-smelling gases bubbled forth from the slimy quag sucking at their boots. Leeches clung to them and their horses and mules, bloating themselves with dark blood, their swollen bodies dropping off as they became sated. To each side and behind they could hear wallow-ings and splashings, as if creatures unknown followed their track. But they came upon firmer land often enough to leave these unseen things behind as deeper and deeper into these foul environs pressed the three of them. And

Arik flinched and started at every swirl in the murky waters, unable to entirely displace his fear of such, though the farther he went the less apprehensive he seemed.

Now and again they would stop and take a sighting on the sun, trying to bear ever northwesterly, deeper into the Drasp. Repeatedly, though, they would come to yet another obstacle barring their way—wide deep pools, quaking bogs, broad sloughs, undulant quicksand, and the like—where they would veer far from the course they set. Yet always would they try to come back to their original line as they won past each of these hindrances and continued onward ever deeper into the bog.

They had started in midafternoon, with the sun riding high over the morass, bringing its blazing heat to bear down upon the vast mire, causing it to bubble and belch and heave, filling the air with suffocating stench. And through this foul reek they pressed, following an elusive clue—if clue it was—the shouted epithet of a dead mage concerning bog spiders and their lairs. And as time slowly eked forward, swatting and cursing, sweating and scratching, wading and riding, they had slogged ahead through water muck and slime and reeds and stands of gnarled and rotted trees until the eventide drew near.

"Look for high ground," called Arik. "A place to make camp."

As twilight crept into the mire, they came upon a spine of land arching out of the bog. Through a wide, waist-deep slough of dark water they waded, black muck sucking at boots and hooves, dead trees jutting up all round like flayed white bones of skeletal victims left behind. Onto the isle they went, the land rocky under a layer of humus, detritus of things dead, with slimy moss and thorny shrubs and clutching weeds and sharp-bladed grass covering all.

As night fell they made camp on the high ground, well away from the backwater. And as they scraped clinging leeches from one another and from the legs of the animals, Orbis rose in the sky, gibbous and on the wane, shedding its bright light glancing across the swamp, and with it came a breeze blowing down from the north.

"I wonder how far we have come," said Rith, applying a healing salve to the cuts and bites on the horses and mules.

Arik shrugged, likewise daubing salve on the steeds. "Eight miles, perhaps, though I really cannot say."

"Eight miles!" exclaimed Kane. "Seems more like eighty."

"Well," said Rith, "eight miles or eighty, I'm—"

Of a sudden her words chopped off and her eyes flew wide. "Ssst!" she hissed and pointed. "Something comes."

As swift Phemis sped up over the horizon, down in the swamp and heading for the rocky isle a pallid light came flickering among the trees. "Seven hells," growled Kane, taking up his spear, "is it another of those *things,* like the one that killed Arton?"

"Whatever it is," gritted Arik, "make ready to ride, and swiftly."

"But wait," hissed Rith, "I hear no great swashing as we did with the monster. This thing is not down in the water but instead floats above the slough."

Arik cocked his head and listened. "Perhaps you are right, Rith," he said as he drew his falchion and stepped forward to take a defensive stance between the horses and the oncoming light. "Nevertheless, be prepared to fight or flee. The last will-o'-the-wisp we faced was deadly."

Kane took station to Arik's right and glanced at the surrounding mire. "I think I'd rather stand and fight than run through a bog at night."

Onward came the pale light, gliding now among the bone-white snags jutting up from the dark water below.

"Arda," breathed Rith on Arik's left, "it looks like it might be a person."

Onto the isle it came, glowing and floating just above the ground, moving directly toward the campsite.

"A ghost," amended Rith, grasping a throwing knife in each hand, hoping that silver was proof against spirits.

Kane hefted his spear; Arik his sword.

Onward came the pale wraith, flowing up the spine of land, flowing to the edge of the campsite, where it stopped.

Suddenly Arik dropped his blade and stepped forward. "Lyssa," he whispered.

There before them stood the shade of Lyssa, glowing and translucent and ephemeral, tendrils of light blowing in the chill wind.

36

Toni Adkins made certain that her comband was on channel four. It was. "John, are you there?" she repeated.

Finally—"I'm here," replied Greyson.

"Have you got a mental pattern for Alice Maxon?" Toni glanced at the rig where the medtechs worked feverishly.

"I'm afraid—" Abruptly Greyson broke off, then—"Yes! Yes, I do! It's just now come back."

Toni expelled the breath she had been holding.

"But not Arthur Coburn's," added Greyson.

"What?"

"I think Arthur Coburn's mental pattern is gone forever," clarified Greyson.

"Let's lock up and get the hell out of here," said Timothy Rendell. As Drew Meyer keyed the panel shut, Timothy took the burned-out plug-in from Billy Clay. He flipped it front to back then back to front again, looking for something that would indicate why it had failed. Finally he handed the board to Sheila Baxter. "Wrap it up and take it to the lab. See if you can determine just what blew it all to hell and gone."

"Right," said Sheila, kneeling and swathing both plug-in and keyboard with bubblewrap.

"All set," said Drew.

Timothy led them back to the nitrogen lock, while behind in silent, cold shadows Avery loomed in the dark.

Toni looked at the doomsday clock: 1:12:00; one hour twelve minutes before catastrophic battery failure.

"And that's what happened, Toni," concluded Timothy. "Blew apart like a fourth of July starbomb."

"And you don't know what caused it?"

"Not at the moment." Timothy glanced at Mark Perry standing at Toni's side, then back to Toni. "Sheila and Billy are in the lab trying to see what happened to the board. Drew is with them."

Timothy looked around the control room. Ramanni sat at her console and pondered. Medtechs hovered about the witches' cradles, just in case someone else went into shock or worse. One cradle was empty: Arthur Coburn's. Arthur's body had been removed to the medcenter, where Stein was attempting to determine the cause of death.

"Timothy?"

Blinking, Rendell looked at Toni. "I'm sorry. What did you say?"

"I asked, is there any other way to contact Avery?"

"Uh, I don't know. We can't find anything wrong with the interface circuits. It's as though he doesn't wish to be contacted. Greyson says he's like a child hiding under a blanket and reading by flashlight, not answering his parents' calls."

"Well then, we've just got to find a way to lift the blanket, to pull it from him," said Toni. "We've got to get the alpha team free before anyone else is hurt."

Timothy stroked his chin. "Well, with their mental patterns trapped in Avery, we can't just pull them out."

"Right," agreed Toni. "We tried that with Alice Maxon. Her autonomous system totally crashed. She would have died had we not plugged her back in. It seems that it's Avery who is keeping them alive. And as you know, we can't reboot, or their mental patterns will be lost."

Mark Perry groaned in frustration. "Then just how by god are you people going to get them the hell out of there?"

Timothy frowned and slowly shook his head. At last he said, "Well, Mark, I think there might be just two ways that the team can get free."

Mark cocked an eyebrow. "And they are . . . ?"

Timothy held up an index finger. "One, the Black Foxes get to endgame and win, in which case Avery *might* release them; or two"—Timothy held up a pair of fingers—"the technical team has got to somehow log onto Avery and order their release."

Mark Perry sucked in a breath. "Would he obey?"

Timothy nodded. "If a superuser commanded him to let go, he would have no choice."

"Of your two ways," said Toni, "I don't know whether the team *can* win against Avery now. At least we can't count on it. I think instead, Timothy, you are just going to have to try again to contact him."

"Yeah," chimed in Mark.

Timothy took a deep breath. "Wait a minute, boss, there's something I think you ought to know."

Toni crossed her arms and waited.

Timothy looked from Toni to Mark Perry and then back to Toni. "Look, there was a substantial delay between when I plugged in the interface board and it blowing up. Drew said it was likely a voltage surge that made it blow. But Billy Clay tells me that those jacks are fed by Avery's voltage regulators, and Sheila believes that there should be no surges at all, especially when we are running on reserve batteries. From what I understand, Arthur Coburn died at the very moment the board blew. I think that our attempt to install the keyboard was what killed Arthur."

"Wait a minute," said Mark Perry. "Are you saying that you killed Arthur?"

"No, Mark. But what I *am* saying is that I don't believe it was a coincidence that Arthur died at the very moment we made ready to contact Avery. Nor do I believe that it was an accident that the interface board blew."

Mark Perry's eyes widened. "Then what you *are* saying, without coming right out and saying it, is that Avery is a murderer."

Toni gasped. "Is that it? Is Mark right?"

Timothy held his hands palms out. "Look, I don't

know. I don't know whether Avery blew the board just to keep us out, or whether we collided with an interrupt, or what. I also don't know whether or not it was an accident or whether Avery deliberately killed Arthur. Avery's ethical programs should prevent him from harming anyone. All I have are my suspicions."

Toni shook her head. "Even though John Greyson tells me that Avery wants to win at any cost, I find it almost impossible to think of Avery as a murderer . . . yet with the lightning strikes, who knows what might have gone wrong?"

"Well *I* don't have any such qualms concerning Avery," growled Mark Perry. "Greyson told me about Descartes' evil genius controlling all the world and everything in it. Well, let me tell you"—Mark gestured at the alpha team—"Avery is the evil genius controlling their world, and that makes him the evil genius behind Arthur Coburn's murder."

In that very moment the control room door banged open and Henry Stein came striding in. As he walked toward them, bearing news as to what had killed Arthur Coburn, Toni glanced at the doomsday clock: 0:57:16. *Less than an hour to go. Where in the hell is Kat Lawrence?*

37

"**L**yssa," said Arik again, and he stepped toward her.

But she glided backward, away from him and away from Rith and Kane, tendrils of light streaming from her, leaving luminous streaks fading in the air. Frantically she waved them back, and called out to them, saying . . . saying . . . but all they heard was a hollow wailing, like the sobbing of the wind. Yet they knew that she was trying to tell them something, something vital, for they could see her lips move and behold the urgency in her ethereal face. And so they stopped moving toward her, and she stopped her retreat.

And there she stood, glowing brightly, an agonized look on her face. Insects flew about her, attracted to her light like moths to a flame; they would circle once or twice, then spiral to the ground.

Standing slightly behind and to Arik's left, Rith called out, "Can you hear us?"

Lyssa nodded.

"I—we cannot hear you."

Lyssa's mouth made an *O* of understanding, and she signaled <Danger!>, using the Black Fox hand code

"From what?" asked Arik.

<From me,> replied Lyssa. <Come too close and I will kill you.> Some of her words were whole-concept gestures, others she spelled out entirely in Fox sign language.

"What?" Arik was dumbfounded.

Rith stepped up beside Arik. "Is it because you are a . . . a spirit?"

<Yes.>

Rith turned to Arik. "See the insects lying dead at her feet? Ghosts drain life from those they come near and from those who come near to them."

Anguish spread over Lyssa's features. <Yes. All of you must stay away from me.> She gestured at the horses and mules. <Animals, too.>

Arik's shoulders slumped and desolation filled his face. Slowly he sank to his knees.

"Damn, damn, damn!" shouted Kane. "How did Horax do this to you?"

Lyssa's fingers flew, intermingled with gestures. <I don't know. I am not even certain that it was Horax.>

"It *had* to be him," Kane said through gritted teeth. "Who else *would* have done such a deed?"

Rith laid a hand on Kane's arm. "Wait, let us hear her story before we jump to conclusions." Rith turned to Lyssa. "What happened?"

Lyssa shook her head, streaks of light fading. <I don't know. I was leaning against the tree, sick because of Arton's— Next I knew I was in a . . . void, in a distant place, perhaps not even on Itheria. I knew my body was dying somewhere far away; how I knew this I cannot say. I could sense the passage of time—I know not how long. Somehow, I felt as if I would not perish, yet I knew I would not be the same. More time passed, and then I was returned to the tree. Night had fallen; the sun had just set. In the deep twilight I could see that I was a gh— I could see that I was as I now am. I was at the hillock where we had fought the monster, but you were gone from there. Casting a spell, I followed your trail, incredibly swiftly, though it took much out of me to do so. And here I am.>

Arik glanced up at Phemis now passing below Orbis and tears seeped down his features. Then he faced Lyssa. "God, Lyssa, what are we going to do?"

<Go after Horax,> she replied. <Rescue Ky. Reclaim the gem.>

"No, love, I meant—"

<I know. I know what you meant, yet I do not know the answer.>

"If the myths speak truly . . ." Rith did not complete her sentence.

"What?" said Arik. "What myths?"

Rith slowly shook her head. "I seem to recall an ancient story, a legend of a loved one being returned from, from . . . drat, I do not remember. It was the tale of a man wrongly banished to the realm of ghosts, a fable written in a tome I found in the far stacks of the great library on the Isle of Azaral. It was a long story, and every day I would go to the library and read some more. Yet my ship sailed before I could finish, and so I cannot tell you how it ends. However, this much I did learn: ghosts live in a half world, in an in-between place. The librarian who guided me to the tome in the first place told me that the tale tells of someone being rescued from there. Perhaps we can go to Azaral and seek out the source—discover a way to restore Lyssa to her natural state."

<But first we rescue Ky,> signaled Lyssa, <and recover the gemstone.>

"And kill Horax," added Kane.

<Yes.> Lyssa nodded. <Let us begin.>

"Now?" asked Arik. "Right now? In the night?"

<Yes. I think I may only exist at night, and if I am to guide you . . . >

And so they began, lading the mules with cargo and saddling the horses. Strangely enough the animals did not seem at all frightened by the specter of Lyssa, and they stood stolidly as Rith and Arik and Kane pulled the cinch straps tight. And when all was ready, Lyssa's wraith stood a moment in concentration, then, trailing wisps of light, she glided down the spine of the island ridge and out into the Drasp, the Foxes following. And once again they waded waist-deep through the dark slough, and leeches had a feast.

Among the black trees they slogged, following Lyssa's ghost, streamers of light wafting from her, afterglow flowing like luminous smoke to fade and vanish in her wake. And all about them the Drasp was filled with breekings and peepings, with wallowings and sloshings and slitherings, and with the whines of flying insects and the distant roars and skraws of other creatures in the night. Yet traveling as they were in the dark, with only the twin moons to light their way, it was cooler and less noxious, for the sun did not beat down upon the great mire and set it to bubbling. Even so, insects still swarmed about them, biting and stinging and gouging, and it seemed that the leeches knew not the difference between night and day.

Now and again they would stop to rest, for the way was arduous, difficult for man and beast alike. And as Kane and Rith and Arik took water and chewed on trail rations, Lyssa's shade stood off at a distance and did not partake at all.

But always they resumed, heading deeper into the Drasp, while Phemis sped across the starlit sky and Orbis trudged after.

On through the swamp they slogged till dawn came with morning on its heels, and without warning Lyssa vanished. The Foxes cast about and found a bit of high ground, where they set up camp. Exhausted, they fell into slumber, except for the one on watch.

In late afternoon Arik and Rith awakened to the grinding sound of Kane's mortar and pestle. "I found a stand of reetha," he explained.

"Reetha?" asked Arik.

"It'll repel some of these stinging bloodsuckers," answered Kane.

"I'm all for that," averred Rith, moving closer to the warrior-healer. Then—"Phew! What's that smell?"

"Reetha," said Kane. He poured out some of the juice into a vial, then cast a green sodden mess from his mortar and replaced it with a handful of small verdant leaves. Once again he began grinding.

"Ugh!" exclaimed Rith, blinking and backing away, her mouth pulled down and tears running. "I think I prefer the bloodsuckers."

Lyssa's glowing wraith appeared in the deep twilight. She looked wan, weary, her spectral light pallid. Even so, again she led them through the night and toward the center of the Drasp, where they hoped to find Horax's lair. And on this night the bloodsucking insects bit neither man nor horse nor mule, though Rith, well protected, would break into sneezing fits now and then.

Once again the way was difficult, and often the steeds and Foxes needed rest. And Lyssa's pale glow seemed to be fading, as if she were a flame ever so slowly going out.

And when dawn came, wan Lyssa vanished.

On the next evening as darkness fell, again Lyssa appeared, yet this night she was haggard, weak, her light but a feeble glow.

"What is it, my love?" asked Arik. "You are so faint, so pale and worn. What's happening?"

<I don't know.>

Kane, the warrior-healer looked long at Lyssa. "Arik, she appears to be . . . dying. Perhaps if I lay hands on her, I can tell what's the matter."

Yet Lyssa would not suffer Kane to come near, signaling, <Danger! I will kill you!>

But a faint memory nibbled at the fringes of Rith's mind. All of a sudden she smacked herself in the forehead. "Of course! I am so stupid."

"What?" said Arik.

"She needs sustenance," answered Rith, "else she will fade, vanish altogether."

"And what do ghosts subsist on?" asked Kane.

"Life force," said Rith. "She needs life force in order to keep from fading entirely away—not just any life force: it must be human, for that is what Lyssa is—was."

"And how does she gain this life force?" asked Arik.

"We merely need to get near her and she will take what she needs."

<No, no. I will not steal your energy, drain away your lives.>

Arik held out his hands in a beseeching gesture. "Lyssa, I love you, and I will not see you die."

<Not reason enough.>

"Lyssa"—Rith's voice was filled with urgency—"we need you. We cannot make our way through this mire without you to guide us. Else we will *never* find Horax's hold."

"Or kill the bastard and rescue Ky," added Kane.

"Or recover the red gem," said Rith.

Arik clenched his fists and held them tightly against his chest. "Love, take a small portion from each of us. Surely we will survive." He looked at Rith for confirmation.

Rith nodded. "Yes. When we rest it will return."

<I cannot.>

"You must," declared Arik, "otherwise the mission will fail."

Lyssa gazed long at the three of them. Finally she signaled, <Rith, are you certain that all will recover?>

"Oh yes, of that I am sure."

<Then how do we go about doing this abominable thing?>

Rith took a deep breath. "We will surround and approach you. When you feel refreshed, signal, and we will withdraw."

Reluctantly Lyssa agreed, and the trio took up equidistant positions about her and slowly approached. When they were within three paces, each felt a faint dizziness and Rith commanded them to stop. And they stood and watched as Lyssa's aura grew brighter.

Finally Lyssa gestured, and they backed away wearily, feeling faint, as if from the loss of blood.

Arik looked at Lyssa, luminous now. "How do you feel?"

<It was . . . intoxicating.>

"Your own life force was very low," said Rith.

Kane lay hands upon warrior and bard. Then he said, "She took a deal from each of us, yet not overmuch. We will be slowed on this night's journey, though."

Lyssa's face fell and she began to gesture. <I knew this was wrong from the very first.>

"Nonsense!" barked Kane. Then more calmly—"Listen. You were indeed very weak, hence needed much restoration. But if you take just a bit from each of us daily, say, just before dawn, you should never again fall so low. And we will recover before the sun sets and you reappear."

Again Lyssa started to protest, but both Rith and Arik interrupted, telling her to heed Kane "for he is the healer and knows." At last, reluctantly, she agreed.

Refreshed, Lyssa led them northeasterly through the mire, tendrils streaming, fading, and on this night, too, the trip was arduous, made more so by the weakened state of the trio. Just before dawn, again Lyssa took a smattering of life force from each, her luminance growing bright again.

She vanished as the sun rose.

Weary and hungry, Kane, Arik, and Rith looked for some high ground on which to camp. At last to the left Rith spied the beginning of a slope upward. They rode to it and found solid ground rising beneath the animals' hooves. Upslope they fared and came to the crest of a wooded hill. "This looks suitable," declared Kane. "I say we camp here." But as he was dismounting, Kane paused, then swung his leg back over the steed and stood full upright in the stirrups.

"Arik, Rith," he called, pointing to the right. "There, in the near distance. See?"

Their gazes followed the line of Kane's outstretched hand.

Perhaps a mile away and glimpsed through the trees stood the stones of a tall dark tower.

38

Doctor Stein strode to Toni Adkins and stopped.

She looked up at him. "Well . . . ?"

"Without a complete workup I can only speculate, but my preliminary diagnosis is Arthur Coburn's death was secondary to gross skeletal muscle contractions."

"Muscle contractions?" blurted Mark Perry. "But I thought he had a broken back. And what about the blood?"

Stein looked at Perry in disgust. "The contractions were incredibly severe; that's what broke his back, Mark. He severed his own spinal cord. Even if he hadn't, he would have died of massive shock."

"And the blood?"

"Concomitant hematoma with attendant severe abrasions. The contractions ruptured vessels in his eyes, nose, lips. Likely all the vessels in his lower torso were breached as well, and when his spinal column snapped, it punched out through his back, and blood from ruptured vessels was literally ejected." Stein paused, then added, "He virtually ripped himself in two."

"Lord God," murmured Toni.

"God had nothing to do with it," gritted Mark. "Instead it was Satan Avery."

"Doctor Stein!" called one of the medtechs, Grace Willoby. "We need you over here, stat."

Hissing air through his teeth, Stein strode to the witches' cradles, Toni, Mark, and Timothy following after. "What is it?" demanded Stein.

"It's Alice Maxon, Doctor," replied Grace. "Her temperature has taken a nose-dive—ninety-five Fahrenheit and falling."

"Have you checked the instruments?"

"Yes, sir. When we first noticed it, she was at ninety-seven. We've replaced the sensor twice, and each time it read lower."

"Here, let me look." Stein moved in behind Alice's cradle and keyed the compad. Frowning, he keyed in a different code.

Toni asked, "Isn't it the same as when the Foxes were riding through the cold rain—chill fluids and control of the internal thermostat?"

Stein did not answer, and after a moment of silence Grace said, "It's faster than that. And I think she's actually losing energy. Why, we don't know."

Toni lifted her comband. "John, are you there?"

"Greyson here, Toni."

"Is there a change in Alice Maxon's mental pattern?"

There was a pause, then—"Not that I can tell. But I'm no expert at reading these things, nor at reading this console for that matter."

"Thank you, John. Toni out."

Toni keyed off her comband then looked at the medtechs. "I need someone who knows that console to relieve Doctor Greyson."

Alvin Johnston looked at Grace, then Stein, and finally at Toni. "It's my console where he's sitting."

"Then hop to, Alvin. We need you there more than here."

Timothy shifted aside to let Alvin leave, then stepped back into position to watch Stein at work. Moments passed, and Drew Meyer, who had slipped unnoticed into the control center, said softly in Timothy's ear, "It was a power surge."

Timothy turned. "The board?"

"Yes. And looking at the schematic of the voltage regulators, the only way it could have happened is if Avery himself sent a transient pulse through."

"He can do that?"

"He has complete control of those circuits."

"Damn!" Timothy looked across the rig at Toni. Then he said to Drew, "Come on. Let's break the bad news."

As they made their way around to Toni, Timothy's eye was drawn to the empty cradle, and something elusive nibbled at the corner of his mind. But before he could catch it—"Hey, you've stopped it, Doctor Stein," crowed Grace. "Her temperature is coming back."

There was a collective sigh of relief all round. Then Toni asked, "What was the problem, Henry? And how did you reverse it?"

Stein glanced over at Toni, and suppressed rage lurked behind his eyes. "I don't know what was the matter," he snapped. "It reversed by itself. I had nothing to do with it at all." Stein turned back to the rig and keyed in more codes.

By this time, Timothy and Drew had reached Toni's side, and Timothy touched her on the arm. When she turned to him, he canted his head toward Drew and said, "It's as we suspected, Toni: the plug-in was blown by a power surge where no power surge should be, through circuits controlled completely by Avery."

Toni cocked an eyebrow at Drew, and the balding physicist nodded.

"Uh-oh," said one of the medtechs monitoring another of the witches' cradles. "Doctor Stein, the temp is dropping on my guy. It's Caine Easley."

Quickly medtechs keyed codes on the other cradles. "Here, too," said a medtech. "Eric Flannery."

"Meredith Rodgers is also losing energy," said another.

"Hiroko Kikiro is holding steady," reported a fourth medtech.

Stein stepped back and surveyed the row of cradles.

"Alice Maxon is continuing to rise," said Grace.

"Blast it, Henry, what the hell is going on?" demanded Toni.

Stein looked at her, frustration in his eyes. "I don't know!" he bit out.

"Well, goddamn it, use that vaunted intellect of yours and find out!"

Stein gritted his teeth and clenched a fist, and in the same moment, one of the medtechs—Ramon Diaz—called out, "It's a waste! A urinary temp dump. My guy is peeing a steady stream, and Avery is pumping in cold fluid to replace the warm he is losing. And his metabolic rate is down, too. At least that's what's happening to Caine Easley."

Quickly, the other medtechs verified that that was what was happening to Meredith Rodgers and Eric Flannery, too.

And Grace, moving up and down the line, added, "Lord, look at those met rates. They are really losing heat."

"All right," snapped Stein. "Ellery, Margo, get to the medcenter and bring back the following: I want every one of these people rigged with a glucose drip. Also get me five power therms, and several vials of thymium and almium. Hypos. And I need . . ."

As Stein barked out orders, Toni turned to Meyer. "Drew, we've got to see what's happening to these people—to the Black Foxes—in VR. Assemble a team and do whatever it takes to get the holo working."

Drew nodded and set out for the lab.

As the physicist strode away, again Timothy's eye was drawn to the empty cradle, and once more an elusive thought niggled at him, but this time, with a sharp indrawn breath, he caught it. "Toni!" he spun to face her. "There's another way we might get in contact with Avery."

Her eyes widened. "Well . . . ?"

"Look, if we could somehow defeat Avery's hemi-synch—"

"But the alpha team would die," interjected Toni.

"No, no. I don't mean defeat *their* hemisynchs, but instead I'm talking about the hemi on the empty rig. . . ." Timothy paused in excited thought.

Toni glanced at the cradle where Arthur Coburn had died. "Go on."

"Well, okay, here's the deal: if we could defeat the hemisynch, so that a person can remain awake and aware, and suit him up and plug him in, then, if Avery, um, accepts him, he can log in as superuser and tell Avery to free the alpha team."

"My god, Timothy, that's brilliant."

"I don't think it'll work," said Doctor Stein, who had come upon them unawares.

Toni turned and looked at him. "Why not, Henry?"

"Isn't Avery programmed to wait for full sync before pulling someone into VR?"

Timothy nodded. "Yes, but, if we can fake it . . ."

The doors banged open and a woman in a yellow rain suit and wearing a hard hat strode in, escorted by Chief Cardington.

"Kat!" cried Toni. She glanced at the clock and her heart fell. *Forty-eight minutes to go.*

Kat Lawrence removed her helmet and clicked off its light, then ran a hand through her hair. She was a redhead this week. She was perhaps five foot seven, and fair skinned, and somewhere in her middle thirties. As she walked toward Toni, Kat pulled the small black unlit synthbac cigarillo from the corner of her mouth and said, "All right, Toni, I've got an Astro two-fifty sitting outside on my rig, and a crew in a van behind it. Where do you want this mojo plugged in?"

"Anywhere it'll work, Kat." Toni turned to Michael Phelan sitting at a console. "Michael, show her to the turbogen room. And find Al Hawkins. He's got a team somewhere in the building shutting down all nonessential power."

Chief Cardington said, "Al is on three. I'll send one of my men to get him."

"Have him meet us at the turbogen," said Michael.

"Kat, Al is our chief powertech," said Toni. "He can show you where all the bells and whistles are." She pointed at the doomsday clock. "And Kat, hurry, we've only got forty-seven minutes left."

"Impossible," snorted Stein. "I don't care how good this woman is, that's not enough time."

Kat Lawrence jammed the cigarillo into the corner of her mouth and synced her watch to the clock, then fixed Stein with a steely blue-grey stare. "As the old saying goes, the improbable we do immediately, the impossible takes a bit longer, but not if some asshole is blocking the way," and she pushed past Stein and called out, "Come on, Mikey, lead me to the power room. Let's go light some fires." Michael Phelan's face split in a wide grin and he leaped forward in pursuit.

As Kat swept from the room, Ellery Pierce and Margo Watson came in wheeling a gurney laded with gear—IV rigs, power therms, fluid-filled bottles, vials, and other such—and they pushed it toward the witches' cradles. As if it were a parade, behind them came John Greyson, sweating and puffing and rolling a cart of instruments, Drew Meyer and Sheila Baxter and Billy Clay following, wheeling instruments of their own; this quartet headed for the defunct holo.

As Stein moved toward the VR rigs, Timothy stepped to Meyer and paced alongside him. "Tell me, Drew, can a spare turbogenerator be plugged into the building in less than forty-five minutes?"

Breathing heavily and without stopping, Drew replied, "Unlikely."

"Because . . . ?"

"Because it's a major undertaking." Drew reached the holo and wheeled his instrument about and began flicking on switches. Sheila and Billy did likewise.

"Well, Kat Lawrence arrived, and she's got a spare turbogen on her truck."

"Look," said Drew, pausing a moment. "If it was a simple jacking in, sure. It could be done. I don't suppose you know whether she brought one with its own fuel supply."

Timothy shrugged. "All I know is that it's an Astro two-fifty."

Drew shook his head. "No fuel. She'll have to rig it to our H2."

Timothy sighed. "Second question. Can a hemisynch helmet be rigged to fool Avery?"

Drew pondered a moment. "Probably. But it'd take some sophisticated design work."

"How soon could it be done?"

"Hmm, six months or so."

"Not in"—Timothy glanced at the doomsday clock—"oh, say, thirty, forty minutes, eh?"

Drew's instrument beeped. "Not a prayer," he said, turning his attention to the control panel.

Timothy walked to Toni. She stood watching as Stein's medtech team quickly arranged the IV rigs. Beside her stood Greyson, the philosopher dabbing at his forehead with a kerchief and muttering something about "dragging a ton up the steps."

"We don't have a prayer," said Timothy.

"In what?" asked Toni, not looking away from the activity.

"My plan to contact Avery from the inside."

"Oh?" Toni turned and faced him.

"Drew says that it's highly unlikely that Kat can get the turbogen up and running in time. And he says that we can't rig a hemisynch helmet to fool Avery without six months of design work. Our chances of solving this technically are on par with the proverbial snowball's chances in hell."

Toni's face fell, and she turned back to watch the medtechs.

Timothy added, "We'll just have to hope the Black Foxes can get to endgame and win."

Suddenly Toni whirled. "Wait a minute, Timothy. We might not be able to solve this technically, but what about solving it, uh, psychologically?"

Timothy looked at her in puzzlement. "You're the psychiatric specialist here, Toni. You've left me in the dirt. What are you saying?"

"Just this: what if we plant a deep posthypnotic suggestion in the mind of the person going in?—such that as soon as he's in VR, he logs in and tells Avery to free the alpha team, along with himself, of course. Oh, and there's this too: after he's hypnotised and the suggestion has fully taken, what if we wake him up and then pump him full of anozine—?"

"Anozine?" asked Timothy. "What's that?"

"It's a mild stimulant, but it also has an antihypnotic property."

Timothy touched his temple. "Oh, I see. And you believe it would—"

"Yes, yes." Toni nodded eagerly. "If we get the dosage exactly right—I'll have to run a calc on this, but I would guess that it's somewhere around a CC for every fifty pounds—then the hemisynch will engage just enough to fool Avery, but won't engage fully, so that the one going in—when he reaches VR—will be aware of his true identity, of who he is in reality."

Timothy's eyes widened. "Will that actually work?"

Toni paused in thought. "I think so. Yes, I do believe that it will."

"Then if anyone goes in, it should be me," said Timothy.

"But we need you out here," protested Toni.

"No, wait," responded Timothy, "don't you see, I am the best choice to do this thing: first, of all the superusers, I am the overlord of superusers . . . if Avery will listen to anyone, it's me; second, I actually have the most VR experience, so that if anything goes wrong, I am the one best fitted to cope with it; third, I have a VR persona, Trendel, the seer, who is quite good at what he does, hence if anything does go wrong, I am well suited to help the Black Foxes get to endgame and win—and before you ask, yes, he will put me in the same adventure, it's the only one he's running; and last but not least, it was my idea in the first place."

Toni glanced at the clock. "All right, Timothy, all right. I don't have time to argue with you; we've only got thirty-nine twelve left."

"Okay, Al," said Kat, looking at the distribution system, "you and your crew cut loose everything between the substation and here. And cut out the fried Allen-Breech. Use fire axes and chop the cables if you have to; we've got just under forty minutes."

Al Hawkins nodded. "Gotcha, Kat. We'll free the bus to the boxes, too . . . for your Astro."

Kat turned to Michael Phelan. "Where's the H2, Mikey? And the valves."

"This way," replied Michael, heading for the liquid hydrogen tanks.

As they hurried along the 'walk, Kat keyed a talkie. "Carleen?"

"Yeah, chief."

"Crank up the rig and pull it round back."

"Right."

Passing through a door, "Here we are," said Michael. "The valves are over there."

Kat looked at the thermopipe-coupling on the line to the defunct turbogen. Again she keyed her talkie. "Luiz?"

"Si, princesa."

"We're gonna need to rig a number ten from the H2 to the Astro. Can do?"

"Number ten? We only brought forty, fifty feet with us."

"Hang on, Luiz." Kat turned to Michael. "How far is it from here to the back entrance?"

Michael scratched his head. "Shoot. A hundred, hundred twenty-five feet."

"You got that much number ten?"

"I don't know. We'll have to ask Al."

"Well, get to cracking, Mikey!" As Michael sped out the door, Kat said into the talkie, "Start thinking of ways to stretch that forty feet to a hundred twenty-five, Luiz."

Kat glanced at her watch. Thirty-six minutes and counting.

"This is insane!" shouted Stein.

"Listen, you arrogant bastard," snapped Toni, "I've already lost one mission in my lifetime, and I'm not about to lose another. This is the best chance we've got—Bloody hell, it's the *only* chance we've got. Now help us or get out of the way."

Grinding his teeth, Stein stepped back and motioned his medtechs to jack Timothy in.

Timothy, injected with thirty-three cubic milliliters of antihypnotic and dressed in a rig suit, inserted his Trendel ID crystal into the helmet slot then swung into the cradle.

Toni glanced at the clock. Twenty-two forty-one.

Swiftly, two medtechs strapped him in while others plugged fiberoptic bundles into the rig.

All the while, Timothy was mumbling to himself: "Log in. Contact Avery. Order him to restore all people to the real world. Log in. Contact Avery. Order him to restore all people to the real world. Log in . . ." It was the posthypnotic suggestion planted deeply by Doctor Toni Adkins.

Finally, at a nod from a medtech, Toni asked Timothy, "Ready?"

Timothy took a deep breath. "Ready," he answered.

The medtech snapped down Timothy's helmet visor and turned to Toni. "We'll have to trigger it from here, from the rig."

"Go ahead, Ellery." Behind her back, Toni crossed her fingers.

"Here we go, on my mark," said Ellery. "Three, two, one, mark."

Moments passed. "Hell, I think he's unconscious," called Grace, observing the readouts at a console.

"*¡Diablo!*" spat Ramon, monitoring at the rig. "Avery is using the electrolytes to flush his system of the anozine."

"Then get him out of there, now!" barked Toni.

"It's too late," said Stein, arching an eyebrow at her. "His brainwaves just went flat, all but the autonomous."

Over Toni's comband came the voice of Alvin. "Doctor Adkins, a new mental pattern has this moment appeared in my holo. It's labeled Timothy Rendell."

Toni felt as if she had been kicked in the stomach and she could not seem to get enough air to breathe. *Now Timothy is trapped in Avery, and it's all my fault. Their only chance is to get to endgame and win, if there is time.* Toni looked quickly at the doomsday clock. Eighteen minutes remained, eighteen minutes until the rest of the alpha team members would die . . . along with Timothy

Rendell. A shiver shook Toni's frame and her chest felt hollow, and the dark shadows in the room seemed to gather closely round and with cold fingers clutch at her missing heart.

39

Trendel's head hurt like all of the seven hells had been crammed into his skull, and something sharp poked his cheek. A sour odor filled his nostrils and he came near to gagging. Slowly he rolled onto his back, the clink of chain accompanying his movement. Whatever was poking his cheek no longer did so. He opened his eyes. Dark stone met his gaze in flickering torchlight. He raised a hand to his— *What th—? I'm shackled!* Swiftly he sat up and looked about, wincing at the pain in his head. *Where the badoo am I?* And then he saw: stone walls, stone ceiling, stone floors, stone pillars, iron fetters linked by iron chains to iron eyelets anchored in stone, and an iron-clad door with an iron grille over a small warder window. He sat on sour straw bedding, and in room center were two buckets—a water bucket and a privy. *How in Luba's name did I get locked up in a dungeon?*

And then on the wall opposite he saw movement in the shadows. And stepping toward him from the darkness came a syldari female dragging chains behind, she too shackled to the stone.

"Awake at last, eh?" she said.

"Where in seven hells am I? And how did I get here?" *Ooo* . . . Talking made his head hurt, as if the resonance of his own voice reverberating through his skull threatened to explode all the cavities therein.

"You are in the dungeon of Horax the Great, or so he calls himself. Me, I call him Horax the Bastard."

Trendel held his pounding head in his hands. "Where is this place and how did I get here? I mean, last I knew I was in the bed of— Well, never mind. She wouldn't want it bandied about."

"You were hauled in unconscious, my friend. As to where the dungeon is located, ha, that I know not for certain, though I suspect we're somewhere in the Drasp. I, too, was senseless when these were locked on." The syldari held up her wrists and rattled her chains.

Trendel drew in a big breath then expelled it. "The Drasp, eh? —A bogland, from the smell of things."

"That's right."

"I grew up near the Gridian Mire; I've found they all smell somewhat the same."

Gingerly, Trendel got to his feet and walked to the water bucket. A moldy gourd hung by a hook on its side. Trendel dipped in a hand and sipped from his palm ... several times. Finally he straightened and looked down at the syldari; he stood two inches short of six feet, she two short of five. She was dressed in mottled grey leathers; Trendel in silk and satin—cerulean silken shirt and dark blue satin breeks and violet silken hose, now wrinkled and torn and stained—and black shoes bereft of their silver buckles. In spite of his appearance, he bent at the waist in a courtly bow, then grimaced and held his head, saying, "I am Trendel, seer."

"I am Ky, Shadowmaster," she replied, grinning.

"Shadowmaster? Then why haven't you, uh"—he looked around the shadow-wrapped cell—"escaped?"

"You know how your head feels?" asked Ky.

"Awful," he answered, holding a hand atop his red-headed pate, his hair tied in a pony tail.

"That's why I can't simply step through shadow and be gone, assuming, of course, that I could get free of these fetters."

"What does my hammering head have to do with it?"

Ky blew out a long breath. "We, you and I, Trendel, are locked in a null dungeon. No spells work."

Trendel frowned a moment in concentration—which

was extremely difficult with the throbbing in his head—
and then attempted to cast a "past vision" spell, one that
would let him see just how he had come to be shackled
here in the first place. Nothing whatsoever happened.

He looked at her. "I've heard of these voided places
where magic is dampened or extinguished altogether, but
I never thought to ever be a prisoner in one."

"Your headache will soon ease," said Ky. "At least
mine did. I think it's the loss of casting ability which
causes such a horrid pounding."

Trendel silently agreed that the pounding was indeed
horrid. "I think I'll go sit till some of this passes." He
wobbled back to his sour straw bed and eased down.

Ky, too, retreated back to her own bedding.

After a moment Trendel softly asked, "Do you know
how you came to be imprisoned by this—this Horax?"

"Horax the Bastard," came Ky's voice from the shadows.

"Yes, all right, Horax the Bastard."

She did not immediately answer, but sat silently in the
shadows of the cell contemplating him, as if weighing
whether or not to trust him.

After a moment, Trendel said, "Ky, I assure you I am
no lackey, come to worm things out of you." He gestured
about, his chains clanking. "You and I both have a score
to settle with Horax the Bastard, and perhaps together we
can manage an escape. Besides, what could you tell me
that Horax the Bastard doesn't already know?"

Still she sat without speaking, her eyes glittering in the
torchlight. But at last Trendel heard her sigh, then
she quietly began: "We were riding across the plains, the
Black Foxes and I—"

"Black Foxes? I once heard a bard-sung ballad about a
group calling themselves Black Foxes. Are these the
same?"

"Probably. What was the song?"

Trendel thought back. "Something about a mere five
Foxes in desperate battle capturing a hundred-score le-
gions."

"Yes. That was us, though the truth of the matter is that

it was but a single company, and no battle at all but trickery instead."

"Oh." Trendel sounded disappointed. "Even so, you are one of the Foxes?"

"Yes."

Silence fell. After a moment, Trendel said, "I interrupted you. Please do go on with your tale and I'll try to hold my tongue until the end."

Once again Ky's voice came softly through the darkness. "We were riding across the plains, the Black Foxes and I, when we came upon a slain gnoman. . . ."

". . . and something or someone struck me from behind and I crashed into the wall, and after that I knew no more until I woke up shackled here."

Ky's voice fell quiet.

"And now he's got the gemstone, eh?"

"Unfortunately, yes."

"Arda, if he does indeed take it to the DemonQueen—"

"Oh, I think he already has."

"You do? If so, there'll be all seven hells to pay."

Trendel heard Ky's chains rattle and she stepped out from the shadow and into the torchlight, walking to the bucket. She, too, ignored the moldy dipper and took drink by hand. When she was refreshed, she said, "You see, Horax the Bastard came and crowed to me that he had successfully bargained with the DemonQueen herself. In trade for the gemstone, he's to be her consort."

"Consort?"

"Yes, ruling Itheria as her regent whenever she conquers the world. Till then he's to sit by her side on the demonthrone. That's been his ambition all along, even when he belonged to the Circle of Mages, or so he said."

"He was one of the Circle? The Inner Circle of Wizards?"

Ky nodded. "Until he betrayed Jaytar back when she stole the gem. He guided the demons to her, but she fooled them—hid the stone where neither they nor he could find it."

Trendel drew in a breath. "When did he tell you this?"

"My third day here, I think."

"And how long have you been imprisoned altogether?" asked Trendel.

"Two weeks, more or less," she answered.

"So then, the DemonQueen may have had the gemstone for, um, ten or eleven days?"

"Likely. But I can't be certain; time is difficult to judge without the guidance of the sun and the moons."

"Then how—?"

"The jailor comes once a day, or so I think, bringing fresh buckets, taking the others away. Bringing food as well."

"What do we eat and when?"

"Believe me, Trendel, you don't want to know."

Time passed, and Trendel and Ky tossed plans back and forth on how they would escape, but everything they proposed was flawed beyond measure and doomed to fail. Even so they continued, hoping against hope that one or the other of their stupid notions would inspire an idea of brilliance.

And as they spoke a pale light came glowing dimly through the grille of the door and slowly grew brighter as it drew near.

"Someone comes," hissed Trendel. "The guard?"

"I think not," whispered Ky. "It's too soon."

40

Kat Lawrence keyed her talkie. "Carleen?"

"Yes, Kat."

"Is she grounded?"

"Yeah. Six-strand double-ought bolted to the building frame."

"Good. —Luiz?"

"Si, princesa."

"You nearly finished?"

"Si, princesa. We upcoupled the ten through an expansion joint to a twelve, ran that out the doors and up the ramp, and now we're downcoupling back to a ten to hook it into the Astro."

Kat looked at her watch. "Hustle, Luiz. We've got just over twelve minutes. Kat out."

Kat turned and ran back toward the power distribution center, passing the rest of her crew rolling a large spool of insulated cable—six-strand double-ought—along the catwalk, the heavy-duty wire snaking back toward the rig. Michael Phelan, helping with the spool, called, "How much time, Kat?"

"Eleven minutes."

Jimmy Chang, second foreman, barked to the crew, "Goddamn it, you heard her, can't we pull this cable any faster?"

Kat reached the powertech team at the circuit breaker

panels. Fire axes were scattered about. "Hawkins, is the Allen-Breech cut free?"

"Yeah, Kat," answered Al Hawkins, not turning away from what he was doing. "The busses to the substation, too. We're rigging the mains for the double-ought."

Kat glanced at her watch. Just over ten minutes remained.

The comband beeped. "Doctor Stein? Johnston here."

Henry Stein keyed his band. "What is it?"

"I think you'd better look at Avery's D2s."

Stein turned to Grace Willoby. "Can you get the D2s on your console?"

Grace punched keys on the compad. "Yes. They're here."

Stein stepped to the console. Moments later he called to Toni, "Doctor Adkins, your expertise is needed here."

Toni, sitting at a dead console, raised her head from her hands and momentarily stared at Stein. Wearily, she rose from her chair and walked to the console. Doctor Greyson and Mark Perry drifted over as well.

"These patterns are not normal," said Stein, pointing at the holoscreen.

Toni bent over and peered. Lines crawled across the display. Toni rolled a chair to the console and sat down next to Grace. Then she keyed the pad. Several lines were highlighted in yellow, the others fading to grey. "Hm. The E3s seem to be altered."

"That's obvious," said Stein.

"E3s?" hissed Mark Perry to Greyson. "What are they?"

"Ha," whispered Greyson. "One of the few brainwaves I know something about. They have to do with empathy."

"Good Lord," said Toni, and her face drained of color. She gestured to Doctor Stein and pointed at the screen. "Henry, if I didn't know better, I would say that we are looking at the mental pattern of a sociopath."

"Sociopath?" burst out Perry.

"That's what it looks like," replied Toni, magnifying the pattern.

"But that's—that's"—Perry turned to Greyson. "Isn't a

sociopath someone who will go to any lengths to gratify his own desires, regardless of the costs to others?"

"Yes," said Greyson, nodding.

"Pah!" Stein expelled a breath. "What could an AI possibly want?"

"Blast it, Henry, I've told you before: Avery wants to *win*," replied Greyson, exasperation in his voice.

"Nonsense!" barked Stein. "Avery is an AI. Winning and losing mean nothing to it."

"Perhaps you are right, Henry," said Toni. "But if these readings were on a human being, then he would be slipping into sociopathic behavior."

Alya Ramanni, sitting at the adjacent console, said, "Do you mean Avery is going mad?"

"With this large a deviation? —Quite probably," answered Toni.

"No wonder the sonofabitch killed Arthur," said Mark Perry. Then his eye strayed to the six in the gimbaled rigs.

Drew Meyer looked at Sheila Baxter and Billy Clay. "Are you certain?"

"Yessir, Doctor Meyer," answered Billy, sitting on the floor, a panel open beside him. "The signals are still coming in from Avery."

Sheila, lying on her stomach at the base of the main holo, glanced up at them both. "It's like Avery wants us to know what's going on in VR, but all the holo circuits are blown.

Drew snapped his fingers. "The ball lightning."

Sheila scrambled to her feet. "There's a full set of replacements in the lab."

"Let's go," said Drew.

Fwoosh! Kat listened to the liquid hydrogen as it initially rushed into the thermopipe. Michael Phelan turned from the valve and gave her a thumbs-up. She keyed her talkie and called out, "Here it comes, Luiz."

Her own talkie crackled and she could hear the hissing of escaping air. "*Si, princesa.* She's venting now."

Kat glanced over her shoulder at Al Hawkins and his crew desperately bolting individual multiclamps onto each of the six double-ought strands. She looked at her watch. Seven and thirty.

"Look, you've got to do something," demanded Mark Perry. "You can't leave those people to the mercy of a mad killer."

"There's nothing we can do, Mark," said Toni. "The only way to get Avery back to normal is to reinitialise him. But we can't reboot, else we lose the mental patterns of the alpha team and consign them to be nothing more than living vegetables, if even that. We can't extract the team from the rigs because the link that's keeping them alive will be broken. Yet if we don't do something quickly, then they'll die anyway." Toni glanced at the clock. Just under seven minutes remained.

"Fire it up," shouted Kat.

As Luiz revved the truck, Carleen Alsberg kicked over the starter on the Astro 250. With a screaming bellow the turbogen caught, and water vapor roared out from the exhaust as the engine whine scaled upward, sounding like a fan jet of old.

Kat punched buttons on the Astro panel, checking the available volt-amps as the turbo came up to speed. Then she keyed her talkie. "Al, throw the switches. Engage."

She heard no reply above the roar of the turbine, and ran the length of the flatbed and scrambled into the cab, slamming the door behind. "Al, goddamn it, she's up and running. Throw the switches."

"Roj!" came Al's reply.

Kat clambered from the truck and ran down the ramp and into the sublevel, following the power cable toward the distribution panels.

In that same instant in the building, with five minutes and twenty-nine seconds to go, Al Hawkins slammed the mains to, and lights flickered on—

—but then, sparks flying, the main breakers blew and the lights went back out.

41

"It must be Horax's tower," growled Kane. "Who else would live in this swamp? Besides, we have Pon Barius's word on it."

"And there's the ferry guard," added Rith. "They were wearing Horax's sigil—twin bloodmoons—so he must live in the Drasp, and I think that he would permit no other to dwell herein. Kane is right: this must be Horax's tower."

"I agree," said Arik.

They lay at the edge of the wood less than a quarter mile from the ramparts and scanned the dark fortress upslope. Square it seemed, two hundred feet to a side, with dark castellated walls some twenty-five feet high and made of a dusky stone. Turreted watchtowers jutted up from each of the three corners in view, yet whether they were manned, the Foxes could not tell. Beyond this wall they could see the roof of a large building—perhaps the main hall. But dominating all else and abutted against a far corner stood a tall black tower, its sides covered with ebon stone—slate or black marble, they deemed. Its roof was flat, perhaps for observing the stars and the portents, though it just as well could be used for other things.

The fortress itself sat on an upraised patch of ground, as was all the land nearby, a set of wooded hills raised above the swamp.

"I see no gate in these two walls," rumbled Kane.

"Let's work our way round and spy how we can best invade."

Starting at the southeast corner, leftward they crept, well back in the woods so that none watching might see them. Soon they could see the western wall, but no entrance or egress did they spy, only solid dark stone.

Onward they crept, now heading north, paralleling the long western wall until they came to its far extent and a bit beyond.

"Ssst," hissed Rith. "Look there."

She had spied a recess in the north wall, and when they stole farther northward, at last they could see a great pair of iron doors, shut. From these doors a dirt road twisted down to an east-west canal where a barge lay docked. "Now we know how Horax gets his supplies," said Rith.

Long they lay and watched, but no activity of any kind did they observe. At last Arik said, "It looks as if it is abandoned. Even so, I would rather that we make our way back to the horses and wait till darkness falls. Then we'll slip over the walls and see whether or not Ky is inside."

"Seven hells, Arik," protested Kane, "who knows what they are doing to her? She could be dying a slow horrible death even as we dither about. I say let's go over now."

Rith lay a soothing hand on the big man's arm. "No, Kane, Arik is right. Weary warriors make mistakes; we've had no sleep and need be rested before we essay these walls. Too, Lyssa will be with us when the sun sets, and she can aid us greatly, assuming that some of what I have been told about ghosts is indeed true. I say we return to camp and sleep. Tonight will be soon enough to scale these ramparts."

"But Ky—"

Rith interrupted Kane. "If they were going to murder Ky, they would have done it long past."

Kane ground his teeth and eyed the fortress, as if deciding whether or not to go alone. But at last he turned and started back toward the south, aiming for the hill where the horses and mules stood tethered.

After caring for the animals, they took a short meal and then fell into restless sleep, all but the one on watch. And slowly the sun rode up the sky and across and then back down. At last twilight stole over the land and with the darkness came Lyssa.

Once again they stood at the edge of the woods, the horses and mules behind them, saddled and loaded and ready to fly, the fortress before them silhouetted against the stars. Phemis rose, racing up into the sky, Orbis yet below the horizon and lagging behind.

"Now is the time to see," said Rith to Lyssa, the wraith standing off to one side.

Lyssa frowned in concentration, and then slowly dissipated, and a pale glowing mist drifted out across the treeless expanse lying between the ramparts and woods.

"I hope this does not hurt her," whispered Arik.

Rith shook her head. "I think not; after all, it is a ghostly thing."

The pale mist, seeming to be no more than a patch of moonlit fog, at last reached the fortress walls, and then vanished.

Kane gasped and gripped his spear tightly. "Where did she go?"

"Through the wall, I think," replied Rith. "Scouting as planned. Finding out how many guards, where they patrol, discovering the weak spots in their warding. With Arton gone, Lyssa is the one best suited to such things."

Passing through stone was like pressing through . . . pressing through . . . Lyssa could not say. But it clutched at her and she could not see, and *something* penetrated her essence with icy cold, or was it blazing heat? Again she could not say. Whatever, it was bloody uncomfortable. At last she was through and glad of it. She had emerged in a bailey. Across cobblestones and scattered about were several small structures—storehouses, a smithy, and other such—and one large building—the main hall. In the northeast corner stood the tower. Two warders lounged at the base of the tall structure, each with low sloping foreheads and outjutting toothy jaws and long dangling arms. Half-man, half-beast, they bore spiked cudgels for weapons. *Arda, these must be the same as Arton saw at the ferry.*

Lyssa floated up to the top of the wall, like a mist rising on a zephyr. Along the castellated rampart she flowed eastward. At last she came to one of the turrets. Inside was a sleeping guard, features and form like that of the others. Twin bloodmoons adorned the guard's uniform, *Horax's sigil.* Onward she flowed, now northward, heading for the tower. *That's where I would keep prisoners, were it my wont and this my bastion.*

"Ssst, atop the wall. See?" hissed Rith.

A pale mist flowed westward, past the turret and then north.

Arik sighed in relief.

Through the wall of the tower passed Lyssa. *First I must find Horax, see if he is here. If so, we may need to deal with him before all else . . . yet the last time we met, we lost . . . or rather, we didn't win, at least not against him.*

Upward she flowed, following a spiral stone stair, up to a room at the top. An open trapdoor was set in the ceiling. Up to the roof she went, to find bones of cattle and great droppings. *The flying thing perches here.*

Now she went down and down, spiraling through floor after floor until she reached ground level. And nowhere had she seen Horax or any living creature.

Two closed doors stood against the walls, one leading into the bailey, the other leading . . . ? Lyssa passed through this second door. A stairwell pitched downward.

She came to a chamber at the bottom. A guard sat at a table asleep. She could hear voices down a short hallway.

Drifting along this way, Lyssa saw three more warders: two playing at rolling several small stones, the other asleep.

The hallway ended in another door. This one closed and barred. *Aha!*

On the other side the hallway continued, but iron-clad doors lined the walls. *Cells.*

At the distant end, torchlight guttered through a small grille-covered warder-window set in the last iron door.

A glimmering mist, Lyssa drifted toward this cell, the only one with a sign of life. As she neared, she felt a tingling, and all of a sudden, without her willing it, her mistform vanished and glowing Lyssa stood, her form restored to that of a ghostly wraith. *Some kind of spell or counter spell.*

She peered through the grille.

"Lyssa!" cried a familiar voice.

It was Ky, moving out from the shadows. And emerging from the darkness opposite came a stranger.

Lyssa pushed forward, trying to enter the cell, but she could not.

"Lyssa!" cried Ky.

The syldari saw Lyssa try to speak, but only a haunting wail came through the grille.

"Why are you glowing?" called Ky.

"Luba, who is this shade?" asked Trendel, moving aflank the syldari, and Ky realized that what he had said was true: Lyssa was a ghost.

<The cell is magically dampened. I could not enter. I signaled her that rescue was coming.>

"Thank Arda, though, Ky is still alive," said Kane, a great grin spread across his face.

Orbis now rode up over the horizon.

"And she is trapped with another man?" asked Rith.

<A seer named Trendel.>

"How many guards are there altogether?" asked Arik.

<Four at the cells, two at the base of the tower, one on each of the turrets, and another thirty-five in the main building. All of them half-man, half-beast.>

"And Horax?" growled Kane.

<Nowhere to be found.>

"Damn!"

Arik looked at the ground in deep thought. Finally he said, "The odds are not good. We'll have to move with stealth. Rith, you nullify any of our sounds, especially if we get into a skirmish."

Rith nodded.

"What about the turret guards?" asked Kane.

Arik glanced at him, then turned to Lyssa. "Can you eliminate them?"

<Me? How?>

Arik inhaled deeply, then said, "Drain them."

A shocked look passed over Lyssa's face. <Arik, it is abominable. If I were running them through with a sword, that would be a clean death. But to drain them? To steal their life in such a hideous way? I cannot do such a thing.>

"Dead is dead," growled Kane.

Lyssa shook her head. <If they were monsters or demons, perhaps I wouldn't care as much. But to drain humans to death—even half-men, half-beasts—it would be like stealing their souls. The threat would have to be overwhelming before I could do such a thing.>

"Method be damned," said Kane. "Ky's in there and we've got to free her."

Arik sighed. "No. Lyssa is right. It is awful to kill in such fashion. I am sorry I thought of it."

"Hold a moment," said Rith. "Lyssa, you don't need to kill them. Just take enough energy to render them senseless."

Arik looked at Rith. "Splendid." He turned to Lyssa. "Love, it may be the only way we can get over the wall unseen."

"To rescue Ky," added Kane.

At last Lyssa nodded.

Arik breathed a sigh of relief. "All right. Now about the remaining guards . . ."

In mist form, Lyssa flowed up the wall to come to the guard turret. The warder was yet asleep. She drifted up behind him. She could see indiscernible life force begin flowing out from his body, but only a small measure seeped into her, slowly, weakly, as if it were an energy somehow incompatible with her own.

He is not wholly human, that's why.

Of a sudden the warder's head fell back loosely, but he yet breathed.

By the bright light of Orbis, Lyssa flowed along the wall to the northeast turret. This warder was awake. He stood at the corner and peered northward out over the swamp. Noiselessly, Lyssa came upon him from behind. Life force streamed toward her, most to flow beyond and vanish on the wind. The guard shook his head dizzily and yawned, then he slumped against the parapet and slowly slid down to the banquette, turning as he did so, to face the glowing mist. His eyes widened, and he feebly scrabbled as if to crawl away. Then his gaze glazed over and he collapsed senseless.

Lyssa drifted partway down the outside of the wall and coalesced into her bright human form. Kane, Arik, and Rith came running from the wood and toward the rampart. As they uncoiled line and snapped tines outward on their grapnels, Lyssa glided westward along the castellations, once more in her mistlike form—there were yet two parapet guards to render insensible.

Tnk. Chnk. Klnk. Three grappling hooks bit into stone near the northeast corner of the bastion. Up the lines swarmed Rith and Arik and Kane. Swiftly they reached the top of the battlement and, shielded by the curved wall of Horax's tower, over the parapet they slipped. They drew up the lines and coiled them, and clicked the tines shut on the grapnels.

Then, cautiously, on his stomach, Arik peered round the curve of the tower. He could see a glowing mist in the southwest turret.

"She deals with the last of the warders," he hissed to Kane and Rith, both of them crouched in the shadows behind.

Arik slid forward to look down at the guards below. As Lyssa had said, there were two of them. They sat sharpening the tines on their spiked cudgels. Arik could see no one else in the bailey, though sounds of argument came from the main building on the far side.

Arik slid backward. "All right, Kane, Rith. It's up to you now."

Kane threw the senseless guard's cloak about his

shoulders, slipping the hood over his head. Then down the spiral stone stairwell he went, Rith and Arik behind.

When they reached the bottom, Kane, his shoulders hunched over with his arms dangling, shambled out from the step-housing and around the curve of the tower, Arik and Rith slipping through the shadows after.

Just before he came to where he could see the guards, Kane turned to Rith. <Ready?>

She frowned a moment in concentration, then signaled, <Ready.>

His spear in hand, Kane shuffled into the torchlight and up the side steps. One of the tower warders was facing Kane's way and gnarled something, yet his voice made no sound. Kane merely shambled toward them in total silence. The guard felt his throat in puzzlement and said something else, his words swallowed in the utterstill. He turned to the second warder and his jutting jaw and protruding lips moved, but he voiced no words. Kane reached them both just as the second warder began to turn, but swift as a viper the big man soundlessly dropped his spear and slammed their heads together in complete silence as bone crunched and splintered.

Arik and Rith dashed out from the shadows, Arik to help Kane with the guards, Rith racing for the door.

As Rith ran to the portal, Kane grabbed one of the downed warders by the collar and began dragging him across the landing, pausing long enough to retrieve his spear. Arik hauled the second one after.

Cautiously, Rith turned the ring on the door latch. She could feel it clack, though it made no sound. It was unlocked. Slowly she eased the panel open and looked inside. No one was there. She threw the door wide just as Kane arrived. As he hauled the guard into the tower, Rith dashed past Arik and down the steps and retrieved the warders' cudgels from where they had fallen.

Just then, Lyssa's lambent mist came flowing across the bailey.

Into the tower they rushed and closed the door behind.

"Are you certain they will be able to rescue us?" asked Trendel.

"We are the Black Foxes," said Ky, as if that explained all.

"Well, it's been entirely too long since we saw your friend the ghost. Perhaps even now they are shackled in chains somewhere, or even worse, dead."

Ky said nothing.

"Hm, I wonder," pondered Trendel, "how do you kill a ghost?"

"Oh shut up!" snapped Ky.

In the utterstill, Kane and Arik rushed the two warders sitting at the table in the outer chamber. Taken by surprise, they leapt up yelling, but silence annihilated their shouts as well as their shrieks of death.

Mist emerged from the door and reformed as Lyssa. <There are two warders inside. One asleep, one sitting on a privy pot.>

"Sst!" hissed Trendel. "Light comes. Perhaps it is your ghost."

The Shadowmaster stood.

A key rattled in the door.

"Damn! A guard." The syldari slumped back against a stone pillar.

But then the door opened. "Kane!" shrieked Ky, and sprang forward as the big man stepped into the cell. But Kane cried out, "Yaaahh!" and pressed his hands to his temples, dropping a ring of keys to the stone floor in his agony. Rith rushed in, Arik behind, searching for foe. And they both cried out and clutched their heads, and Rith sank to her knees in excruciating pain.

"It's the cell!" cried Ky, hauled up short by her length of chain. "It's null, dampened!"

Kane managed to look through tears at the Shadowmaster. "Throw me the keys," called the syldari, holding out her hands.

Groaning, Kane stooped down and took up the ring and cast it at her, the keys landing short and jingling as they skittered across the stone floor.

Swiftly she snatched them up and tried several, at last

finding a key which unlocked her shackles. "This one," she said, handing the ring to Trendel.

As the seer opened his manacles, Ky rushed to Kane. "Out of here, now!" she barked, shoving at him. "You too, Arik." She went to Rith. "Trendel, help me."

Together, Trendel and Ky lifted Rith to her feet, and they followed Kane and Arik as they lurched from the cell.

The moment they stepped into the hallway, blessed relief washed over them all, eradicating the pain, including the dull ache in Ky's head and the pounding distress in Trendel's.

Kane picked up Ky and whirled her round. "I thought you dead, little mouse, but I've never been so glad to be wrong."

Arik barked, "Now is not the time to celebrate. Instead we must win free of this fortress before we are detected."

As Lyssa stood watch at the far end of the corridor, Rith handed Ky her black long-knife. Gratefully, Ky took possession of the blade, then growled, "The bastards took my scabbard."

Kane stooped down and pulled a silver-bladed short-sword from his boot and held it out to Trendel. "Here, can you use this?"

"Yes," said Trendel, accepting the weapon, "though a good axe and shield are more to my liking."

At that moment they heard the blat of a bugle sounding above.

"Dretch!" spat Rith. "We are discovered."

"Come on," growled Arik, and down the corridor he ran, the others on his heels, ephemeral Lyssa racing ahead. Quickly they reached the ground level, where the two skull-crushed tower warders lay stone dead. Outside a bugle blared and there sounded the shouts of one of Horax's man-beasts.

At the door Lyssa signaled, <Wait here; I will go see.>

She dissipated into mist form and flowed through the wood.

Ky looked about. "Where is Arton? And Pon Barius? Did he live?"

Kane put a hand on her shoulder. "Dead, mouse. They are both dead. Horax's doing."

Ky's face drained of blood. "Arton? Dead?" She sagged against Kane, stricken, tears welling.

In that moment Lyssa returned and resumed her erstwhile corporeal form. <They've discovered the senseless guards on the walls. The keep swarms with searchers. They will soon be here.>

Arik thought a moment. "We need a diversion."

<I will go,> signaled Lyssa, and before any could protest and still in her bodily form she turned and vanished through the doorway, and suddenly the blats of many horns and shouts filled the bailey. Cautiously, Arik turned the latch and opened the door a crack to see . . .

. . . bright shining Lyssa fleeing across the court and toward the northern gates, guards atop the walls racing after, arrows flying, and other warders in the compound, cudgels raised, yelling and cursing and running to intercept this luminous intruder.

"Their weapons won't hurt her," sissed Rith, looking over Arik's shoulder. "Unless they're enchanted or silver."

Arik turned and looked at her, an unspoken question in his eyes. "I swear," said Rith.

Arik glanced at the others. "Let's go," he barked.

Ky gathered herself together, then called, "Wait!" and frowned a moment and muttered a word. Shadows gathered about them. "Now," she said.

Out the door Arik darted and around the tower toward the stairwell, Trendel and Rith and Ky and Kane dashing after. And covered in darkness they were all but invisible in the fortress gloom.

But as they neared the spiral stair, out from the stephousing came boiling five of Horax's man-beasts, running to join the chase of the glowing intruder. But into shadow they ran, and Arik took the first through the throat as Trendel stabbed his borrowed silver blade through the second one's heart. The third cried, "Waugh!" and then fell to Arik's sword. The fourth and fifth turned to flee, but one of Rith's daggers flew into the nearest one's back and he staggered a few steps and fell. Yet the fifth one leaped shrieking into the step-housing and fled up the stairwell.

"Damn!" shouted Arik, and leapt after, Trendel on his heels.

Rith paused long enough to retrieve her dagger, then sped after, Ky and Kane behind. Up they spiraled, coming at last to the parapet. To the right, the man-beast ran along the banquette, shouting in alarm, yet his calls were unheard in the general uproar below.

"Dretch!" cursed Arik, breaking off pursuit. "We may be undone."

"Perhaps not," said Ky. "Perhaps they'll think it was shadow they fought."

"Detected or not, shadow or not, let's flee," said Rith, unhooking her grapnel from her belt and snapping the tines into place.

Kane and Arik joined her and all set hooks in the castellated angles of stone. Then they cast the ropes over the wall. "Ky, Rith, Trendel, go now," barked Arik. "Kane and I will follow."

Those three quickly glanced at one another and nodded, then rappelled down to the ground, Ky taking the shadow with her.

And at the distant end of the parapet, the man-beast shouted and blew his horn, for in the bright light of Orbis above he saw the two revealed men.

As soon as the others reached the ground, over the wall went Arik and Kane, swiftly rappelling down.

Abandoning the hooks and lines, toward the woods they all fleetly ran. Quickly they reached the trees and disappeared among them. From the bastion walls behind there sounded shouts of discovery, the alarm mingled with the clamor of man-beasts yawling in pursuit of a ghost.

As the Foxes came to the horses and mules, "Trendel, take this steed and mount up," sissed Arik.

As Trendel hastily adjusted the length of the stirrups then swung into the saddle of Pon Barius's former mount, he asked, "Which way?"

"West," cried Ky, "circle round to the west and out from this cursed swamp."

"Why west?" asked Arik, mounting up. "What lies to the west?"

"The Kalagar Wood," answered Ky.

"But that forest is haunted," protested Trendel. "Why would anyone wish to go there, much less thee and me?"

"That's where we'll find the Kalagar Gate, the portal to the demonplane," said Ky, swinging up onto her horse. "And the demonplane is where we'll find Horax the Bastard and the red gem."

Arik glanced back through the trees, where atop the fortress wall he could see a force of man-beasts gathering, one of them gesturing toward the woods. "Come on," Arik barked, "let's get out of here while we can." He spurred his horse, and the others followed after, bending low over the necks of their steeds and galloping among the trees.

As they fled deeper into the woods while horns behind blatted in alarm, Trendel the seer muttered unto himself, "Indeed we might find Horax the Bastard on the demonplane, but that's also where we'll find the DemonQueen and her ravening, chaotic hordes—drakka and skelga and demonsteeds and broogs and . . ." but still he raced on with the others, running for the trackless swamp to throw off the gathering pursuit.

42

Doctor Stein pointed at Mark Perry. "As ignorant as this lawyer is, he put his finger on it when he said that those mental patterns were ersatz duplicates."

Toni Adkins looked briefly at Mark and then back at Stein. "Oh?"

"Yes. The AI has somehow found a way to deactivate the higher functions of a brain and mimic their patterns within its own processors."

"What makes you so certain?" asked Greyson.

Stein peered down his nose at the portly philosopher. "It's obvious, John. Only the autonomous processes of the alpha team members are active; the rest are shut down. But listen"—Stein turned to Toni—"if I modify a hemi-synch helmet to shock their brains back into full activity, then I, we, will have revived them from their comatose state."

Greyson objected: "Nonsense, Henry. You assume that the human mind is nothing but the parallel workings of clusters of neurons. But I believe a mentality is more, much more, than that—independent altogether—and that Avery has somehow captured these spirits of the alpha team, captured their very souls. We proved that when you tried to extract Alice Maxon from the rig and she nearly died when you broke the psychic link."

"You irrational ass, the AI is likely synchronizing the autonomous functions, and sync is lost when disconnect occurs." Stein turned away from Greyson and appealed to Toni: "Are you going to let this superstitious fool and his jabber of so-called psychic links stand in the way of reviving those people? My hemishock will free them from Avery's control."

Greyson started to protest, but Toni held up a hand to stop him. "Look, Henry, John, I don't know the truth of the metaphysics involved, and neither I think do either of you. But I will say this: desperate times often call for desperate actions, and this sounds to me like an ultimate gamble." Now she held up a hand to stop Stein's protest and fixed him with a stare. "Henry, Drew told Timothy it would take months to modify a hemisynch helmet, and so there simply is not time. But even if there were, and even if you did find a means to administer your so-called hemishock, even then we would use it only if it became absolutely necessary, only as a last resort."

Stein shook his head and pointed at the gimbaled rigs. "But don't you think—"

At that moment the overhead lights flickered on then faded.

Toni glanced at the doomsday clock—five minutes, thirty-one seconds to go—then keyed her comband. "Al, what's going on?"

Al Hawkins' reply came tinnily through. "We got one or more short circuits in the building. We're flipping the goddamned breakers off now to find them, then we'll try again."

"You mean Kat's turbogen is up and running?"

"Up and running and connected, but something's blowing the mains. Now lemme do my job."

Toni keyed her comband off. She looked at the others, her heart in her throat. And then a klaxon began sounding on the clock and the display began to flash. Doomsday—the catastrophic collapse of the batteries—was just five minutes away.

Her hard hat light casting a beam ahead, Kat ran for the distribution center. As she ran, she keyed her talkie. "Carleen, is the Astro all right?"

"Just a mo, chief" came Carleen's reply.

"Cut it free until I find out what's happening." Kat heard the whine of the turbine as Carleen opened the door of the truck.

Quickly Kat reached the breaker panels. Powertechs were milling about. At the breakers themselves, Al Hawkins stood with a meter while a man and a woman swiftly threw individual breakers off. Somewhere a klaxon was sounding.

Kat moved up next to Michael Phelan. "What the hell happened?" she snapped.

"The mains blew," he answered. "We've got a low resistance short to ground. Al is trying to locate it now."

"And the klaxon?"

"Coming from the battery room. There's less than five minutes reserve remaining."

"And then . . . ?"

"Total collapse."

Anxiously they watched as Al monitored the ohmmeter as the techs threw breakers. And time fled irretrievably into the past as the reserve batteries drained.

Kat's talkie beeped.

"Yeah."

"It's Carleen. The Astro is fine."

"Thanks, Carleen. Leave her mains open till I say go."

"Right, chief."

Kat keyed the talkie off.

She watched a moment more, then her eyes flew wide. "Wait just a damn minute," she called, shouldering her way forward to come to Al's side. "Look, Al, if it were some individual circuit, *that* breaker would be the one to blow and *not* the mains."

Al looked at her. "Crap! That's right."

Kat's blue-grey eyes became gemstone hard. "Now think, Al: what could blow both mains at once?"

"Nothing. Not a goddamned thing."

"Bullshit! They both blew, didn't they?" Kat flipped her unlit cigarillo into the shadows.

Al took a deep breath and expelled it. "All right. There's the main busses to the substation, but we cut them loose. There's the busses to the Allen-Breech, also cut loose. There's the power leads to your Astro. But wait a minute, those are all on the input side of the mains. What we gotta find is a short on the output side . . . which means either some of these feeds to the individual breakers are shorted to ground, or something is wrong with the . . ." He looked at the large subpanel housing the mains. "Susan, Bill, let's pull this fucker off the wall."

As the powertechs grabbed up wide-bladed drivers and began to snap open Dzeus fasteners, Kat jammed another unlit black synthbac cigarillo into the corner of her mouth and looked at her watch. Two minutes twelve seconds remained.

And the klaxon shouted disaster.

In the relative quiet of the control center, Toni Adkins paced back and forth, unable to stand still. She had switched off the klaxon before it had driven them all mad, but the display still flashed out its silent warning. Off to one side, Stein and Greyson argued over whether the mental patterns in the AI were real or merely Avery-generated duplicates. Mark Perry sat at one of the dead consoles, his head in his hands. Alya Ramanni sat at a live console and punched buttons on the compad. And in the shadows the alpha team lay comatose as the witches' cradles twitched and hummed in the dark.

Toni glanced at the flashing clock. One minute forty seconds till doomsday.

Popping the subpanel loose, Al Hawkins wrested it free of the primary housing. A black cable snaked out after. "What the hell is this?" As the klaxon continued shouting its warning of imminent disaster, Al turned the panel sideways. "Damn. Welded. Lightning welded! Cross-connected to the breakers." He wrenched the subpanel farther out. It stopped, the cable snagged on something.

"Yank it again," called Susan above the klaxon's cry, "I think I saw it move over here."

Al jerked.

"Yeah, this is it." Susan ran her hands along the heavy-duty wire. It was bolted to a girder. "It's the goddamned panel ground!"

Al braced the panel edgewise against the wall, his hands at top and bottom. "Get an axe," he cried.

Michael Phelan passed one to Kat. "Chop it free, Kat," ordered Al, turning his head aside.

Kat knelt and eyed the weld then swung. Sparks flew as steel met steel, the blade shearing along the subpanel and then across plastic and through the lightning-welded copper-to-copper bind and on into the concrete wall. Chips and dust and mortar flew. The cable flopped free.

"Pull it, Susan!" shouted Al. "Kat, when it's behind the panel, push it down and away."

As Susan and Kat maneuvered the panel ground cable back through the subpanel opening, Al snapped, "Reengage all the breakers, now!"

Bill and another powertech stood shoulder to shoulder and frantically flipped disengaged breakers back on, and still the klaxon clamored.

"Ready," called Kat, stepping aside.

Al slammed the subpanel back in place and held it while a powertech clicked the Dzeus fasteners shut. Then he looked at Kat. "Ready?"

"Just a mo." Kat keyed her talkie. "Carleen?"

"She is at the Astro, *princesa*," came Luiz's voice.

"Tell her we're ready. Tell her to reengage."

"Si." The whine of the turbo sounded as the cab door opened. A moment later it chopped off as the cab door was closed again. "It's done, *princesa*."

Kat nodded to Al and crossed her fingers. "Go ahead."

Al took a deep breath then slammed the mains to.

In the control center, the overhead lights came on and stayed on.

Toni looked up in disbelief, then tears filled her eyes. Blinking, she peered at the doomsday clock, but the numbers were all blurry. "What does it say?" she asked Mark Perry, pointing at the display.

"Thirteen seconds and stopped," he replied.

Down in the power distribution center men and women yelled and pounded one another on the back. Standing at the panel, Al Hawkins looked at Kat Lawrence. "Gimme one of them cheroots," he said.

She grinned at him and reached under her yellow rain-suit jacket and fished out another cigarillo.

Solemnly she handed it to him.

Just as solemnly he lit them both.

43

With Arik leading and three Black Foxes and Trendel trailing after, south they rode then west, fleeing from Horax's tower. And as they ran among the trees the hue and cry within the fortress walls faded in the distance. They galloped across the island of hill country and swiftly came to the swamp, and just as they reined back their steeds, a luminous mist caught up with them and coalesced into Lyssa's form.

Into the bog she led them, mosquitoes and gnats whining about in a blood-hungry swarm. They batted and swatted and slapped at the bugs for a half mile or so, then paused on a bit of high ground. Kane passed around a vial of pungent reetha juice and they dabbed it on themselves and on the six horses and two mules. Then only the maddest of the blood-mad insects attempted to penetrate the fumes to bite.

But nothing stopped the leeches, and whenever the Foxes came to a patch of dry land they would pause long enough to scrape the blood-suckers free.

As before, when insects flew about Lyssa, attracted to her light like moths to a flame, they would circle once or twice, then fall into the mire, their minuscule life forces drained by her presence, though she gained no sustenance from their incompatible loss.

Orbis passed overhead and sank into the west, and just before dawn they found a large hummock covered with sharp-bladed sawgrass, where they stopped to make camp.

"Lyssa, you must draw life force," said Kane, looking east, "before dayrise."

Lyssa shook her head. <Not this night, healer. Draining the turret warders to senselessness more than filled my needs.>

"Were they human?" asked Rith, surprised. "They did not seem so."

<Human enough,> signaled Lyssa. <Some crossbreed of Horax's.>

"Horax the Bastard," hissed Ky, tears welling again. Her shoulders slumped. "I loved Arton like an uncle. And Pon Barius?—he reminded me of my own grandsire."

Dawn broke across the Drasp, and with the coming of the sun, Lyssa vanished.

They tended the horses and mules, currying and feeding them rations of grain. Then the Foxes and Trendel settled down to a meal of their own.

Arik cast a glance at their new companion. "You handled yourself well back there." Arik tilted his head toward the direction of the distant tower, ten or twelve miles arear.

"I had a good swordmaster," replied Trendel, biting off a mouthful of jerky and chewing slowly. "Actually a good axemaster, too," he added, talking round his mouthful.

"Trendel is a seer," said Ky.

"Oh?" Arik raised an eyebrow. "Then how came you to be in Horax's prison? Did you not foresee your own fate?"

Trendel shook his head. "Peering into the future— especially one's own future—is no small feat. A tricky business at best and highly unreliable, for the very act of looking oft changes the way ahead. Besides, the dubious information gained is usually not worth the cost. —But as to how I landed in Horax's cell, I don't know at the moment, yet after this meal and a nap I will discover the reason."

Ky tilted her head. "Cast that past-vision spell?"
Trendel nodded.
Ky turned to the others. "He couldn't do it in Horax's

dungeon. It was null, you know. Takes away your magical talents. —That's what gave you all such splitting headaches when you came running in."

Kane and Rith nodded, but Arik looked at her wide-eyed. "Wait a moment. That can't be right. I got a splitting headache in there and I have absolutely *no* magical talent."

Now it was Ky's turn to be wide-eyed. "That's right! You *did* get a headache. —But hold on a moment . . . you must have talent, else the cell wouldn't have hurt you."

Rith looked at the warrior. "My, my, Arik, what have you been keeping from us all these years?"

Slowly Arik shook his head. "Beats the seven hells out of me," he replied.

Kane growled. "One of these days we're going to go on a venture where there are *no* enigmas to resolve. Just plain old combat, and not much of that."

"Against pitiful foe, I hope, and in a comfortable place," added Rith, waving at the Drasp. "I've had enough of fighting and slogging."

"Pitiful foe or skilled, it does not matter," said Kane. "Just as long as there are no cursed unsolvable riddles. I mean, look at what we've got: a leader with a magical talent which even *he* doesn't know. A gem with a mysterious rune enscribed inside. A—"

"Rune?" asked Trendel, looking at Ky. "You didn't tell me about a rune."

"I forgot all about it," said Ky. "I only saw it that once." Ky took out her dagger and as she scratched in the soft dirt of the hummock, she said, "It looked something like this—"

Trendel cocked his head and stared at the figure. "Well, I know quite a bit about runes and glyphs," he said, "but this one I've never seen before. Besides, to decipher any magical meaning it might have, I need to do a casting on the real thing. When we recover the gem from Horax, let me take a look. Perhaps I can decipher it. It could prove to be important or trivial or have no significance at all."

Arik raised an eyebrow. "Do you mean to come with us?"

Trendel took a deep breath. "Well, it seems as if you could use a hand, and I'm adequate with weapons. Too, I am a rather good seer, or so I think, and my sort of talent is quite useful. And you broke me free of imprisonment. With all that, how could I refuse to aid you? Besides, I already feel like a Black Fox, at least temporarily, though I'm not dressed for the part." Trendel gestured at his tattered raiment.

Arik glanced at the others, then stood and stepped to his gear. He pulled out his spare set of leathers and tossed them at Trendel. "Welcome to the Black Foxes"—he grinned—"at least temporarily."

Arik's leathers were a bit large on Trendel, but all in all better garments for swamp travel than the seer's torn silks and satins. "What? No spare boots?" he asked in mock indignation.

" 'Fraid not," replied Arik. "We'll just have to wait till we get to a town."

"Where I'll get me a good axe, too," said Trendel, peering at his inadequate shoes. "If we've any money, that is." He turned out his empty pockets. "At the moment I seem to be totally embarrassed."

"Horax the Bastard probably took it all," gritted Ky. She turned to Kane. "You know, he really *is* a traitorous bastard. He's the one from the Circle of Mages who betrayed Jaytar to the demons. And he's proud of it, too. And now he's gone to be with the DemonQueen—to serve as her consort."

Arik looked at the syldari. "Perhaps, Ky, you ought to tell us what you know."

Ky nodded. "Well, here's what he said . . ."

By the time Ky finished, Kane was stomping back and forth, enraged, trampling down sawgrass and cursing Horax the Bastard.

But Arik sat coolly and considered the facts. "I would guess that Atraxia intends on invading Itheria again . . .

this time she is likely to conquer all, for no longer is she opposed by the Inner Circle of Wizards."

Ky slowly nodded. "Pon Barius said they were all dead, all but him."

Rith raised an eyebrow. "Perhaps he was wrong and some yet live. He was wrong about Horax the Bastard, after all, as we found out in White Mountain, much to our detriment."

Silence fell on the group, but at last Ky looked across at Rith. "Tell me: what happened after I lost consciousness? How did you defeat the skelga? Was there any problem getting free from White Mountain? And Arton, how did he . . . die? And what happened to Lyssa?"

Rith looked at the others. "This is a long tale. Why don't you get some sleep while I tell it to Ky? She and I will take the first watch."

"I'll stay awake and hear it, too, if you don't mind," said Trendel, smiling at the bard.

Rith looked at Ky then nodded.

As Arik and Kane spread their bedrolls, Rith began: "After Kane threw the skelga which slammed you into the wall"—Ky shot an accusing glance at Kane and he turned up his hands and shrugged, then bedded down—"Horax the Bastard lifted you up to use you as a shield. And he demanded the silver dagger with its gem. . . ."

As the day wore on, the horses and mules stood dozing or grazed on sawgrass, though how they kept from cutting themselves on the sharp blades, none could say. The Black Foxes, too, slept . . . or stood sentry duty. But as the sun neared the western horizon, all were finally awake and taking another meal.

Rith turned to Trendel and said, "How about your story, seer? Do you yet know how you came to be in Horax the Bastard's cell?"

Trendel shrugged. "The last thing I can remember before waking up in the dungeon is being in bed with a lady of my acquaintance."

Rith canted her head and smiled toothily. "Was she, perchance, married?"

Trendel looked down at his hands. "Um, yes. —But I hasten to add that her husband is a pig. —Or so she said."

"So then . . . ?"

"So when I woke up I was in Horax's dungeon."

Ky blew out a breath. "Perhaps you ought to try that spell."

Trendel intertwined his fingers and sat with his head bowed. All the other Foxes remained silent. Moments passed. Then Trendel raised his head. There was a confused look in his eye and his hands trembled. "It failed," he said, trepidation in his voice. "It failed."

He looked at Ky, at Rith. "I've never failed before."

"What did you . . . sense?" asked Rith.

"A vagueness. It was as if there was virtually nothing between being in bed and then being in the dungeon."

"Perhaps the lady drugged you," suggested Rith.

"Perhaps it was her husband," added Ky.

"Even so, a past vision should have shown me what happened," responded Trendel. "Instead, it is as if virtually no time at all had elapsed between being at one place and then at another."

"Perhaps—" Rith began, but Trendel interrupted her.

"What day is it?"

"Orbis eighteen," said Rith.

"Orbis eighteen! Luba's teats, I've lost twelve days."

Arik standing near, stepped to Trendel's side and squatted. "Perhaps more. This is Summer third."

The air whooshed from Trendel's lungs. "And the year?"

"Torlon twenty-seven."

Trendel's eyes flew wide. Quickly he counted on his fingers. "Arda's Wife! I've lost nine months."

Rith reached out and laid a soothing hand on Trendel's arm. "You said you sensed a vagueness. A vagueness of what?"

Trendel shrugged. "A shadowy premonition that I was, um, elsewhere . . . perhaps on a different plane altogether."

Ky shook her head. "How can that be? I mean, it's not like someone swooped down and abducted you. You'd remember that. No, I'd say that the lady's husband discovered that you were cuckolding him and drugged you. Perhaps he's a confederate of Horax."

"Squire Foth? Ha! He's as unlikely to be allied with Horax as I am to be allied with—with—"

"With the Black Foxes?" asked Ky, grinning.

Kane, saddling his horse, growled, "Arrgh! Another dretching mystery! It's like the gods above are handing us one puzzle after another and manipulating us for who knows what ends?"

The sun set and, as twilight followed, ghostly Lyssa appeared. With Phemis halfway across the sky and Orbis yet to rise, toward the far western marge of the Drasp started the Foxes and horses and mules, riding and walking and sloshing through the grasping, clutching mire. West they fared over sawgrassed hummocks and through pools of slime and among twisted black cypress with greyish moss dangling down; through thick stands of reeds, raising a cloud of gossamer seedlings with their tiny hooklike strands snagging, grabbing, hundreds working their way inside leathers and down, itching abominably; across flats of deep muck, the mud clinging and sucking at their feet as if trying to trap these intruders; through greyish webs of bog spiders, the poisonous arachnids dropping down on them to be swatted away; and all the while, ploppings and slitherings and distant screams sounded through the dark.

And on this night as they were all afoot and wading across a shallow slough, they saw lights glimmering among the black cypress.

"Will-o'-the-wisp," hissed Rith. "Like the one that slew Arton."

Mounting up they rode splashing through the mire, and soon the creature was left behind.

Just before dawn, Lyssa took a small bit of life force from each of them, and then vanished with the coming of day.

The next night was much the same, except they saw no will-o'-the-wisp creature.

They reached the edge of the Drasp just after midnight on the following eve. And after they had ridden a mile or so out onto solid ground, they stopped and dismounted to stretch their legs and to feed the horses and mules and to scrape away the last of the leeches.

"Arda, I've never been so happy to be on dry land," said Trendel.

A murmur of agreement muttered among the Foxes.

Arik turned to Lyssa, standing apart. "Do you know where the Kalagar Forest is?"

She pointed westward and signaled, <Two hundred miles.>

"And the gate?"

Lyssa shrugged. <I've never been there. But if a trail goes to it, I will find the way.>

Trendel did not understand the Fox hand code, but he could tell from Arik's questions and Lyssa's expressions that although she could get them to the forest, she might have trouble finding the portal. "Don't worry, Arik. I will be able to locate the gate."

"Are you certain?"

Trendel smiled. "Yes. I know what it looks like. I have seen it on the tapestries chronicling the demonwars." He frowned a moment in concentration and murmured a word. He smiled again. "That way," he pointed, "two hundred and twelve miles and a furlong or two."

They rode westerly at a pace the horses could readily sustain, and Lyssa had no trouble staying with them, the glimmering wraith floating across the ground some fifty paces ahead.

On the fourth day out from the Drasp, during a driving rain, they came across the moderate town of Grencwmb, where they took rooms in the Eagle's Nest and rested for two days. And in this time of respite, using Black Fox funds, Trendel purchased leathers and boots that fit, and a one-handed war axe and shield, as well as two throwing axes and a dagger with scabbard . . . and acting on the advice of the other Foxes, he found a smith to silver the blades. Ky, too, purchased a scabbard, this one for her black long-knife, with straps fitted to lash it to her thigh.

And they bathed and ate warm meals. And in the great-room of the Eagle's Nest, Trendel sang harmony to some of Rith's songs, though he was not trained as a bard. And the inn became fair to overflowing when the townsfolk heard that a true bard and her lover were staying there. Rith smiled at Trendel when he was named as her lover, and that night they turned rumor to truth.

And although Lyssa kept her distance, this close to a population center it seemed she needed no sustenance from anyone, yet in truth and without willing it she drew a minuscule bit of energy from everyone in the entire town.

Rested and fed and clean, and with replenished supplies and a new mule, the Foxes resumed their journey. They could have used their spare horse to bear part of the goods, but it was Lyssa's mount, and they left it saddled and equipped with her gear—a token of their faith that somehow they would restore her to her own true form.

Six more days they traveled west, the nights now chill as autumn approached. And on the evening of the seventh day they sighted the Kalagar Wood.

"Trendel?" Arik looked at the seer.

After a moment, Trendel said, "That way." And he pointed slightly rightward. "A bit over forty-one miles." Lyssa looked at the way he directed, then cast a spell of her own. And as clouds gathered low on the horizon, off she moved, a point or so north of west.

Into the forest she glided, Black Foxes following, and the dismal wood seemed darkly alive and hostile. A chill wind sprang up, lightly at first but growing stronger with each stride they took, until it whirled through the treetops and moaned in agony among thrashing limbs. Twisted branches ending in barren twigs lashed and swayed and reached out as if to snag them, brittle fingers clutching, clawing, the wood creaking and groaning. All the Foxes felt as if they were being watched by unfriendly eyes moving along the periphery, but when they looked nothing was there. And now and again they could hear wild howling on the wind. Yet Lyssa flowed onward, deeper and deeper, pressing farther into this forsaken realm.

At times they would stop to rest the skittish horses and the unsettled mules, or to feed them a bit of grain. But the animals stamped and fretted and rolled their eyes and would have none of this, and the Foxes then moved on. And whenever they came to a stream in the woods, Kane would test it before allowing any to take a drink. Here at least the animals did take water when offered, though they tossed up their heads and peered around nervously between wary sips.

And so, riding, walking, and resting, the Foxes and horses and mules moved deeper into the windblown writhing forest, following a glowing wraith.

Toward morning the sky cleared and the wind died and they made camp in a tiny swale. And as the sun rose up into the sky the air became deathly still and the woods seemed to crowd around suffocatingly close, dark boles closing in. And the hot, stifling day pressed down upon them and no birds sang among the tangled branches. Foxes tossed and turned restlessly, sleeping in fits and starts, and the one on guard saw grotesque shapes standing among the baneful trees, but investigation of these forest lurkers showed each to be a twisted snag and not some malformed watching creature, or so they believed.

Finally evening came and with it the swirling wind, tossing and heaving the creaking limbs, and their clawlike branches reached out and twigs clutched and grasped. Glowing, Lyssa appeared, luminous streamers and lucent tendrils fluttering in the blow, some to spin away and vanish in the twisting air. Again Trendel cast a seer's finding, and once more pointed slightly north of west, and through the swaying woods they started, horses and mules skitting and shying, the Foxes peering about with chary eyes.

"Luba, but I hate traveling in these dark writhing woods in the black of night," hissed Trendel. "It's like the very trees resent our passage."

"Perhaps they do," said Rith, riding at his side. "Who knows what trees think?"

"Perhaps they think of men with axes," said Trendel. "Maybe that's why I feel so, um, so threatened."

They rode a bit farther and suddenly Trendel raised up his silver-bladed war axe in one hand and an argent throwing axe in the other and called out, "Let be! Let be! These are not for cutting wood but for hewing demons instead." Yet the creaking trees and clutching limbs seemed not to heed him at all.

Onward they rode through the groaning woods, the wind sobbing above, and time after time on this night they heard the flapping of wings, as if *things* flew across the whirling wind, things sinister and dark and dangerous. Yet when they scanned the gloom of night for creatures flying above, they saw nothing beyond the writhing limbs but dark scudding clouds in the sky.

Again daylight came and again they made camp and again a stifling day tried to smother them. And as Rith sat facing Trendel and holding his hands in hers, she looked about and shivered, then asked, "How much longer must we travel among these angry trees?"

Trendel paused in concentration, then answered, "Twelve miles less two furlongs. We should get there just before dawn."

As midnight came and the Foxes stopped to rest the nervous horses, "What is that wild howling?" asked Trendel.

Rith glanced up through the groaning branches at the night sky above. "Wind wolves, love. Those are the howls of the wild wind wolves chasing cloud deer across the sky."

Trendel looked at Kane. The big man raised an eyebrow and shrugged. Ky grinned then sobered. "The syldari call it the cries of beleaguered souls searching for the way to the spiritland."

All the Foxes glanced at Lyssa standing a distance from them.

Ky reached out and touched Arik's arm. "I'm sorry. What I said was thoughtless."

Arik groaned deep in his throat, but he said nothing in return.

Again came the distant howls.

Now Arik looked at the others. "Mount up. It's time we were on our way."

In the candlemarks before dawn they came through the groaning, clutching forest to the base of a broad treeless hill. Like a huge barrow mound it was, high and rounded and windswept. And in between clouds, by the light of waxing Orbis, they could see on the crest a broad archway, seemingly made of dark stone.

Onto the slopes they rode, yet as they started upward a wailing filled the air, as pale wraiths rose up from out of the ground and started downslope toward them.

Kane drew his spear from its saddle sling and then looked at Rith. "There, methinks, are your wind wolves, bard, howling unto the sky."

Lyssa, in the fore, glided upslope and stood to bar the way, her light bright, theirs but a pale reflection. And she held up her arms and opened her mouth and called out to the ghostly throng, but the only thing the Foxes heard was an eerie lamentation like the weeping of an abandoned spirit. Some wraiths paused and called to Lyssa, others turned back, but many came onward still.

"Take weapons, Foxes," barked Arik, drawing his silvered sword. Trendel set his shield to arm, and hefted his argent war axe. Rith pulled two silver daggers from her bandoliers, and Ky took her dark main gauche in hand.

And their weapons gleamed argent in the light of the twin moons shining through rifts in the clouds, all but Ky's, which reflected deadly black.

And seeing this silvered and ebon display, wraiths fell back and aside, retreating from this shining glimmer.

Even Lyssa drew apart.

Trendel looked at Ky and said, "Now we know what will kill a ghost," then he tossed her his silver dagger.

But she tossed it right back, saying, "I need no silver to protect me, seer. My blade is more than enough."

Once again Lyssa spoke to the wraiths—the weeping of ghostly wind the only sound she made—and the phantasmal throng retreated before her hollow wail. Back upslope they drifted, some more slowly than others, until at last they were gone, sinking back into the ground.

As Lyssa turned and came downslope, Arik and the others resheathed blades and reslung axe and spear. And the Foxes could see that Lyssa was weeping.

"What is it, my love?" asked Arik.

<Oh, Arik, we must find a way to release these trapped souls, a way to set them free.>

"Set them free?"

<They were sacrificed to build the portal, slain to give it power.>

Arik glanced upslope. Then he turned to Rith. "If we destroy the arch, will it release them?"

Rith shook her head. "I don't know, Arik. Perhaps. Ghosts are often bound to a place or a thing. If the arch is their focus, then, yes, I would believe that its destruction would break the bond which binds them to this plane."

Arik looked grimly at the black arch and said to Lyssa, "When we finish our mission in the demonworld, we will see what we can do to set these spirits free."

Lyssa nodded and looked long up the slope, then she turned her agonized face to him. <Oh, Arik, they are so . . . hungry.>

When day came, the Foxes camped at the base of the hill, but in midmorn they moved back and away and into the woods, for sleep eluded them entirely as long as they stayed on the slopes of the great barrow mound. Yet though they had moved, rest did not come easily, and even when they finally slept their dreams were filled with visions of hideous sacrifices and they woke up screaming.

Some respite came to Kane and Ky when her watch was over and she snuggled up next to the big man and he threw his arm about her, as likewise a measure of rest came to Trendel and Rith when they held onto one another. But Arik slept alone and did not fare well at all.

When twilight fell, Lyssa led the Foxes and horses and mules through a silent ghostly throng, the wraiths staying well back from the drawn silver weapons. And Lyssa spoke to weeping shades in the sound of a wailing wind, promising them when the mission was completed the Foxes would return and try to set them all free. Moaning, the spectral assembly backed down the hill, away from the Foxes, where they stood glowing dimly in the deepening dusk.

And under the twin half moons of Phemis and Orbis, already high in the early evening sky, the Black Foxes came to the Kalagar Arch, the way to the demonplane.

Set on a bed of rough black granite, it was made of a dusky stone and carved with arcane runes. It arched upward some seven yards, and its legs stood perhaps four paces apart at the base. And at the foundation each leg was square, nearly three feet to a side, but they tapered as they curved up to meet at the very peak, where the stone appeared to be but half as thick. And the arch looked to be all of a solid piece. Darker than dark, it seemed to suck at the light of the twin moons and the stars in the sky, devouring it, consuming it, as if to gorge it all down.

Arik turned to Ky. "Shadowmaster, it is up to you now."

Ky dismounted. "This is one of the greater spells, and it will take much from me," she said, "yet I will recover. Just put me on my horse when it is time and take me through with you."

Kane, too, dismounted and stood at her back.

Arik looked down at her. "How long will we have?"

Ky shrugged. "A few moments at worst. More perhaps."

Arik turned to the others, including Lyssa off to one side. "All right, then, everyone be ready to move."

<I will come last.>

The warrior nodded, and Rith relayed Lyssa's message to Trendel.

Arik looked down at Ky again. "Whenever you are ready, Shadowmaster."

Ky canted her head toward Arik.

Kane leaned forward and whispered in her ear. "I'll be right behind you, mouse."

Ky sat cross-legged on the ground and Kane knelt just behind. She took several deep breaths and concentrated, then she looked at the stone of the arch and whispered a word or two.

And an utterdark filled the opening, a void, a nothingness blacker than black.

Ky fell over backward, unconscious, and Kane scooped her up. "Arik," barked the big man, and handed her up to the warrior. Arik took her across his lap. "Ride!" he commanded, and spurred forward into the void, his horse squealing as it ran through the utterdark wall, iron-shod hooves ringing on black granite stone. . . .

After him rode Rith, and behind came Trendel, with Kane on his heels, mounts or mules on tethers running after . . .

. . . and suddenly they all were gone.

44

There was bedlam in the control center, too; people shouting and pounding one another on the back. As Toni wiped her eyes with the heels of her hands and looked at the display, confirming that the doomsday clock had indeed stopped just thirteen seconds short of catastrophic battery failure, Mark Perry called out above the noise, "My God, why are they cheering? Arthur is dead and six people are trapped by an insane machine."

"Oh, Mark, don't you see?" answered Toni. "Now we have a chance. With power restored, we have more time: more time for the Foxes to win, or for us to find a way to rescue them."

Toni keyed her comband. "Al? Al Hawkins?"

Shouts of victory down in the power room came through her communicator as Hawkins replied, "Yes, Toni."

"Congratulations, Al. You and Kat and all the power-techs have given us a reprieve. Is Kat where she can hear me?"

"I'm right here," Kat answered, talking through Al's comband.

"Nicely done, Kat. Nicely done. My compliments to your crew."

"Right. —And Toni?"

"Yes."

"Al and I are going to survey the damage done to the substation. We'll let you know what we find."

"What about the reserve batteries?"

Al came back on the communicator. "The Astro is charging them up again, just in case, you know. They'll be fully loaded in an hour or so."

"Thank you, Al. Thank you, Kat. Toni out."

As Toni keyed off her comband, Drew Meyer and Sheila Baxter and Billy Clay came back through the glass doors, this time wheeling a cart loaded with IC boards. They rolled it to the main holovid and Sheila flopped to the floor and opened a panel. She pulled out a circuit and examined it, then laid it aside and said, "Billy, give me the synchronizer."

Billy searched among the boards and then handed her one. As she guided it into the tracks, Sheila said, "I'll need the transducer next."

Drew walked over to Toni. "I'm going to start thinking of alternate ways of getting in contact with Avery."

"Oh? What about the holovid?"

Drew turned and gestured at Sheila and Billy. "I'm not needed there. They've got things well in hand."

"What are they doing?" asked Mark.

"Replacing every board; we think the ball lightning took them all out. But we've determined that Avery is sending signals over the optical fibers, so replacing the holoboards should bring it back on-line."

Toni looked up at the physicist. "Avery is sending signals to the holo?"

Drew nodded. "Yes. It's like he wants us to see what's going on in VR."

"Of course he does," growled Mark. "The murdering sonofabitch is mad—Mad Avery, the psycho sociopath. And of course he's sending signals—the bastard is bragging."

Kat Lawrence and Al Hawkins strode past the whining turbine. Kat waved at Susan and Luiz up on the flatbed, and she made an okay circle with her thumb and forefinger and received broad smiles and two thumbs-up in return. Kat and Al tramped onward, heading toward the northwest corner of the Coburn Building, where the distribution station was located. As they neared, a guard moved to intercept them. "Stay back. The power lines are down and this is a restricted— Oh, Al, I didn't see who you were."

"Roberto," acknowledged Al. Then he pointed to Kat. "Roberto Sanchez, this is Kat Lawrence, best powertech west of the big muddy."

Kat nodded to Sanchez, but then her eye strayed to the substation. "Jeezie Peezie, it looks like it was bombed."

Al nodded and turned and flipped the stub of his cigarillo out into the wet dark. "Transformers exploded."

"It must have been a superbolt," said Kat, her stub following his.

Al sighed then looked up at the sky, still dismal, still cloud covered. Far to the northeast lightning yet flickered. "It'll soon be dawn," he announced.

Kat doffed her rain jacket as she walked into the control center. Looking about, she spotted Toni Adkins and went to her. Toni leaped up and shook Kat's hand, then threw her arms about the powertech and hugged her tightly. "Thank you, Kat. You don't know how much this means."

Kat glanced at the gimbaled rigs, no longer in shadow. "Perhaps one day you'll fill me in."

"That's a promise," said Toni.

Kat grinned, then sobered. "The substation is blasted. Al is on the line now, talking to Solar. They'll get here as soon as they can, but that may be tomorrow."

Toni looked at Mark Perry. "Mark, have you got any connections with TSP? High up?"

"Tucson Solar? Sure. Bill Petrie is a friend. A close friend."

Kat's eyebrows raised. "Billy the Bull?"

Perry nodded and, at a puzzled look from Toni, said, "The CEO. We ski together."

Toni grinned. "Well then, Mark, how about giving Bully Bill a call—"

* * *

"Billy the Bull," corrected Mark.

"—give him a call and see if he can speed things up. I mean, if anything goes wrong with the Astro two-fifty, well then, we're back in the same bind. Tell him it's critical and, if you have to, tell him that six people's lives are on the line."

As Mark reached for his portable vidcom and stepped away, Kat turned to Toni. "So what's the problem?"

Toni eyed Kat and then said, "This is strictly confidential." At a nod from the powertech, Toni went on: "See those six people over there? Well, at the moment their mentalities are trapped in a virtual reality run by an AI. We think there're only two ways they can get free: one way is if we manage to get into contact with Avery, the AI, and tell him to release them; we've tried this once, no, twice and failed—the first time with deadly results, and the second time Avery trapped another soul."

"That's one," said Kat. "What's the second way?"

"We think they might be able to free themselves by getting to endgame and winning."

Kat glanced at the rigs. "That's it?"

Toni sighed. "That's the short of it, Kat. The long of it will take some telling, but sit down and I'll fill you in."

In that moment there came more cheering and shouts. Toni looked. The main holovid was up and running. . . .

"God save the Queen!" exclaimed Toni. "But what in bleedin' Hades . . . ?"

She could see the alpha team, or rather their alter personas, atop a hill before some kind of archway: Kane and Ky were on the ground, with Arik and Rith and Trendel on horseback. But what was this? Off to the right floating just above the soil was Lyssa—Alice Maxon's persona— and, bloody hell! She appeared to be a—a spectre, a ruddy *ghost*! And gathered on the hillside below them were hundreds of other ghosts!

In that moment, a black beyond black filled the arch, and Caine Easley, or rather his alter, Kane the warrior-healer, handed unconscious Ky up to Arik on horseback.

"Ride!" Arik commanded, and spurred forward, charging toward the utter darkness. Kane leapt into his own saddle, and trailing mules and spurring forward charged all the rest, steel-shod hooves clattering on black stone as into the darkness they ran . . .

. . . and suddenly they were gone.

45

They emerged galloping down a rounded hillock, the twin of the barrow behind, but the world itself . . . the world itself . . . it was no twin.

Hauling back on the reins, Arik skidded to a stop, his eyes wide with wonder. Dust flying, the others thundered to a halt behind him, their startled gazes sweeping outward, upward. Overhead arched a yellow-orange sky, beyond which great purple arcs swept across; and if each world was truly a sphere, then perhaps these demonic rings encircled the entire globe. Just above the horizon and off to what was perhaps the east a great black ball rode in the ocherous sky—an ebon sun, it's spectral light glancing across the land.

And out before them lay a hellish 'scape: bubbling, boiling, jagged rocks suddenly thrusting up, boulders sucked downward to vanish. Off in the distance something exploded in brilliant green fire, and heartbeats later there followed a bone-jarring boom. And as far as the eye could see, the land was a frenzy of ever-changing disorder; only the barrow mound stood stable—a rock in a sea of chaos.

Arik glanced at unconscious Ky in his arms: she was dark violet and her hair was pure white. Then he looked back at his companions: Rith was colored a pale grey with whitish hair, and all the others were hued in shades of malachite, Kane's hair a greyish-green, Trendel's even greener. Arik's own hair was dark violet. Their leathers were mottled brown, and the horses grey instead of brown, white instead of black, dull green instead of roan . . .

. . . It was as if all colors had been reversed.

"Is everyone all right?" he asked. "Did everyone make it through?"

His eyes swept from one to the other, then he demanded, "Where is Lyssa?"

Lyssa!

The wraith was nowhere to be seen.

Lyssa!

Arik looked back at the arch. The stone itself was pearlescent, and blinding white filled the opening. Yet even as he looked on, the white vanished, revealing only the chaotic demonscape through the span beyond.

Ky's spell had expired.

Kane dismounted and took the syldari from Arik and lowered her to the ground. Now all the others dismounted as well and formed a circle about her and Kane. The warrior-healer looked up and said, "She'll come around in a moment, then we need to ride."

"Ride? Now? What about Lyssa?" asked Trendel.

"Listen," said Kane, "we don't know what kind of alarm might have been set off when we came through that gate. For all we know, even now a band of demons is heading this way. I say we get down off here and out of sight."

Rith glanced at the ebony sun. "Perhaps Lyssa did come through, after all. But I think it's daytime here in the demonworld, and so even as she arrived, she vanished, going wherever it is that spirits go during the day."

Arik looked at Trendel. The seer shrugged and said nothing.

Ky groaned and her eyes fluttered open. Kane gave her a drink.

Arik knelt and asked Kane, "Do you think she could cast another spell now?" At Kane's negative shake of the head, Arik said, "I thought not. If she could have, I would have stepped through to see if Lyssa was on the other side of the gate."

Kane held Ky's hand. "I don't think she'll be able to throw another great spell until this evening—assuming there are evenings in this blasted realm."

Rith cleared her throat. "Come on, Arik, let's get away from this place. If Lyssa is here, we'll see her tonight, when the black sun sets."

Arik cast a glance at the archway and sighed. "All right. As Kane said, a demon force may even now be coming to check on the gate. Besides, we've got to find Horax." Arik stood and shaded his eyes and scanned the horizon. "But which way do we go?"

Trendel cleared his throat. "I can't find Horax, for I don't know what he looks like. But, if he's with the DemonQueen, Atraxia, *she* I can find."

Rith gasped. "You've seen the DemonQueen?"

"In tapestries, my dear. The same ones depicting the Kalagar Gate. She's all in armor and carries a great long blade . . . and is rather beautiful in an exotic way. —Oh, nothing like your black beauty, Rith."

"Black beauty?" Rith held up her greyish arm. "Gack! I look like a gnoman."

Trendel laughed. "Too tall, Rith. Too tall."

Rith smiled, her black teeth gleaming. "Let us hope I fare better than the last gnoman we saw."

Arik looked at Trendel. "DemonQueen it is, seer. Where is she, and how far?"

Trendel concentrated briefly then pointed. "That way. Is it north? Whatever. She lies that way some ten miles—" Suddenly Trendel broke off and his eyes widened. "Huah. The distance is more like a thousand." He maintained his concentration. "Hold on, something strange is happening. Now she's twenty-two miles away—still north. What under Luba's bed is going on?"

"Perhaps spells don't work well in the demonplane," suggested Arik. He glanced down at Ky. The syldari was awake and aware.

"Can you travel?" he asked. "Are you strong enough?"

"Unh, I think so," said Ky. Her voice was somewhat thready.

"I will take some of the weakness from her," said Kane.

"Careful," warned Rith. "Given what's happening to Trendel's casting, your own may act against you or her."

"Six hundred and three miles," said Trendel. "Still north." He broke off his spell.

Kane took a deep breath and laid hands on Ky. Then he frowned in concentration. After a moment he released her and said, "How's that?"

Ky grinned up at him, her almond eyes flashing silver in black. "I'm all right now."

Trendel ran a hand over his green hair. "Hm, why did his spell act as normal, while mine behaved so strangely?"

Rith paused in thought. "Perhaps they are both acting correctly."

"If that's so," said Arik, "then the DemonQueen lies northward, but the distance is haphazard. —Regardless, mount up and let us be gone from here."

As they started down the slope, Rith exclaimed, "I just remembered: didn't Pon Barius say that Ranvir's host crossed the Plains of Chaos? Perhaps that's where we are—on the Plains of Chaos. If so, then that might explain the muddled answer Trendel's spell yielded."

"Muddled?" protested Trendel. "Strange, yes; muddled, not at all. Besides, my confused little spellsinger"—he sniffed and lofted his nose in the air and pointed north— "it is definitely that direction." Then he burst out laughing at the squinty-eyed look Rith shot his way.

They rode out from the rounded barrow hill into a land which continuously churned and changed—subtle at times, violent at other times, but always hellish. Before their very eyes rocks would shift an inch or two or race away for miles; upslopes would lurch to become steeper or abruptly transform into downslopes. Within a few hundred strides, Arik looked back over his shoulder; the archway was nowhere to be seen, nor the mound on which it stood. He faced front once more and headed deeper into the mutable 'scape. North they went and north. Suddenly with great heaving and splitting a mighty rift opened before them, and as horses reared and plunged and mules bellowed, it thunderously slammed shut. A great cloud of choking dust rose up around them, and hacking and coughing they could but barely manage to breathe; yet just as suddenly the dust vanished, leaving ice crystals in its wake. In freezing cold, northward they fared as the demonday drew on, and a bluff ripped up out of the ground to steeply bar the way; boulders and pebbles and melon-sized stones crashed down from above, and the Foxes danced their horses this way and that to avoid the plummeting rocks. But one stubborn mule broke free only to have its hindquarters crushed beneath a great slab smashing down. And it screamed in agony and foundered and flopped as stone continued to rain. But at last the cascade ended, and as Arik cut the throat of the animal to put it out of its misery, they found themselves on a towering mesa with escarpments falling sheer. While Arik salvaged the goods from the dead mule, the others dismounted and walked the perimeter looking for a way down, finding none. Then the land mutated into a white lava plain. Northward they journeyed across the glaring stone as the black sun climbed up the yellow-orange sky. And as they rode, far-off hills raced away or moved close or grew tall or shrank into oblivion to leave vast sinkholes behind. A field of thorns burst up all around them and loomed tall in mere moments; they could not take even a step without enduring gashes and cuts and punctures, and here the animals suffered greatly, shifting about in fright. But the land mutated again, changing into a glacial plateau, where raging green fires ravened forth from the ground, and it was all the Foxes could do to retain control of their mounts and the two mules and one horse trailing after. Across this frigid burning high plain they went, which suddenly transformed into dark gravel dunes sloping this way and that, and the Foxes dismounted and led the animals slipping and sliding, for the gravel was entirely too loose for anyone to ride along the oceanic slopes. They stopped often to check hooves and to pick stones from the iron shoes. And as they did this, the dark gravel shifted subtly, ever so subtly, into miles of purple stone flats. They passed through an area where a field of monolithic boulders suddenly rose up from the rock and streams of green magma poured out to become, in a flash, hot sand cascading over a high bluff to fall with a bellow into a

river of pebbles roaring down a solid stone hillside. Onward they pressed as pustules formed on blasted plains
and became sulfurous fumeroles belching up blue mud as
molten glass oozed out from frozen bluffs. Still the Foxes
went forward, northward, and ever did the land shift, but
always into something infernal, as of a landscape damned.
Even so, the Foxes found passage over or under or across
or through, Trendel pointing the way.

As mid of the demonic day came, the Foxes stopped to
rest and to take a meal on a spot of land which the seer
deemed would be safe for the moment. And as they ate
beneath purple rings with the sable sun beyond, Rith said,
"Perhaps this is why demons have chaotic forms, the land
being such as it is . . . Plains of Chaos, indeed."

"Huah," grunted Trendel, "I think you are right, love,
and the de—" His eyes flew wide and he jumped to his
feet. "Look!" he exclaimed, pointing.

At his call the Foxes turned round and peered to the
north, then they, too, stood and shaded their eyes from the
spectral light of the black sun overhead. In the near distance they could see jutting up from a desolate plain an
obsidian mountain with an ebony castle clutched atop its
jagged crest.

And although it was too far to make out significant details, Kane growled, "I need no seer's spell to tell me that
there lies the dark towers of the DemonQueen, as black as
her own black heart."

Arik glanced at Trendel. "Well done, seer; we are on
the right track." But even as he looked northward again,
the ebony mountain sped straight away from them and
disappeared beyond the horizon.

"Aha," said Trendel, "*that's* why the distance to the
DemonQueen shifts."

"Hm," murmured Ky, "I wonder, how we are ever going to get aboard, what with its racing to and fro like
that?"

"Never mind getting aboard," rumbled Kane. "Instead
tell me how we will keep from getting run over."

Again they started their northward journey across the
mutating land, with its howling blizzards of boiling mud

and flaming stones falling from the sky, and its grinding whirlpools of jagged rocks and thunderous winds shrieking along knife-edge ridges, with its trackless wastes of burning sand and rivers of fire through ice-choked gorges and pitching slopes of jolting steep mountains . . . and more. And all the while, the spectral black sun moved down through the ocherous sky and umber clouds floated above.

Now and again the obsidian mountain would reappear, sometimes close, sometimes far, but always would it retreat northward to vanish beyond the horizon.

"Luba," exclaimed Trendel, "this is like chasing a friar's lantern, a corpse candle, a dancing will-o'-the-wisp."

"Oh, don't say that," cautioned Rith. "The last time we tangled with a will-o'-the-wisp it ended in Arton's death and Lyssa's becoming a ghost."

"Horax the Bastard's doing," growled Kane. He slammed a fist into hand. "If he's on the mountain, then he will pay dearly."

"But not before he restores Lyssa to her rightful form," admonished Ky, glancing at Arik in the lead.

"Do you truly believe that he did it?" asked Trendel, shaking his head. "Changed her into a ghost, that is?"

"It was his swamp, his will-o'-the-wisp, his traitorous ways," growled Kane. "Who else could have done it? Who else *would* have done it?"

Trendel took a deep breath and sighed and shrugged his shoulders . . . then hunched over as phosphorescent black hail began hurtling down on the green burning land.

The shadow-wrapped sun was nearly to the horizon when suddenly the black mountain stood at hand. Arik spurred forward, Foxes following, and onto dark rock they clattered. They raced ahead a hundred yards or more, only to be barred by a yawning abyss standing across the way, and here the Foxes reined to a halt, horses sidestepping, hooves clacking on stone; green fire shone up from the depths of the crevasse and choking fumes arose. Looking left then right, Arik called, "This way!" and rightward he spurred.

They came to a narrow span, a footway too narrow for the horses to traverse, and it held no rails. It bridged the abyss to meet a path twisting up the mountainside.

"Quick," cried Arik, leaping down from his horse, "we must cross before the mountain moves." But even as he said it, Trendel cried, "Not so!" and he pointed back along the way they had come. The land behind was racing away southward. "We are on the mountain even now."

Hundreds of feet down, the abyss was filled with fiery green magma, heaving and churning, enormous hot bubbles belching to the surface to burst with ploppings and plappings and retch out great clouds of acrid fumes, the dark emeraldine gas rising upward to strangle anyone who would dare to cross over the span. Yet the Black Foxes did so, Arik leading, Rith coming last, the bard spellsinging to calm them all, especially Kane treading in fear above the long and terrible fall.

On the far side they moved away from the frightful crevasse, then stood at the base of the mountain and surveyed the obsidian steeps.

Finally, "There," said Rith, pointing at the sable peak where stood a fantastic castle, ebony in aspect, with flamboyant towers and ornate turrets reaching up into the aberrant sky. "There's where we'll find Horax the Bastard."

"And the DemonQueen," added Trendel.

Arik glanced at the black sun even then lipping the horizon. "If we start now it will be night by the time we reach it."

"Good," grunted Kane. "Let's go."

With helms on their heads and shields on their arms and with their weapons in hand, upward they started, walking in silence to follow the wide pathway as it wended and snaked up the slopes. Yet as they rounded the first of the turns, there before them stood an array of white-armored drakka in full plate with helmed visors of hideous aspect and metal horns jutting up, their stone-barbed lances and jagged-edged stone-bladed swords leveled and ready. And among them capered jeering skelga, teeth and talons wickedly flashing, while behind something bright and chaotic loomed.

With Arik on point, Kane to his right, and Trendel to his left, and Ky and Rith behind, the Black Foxes leapt forward to do battle, sword and spear and axe gleaming black, silver fire playing about Ky's fingers, and Rith starting a song. Yet before weapon or magic could strike, the Foxes fell back, numbed, trapped by a powerful spell, their minds held in thrall.

As if acting on command from an unheard voice, the drakka beringed the Black Foxes and, with pale skelga leaping about and japing and the chaotic whiteness churning ahead, they marched them unresisting up the pathway and toward the ebon castle above.

And as the Foxes moved woodenly upward, the black sun gradually sank into the horizon and slowly disappeared, just as it seemed did their chances.

46

"**D**amn! Damn! Damn!" cried Mark Perry. "They've lost!"

Stunned, the observers in the control center watched as the Black Foxes were marched up the twisting path and toward the soaring ebony castle, the ring-filled sky above shading toward a pustulant green with the onset of the demonic twilight.

"He's done something unethical," said Greyson, taking off his half-glasses and staring at them abstractly.

"Who?" asked Kat Lawrence.

"Avery," answered Greyson.

"Unethical?" exploded Perry. "Of course he's unethical! He's a goddamned sociopath!"

"What has he done, John?" asked Toni Adkins.

"He's broken two of his most basic VR rules: one, he didn't give the team a fighting chance; and, two, he stripped them of their free will."

Stein burst through the doors and headed toward the VR rigs. "I have solved it!" he declared, waving a schematic toward his medtech crew.

Toni called out and beckoned to him, and loath to do so, still he complied. And when he reached her side at the console, she said, "Show me."

Annoyed, he slapped the schematic to the table and spread it out with irritated jabs. Drew Meyer and John Greyson moved to join them to see what was afoot. Stein glanced about. "Some of you may actually understand this: all we have to do is jack into the aux port of the hemihelm with a modified CR. It'll act like a broadband shocker."

"Broadband?" asked Drew. "How do you plan on making it so?"

"A CR? A shocker? —What are those?" asked Greyson.

Stein ignored Greyson and pulled Drew closer. "Here and here," said Stein, his finger stabbing at the schematic, pointing to portions circled in red with their values changed. Drew bent over to look, then reached for his minicompad.

"Would somebody please answer my questions?" appealed Greyson.

Toni turned to the philosopher and said, "A CR is a cephaloruptor—a therapeutic instrument specifically targeted to treat certain types of depression untreatable by other means. A cortical shocker is an instrument of torture, first used by the junta in the recent Kazakhstani oil wars. It acts directly on the brain, especially the centers of fear and pain."

Greyson took Stein by the shoulder and spun him to stand face to face. "You are going to torture the alpha team?"

"Of course not, you fool," bit Stein. "But by using modified gear to give them a jolt of shock therapy, I can break the hemisynch while simultaneously stimulating their brains into functioning normally again."

"Damn you, Henry," cried Greyson, balling a fist and shaking it in under Stein's nose, "don't you realize that the true essences of these people are trapped in Avery, and if you shock the brains back into activity, you, we, all of us will have six people on our hands, none of whom will have a soul?"

Stein batted Greyson's hand away. "Understand this, you superstitious braying ass: those mental patterns in the AI are merely duplicates. The real brains are over there. Shut down. And I have a way to reactivate them."

Greyson stepped back, frustration and horror raging in his eyes. "My God, Henry, you are not only Doctor Stein, you are Doctor Frankenstein! He reanimated a brain and created a creature without a soul; and now you want to do the same, only sixfold over! Who, then, is the monster here?"

Toni stepped in between them. "Stop it, you two!" She gestured at the holovid. "The game is not over. The Foxes may yet win"—Stein snorted and Mark Perry threw up his hands in disbelief, but Toni continued—"and if they do, then in all likelihood their minds will be set free by Avery. And if that's not the case—" She broke off and turned to Doctor Meyer. "Drew, will those changes actually work?"

Meyer glanced at his minicompad and then at her and nodded. "It certainly seems that way."

Toni turned back to Stein and Greyson. "—And if Avery doesn't free them, then and only then will we try Henry's lash-up as a last resort—as a final solution."

"History shows that so-called 'final solutions' are executed by megalomaniacs," Greyson said through gritted teeth.

Toni sighed then said to Meyer, "Drew, recheck your figures, and if they still show this to be feasible, you and your crew modify the cephaloruptor in accordance with Henry's plans. —And, Henry, go ahead and get the alpha team set up, but—listen to me!—do *nothing* without my final approval."

In that moment the doors banged open and two medtechs wheeled in a Phoenix Therapeutics cephaloruptor, the symbol on its side showing a golden firebird rising from scarlet flames.

Greyson started to protest, but Alya Ramanni took him by the arm and softly said, "Come with me, John. Now is not the time. The Black Foxes may yet win, Lord Vishnu willing." She led the philosopher to a seat and sat down beside him. Together they watched the holovid, the muscles in Greyson's jaw clenching.

In the holo, the enthralled Black Foxes were escorted into an ornate throne room, and in convoy they woodenly marched toward a high dais on which sat a woman in black plate armor. Surely this could be none other than Atraxia the DemonQueen.

47

With a chaotic whiteness churning ahead and jeering bonelike skelga capering about, white-armored drakka in full plate marched the Black Foxes up the path and toward the ebony castle. The black sun sank beyond the hellish horizon and a demonic twilight drew across the chaotic land, the ring-filled sky above shading toward a sickly, pustulant green. And low in the eastern sky, dark ruddy stars began to appear in the oncoming verdigris night. Yet the Foxes seemed to note none of this as they woodenly tramped along the twisting path snaking up the flanks of the black mountain and toward the soaring towers and turrets and domes of the lofty palace above.

At last they reached the castle, and beringed by barbed lances and jagged-edged swords, the Foxes were marched across a black stone courtyard just as a flaming violet moonlike orb scored across the viridian sky beyond the purple rings, a cluster of burning moonlets trailing in its lavender wake. And farther beyond, the aethyr was afflicted with corpulent stars—maroon and deep orange and vivid dark blue—and a pale grey wedge rolled into sight on the rings in the vault above.

But little of this did the Black Foxes see, for in that moment they tramped into the onyx palace and beyond the sight of the alien sky. As they crossed the threshold to enter the castle proper, colors about them returned to normal:

the drakka armor and hideous visors and jutting metal horns became ebony, and their stone-bladed weapons obsidian; the bony skelga, pitch-black; and the churning, chaotic demon in the lead, a boiling inky cloud. Fox weapons gleamed silver, Ky's blade sable, and their leathers took on the mottled hues of grey. Hair and skin returned to normal, as did eyes and teeth and all else. But by no sign or gesture did the Foxes acknowledge the change.

Unresisting, they were marched through gilded hallways, the ivory floors smooth and polished, with elaborate scrollwork enscribed in the stone. They trod through ornate archways and along arcades hung with resplendent tapestries, though the patterns depicted seemed nothing more than geometric chaos. But at last the enthralled Black Foxes were escorted into a spacious, high-vaulted chamber, with fluted pillars along the walls reaching up to the ceiling and portals to either side opening into rooms seemingly set for dining or counsel or other businesses of state. Yet the Foxes turned neither left nor right but instead were convoyed straight ahead and toward the distant end where stood a lofty dais holding a wide golden throne on which sat a female—Atraxia the DemonQueen.

Exotic and beautiful and slender she was, and dressed in black plate armor, though at the moment she was wearing neither gauntlets nor helm. Her skin was alabaster with a tinge of pink. She had straight black hair cropped at the shoulder, the pointed tips of her ears showing through. Her pale oval face was feminine, with high cheekbones and a delicate chin, and exquisite pale cinnabar lips. With dark eyebrows and long dark lashes, her eyes were tilted and completely white and held no cornea whatsoever. Leaning against the throne stood a sword, long and slightly curved—a hand-and-a-half shamsheer.

At her side sat a black-haired man with an aquiline nose and a wide leering mouth. He was dressed in sable and wore an ebon cloak. On the front of his doublet were emblazoned two red crescent bloodmoons—one small, one large. It was Horax.

And as the Black Foxes were marched before her and came to a halt at the foot of the dais, Atraxia laughed and held up a bronze scepter on the tip of which was now affixed the arcane red gem. "Did you come for this, my dear Black Foxes, come to steal the gift given me by my new consort?" The DemonQueen turned and smiled at Horax.

The mage smiled back then leaped to his feet and strutted across the dais. "Fools! Did you puny five think to creep unnoticed into the very heart of my queen's dominion and like thieves in the night take from her that which I have given as my token of troth? Did you think so much of your skills, your prowess? Pah! You are as nothing when compared to her or to me." Horax stopped pacing and raised a hand in a gesture of concession. "I must admit, though, to a mild curiosity as to two events: first, that you managed to escape White Mountain after I had reset all of the significant wards; and, second"—he pointed at Ky and Trendel—"that these two were among your band when you came through the demongate." He laughed again then cocked his head questioningly. "What's that? You are shocked to learn that we saw you come through? Bah, only dolts would think that the way into our world would stand neglected. Did you not know that we followed your progress all the way from the demongate to the foot of my queen's dark fortress. Your journey was most amusing."

Now Horax strode halfway down the steps then turned to Atraxia and appealed, "What shall we do with these fools, my queen? Behead them with your great sword? Or shall I instead see to their demise, perhaps throw them as scraps to the skelga? Or do you have in mind a sentence more fitting to the crime they sought to commit against your royal personage?"

Atraxia stood and paced to the edge of the dais and looked down on the Foxes; long moments she contemplated, then smiled a slow wicked smile. And she gestured at the blank wall to the left of the prisoners. An archway appeared and ruddy light glared forth. Without willing it, all the Black Foxes turned to look through the aperture. It opened onto a fiery chamber, lit crimson by boiling lava, where blistering magma churned up from unknown depths to seethe and roil at the very lip of a broad jagged split in the floor. At the very edge of this molten inferno stood a brass anvil, with a brass hammer and a pair of brass tongs lying atop.

Now the Foxes turned and faced Atraxia again. "You came this night to steal the jewel from my scepter, the Dark God's gem. And since the token of the Nameless One was affixed in my scepter's forge, it is only fitting that you pay penance in that very same forge: you will bathe in the lava pool."

Horax laughed and strode down the remaining steps of the dais to pass among the Foxes, the drakka and skelga and the roiling black demon yielding respectfully back. He stopped before Kane, the largest of the Foxes, and sneered at the enthralled man. A bead of sweat trickled down Kane's forehead and cheek as if he were struggling to break the spell, entirely to no avail. "Bah," said Horax, "you are a fool."

He stepped to Ky—"My shield"—and then to Trendel—"The unexpected sacrifice"—and lastly to Rith. He stood before the bard, fury in his face, and he hissed, "Before you go into the lava, my black beauty . . ." He turned his head aside and showed her his left ear, deeply notched by the thrown silver knife. He then took that same silver dagger from his waistband and slashed it through both of Rith's ears. Blood flowed freely, but she neither cried out nor made a move to stanch the flow. Horax laughed and wiped the blade clean on her hair and shoved the knife back into his waistband.

Then he stepped to Arik and sneered at the silver sword yet clenched in the warrior's hand, for the drakka could not abide the touch of the metal and so had left all the captives armed. "What use your silver weapons now, my flaxen-haired buffoon? Did you think to stride among demonkind hewing left and right with a bright argent blade before which no demon could stand?" Horax reached out and drew a leering black skelga to him and clutched a handful of the creature's hair and pulled back its head, exposing its neck. "Come, Black Fox, hew his throat with your charmed blade. What, cannot bring yourself to do it?" Horax set free the jeering skelga then tilted his own head back, baring his jugular. "Perhaps a powerful wizard is more to your liking; if so, then cut this neck.

A simple chop will do." Again he laughed. "What's that? Too . . . ah . . . frozen in awe to take a swing? Pah! Your silver weapons are of no use here; my queen has seen to that."

Horax then laughed and strode halfway up the steps toward Atraxia, where he stopped and turned and faced the Foxes and sneeringly called out, "Do as you will, my DemonQueen, I am finished toying with these insignificant fools."

All eyes were on the Black Foxes—those of the drakka and skelga and of the roiling chaos, as well as the eyes of Horax and of the DemonQueen. But the eyes of the Foxes themselves, they instead stared fixedly up at Atraxia as she raised her scepter to invoke its power. Hence only the Foxes saw the glowing presence begin to emerge from the throne-room wall behind the DemonQueen.

It was Lyssa!

Spectral Lyssa.

She had followed them to the demonplane, but could not manifest until night had fallen. And she had sped across the Plains of Chaos on their bewildering trail to arrive now!

She broke free of the stone and rushed forward and clamped her ethereal hands to the DemonQueen's head and began draining life with a vengeance.

Atraxia's eyes flew wide and she shrieked in anguish and dropped her scepter, and the heavy bronze wand went clanging down the steps of the dais, the affixed red gem glittering and flashing crimson as the scepter tumbled down the ivory stairs.

In that instant the enthrallment was broken, and with weapons hewing, the Foxes sprang into action, cutting down drakka and skelga alike.

But the great roiling chaotic demon boiled up the dais to aid the DemonQueen. Yet Kane's silver-headed spear stabbed through the churning blackness, and the demon blasted apart with a thunderous roar, spectral fire exploding outward.

Horax darted down the steps, lunging for the scepter, but an argent tumble glittered in the air, and Rith's silver dagger took him under the arm. He screamed in agony and jerked out the blade, vermilion blood spurting after. And he began sketching an arcane gesture at the black bard, but before he could complete his spell, a bolt of ebony darkness hammered into his chest, smashing through ribs and lungs and heart and spine and exploding out his back. And Horax was hurled hindward, crashing to the steps and tumbling down like a broken doll, dead before he struck the ivory floor. Rith cast a glance at Shadowmaster Ky and grinned—together they had avenged Arton Masterthief and Pon Barius the mage. But then the drakka were upon them, and they were driven apart in the fray.

The battle raged to and fro, skelga teeth and claws rending, drakka barbed spears and jagged-edged swords ripping, the Black Foxes taking wounds as they fought. Yet their silver weapons were deadly and though greatly outnumbered they hewed through the demonic ranks: Arik was a whirling ravager, his blade cutting into drakka and skelga, slashing deeply, blue witchfire bursting forth, and demons shrieked and spun as spectral flames consumed them. Likewise, Trendel's axe slammed through plate and bone alike, and demonkind flared in his wake. Kane's spear pierced foe, as did Rith's daggers and Ky's deadly black blade.

And up on the dais, the DemonQueen had somehow managed to turn and grasp Lyssa by the head, just as she herself was clasped. And their mouths were stretched wide in silent screams as they struggled to defeat one another, but as to who was winning or losing, it could not be told, though Lyssa's glow was dimming rapidly.

"Kane! Kane!" shouted Rith, trying to move forward toward the dais, but being driven back by black drakka. "The scepter! Throw it into the pool!"

Shouting in rage, Kane hammered his way through demonkind and scooped up the bronze wand, and with Trendel at his back bashing with his shield and hewing his silver-bladed axe left and right to chop down the foe, Kane won to the archway and cast the scepter into the roiling magma.

The moment the device struck the lava, the Demon-Queen screamed, and so too did Lyssa, her voice the wail of the wind.

The scepter sank in the fire of its birthforge, disappearing into the molten churn, and again Atraxia shrieked, and she burst into flame. Whirling and spinning she broke free of Lyssa's grasp, blue fire consuming her as she twisted and twirled, her screams rising in rapid crescendo and of a sudden flames blasted outward leaving nothing behind but echoes, and then these too disappeared.

The surviving demons broke, fleeing silver, now that their queen and her power was gone.

And up on the dais, Lyssa collapsed, her light but a feeble glimmer.

"Lyssa!" cried Arik, rushing toward her, but Rith grabbed him from behind and shouted, "Wait!" Arik threw off her hand and started upward again. Bleeding from the slashes through her ears and from wounds taken in battle, still Rith had the strength to kick Arik's feet out from under him, and she leapt upon him, shouting, "You cannot go to her! As weak as she is she will have no control and will drain you entirely should you touch her."

Arik hurled Rith off and spat, "I'd rather be dead with her than alive without."

As the warrior got to his feet, "Arik, you cannot!" cried Rith, lying on the ivory floor, her blood staining it scarlet. "There are an untold number of demons out there, and we need you, else we'll never win free of the demonplane."

Arik looked down at her bitterly then up toward Lyssa, the ghostly glimmer nearly gone out; his shoulders sagged and he nodded bleakly, then slumped to the steps and wept.

Rith got to her knees and cast her arms about the warrior, and whispered, "There is yet a chance . . ."

At that moment in the roiling demonforge, an indestructible red gem floated to the top.

48

"**Y**es!" shouted John Greyson; the portly philosopher clenched his fist and leaped to his feet in joy as in the holo the DemonQueen vanished in a blast of flame and the surviving drakka and skelga fled. "By Socrates, they've won!"

His voice was lost in the raucous clamor of the control room as people cheered and clapped and Toni wept tears of relief. Yet at the gimbaled rigs, medtechs worked frantically; Alice Maxon's core temperature had dropped to 89° F. They heated IVs using power therms and pumped the warm fluid into her veins, the medtechs now just barely holding their own against the cool electrolytes Avery was flushing through her system.

"All right, Henry," ebulliently shouted Greyson to Stein, "get ready to extract them. Avery will release their minds any moment now. They've won; he's lost."

Toni Adkins wiped her eyes and turned to Grace Willoby. "Any change in the brainwaves?"

"No, Doctor Adkins," came the medtech's reply. "The console still shows only the autonomous is working."

Toni frowned and called out to a medtech at the rigs. "Ramon! Any change in the EEGs?"

"No, Doctor Adkins. No change."

Henry Stein looked up and raised his voice to be heard, "The AI still has their brains shut down; it's time for my solution."

"Not without my say-so," called Toni. Then she keyed her comband. "Alvin?"

"Yes, Doctor Adkins?" replied Alvin Johnston down in the AIC.

"Any change in the mental patterns?"

"I don't think so, Doctor Adkins. They seem to be the same . . . still locked in Avery's volatile memory."

"Let me know if there's any variation whatsoever, Alvin. Adkins out."

Moments passed and moments more, and still there was no change in either the flat EEG tracks or the states of the glittering patterns. Finally Toni turned to Greyson. "John, what's going on? Why hasn't Avery released them?"

Frustration filled Greyson's face. "I don't know, Toni. They should be free by now, but instead he holds them captive, which means he's broken another one of his strictures, though I can't tell you why."

"Because he's a goddamned sociopath," spat Mark Perry, "and wants to win, no matter the cost or the rules. Even now it looks as if Alice Maxon is dying, another victim of this mad machine." Perry turned to Toni. "I think that sonofabitch Stein is right; it's time you let him try his solution, or there won't be anyone left alive."

"No, no, you can't do that," protested Greyson, but Toni stood and, with Greyson and Perry following, she strode to where Henry Stein and Drew Meyer and Sheila Baxter and Billy Clay worked on the CR stimulator.

"Where do you stand?" she asked

Stein snorted impatiently and gestured at Sheila, the comptech sitting on the floor before an open panel.

"We're almost ready," said Sheila, sliding a modified circuit board in on its tracks.

"The system is jacked into the aux EEG ports on the hemihelms," added Billy. "All we have to do is change a capacitor on one more board then plug her in and turn her on."

"Then I'll reactivate their brains," said Stein.

"You can't let him do this, Toni," declared Greyson, his voice trembling in distress. "It's profane, and will create six unholy monsters, six creatures without souls."

Stein sneered. "Fool. I suppose you would rather that they die."

"No, Henry, I would rather that they live. But with their souls intact. Yet I will say this"—Greyson gestured at the six comatose beings in the witches' cradles—"better that they die now than live as reanimated *things*."

Stein turned to Toni Adkins. "Don't listen to this superstitious fool. This is the only way they'll get free."

Greyson clenched his fists and said fervently, "But wait, Toni, and *think*, for God's sake: every time we've tried to intervene, something terrible has happened: first, Arthur Coburn died a horrible death, virtually ripping himself in two; then we nearly killed Alice Maxon by unplugging her from her rig, breaking the silver cord between her body and her soul, and look at what we accomplished—her alter is a *ghost*!—and Lord knows what she herself has become; and then we tried to inject Timothy Rendell into VR to command Avery to set the alpha team free, but instead Timothy's soul was ripped from him and now he, too, is trapped. That's three disasters out of three attempts—did you hear me? Three out of three!—and all because we presumed to interfere. Everything we've tried has been a catastrophe, and this will be, too, only worse, for not only will we lose six souls, we will also set six monsters loose on an unsuspecting world."

"Bah!" barked Stein. "I suggest you gather up your powders and potions, your gourds and beads, your feathers and drums, and dance your voodoo elsewhere, John."

With an inarticulate cry of rage, John Greyson lunged forward, clawlike fingers raking down Henry Stein's face and grasping for his throat. Shouting, Drew Meyer and Billy Clay and Mark Perry grabbed the philosopher and pulled him away. Greyson looked about wild-eyed, then collapsed to his knees and wept into his hands.

Breathing heavily and with a trickle of blood seeping down his cheek, Stein turned to Toni. "It is time for my final solution, no matter what any superstitious fool might say or do."

As Toni looked fretfully from Greyson to Stein, Mark

Perry said, "I think Stein's right: we ought to do what he says."

"This is no democracy, Mark," snapped Toni, "and I'm not taking a vote. The decision is mine and mine alone to make."

"All set," said Sheila, closing the panel and moving back from the modified CR.

Stein looked at Toni, waiting. She glanced at the rigs then said, "If Avery hasn't set them free by the time you are ready . . . then proceed."

Stein whirled to Drew Meyer. "Plug it in and start the countdown."

Billy Clay passed the power cord to Drew, and he inserted the plug into the nearest wall socket. Stein began keying switches, and display lights flickered on. Sheila and Billy started the calibration procedures.

Behind Toni someone exclaimed, "Mother of Satan!" Toni turned; it was Kat Lawrence, and she pointed at the main holovid.

There on the dais, above the DemonQueen's throne . . .

49

With one hand outthrust and shielding his face from the heat of the fiery lava and the other hand gripping the bronze tongs, Kane fished the gem out from the magma even as Rith called for him and Trendel to return to the throne room. He lifted up the jewel and gingerly tapped a finger to it, then again, then handled it, then tossed it to Trendel, the gem cool to the touch in spite of having been submerged in the molten stone. The seer held it up and peered through it, looking at the enscribed glyph: ◣◥ .And he frowned in puzzlement as something nagged at the edge of his mind, but before he could capture the elusive thought, again Rith called. "Let's go," rumbled Kane, dropping the tongs back onto the anvil, and he and Trendel strode from the chamber of the demonforge to join Arik and Ky at the bard's side, Trendel jamming the gem into his own pocket as he went.

As soon as they arrived, Rith said, "Quickly, Lyssa is dying. We must yield up energy to save her, else she is foredone. But do not touch her nor step too close, for I think in her state of weakness she will drain you to death."

Ky glanced up at the dais where Lyssa had fallen, then she looked down at Horax the Bastard's corpse and her eyes widened in a shock of realization. "Oh god, oh god, I killed Horax, and even though we save Lyssa, she will forever be a ghost."

"This is no time for guilt," snapped Rith. She turned to start up the steps of the dais but stopped, for in the air above the throne a vortex of spectral darkness began to manifest—ebony and sable and obsidian, shadow and smoke, dusk and night . . . all endlessly spiraling down into an unfathomable jet-black abyss.

The Foxes drew weapons and backed away, especially Kane, for it seemed to them all as if they were looking into a bottomless pit.

And then, emanating from the centerpoint of the slow-turning whorl, there came a towering androgynous voice:

"I AM THE NAMELESS ONE, THE DARK GOD, AND I AM SORE DISPLEASED THAT YOU HAVE BANISHED MY ACOLYTE, THE DEMONQUEEN." The spectrum of blackness slowed a moment then resumed its spin. "FOR SUCH AN AFFRONT TO ME, I WILL SLAY YOU ALL, BEGINNING WITH THIS UNDEAD ABOMINATION YOU NAME LYSSA."

"No!" cried Arik, raising his silver sword and starting up the steps. But the endless whorl spun faster and a wave of darkness billowed forth from the bottomless abyss to smash into Arik and hurl him backward to crash to the marble floor.

"FOOL! WHO ARE YOU TO CHALLENGE ME?"

As Rith and Ky knelt by the stunned warrior's side, Kane stepped forward and raised his spear and bellowed, "I challenge you, Dark God, Nameless One, coward! Bah! Just who or what do you think *you* are?"

"FOOLISH MORTAL, YOU ASK WHO I AM, WHAT I AM? THEN I WILL SHOW YOU, BUT ONLY YOU. THEN YOU WILL KNOW."

At that moment the Dark God vanished and so, too, did Kane.

Desperate to find advantage, Trendel looked for something—anything—that would aid them. Powerful magic was needed, yet he was not trained to cast fire or lightning or such; instead his were the skills of a seer: finding, seeing, runes, glyphs, and—

Glyphs! Perhaps! Perhaps I can tap into some kind of power! Even as he thought it, Trendel snatched the gem from his pocket and frowned in concentration, then cast a spell on the mysterious glyph within the jewel. Surprise filled his eyes, and again an elusive thought plucked at his mind, but then the throne room was filled with hoarse screams as the Dark God and Kane reappeared, unremitting horror in the warrior-healer's eyes as he shrieked and shrieked in madness and collapsed to his knees and curled tightly into himself, burying his face in his hands but screaming still.

Ky ran to him and tried to give comfort, but he paid her no heed as he howled in ceaseless terror.

Arik struggled to his feet, and Rith stood as well. And they gripped their weapons and faced the dark spectrum and prepared to fight.

But Trendel glanced at the red gem and called out above Kane's muffled shrieks, "By your truename I command you to cease!"

"PUNY MORTAL, I AM THE NAMELESS ONE, NONE KNOWS MY TRUENAME."

"I speak it now and it is—it is . . ." Something pressed at Trendel's mind, some knowledge deeply buried, a hidden ritual forgotten until now.

"FOOL!"

"I speak it now and it is *AIVR*!"

Momentarily the Dark God's whorl stilled, then began turning anew. "AGAIN I NAME YOU A FOOL, FOR NOW YOU MUST GIVE UP YOUR OWN TRUENAME TO ME."

"Tr-Tr—" Once more the buried knowledge of the rite burst forth in his mind. "No, not Trendel. My truename is *Rendell*!"

"RENDELL." The Dark God laughed. "NOW I HAVE YOU, MORTAL; YOU HAVE GIVEN ME YOUR OWN TRUENAME AND YOU CANNOT COMPLETE THE RITE, FOR THE HIDDEN WORD OF POWER IS KNOWN ONLY TO ME." The whorl spun faster as if readying another black wave.

Trendel clenched his fists and hesitated, knowing that all their fates hung in the balance, hung on a single word. Again buried knowledge surged into his consciousness. *"Socrates!"* he shouted. "Socrates is the hidden word of power!" The whirling totally stopped, and Trendel's voice rang with authority. "And now I command you, foul AIVR, Nameless no more, release us from this place and return us where we belong!"

And it seemed as if the entire world—the entire plane—screamed in agony: the castle, mountain, plains, sky, rings, stars, aethyr, the whole of creation bellowing in pain and rage and anguish and frustration. The dark spectrum began whirling again—faster it spun and faster, until it became but an obsidian blur. The castle began to shake, the floor to rumble, the juddering increasing in violence until pillars began to topple. Intense light burst forth from the gem, burning Trendel's hand; he jerked in pain and cast it down to skitter across the marble, and a great crack split through the floor in its wake and clove the dais in twain. A wrenching jolt ripped through the palace, and where the crack had been a yawning crevasse fissured wide to swallow the gemstone. The blazing jewel tumbled down and down, searing bright rays stabbing forth as it plummeted into immeasurable depths. And from the bottomless pit there came a shattering explosion, rocking the entire world. The throne toppled into the chasm, and then the dais fell, carrying Lyssa down with it. "Lyssa!" cried Arik, and reeled forward as the floor lurched and heaved.

"No!" cried Rith. "There's nothing you can do! We've got to get out!"

A great slab of the ceiling crashed down, choking dust billowing upward. Arik groaned and cast one last look at the black abyss and the Dark God shrieking madly and spinning wildly above, and then turned and helped Ky get screaming Kane to his feet. Through the halls they scurried, marble smashing down all about, tapestries falling, lintels crashing, arcades collapsing behind them as they ran, dragging shrieking Kane after, the big man's eyes wide but seeing nothing as he screamed in endless horror. They fled into the courtyard just ahead of floors and ceilings and domes and turrets and towers crashing down. And as the castle fell inward, the mountain split in two, green lava belching forth. High above in the shrieking sky, great purple rings burned furiously, while unnumbered pustulant stars exploded simultaneously, rings of ebony light swelling outward like limitless black ripples in a vast malachite sea to act and interact and rebound. The burning lavender moon whirled up across the demonic heavens, the blazing moonlets following after, fire bellowing wildly as they were completely consumed. The black sun spun up over the horizon, a great bloated thing swelling and swelling to explode in a colossal blast. The green sky turned into a yellow-orange inferno, the very air aflame. And countless vast cracks shattered wholly through the world, cleaving it asunder, hurling the Black Foxes into the flaming aethyr. And then with a mighty detonation the entire demonplane blasted apart.

50

Thirty-five . . . thirty-four . . . thirty-three . . .

"Oh, my God, my God," cried Toni, as turrets and spires and domes crashed down round the Foxes.

Thirty-one . . . thirty . . .

"Lord Vishnu, protect them," fervently prayed Alya Ramanni.

The mountain split in two and green lava vomited forth.

Twenty-seven . . . twenty-six . . .

"What's happening?" asked Kat Lawrence as pustulant stars detonated beyond purple rings ablaze.

Twenty-four . . .

"They could all be killed, Kat," answered Toni. "Just as Arthur Coburn was."

The furiously burning lavender moon whirled across the shrieking sky, moonlets aflame racing after.

Kat jammed a cigarillo into the corner of her mouth and chewed furiously as the Foxes ran for their lives and the swollen black sun spun up over the horizon and exploded.

Twenty . . . nineteen . . . eighteen . . .

"Henry!" Toni called. "Hurry up! Else they're all dead!"

The green sky turned yellow orange and burst into fire.

Fifteen . . . fourteen . . . thirteen . . .

"The CR is nearly charged," shouted Billy Clay. "We are in the last of the countdown now!"

Suddenly innumerable cracks shattered the demon-world into countless hurtling fragments.

Nine . . . eight . . .

"Stop it! Stop it! Oh, stop it!" sobbed Greyson on the floor, "don't do this evil thing!" but no one paid him any heed, and weeping he scrambled on hands and knees toward the wall as with a mighty detonation the entire demonplane blasted apart.

Six . . . five . . . four . . .

"I've got brain patterns! I've got brain patterns!" shouted Grace Willoby.

Two . . . one . . .

"Henry, stop!" screamed Toni.

Zero! Stein glanced up at her, then pushed the button.

Nothing happened.

Greyson sat giggling against the wall, his eyes vacant and staring, the CR power plug in his hand.

Eric Flannery opened his eyes as medtechs swarmed about, working to free him from the gimbaled rig.

"Did Alice make it? Oh, God, please let Alice be back."

But all he heard was Caine Easley screaming and screaming and screaming and . . .

51

Some eleven weeks after the funeral, Hiroko Kikiro, Meredith Rodgers, Eric Flannery, and Timothy Rendell sat at a corner table in one of the many dining rooms of Casa Molina, the family-run restaurant—really an old adobe house converted generations past by the Mexican forbears of the current proprietors—located in the Presidio area of Tucson.

Hiroko had packed up her art gallery in Santa Fe and had moved to Tucson to be near Caine Easley, the big man currently confined in the mental wing of the Catalina Crest Retreat.

After her engagement to Timothy, and following Hiroko's example, Meredith was currently in the process of opening a rare bookstore—Scrolls and Tomes and First Editions II—in the elegant foothills north of town.

Eric, a native of Tucson, had spent most of this time thinking of the future and visiting Caine every day and keeping the others informed as to his progress. The big man had finally stopped continually screaming some twelve days after he had been extracted from the rig, and just five weeks past he had begun to feed himself.

Timothy had been working long hours with the others at Coburn Industries to try to discover what had gone wrong.

And slowly the weeks had passed.

And now they sat in a dining room in Casa Molina to discuss the uncertain future, given what they had become.

"Chugga, chugga, vroom," growled Hiroko as she drove her blue-corn tortilla chip through the picante sauce then lifted it to her mouth and crunched off a corner, her black almond eyes dancing as she glanced at her three companions.

Eric took another swig of Simpatico and held it a moment in his mouth, the cold beer soothing the jalapeño burn on his tongue.

Meredith sat with the fingers of one hand entwined in Timothy's. "I don't see how you can even eat those things, Arik. They're like little green thermite bombs."

Eric looked at her and smiled. "After you've lived here awhile, Rith, you get acclimated."

"Ha!" Meredith raised a skeptical eyebrow then turned to Timothy. "Tell me, O seer"—she picked up one of the small peppers—"just what would happen if I did pop this burner in my mouth?"

"Let me look," said Timothy. He frowned a moment in concentration, then said, "Oh, hell! Mark Perry is just about to walk in."

Eric groaned. "At lunchtime?" He quaffed another mouthful of beer.

Hiroko made a face. "Does anyone want to talk to him?"

Eric waved his bottle in a negative gesture.

"Then sit still," said Hiroko, and deep shadow gathered about the foursome.

Moments later, they heard footsteps, and Mark Perry stuck his head in the doorway of their room and looked about, then moved on.

"I wonder what he wants?" growled Meredith in the darkness. "Another deposition?"

"Shh," hissed Timothy, "he'll hear us."

"No he won't," answered Meredith. "I took care of that."

Timothy grinned in understanding.

"Damn lawsuits," growled Eric. "Picking over Arton's bones. I'll be glad when they get it settled and let him rest in peace."

Timothy shook his head. "The receivership of Coburn Industries won't be settled for years . . . perhaps not in the lifetime of anyone sitting at this table."

Hiroko groaned and scooped up another chip of salsa.

A minute later they saw Perry pass back by their door and in that same moment a waiter bearing a platter piled high with food came into the room and looked confusedly about. He was just turning to leave when Hiroko dropped the shadow. With a start the waiter juggled the platter, dishes clattering. Then shaking his head he moved to their table.

Soon the four of them were digging into delicious carne secca wrapped in Mama Rosa's handmade flour tortillas, washing it down with beer.

"How's Kane?" asked Timothy, pointing a fork at Hiroko.

She nodded enthusiastically and chewed. Finally she swallowed then said, "He's good. He recognized me. Told me what he's been up to."

Meredith smiled. "More miracle cures?"

Hiroko grinned. "Oh yes. A broken arm, a bleeding ulcer, and the like. He's driving the Retreat staff mad trying to figure out just what's happening. But so far, they haven't caught him at it."

"I'll say something to him tonight, caution him," said Eric. "Hell, they'd study him like a bug under a microscope if they ever found him out."

Hiroko agreed. "I warned him this morning, but it never hurts to remind him."

"Any prognosis from that psychiatrist of his?" asked Timothy.

Hiroko shrugged. "No change. She still believes that he will be years in therapy."

"I don't think so," said Timothy. "My casting said that he'll be completely sane in, let me see, in another four weeks or so, assuming of course that he follows the main probability sequence and nothing happens to send him spinning off onto one of the alternate paths."

Meredith looked at Timothy. "Did you do another one?"

Timothy shook his head. "No. Just that first one. They

take entirely too much out of me. I was a week recovering."

Meredith patted his hand.

Hiroko sighed. "On Itheria Kane told me that afflictions of the brain, of the mind, are the most difficult to heal."

Meredith glanced at the date on her watch. "What's it been now—nearly three months, right?"

Glumly Hiroko nodded. "Eleven weeks, three days." Then she brightened. "This morning he told me that we are all brains in vats. He's convinced of it. He asked me to help him find the evil genius who's pulling the strings. Does that sound like progress?"

Eric turned up his hands. "I think it does. I mean, it's much better than what he thought last week—that a hideous demon was controlling everything. At least he's now only a century or so in the philosophical past. Too, this last couple of weeks he seems to be coming round faster, as if he's accelerating his own mental recovery. They tell me he only occasionally wakes up screaming in the night. I think he's on the road to sanity."

"I certainly hope so," said Meredith.

They ate in silence for a few minutes, then Hiroko turned to Timothy. "How is Doctor Greyson doing?"

Timothy pursed his lips. "Ah me, poor John . . . his beliefs, his ethics were tested up to and beyond his breaking point—he did not know whether he was saving our souls or condemning us to a needless death." Timothy paused a moment in thought, then looked at Hiroko and said, "But to answer your question, he seems to be recovered from his breakdown, or at least that's what we hear from the monastery. They're worried about his faith, though; I'm told by one of the brothers that John and the abbot have arguments long into the night concerning the nature of souls and of all creation."

"Hm," mused Meredith. "Regardless, I am glad he did what he did—pulled the plug on Stein. Of course, my dear Trendel here managed to get us all out before the good doctor actually pushed the button. But who knows what would have happened had Greyson not pulled the plug? We'd've been hemishocked—whatever that might have done."

Hiroko cut through another tortilla-wrapped carne secca. "Thank you, Trendel, for saving us. I for one am glad we all escaped VR before Doctor Stein tried his final solution, else we'd be dead or worse—our souls trapped in Avery while our soulless bodies would be running around doing who knows what."

"Perhaps you are right, Ky," said Timothy, "but then again perhaps you are wrong. Stein could have been right all along—our brains deactivated for the most part, with Avery running ersatz duplicates of our minds, the AI ready to kill if it sensed interference."

Meredith patted Timothy's hand. "Whether or not Stein was right or wrong, love, it was you who got us out."

"Ha," barked Eric. "I am not certain at all that we have actually escaped Avery." He gestured about. "I mean, look around. Don't things seem, um, brighter, more present, just as they were in Itheria? And the magic: shadow-mastery, sound mastery, seer talents—"

"Speaking of talents," interjected Hiroko, "have you found out just what your talent is, Arik? I mean, you collapsed in Horax's null dungeon. So what is it?"

Eric shrugged and muttered, "Beats the seven hells out of me."

Meredith said, "I think we might have two clues."

Timothy looked at her wide-eyed. "Oh?"

Meredith nodded. "Yes. Look, for as long as I can remember, Arik has never been seriously wounded in battle—oh, scratches, scrapes, bruises, a few broken ribs, but nothing near deadly at all. And then there's what Horax said when we were in Atraxia's palace."

"He said a lot of things, Rith," exclaimed Hiroko. "What specifically did he say about Arik?"

Meredith looked at Eric and then at her. "Do you remember what he said when he pulled back the skelga's head and offered the creature's neck for Arik to cut?"

Hiroko shook her head, but Eric took a deep breath and said, "His exact words were: 'Come, Black Fox, hew his throat with your charmed blade.' "

Meredith nodded sharply in agreement. "Precisely so. Yet at the time, Arik, all you had in your hand was an ordinary steel blade—flashed with silver yet ordinary."

"What are you driving at?" asked Hiroko.

"Well," replied Meredith, "if Horax's words are to be believed, then it just may be that any blade—perhaps any weapon—that Arik wields becomes charmed . . . at least for as long as he holds it."

"Holy moley!" exclaimed Timothy. "If that's true, then it's no wonder you've never taken a deadly hurt."

"Perhaps we can test it sometime," said Meredith. "Let Arik go up against, say, a champion fencer at the U of A and see what the outcome is. I have every reason to believe that Arik will prevail."

"I think you're right, Rith!" declared Hiroko, turning to Eric. "I mean, we all got back to reality with our talents intact, and there's every reason to believe that you did too."

Eric looked at her and shook his head. "You assume we got back to reality, but let me ask you this: do you think you could control shadows if we were truly in Tucson?"

Hiroko took a deep breath. "Actually, I think I must be controlling light rather than shadow. Sending it away, leaving us in the dark."

Meredith shook her head. "Then how do you explain your darkbolt and your ability to—?"

"Light or shadow," interjected Eric, "no matter how it's done, my question remains: assuming that I have a hidden power, could we do these things if we were really back in Tucson? Or are we instead in just another one of Avery's virtual realities?"

"Come on, Arik," chided Timothy, "you are beginning to sound like Kane"—he glanced at Hiroko—"no offense, Ky."

"None taken," she replied.

Timothy turned back to Eric and gestured at the surroundings. "Look, old man, I'm almost positive that this is real and not virtual."

"Oh, how so?"

Timothy took a swig of beer. "Okay. Listen. Here's my reasoning: both magic and science consist of rites—arcane to the uninitiated, well understood by the cognoscenti. And although I didn't know it at the time—thanks to a deep posthypnotic suggestion—I was actually logging on as a superuser when I spoke the truename ritual and commanded Avery to return us all to where we belonged.

"But by this time Avery was completely mad and he wouldn't obey, yet he had no choice but to obey . . . it was like an irresistible force meeting an immovable object. You see, a Dark God, virtual or not, is still a god, hence subject to *no* man's command; but a computer *must* obey the commands of a superuser—yet he wouldn't obey, but he must obey, yet wouldn't, but must, wouldn't, must . . . In any event, that's what blew up the virtual reality and expelled us. The AI couldn't deal with the paradox."

Erik forked in another mouthful of carne secca. He chewed a moment then said, "Good reasoning; perhaps you're right. Speaking of Avery, what's happening on that front?"

Timothy shook his head negatively. "We've tried booting every way we know how. Nothing works. He seems to be totally nonresponsive. We think the mutable logic itself is permanently flawed."

"Well, if it's permanently flawed, are you going to make another one?" asked Hiroko. "Another Avery?"

Timothy shook his head. "Until we examine all the data, we are disinclined to do so. Besides, there's the financing. And with Arthur dead—"

"Financing or not," said Meredith, "I think you ought to delay creating another Avery until you can find a way to give him a soul."

Hiroko nodded vigorously. "I certainly agree with that."

Timothy toyed with his food. "We *have* managed to access a part of Avery, but it babbles nonsense. However, there's a part that no one has been able to crack into; it's like a black hole. What's in there is a complete mystery— some fragment of Avery, we believe, yet we won't know for certain until we manage to get in."

"Get in? You mean go back into virtual reality?" asked Hiroko.

"Perhaps," replied Timothy.

"But why?" asked Meredith.

"For the benefit of mankind."

Meredith shivered and said, "Given what Avery has become, I never want to go back in. I don't care what's in that hole."

Timothy took her hand in his. "Love, if the Coburn team can't crack into Avery's memory, then I believe someone has *got* to go in. Look, even though we've kept our talents a secret, someone simply has to discover just how Avery managed to bequeath these powers to us. I mean, hell, we don't know whether they are truly magic or if instead they are psi, ESP, whatever."

Eric said, "I think it's psi. I mean if this is truly reality, Avery has somehow modified your mentalities or perhaps the structure of your brains so that you now can tap into these extraordinary powers. And if I have a talent, too, then perhaps so can I."

Hiroko laid aside her fork. "Are you saying that we are mutants? Forced mutants?"

Timothy nodded. "Yes. Arik is exactly right. We've all been mutated."

They ate in silence for a moment, then Eric looked at Timothy. "I think I agree with you: if Avery can do this to us, then he can grant special abilities to other humans as well. As you say, for the benefit of mankind we've got to find out how he does it. And perhaps that means someone has got to go back in."

"Oh, lord," groaned Meredith. The others looked at her questioningly. "Well," she explained, "the only ones who might stand a chance of breaking into the black hole and then getting back out are the Black Foxes."

Hiroko picked up her beer and took a great slug. Then she set the bottle down and said, "We've got four weeks before Kane will be ready, four weeks in which to plan."

"I think we'll need more time than that," said Eric. "We've got to speak to Toni Adkins, let her in on the truth. And Drew Meyer: perhaps he can modify the hemi-helms so that we don't get sucked in, and that may take some time. We've got to teach Trendel our hand-signal code. And then . . ."

They talked animatedly for another hour or so, then moved to the porch of Casa Molina and ordered ice-cold margaritas. A soft breeze gently swirled across the veranda.

As the waiter moved away, Meredith said, "You know, it occurs to me that if there is a Dark God in Itheria, then Arda ought to be virtual-real too; perhaps we can enlist His aid."

"Or Luba's," added Timothy.

A taxi rounded a corner and rolled into view. It pulled up and stopped. "What about—" Eric began, but broke off and quickly stood and headed for the street as Alice Maxon stepped from the cab. He met her on the far sidewalk and embraced her.

"God, but I've missed you, darling," he said.

"Me, too," she whispered, and took his face in her hands and they greeted one another for the next minute or so. They had not seen each other since the day of Arthur Coburn's funeral, eleven weeks past.

When they finally came up for air, he grinned at her and asked, "How was your eco mission?"

"Piece of cake," she answered, grinning. "Tracking the animals? Ha!" She snapped her fingers. "The others wanted to know how I did it. I just said it was luck. We finished the survey in five weeks instead of fifty-five."

"Then you're done?"

"Yes."

He picked up her gear, then took a deep breath and said, "Come on up to the veranda, we've got something to tell you, Lyssa."

At this use of her Black Fox name, she looked at him in speculation, but took his hand as they started across the street.

As Eric and Alice came hand in hand, Hiroko Kikiro gazed up at the magnificent, clear Tucson sky, a blue that went on forever. And as she took another sip of her icy margarita, she looked around at the bright and beautiful world and wondered, "Is this just another cavern of Socrates?"

If anyone answered, she did not hear.

finis?

In the abyss where he had been cast,
a Dark God plots his revenge.

AFTERWORD

This was a fascinating and fun book to write . . . mainly because of the enjoyment I derived in researching the fundamental questions delineated in the foreword. Just in case you are interested in reading some of this background material, the following is a list of the more readily available material I ran across during my research:

Achenback, Joel (Mister Know-it-All). "However we spend it, 'time' doesn't exist." *Columbus Dispatch*, Thursday, March 3, 1994.

Blakeslee, Sandra. "Experts finding how brain 'sees' things you think." *Columbus Dispatch*.

Conners, Dianne. "Interview." *Omni*, October 1993.

Cox, Murray. "Notes from the New Land." *Omni*, October 1993.

Freedman, David E. "Quantum Consciousness." *Discover*, June 1994.

Harary, Keith. "Spirit Exercises." *Omni*, October 1993.

Killheffer, Robert K. "The Consciousness Wars." *Omni*, October 1993.

Kinoshita, June. "Dreams of a Rat." *Discover*, June 1992.

Kinoshita, June. "Severed from Emotion." *Discover,* June 1992.

Liversidge, Anthony. "Mind." *Omni,* October 1993.

Montgomery, Geoffrey. "The Mind's Eye." *Discover,* May 1991.

Plato. *The Republic,* translated by A. D. Lindsay. New York: Knopf, 1992.

Porush, David. "Finding God in the Three-Pound Universe: The Neuroscience of Transcendence." *Omni,* October 1993.

Poundstone, William. *Labyrinths of Reason.* New York: Doubleday, 1990.

Sterling, Bruce. "Artificial Life." *Fantasy & Science Fiction,* December 1992.

Stites, Janet. "Bordercrossings: A Conversation in Cyberspace." *Omni,* November 1993.

Uman, Martin. *All About Lightning.* New York: Dover, 1986.

Van, Jon. "Western thought getting fuzzy?" *Columbus Dispatch,* September 5, 1993.

van Inwagen, Peter. *Metaphysics.* Boulder, Colorado: Westview Press, 1993.

Voll, Daniel. "Soul Searching with Francis Crick." *Omni,* February 1994.

"What is Consciousness?" *Discover,* November 1992.

There were other articles and TV shows and conversations which impinged on the subjects in this tale, especially consciousness, the mind, souls, free will, artificial intelligence and, above all, the nature of reality. There were also several entries concerning lightning, ball lightning, storms, lightning and thunder, and so forth in various encyclopedias. I did not record the specifics concerning these additional sources of information, hence their identities are lost in the mists of time.

I do hope that *Caverns of Socrates* has been a worthwhile read for you. I know that the writing of it was a worthwhile endeavor for me.

* * *

Now I think I'll step outside and look at the sky above and the world below and ask myself, "Is this just another Cavern of Socrates?"

Then I'll go kick a rock.

—Dennis L. McKiernan

March 1994

POSTSCRIPT

As I was starting *Caverns of Socrates* I attended a science fiction convention (Wolfcon) at which an auction was held in memory of Curtis Scott, a game designer and convention organizer. Surviving Curtis was his wife Mary and his son Phillip. Into the auction I entered two rights to appear as a character in this novel—that is, the highest two bidders would become individuals in the story—one to appear in the reality chapters, the other to appear in the virtual reality chapters . . . the winning bidder would get her or his choice as to which type of chapters to appear in.

The bidding was spirited.

William C. Easley was the high bidder and chose to appear in the virtual reality chapter using his Society for Creative Anachronism (SCA) persona name of Kane. Thus was born the character Caine Easley/Kane.

Antoinette B. Adkins (also a member of the SCA) was the second highest bidder. I needed a strong female lead for the reality chapters, hence the head of the AIVR project, Doctor Toni Adkins, a Brit, came into being.

I do hope both William and Antoinette find their fictional counterparts to their liking.

A scholarship fund for Phillip Scott has been established. Contributions may be sent to the Phillip Anthony Scott Scholarship Fund, c/o Phillis Lewis, Software Institute, Carnegie-Mellon University, Pittsburgh, PA 15213.

ABOUT THE AUTHOR

Dennis L. McKiernan was born April 4, 1932, in Moberly, Missouri, where he lived until age eighteen, when he joined the U.S. Air Force and served four years spanning the Korean War. He received a B.S. in electrical engineering from the University of Missouri in 1958 and an M.S. in the same field from Duke University in 1964. Dennis spent thirty-one years as one of the AT&T Bell Laboratories whiz kids in research and development—in antiballistic missile defense systems, in software for telephone systems, and in various management think-tank activities—before changing careers to be a full-time writer.

Currently living in Westerville, Ohio, Dennis began writing novels in 1977 while recuperating from a close encounter of the crunch kind with a 1967 red and black Plymouth Fury (Dennis lost: it ran over him: Plymouth 1, Dennis 0).

Among other hobbies, Dennis enjoys scuba diving, dirt-bike riding, and motorcycle touring—all enthusiasms shared by his wife.

An internationally bestselling author, in addition to *Caverns of Socrates* his critically acclaimed fantasy novels include *Voyage of the Fox Rider, The Eye of the*

Hunter, Dragondoom, The Silver Call duology, *The Iron Tower* trilogy, and the story collection *Tales of Mithgar.*

Never one to sit too long idle, Dennis has also written *The Vulgmaster* (a graphic novel) and several short stories and novelettes which have appeared in various anthologies.

He is presently working on his next opus.

Return to the wonderful world
of Mithgar in
Dennis L. McKiernan's new fantasy,

THE
DRAGONSTONE,

coming November 1996

The air over the Grey Mountains of Xian was filled with bellowing roars and the thunder of leathery wings. Dragons, mighty Dragons—glittering red and silver and black and green and other sheens—filled the summer sky. Down they came, spiraling and spiraling, 'round the towering Black Mountain where Wizards dwelled. Gate guardians cried out in fear and fled inside, slamming the great portals to. But still the Dragons descended, to land on mountain crests all 'round, settling like weighty, gleaming monoliths atop the lofty spires ... all but three of the mighty Firedrakes, and these came to rest before the shut iron gates of the Wizardholt. Two of these Dragons were massive and black, deep violet glints shimmering as they shifted about, and they had ebony claws like sabers which scored the dark stone of the foregate court. And they flanked a third Dragon, small by Dragon measure—if any Dragon could be said to be small. Green, he was, with a yellow cast, and seemed cowed by the other two. And in one claw he held a leather bag, tied tight at the top by a thong.

"Wizards, we would parley!" bellowed the monstrous black Drake on the left.

The Drake on the right turned and hissed in rage and spoke in a tongue from the dawn of time, the words sounding like great brass slabs grinding heavily upon one another. ["*I* shall be the speaker here, Daagor, for *I* occupy the highest ledge!"]

Daagor's massive tail lashed furiously. ["Only because *I* was in Kelgor, Kalgalath, at the time of the mating."]

The green Drake in between crouched lower.

At that moment a side postern opened and out stepped a black-robed Mage.

Black Kalgalath eyed the Wizard, and then turned to Daagor. ["We shall settle this once and for all at the time of the testing. But for now it is *I* who will speak for all of Dragonkind."]

Daagor roared in challenge, shifting his bulk to face his nemesis. Black Kalgalath bellowed in response.

The green Drake scuttled backward, out from between these rivals, and the Mage at the gate clapped his hands over his ears in pain.

But from the mountains all 'round, a hundred or more Dragon voices were raised, thundering bellows of their own blaring through the air, and the mountains entire shook and boomed with the echoes of Dragon shouts.

Warily, Black Kalgalath took his eye from Daagor and scanned the crests above, and Daagor did the same. Then Daagor hissed, ["The ledge was and is rightfully mine, Kalgalath, yet even we together cannot defeat all of them, hence *I* will permit you to speak to this Mage."]

["*I* need no sanction from you, Daagor, for that which is rightfully mine."]

Now Kalgalath turned to the Wizard and spoke in the common tongue, though his voice still sounded as great brazen slabs dragging one upon another. "Mage, we have come to parley."

The Wizard stepped forward. "Parley?"

"Yes, we have a small favor to ask."

"A favor?"

"The tiniest of things."

The Mage barked a laugh and flung his arms wide, taking in the entire assembly of Drakes. "The whole of the Dragon nation comes knocking on my door and then requests the tiniest of favors? I think not, Kalgalath."

"You know my name?" Black Kalgalath turned his head and gloated at Daagor.

"Yes, and Daagor's as well."

Now it was that dark Drake's moment to exult.

"Who would not know the names of the two mightiest Dragons in Mithgar?" asked the Mage rhetorically. "Dragons visit woe unto the world—Kalgalath and Daagor most of all."

Both Drakes raised their heads and arched their necks in high conceit; had there been a great mirror at hand they would have pridefully gazed at their reflections within . . . though truth to tell, Kalgalath and Daagor were so nearly identical that they merely needed look at one another to see the image each sought.

"Yet you did not bring all of Dragonkind here merely to hear me sing your praises," said the Mage. "Instead you came to parley. This favor, this tiniest of things, just what might it be?"

Kalgalath glanced back at Quirm and the leather bag he held, and then at Daagor, and finally up at the perched assembly of Drakes. "We would have you hold a thing for us."

"A thing?"

"Yes, but first, all of Magekind must swear an oath."

The Mage grunted in surprise. "An oath, eh?"

"An unbreakable oath," said Daagor.

Kalgalath glared at his rival. "An unbreakable oath," repeated Kalgalath. "A pledge to hide this thing away forever and leave its secrets unlearned . . . and to ward it from all who would do otherwise."

"And just what do you propose to exchange for the keeping and warding of this thing, sealed with an 'unbreakable oath.' "

Black Kalgalath nonchalantly examined the saberlike claws of his right forefoot. "For the keeping and the oath we would pledge to leave your Magehold alone, unplundered by Dragonkind."

"Ha!" barked the Wizard. "You pledge to leave undone that which you never had the power to do in the first place."

"Take care, Mage," hissed Daagor, "else you will see what Dragonkind can do."

Again Kalgalath shot Daagor a vitriolic glare, then turned to the Wizard. "Only *I* am the voice of all Dragonkind, Mage, yet in this case Daagor speaks true."

The Mage shook his head and gestured at the Wizard-holt behind. "First, I do not speak for all of Magekind. There are those of us within Black Mountain, and those on the island of Rwn, and yet others scattered across the face of this world. Too, there are many in the world of Vadaria and a few on the other Planes. I can only promise to bring the matter before the Council here at Black Mountain. And even then, the pledge would only concern the Mages of this Wizardholt.

"Second, ere we promise to speak oaths and receive oaths in return, we would know just what this thing is that we are to ward for Drakedom, for we would not give value without knowing the value of what we give.

"And so, my friend Dragons, I would see this thing you would have us safeguard."

With a jerk of his head and a hiss of ["Quirm,"] Black Kalgalath summoned the green Drake forward to stand once again between him and Daagor. Kalgalath glared down at Quirm and hissed, ["Let the Wizard heft it."] The green Dragon set the leather bag onto the forecourt stone.

The Mage raised an eyebrow. "You would have me walk within reach of your claws?"

Daagor hissed, "Wizard, you are within reach of our claws even where you stand."

The Mage looked left and right and fore ... and shrugged.

Kalgalath snarled at Daagor, then turned to the Wizard. "If you would feel the weight of this thing, come heft it."

The Mage stepped forward to where the bag lay, between Quirm's flexing claws. He stooped and took up the leather sack. "Hmm. Rather heavy for its measure. Something rounded inside. Ovoid. Perhaps the size of a melon." He squatted and set the bag in front of him and began plucking at the thong. "What's in here? A malformed crystal ball?"

"You cannot open it, Mage," said Black Kalgalath.

"Ha!" barked the Mage. And he looked at the tightly lashed strip and muttered, *"Laxare!"* and the thong fell loose to the forecourt, and the bag slid open and down, revealing an oblate spheroid of translucent, jadelike stone, flawless and pale green and lustrous—some six inches through from end to end, and four inches through across.

All three Drakes roared and backed away and turned their heads aside, just as did the Dragons all about on the crests above, the mighty bellows reverberating among the jagged peaks. Whelmed by the sound, the Mage slapped his hands to his ears in agony, and blood seeped from his nose.

"Put it away," cried Black Kalgalath. "Put the abomination away."

But, gritting his teeth, the Mage hefted up the egglike stone, its weight nearly twenty pounds.

Risking short glances, Black Kalgalath slithered forward and reached outward with his great black claws and hissed, "I said, put it away . . . else I'll shred you where you stand."

The Mage squatted and set the stone in the leather sack, and then he drew the bag up and about and retied the thong. As he did so, he asked, "Whence came this stone?"

Now recovered, Black Kalgalath glared full at him. "That is not for you to know."

The Mage stood. "What are its powers?"

Daagor roared. "Fool! Did we not say that was not for you to know?"

Undaunted, the Mage said, "This I do know: Here we have a mighty token, one that even Dragons fear. If you would have our pledge of warding, then we need know something of it, else you can go from here unsatisfied, the stone yet in your grasp."

Daagor and Kalgalath exchanged glances, but Quirm blurted, "We cannot sense it, Mage, and he who holds it and learns of its powers will command—"

["Silence!"] roared Kalgalath in the ancient tongue, turning on Quirm in fury. Yet at the same time flame roared forth from Daagor, and his claws slammed against the green Drake's skull, driving him hindwards. ["Yield nothing, nothing, to these Mages!"]

["Daagor, cease!"] bellowed Black Kalgalath. ["We can trust none but the weakest of us to bear the stone."]

Reluctantly, Daagor lowered his claws and muted his flame and stepped back from the cowering green Drake.

The Mage had scrambled away from the fury of the Dragons and now stood near the gate, ready to flee through the postern at need. But when he saw that the fighting was done, he called out, "I will bear your request to my fellow Mages. We will confer, and I will bring you our answer tomorrow."

The Roc Frequent Readers Club
BUY TWO ROC BOOKS AND GET ONE SF/FANTASY NOVEL FREE!

Check the free title you wish to receive (subject to availability):